ECSTASY

K.V. ROSE

To anyone who has ever felt lost. To anyone who has ever helped someone find their way again. To the memories of those who never got to tell their stories.

PLAYLIST

Check out the playlist on Spotify.

It's long. Really, really long.

Don't say I didn't warn you.

This is not a relationship guide.
This is not a recovery manual.
This is not a handbook on mental health.
This is a dark romance that holds a special place in my heart.
Enjoy.

1

Alex

"FUCKING CUNT."

She doesn't back down. "Go fuck yourself, Alex—"

"Nah, Za. I think I'll have some other bitch do that for me."

Her blue-green eyes are narrowed into slits and usually when she gets like this, it scares me—wondering what she's going to do next, who she's going to try to use to fuck me over.

But it's too late for that because she already screwed me over for the last fucking time.

"Get out of my house or I'll throw you out."

She just smiles at me, crossing her arms over her chest. Her pale stomach is exposed, a string bikini tied around her slim hips, a scar across her left one.

I feel my dick growing hard at the sight of her. Knowing I could take her right here. Right fucking now. Even if she put up a fight, no one would hear her scream. The music is so loud downstairs, my bedroom floor is shaking with the bass.

And although at five eight, Za isn't short, she doesn't have shit on me, not to mention she's slim as fuck.

Just thinking about yanking her two white-blonde braids, forcing her to her knees and throat fucking her makes my chest feel tight and my hands curl into fists at my sides.

But I can't do it. She brings out the fucking worst in me and I can't do this.

Not again.

Not anymore.

Not after the shit she pulled last week.

"You don't mean it," she tells me, switching tactics, trying to plead with me. She drops her arms, takes a step toward me. "Don't do it, Alex, I swear I—"

"You swear you what?" I ask, grinding my teeth. If she touches me, I swear to God, I will fucking—

She does it.

She closes the space between us and she fucking touches me, her fingers trail down my bare chest. All the way to my swimming trunks, and then her hand is on my dick, palming me.

Despite my promise to myself that that was the last time, that I wouldn't touch her again after I saw her down on her knees for Jamal Clint, my eyes flutter closed and I just...

Goddammit, I can't fucking stop her.

I try to picture it. Try to think of her, high as fuck as she stumbled down the hall of that house party in Shadow Lakes. Think of how I let her go, how I shot the shit with Dwight, keeping an eye on the hallway, hoping she'd just gone to the bathroom. How I was growing so fucking impatient, but I was going to trust her. Six months together and I never had, but this time, I was going to do it.

But ten minutes passed and even Dwight seemed concerned. He told me to go check on her.

I did.

She wasn't in the bathroom.

She was in the spare bedroom, and Jamal was moaning as she was...

My eyes fly open and she's already on her knees again, trying to pull down my green swimming trunks.

No.

I grab her by the throat, yank her up to her feet. Her fingers rise to my hand, scratching at me. And I know her. I know what she'll try to do if I leave a bruise on her. Zara Henderson is a vindictive, manipulative, lying, druggie whore.

I push her away, letting go of her quickly. "Get. *Out,*" I say again, pointing to the door.

She rubs her hand over her throat, breathing hard. "You're going to regret this."

I laugh, shaking my head. "Yeah, you're fucking right. I'm going to regret not doing this shit sooner. Now get the fuck out of my house."

She stares at me a moment longer before she marches past me, flings open my bedroom door, and slams it shut so hard behind her it rattles the mirror hanging on my wall.

I stare at the space she just occupied, trying to feel good about what just happened. About getting rid of her toxic bullshit. But I have a strange feeling it isn't over. She probably has no intentions of leaving my house at all.

I'm worried I might actually have to call the police and have her forcibly removed. The last thing I want to do is call the goddamn police because I fucking hate the cops.

I head to my bathroom and splash cold water on my face, trying to shake that uneasy feeling that twists my stomach into knots. There's a bottle of vodka on my bathroom counter, unopened, that I forgot to take downstairs. I twist off the cap and down as much as I can without puking.

I wipe the back of my hand over my mouth.

Look myself in the eye.

I'm going to go downstairs, I'm going to get fucking hammered, and I am going to bury my dick into some other chick so I can get Zara off my mind.

Fuck her.

Eli

I see Zara but she doesn't see me.

She's knocking back a shot in the living room, a group of guys around her cheering her on. I glance around the room, seeing no sign of her roommate, Kylie. No surprise, even though she dropped her off. Kylie is a pre-pharm nerd, and Zara...

Zara is something else.

Clearly, all these dudes don't know what went down with Alex and her last week or else they wouldn't be caught dead so close to her in mine and Alex's house.

Especially after Jamal Clint nearly ended up in the hospital.

But I know why they don't know. Alex doesn't have the balls to give her up just yet, and in the grand scheme of things, Jamal was a nobody at Caven. An unsuspecting freshman who happened to have the drugs Zara wanted and the stupidity to let Alex Cardi's girlfriend suck his dick.

I tip my beer up and take a swallow, keeping myself hidden in the foyer, leaning against the doorway. No one is paying me any mind.

I prefer it that way.

It's why having Alex Cardi as my roommate—now house-mate, I guess—is so damn beneficial to someone like me. He's got the hot temper, the loud mouth, and the suspension for the next three football games. Always causing a fucking scene.

I'm a wrestler and while compared to his stats, mine are far more impressive, it's quarterbacks that get the attention in southern towns.

Which is good.

Because I don't want it.

I've been told more times than I care to count that I'm too quiet. That's because when you're quiet, people talk around you. If you never shut the fuck up, like Alex Cardi, you have no idea what's really going on.

And Alex might be my best friend, but it feels strange sometimes to call him that, considering I'm not sure anyone really knows me at all.

But as Zara hops up on the coffee table in the living room and starts shaking her ass in her thong bikini, *Ecstasy* by Young Thug playing way too loudly, I wonder if she could.

Because I know things about Zara Henderson.

Things Alex doesn't.

For a brief moment, I think her eyes find mine, and a small smile pulls at her heart-shaped lips. A secret floating between us.

And then I hear Alex.

Even with the music and the people and the dancing, I hear Alex's footsteps down the stairs, and I can almost feel his anger when he brushes past me to head into the living room, where he sees her on the coffee table. He doesn't stop to talk, but says under his breath, "Don't you dare fucking stop me," so, like a good friend, I don't.

I just watch as the crowd parts for their quarterback and Alex grabs Zara's arm and yanks her down from the table. Putting on a good show, she laughs, and wraps her arms around his neck.

I don't look away from her and I don't stop him when he twists her in his arms, holding her back to his chest. I don't stop him when someone hands him a beer and he guzzles it down even though I'm pretty sure he's already fucking drunk.

I don't stop him as the people packed in our living room cheer, and when a girl I occasionally fuck, Rihanna Martinson, saunters over to me and wraps her arm around my waist, I don't stop her from standing on her tiptoes and trailing sloppy kisses down my neck.

But I don't look away from Zara either.

And when I see exactly what it is Alex is going to do, I

don't say a fucking word. When Zara sticks out her tongue and Alex places a pill on it, then watches as she swallows, I let Rihanna grab my dick in the shadows. When Alex hands Zara a cup, tilts it up to her lips when she doesn't take it and makes her drink the whole thing, I keep quiet.

I let Rihanna's hand cup my balls.

But it isn't Rihanna I'm going to fuck tonight.

Zara

"What're you doing?"

Alex ignores me and I can smell the vodka on his breath. I can smell it and I know by the way he's hanging all over me with a smile pulling up on his lips, that he's fucking drunk.

And that ecstasy on my tongue?

He would've never given that shit to me if he wasn't.

What he doesn't know—or maybe he does, and he just doesn't give a fuck—is that I took an Addie before I crashed his stupid fucking party.

I'm not sure how that's going to affect my MDMA high, but either way, it'll take half an hour for it to kick in.

So why Alex is all over me after that shit he pulled upstairs, I don't fucking know.

But if he wants to put on a show, well, no one does it better than I do.

The people packed in the living room are grinding against each other, and Alex's hard cock is against my back as he wraps his arms around my waist.

People dance near us, *Or Nah* pumping through the mounted speakers. Some girl gets close to Alex and despite his dickish behavior and his half-hearted break up, I shove her away.

She shoots me a glare, realizes it's me, and scurries off.

Alex laughs against my ear, his breath on my skin sending a chill down my spine. "God, I fucking love you."

I want to remind him that he called me a cunt upstairs right before he tried to kick me out of his house.

But I'll indulge him.

I lean my head back against his hard chest, close my eyes as his hands trail down lower, gripping my bare thighs. "I know."

He licks his way down my neck. "You're such a bitch."

I press further back against his dick. "I know."

But clearly, he's a glutton for punishment. I knew he'd do this shit, though. It's why I didn't leave. Yeah, maybe I sucked Jamal off but he's nothing to me. Just a hot guy that wanted what all guys want, and I was only too happy to give it to him.

For two reasons. One, he had something I wanted and two, Alex let Rihanna fucking Martinson kiss him on the cheek after her cheerleading practice and his football practice just before we went to that Shadow Lakes party.

I glance toward the doorway that leads to the foyer in Alex and Eli's house, and I catch sight of Eli.

Rihanna has her tongue on his neck, her body pressed against his. He's so tall, and she's so damn short, it's almost comical to watch.

His eyes connect with mine.

For a long moment, while Alex grinds his dick against my back and Rihanna dry humps Eli, we just hold each other's gaze.

I feel warmth spooling in my core the longer he stares at me.

Eli, like Alex, is fucking fine. But where Alex looks like the all-American asshole that he is, Eli Addison just looks...wicked. Those hand tattoos might have something to do with it.

He's got black hair and dark green eyes, olive skin supposedly from the Greek mother that left him when he was a teenager, and he's just...cold.

Eli is cold.

Alex is hot.

I've always wondered what it would feel like to have them both buried inside of me.

But Alex's voice, loud above the noise of the party, startles my focus away from Eli. "Who wants to see this beautiful bitch naked?!"

The fuck? My blood runs cold as everyone cheers around us. Before I can react, Alex leans down and murmurs in my ear, "Hear that, baby? They want to see your tits."

I grit my teeth, but if he wants to play this game… "Alex, you're going to regret this," I singsong as he runs his hands over my breasts and another cheer goes up around us. People are pressing in from all sides and if he thinks the boys here will be content to look and not touch...

My stomach churns.

Maybe that's not what he thinks at all.

"Nah, princess, I don't think so."

I bristle as his hand slides up my bare stomach, his fingers edging under the cup of my bikini.

"Alex." My voice is strained, and I want to turn around and punch him in the fucking face, but everyone is looking at us with eager smiles, just waiting for Alex Cardi to do something fucking stupid.

And Alex loves to give the people what they want. Fucking coward.

I take a step away from him and turn to face him in the crowded living room as people cheer, some holding up their drinks. "You fucking asshole."

Six months we've been together, since we hooked up at my dealer's house back in March when I transferred from ECU after a stint in rehab. Six months, and all the shit we've given each other, this has to be lowest of the fucking low.

I can't say people didn't warn me. My roommate, Kylie Jones, specifically said, "Alex is trouble. Stay away from him, Zara."

But I don't listen well to anyone, and Kylie, as good and smart and pure as she is, was no exception.

Alex's dark brown eyes are gleaming, those flecks of amber magnified with the flashing lights him and his football friends set up before the party. He's got a smile on his face, and he lifts up his red Solo cup.

"Come back, princess," he says, loud enough to be heard over the music. People around us are definitely staring, and I just want to get out of here. "Come back here." He points at the spot right in front of him that I just occupied.

The molly is making the music *feel* good, and the Addie is making my heart race. I need some water. I need water and I need a bed. A safe place. Or else I'll end up doing something stupid tonight. And with the way Alex is looking at me right now, that something stupid will be him.

"I'm leaving," I tell him, and turn to go. He wanted me out anyway.

But apparently, not that badly. He grabs my wrist, yanks me back to him and another cheer goes up from the dozens of people packed in this fucking house. He pulls me to his chest, my back against him. He wraps his arm around my waist, not letting me go.

"Let's give the people what they want."

I grab his forearm, digging my black-painted nails into his skin. "Let. Me. *Go.*"

I'm starting to feel jittery and my jaw is fucking aching.

I really fucked this all up. I should not have come tonight.

But Alex shifts his hold on me, yanking both of my arms behind my back with one hand, threading his arm through them and pinning me to him. With his other hand, he trails his finger over my chest, toward the material of my bikini.

I stiffen, closing my eyes as everyone seems to be pressing in on me. I try to take deep breaths in through my nose, out through my mouth. Some people are still yelling and cheering, and some people probably aren't paying attention, probably as high as I am, but if he does this...

If he does this, *someone* is going to record it and I will never fucking live this down.

I don't really mind people seeing my tits, but if my mom finds out this happened, she'll yank me out of school and send me back to rehab and that is *not* how I want to spend the rest of the year.

"If you wanna act like a fucking whore, Za, I'll treat you like one," Alex whispers in my ear, his words against my skin.

I try to yank out of his grip but it's a joke. He's a freak of nature, over six feet tall and all lean muscle and *asshole.*

He straightens, yelling loud enough to be heard over the music the same bullshit he called out earlier, *"Who* wants to see this beautiful bitch *naked?"* like he's a fucking sports broadcaster and flashing tits was his specialty back in the day.

Everyone is yelling and screaming, and I open my eyes again, staring over their heads at the high ceiling as if I might just disappear. As if this isn't really happening. As if I could float up to the ceiling and fly out of here on the wave of music pounding through the speakers.

"Stop," I whisper the word, hoping someone might see me say it, but mainly, I'm just saying it for my own satisfaction. That I *did* say it. I can't get out of his grip and none of these people are going to help me because this is Alex's house, and no one tells Alex no, but still.

At least I said it.

Here we fucking go.

But then someone comes to stand directly in front of me. And just as Alex's fingers grab the thin material of my bikini, he says, "Alex."

Eli. He's looking past me, at his best friend.

I can smell him, he's so close to me. Coconut and citrus, he smells fucking amazing. The opposite of Alex's dark and woodsy scent. And he's probably the only guy in here not in swimming trunks. He's wearing black pants and a white, fitted tee instead. This close to me, his body nearly brushing mine, I can see his long, dark lashes. The lighter flecks of green in his eyes.

I swallow, feeling nervous.

Feeling like I wish I was with him right now and not Alex.

Eli is quiet.

When I'm not high as fuck, I like to be in the quiet too.

And Eli never causes a fucking scene like this.

"Oh, you wanna help me undress her, E?" Alex asks in a mocking voice, laughing loudly. I can feel his body shaking with that laughter.

He's fucking drunk off his ass.

I hate when he gets drunk. It's like all the worst parts of his personality come out in full force. I guess I could say the same about myself but fuck.

"Fuck. Off," I growl, and try to pull away again, moving toward Eli, but Alex only holds me tighter.

The crowd is full of dancing, screaming idiots and someone jostles Eli. Caught off guard, he's momentarily bumped out of my view and another guy is in front of me. Someone I've never seen before. Blond hair, baby face, a cup in his hand, the contents of it nearly sloshing over the sides.

He's got a broad, toothy grin on his face, his eyes on my boobs.

"Show him your tits, Zara," Alex says against my ear. And then he runs his hand and forearm down my chest, yanking down my bikini.

The screaming and cheering reach atrociously high levels and the guy in front of me looks like he might come in his pants right here and now, his mouth forming a comical "O" as he stares at my bare breasts.

Comical, except this isn't fucking funny.

My heart is racing so fast it's making my chest hurt, and my cheeks are flushed as Alex keeps holding down my fucking top, spinning me around so everyone can get a good look. And a keepsake video.

I want to go home.

I want to go home and get to my bathroom sink and grab a benzo and fucking knock myself out and go to sleep. I want to get out of here.

But I don't bother trying to fight Alex. What's the fucking point? This will be over soon. He's just getting back at me. It's just, what we do.

"Alex!" I hear Eli's voice again and interestingly, he sounds angry. I don't think I've ever heard Eli sound…anything.

Alex is laughing, but he spins us back around and Eli is in my face, shielding my tits from view. I guess I should be grateful, but as he steps closer, his chest grazes my pebbled nipples and my breath catches in my throat.

I don't think he even notices.

If he does, he definitely doesn't care.

He's staring up at Alex. "Cut it out," he yells at him over the music and the throng of people being obnoxious as hell. I see the veins in Eli's neck straining against his skin. I see his collarbone, too, and I can smell him all over again.

I want him to step closer.

I want to be between him and Alex.

I want more than my breasts grazing against him.

Fuck.

This is not good. The molly is fucking me all up and I shouldn't be thinking about boning my ex *and* his best friend.

I close my eyes again as Alex keeps laughing. *This'll be over soon.*

I just repeat it over and over in my head. *This will be over soon. This will be over soon.*

I've survived far worse than this shit. You know, like an overdose. Besides, tits are nothing to be ashamed of. Fuck him. I won't give him the satisfaction of squirming again.

He dips his head down. "You hear that, princess? Eli

wants me to let you go. If I do, how are you going to pay us back for that?"

His words light a fire under my skin and my eyes fly open.

Eli is staring right at me.

He's still so damn close, I can feel his body heat against my chest. It's like he's caging me in, so no one else can see me. Just him. Just him and just Alex, at my back.

I try to squirm again out of Alex's grip, so I can turn around and face him, but he only holds me tighter. What he doesn't know is that despite what he's doing, I would pay them both back. I'm so turned on the moment, I'd probably let them both take me at the same time. It's not like I haven't thought about it before, and this fucking molly is making me want things I can't have. Things I shouldn't be thinking about. Things I—

"Hey!" Alex's voice suddenly turns cold. He pulls up my top, let's go of my arms and yanks me into his chest, his arm around mine, covering my breasts. "I didn't say you could touch her, you dumb fuck. Get out of here."

Eli's eyes flick from mine to the guy Alex is talking to, right beside him. It's the blond guy with the baby face. I realize his hand is outstretched, reaching toward me. But at Alex's words, his eyes go wide, fear replacing the lust on his face.

It isn't Alex that goes for him, though.

It's Eli.

He grabs the guy by the throat, digging his fingers so hard into his skin the tips of them disappear into the guy's flesh.

The guy is sputtering, his mouth opening and closing but nothing comes out.

My thighs clench together, watching Eli look at this guy with no expression on his face, but he doesn't really need to say much.

And when he does, it's just one word. "Leave."

He lets the guy go, and he starts rubbing at his throat, coughing and choking, red marks against his skin.

But he leaves.

He turns and fucking runs as fast as he can through the mass of people in the living room, some pointing and laughing as he goes.

"Thanks, man," Alex says behind me, and slowly, Eli turns back around, his expression neutral. His eyes lock on mine and I wish he'd step closer. I wish he'd put his hands on me like that.

I wish he'd...

"Yeah." That's all he says before he turns around and threads his way through the crowd, which seems to part for him like he's fucking Moses or some shit.

I want to go after him.

I want him back here with me and Alex.

Alex leans down close to me. "Let's get a drink, yeah?" he whispers in my ear, and before I can answer, he shifts his arm around my shoulder and leads me through the living room. He's so damn big, all I have to do is stick close to him and there's no fighting or squeezing through people. They just move.

Just like they did with Eli.

So many thoughts are whirring in my brain—About my mom seeing a video of my tits. How she'll put me back in rehab so fast I'll be there by sunrise. What the fuck Alex just did. How this might mean we're really over.

And about Eli Addison, grabbing that dude by the throat.

But when Alex leads me into the kitchen and Eli is nowhere to be found, I try to push him from my mind and spin around to face Alex, shrugging his arm off my shoulder.

He grabs my wrist, yanking me closer to him. He knows if he lets go of me right now, I'm going to bolt.

"What the *fuck* was that?" I hiss.

Some dude comes up beside us and I glance over at him, recognizing Dwight Morris. He's the running back at CU, and he has two drinks in his hand. He looks from me to Alex then back to me, offering me the drink.

I stare at him like he's stupid. *Did he not just see what the fuck happened there?*

"Looks like you could use this," he tells me, and he's not smiling, which makes me feel marginally better. His golden eyes go to Alex, but he still holds the cup out to me. "That wasn't cool, man."

That was the wrong thing to say.

I can see Alex's jaw clench, his expression stormy as he turns to his friend. "Do you not fucking remember what this bitch did last week?" he asks, like I'm not even standing here.

I take the drink from Dwight's outstretched hand. Without hesitating, I throw it in Alex's fucking face.

Alex drops my hand, taking an instinctive step back, liquor and soda all over him, running down the front of his chest.

Silence—save for the music in the living room—seems to descend in the kitchen from the few people in here.

Beyond the sliding glass doors, I hear people splashing in the pool, and in the living room, the party is still raging on.

But right here, in this kitchen, the only thing raging is Alex.

His mouth is open as he blinks rapidly, wipes his hand over his face and through his light brown hair. He shakes his hands out, sending drops of liquid splattering on me and Dwight, who takes a step back, his eyes flitting from me to Alex and back again.

I watch him swallow and take another step back.

"I'm just gonna—" And then he walks away, giving me a lingering look.

I turn to face Alex, cross my arms over my chest. "That's the fucking least of what you deserve, you dick."

He reaches behind him, to the sink, and grabs a hand towel, wipes his face and his chest, then throws the towel past me, on the marble island of the kitchen.

Finally, his dark brown eyes connect with mine. "You fucking bitch." Then he moves so fast, I don't have time to react as he picks me up, slams me against the island, bottles and cups rattling and rolling in every direction. His hand cups my head, cushioning the blow before it slams against the marble. Then he yanks his hand out from under me, plants it on my chest, grabs a bottle of tequila, twists off the lid with his teeth and spits it out. I thrash against his hand, kicking, and scratching at his forearm, but he brings the bottle to my mouth.

"Open your fucking mouth or I'll break your goddamn teeth," he growls at me.

I don't know if anyone else is in here, but I hear nothing. No one protesting, coming to my aid.

For one stupid second, I wonder where Eli is.

"Fuck you," I spit at Alex as he leans over me, digging the bottle in deeper against my mouth. But when I say that, he forces it between my teeth and starts to pour it down my throat.

It burns and I cough, turning my head before I choke to death on tequila at this stupid house party that I should've never gone to.

But Alex doesn't fucking let up.

He turns the bottle as I turn my head, and it's still lodged between my teeth. He moves his hand from my chest to my face, forcing me still.

"Taste as good at Jamal's cum, huh, princess?" he snarls at me, his eyes two dark pits. I jerk my head from his grip and *finally* I can breathe. But tequila is burning its way down my throat, into my empty stomach—I don't remember the last time I ate—and I know, with that, and the Addie, and the molly, I'm about to be *very fucked up*.

Usually, with Alex, I wouldn't care. He'd take care of me. He might be a dick and he might make fun of me, but he'd take care of me all the same.

Not tonight though.

Tonight, he's gone way past his usual one-beer limit and tonight he's fucking on one.

I think about calling Kylie. I think about calling my mom. My dealer, Jax. Or fuck, at this point, I'd even call Jamal. Anyone to come pick me up and take me away from this shit, but I don't even know where my phone is. I don't know where my phone is, and my head is already spinning and...

Goddamn, I want a Xanax.

It's an irrational thought, but with my heart pounding so loud I can hear it in my ears and with that look of rage still on Alex's face as he slams the tequila bottle down on the table so hard, all of the bottles rattle against each other, it's the only hope I've got.

At least then I could fucking roofie myself and not have to live through whatever fresh hell my ex has in store for me.

But I don't have a Xannie on me, and my ex is already moving on to the next thing so there's no way I can fucking find one right now.

He yanks my arm, sliding me down the counter, and tosses me over his shoulder.

My head is spinning, the room a swirling vortex of colors and sounds around me as he ducks down so I don't hit my head on the doorway when he goes outside, the smell of chlorine and the warm, September air assaulting my senses.

And that's what it feels like.

An assault.

Because whatever Alex plans to do with me out here cannot be good.

I'm hanging over his shoulder like a ragdoll, and he's got one hand on my back, the other on my ass. His grip isn't overly forceful but I'm working on trying not to puke, trying not to black out so I don't drown in this pool, so it's not like I'm going anywhere.

And when he sets me down on my feet, the rough concrete cold beneath me, I think I'm going to fall over.

But he grips my arms, keeping me upright.

Distantly, I'm aware there are people out here talking and laughing and I hear a few splashes from the pool and music that I can't quite make out.

All I can focus on is Alex's eyes on mine.

He's smiling at me, which can't be good. But his smile is so damn cute, a single dimple flashing in his tan face, his white, straight teeth fucking perfect. I see other things, too. The small dent in his bottom lip, right down the center. The flecks of amber in his dark eyes, and his long lashes.

Why do boys always have such nice lashes?

I want to ask him. I reach a hand out to touch them, but my hand goes to his face instead and his skin is so smooth, so warm beneath my hand.

"Alex," I say his name, and it's heavy in my mouth, like my tongue is swollen or something. "Alex," I try again, and I can hear it, the sound, but I can't quite tell if I'm saying it right.

God, I'm fucked up.

He's still holding my upper arms and I see, past him, a few people looking our way. We're by the shallow end, I know that much. But even with the tiki torches and the underwater pool lights giving off enough light to see by in the darkness, I can't tell much beyond that. I don't know how close we are to the pool. I don't know how close I am to the door to the house.

I don't know how close I am to passing out.

I sway a little in his arms.

"You wanna swim?" he asks me. His words are kind of quiet, but he's got that smirk on his face that means he's up to no good.

I shake my head. "No," I mumble, still touching his face. "That's not a…" I trail off, unable to say what it is I really want to say. *That's not a good idea.*

It's not even that I don't want to swim with him.

It's not even because of what he just did.

It's not even the way I taste blood in my mouth, and I think it must be because he forced that bottle down my throat.

It's that if I get in that pool, I will *definitely* drown.

But none of that comes out. The only words I can force out of my mouth are, "I'm drunk."

Alex smiles, presses his forehead to mine. *"Good."*

And I'm too drunk to feel angry at his words, or to remind him of what he just did. Instead, I swat my hand against his bare chest, and he catches it, threading his fingers through mine. He jerks his head toward the pool.

"Come on, let's swim."

I shake my head, my eyes fluttering closed. My body feels heavy. *I'm messed up.* I tell him that, my words slurred, but he must get what I'm saying because he speaks against my mouth.

"I won't let you get hurt, Zara."

My limbs feel loose and warm with his words. His touch. Alex is safe. *Alex is safe.* The past six months, we've fought and fucked and screamed and yelled but he's safe. He's taken care of my drunk ass more times than I'd really like to admit. He hasn't told my mom that I'm not in recovery.

He hasn't ever let me get hurt. He picked me up on the football field after his first game, the one he was suspended at, and twirled me around and kissed me in front of everyone.

He's safe.

He's safe.

So, I nod my head, knowing as I do that things are going to go downhill fast. But you're only a senior in college once, right? And he won't *really* hurt me. He won't *really* drown me.

He wraps an arm around me and steers me toward the edge of the pool.

I hear a splash, see people sitting on the outdoor couches with drinks in their hands.

I think some people are looking at us, but I'm too drunk to

see them clearly. I can barely see the edge of the fucking pool and I'm worried I'm going to drown sooner rather than later.

I kind of don't care now.

Not right now anyway.

"It's going to be cold, princess," Alex warns me.

Music is playing out here. *Limbo* by Salem. *I love this song.* I try to tell Alex that as I stare at the rippling blue surface of the water.

Alex's fingers skim up my sides, making me shiver.

"I love this song, too," he says softly.

Yeah. I knew that. We don't agree on much, but we like the same music.

"Hey," I mumble as he keeps rubbing my skin, gazing down at me. All I can hear now is the music, like someone turned it up. Or my brain turned everyone else's voices down. I speak a little louder, "I shouldn't do this."

He grins at me, grabs my wrist and trails my hand over his chest, diverting my attention. I take in his six-pack, his lean body and tall frame. His skin is smooth, and I trace one of those freckles under his pec, then down across his abs. I have them memorized.

"Ready?" he asks me, catching my hand again.

I chew my lip, looking up into his eyes. *No.*

But I nod in answer to his question, and he pulls me closer toward the pool. But then we bypass the steps and as I stumble over the concrete, fear starts to creep in past my intoxication.

"Hey, I told you I—"

"And I told you I wouldn't let you get hurt," he cuts me off as we come to the deep end. Eight feet, if I'm seeing the black number on the edge of the concrete correctly.

His toes are at the edge and mine are too, my hand still in his.

"You ready?" he asks me, squeezing my hand.

I shake my head. "No, you get in first and then you can—"

"You know how to swim, Zara." It's a statement, because he's taken me to the beach a few times and we've jumped the waves together and his parents have a pool and he's seen me swim completely naked in it that one weekend when they were out of town.

I nod in agreement but try to pull out of his grip. I don't think I'm explaining myself properly, or he doesn't care.

I think about him breaking that guy's nose on the field, right after the Caven Camels had won the game. Right before he picked me up from across the fence and spun me in his arms. I'd been high on Addie then too, and his coach had been yelling at him because Nate's nose was dripping blood and the paramedics were on the field, but Alex didn't care.

Alex didn't care.

Because Nate was the quarterback for ECU, and I'd fucked him before. I guess he'd been talking shit to Alex during the game and Alex doesn't like when people talk shit.

And I guess he really, really doesn't like when his girlfriend cheats on him because this punishment seems a little...*much.*

I swallow as he pulls me closer to the deep end, my toes going over the edge of the concrete. I try to enunciate clearer, but I know I'm just sounding more and more drunk with each word. It's like trying to speak underwater. My thoughts aren't coming out right, but I give it another try anyway. "Yes, I *can* swim, but *I'm drunk—*"

"Yeah, here's the thing, princess." He leans down close to me, his words against my ear. "You should've thought about that before you put Jamal's dick in your pretty little mouth."

He jerks my hand as he jumps.

I stumble in, too, the water surprisingly warm.

And that's all I can focus on. The temperature of the water.

Chlorine burns my eyes, which are still open, seeing the foggy way the lights shimmer beneath the surface. It burns my nose, too, and I realize Alex is still holding my hand.

Yanking me all the way down.

I turn to look at him, and then he lets go.

I'm at the bottom of the pool.

I feel my feet on the smooth concrete, my head heavy as I blink underwater. I see some people's blurry legs, at the shallow end, and I force myself to walk toward them.

I hear something that sounds like yelling above the surface, and I look up. I can see it. The surface is less than three feet above my head.

I just have to move my legs. Push up.

The chlorine starts to burn. In my eyes. My nose.

My lungs.

I just need to push up, though. That's all. Just push up to that shimmering surface a few feet above me.

I brace myself to do just that, when I see someone splash into the water right in front of me. A cloud of bubbles.

And then strong arms yank me up and I'm breaking the surface, the air much colder up here.

I take a deep, gasping breath, my lungs burning.

But working.

They're working.

Water and mucus pour from my nose, and I take deep, gulping breaths, coughing and spluttering as I do.

"Zara," someone says. Someone who's holding me, my body pressed against theirs. They're wearing clothes, I feel them against my skin.

I start to shiver, rubbing my eyes with my fists, my back to whoever is holding me. The coughing is subsiding, but my throat is burning.

"Zara." It's Eli's voice.

People are peering at me from the edge of the pool, crowded around with wide eyes. A few of them have cell phones, recording me.

Eli's arms tighten around me. He tells them the same thing

he told that baby-faced blond that tried to touch me. "Leave."
He doesn't even raise his voice.

I don't think I've ever heard Eli raise his voice.

The crowd around the pool breaks into nervous laughter,
but they all disperse.

"Zara." Eli again, his voice against my ear.

I'm still shivering but he spins me in his arm as he hangs
onto the edge of the pool with the other.

My eyes lock on his.

"What happened?"

I shake my head, water in my ears. I can hear him, but...
my face feels numb. My lips, too.

God, I'm fucking drunk.

I lay my head on his shoulder, against his wet shirt. "Alex
pulled me in," I manage to tell him.

Eli pulls me closer. "He pulled you in?" he repeats, his
words almost...clinical.

I nod against his shirt, letting my eyes fall closed. I'm still
shivering, but I'll be fine. I'll be fine.

I'm fine.

But my heart is still racing and even though my body is
tired, my mind...

"Here." Another familiar voice interrupts my thoughts.
The one that just...

"You almost drowned me." I'm not sure I'm speaking the
words out loud or just mouthing them as I look up at a
soaking wet Alex, hands on his knees and water dripping from
his thick bronze hair as he smiles down at me.

He extends his hand.

"No." I shake my head, but I still can't tell... Am I actually
speaking? My jaw is aching again, and Eli's fingers are splayed
on my torso beneath the water. I turn to him.

He's glaring up at Alex, but he doesn't say a word.

Then someone lifts me from under my arms straight from
the pool.

I reach my hands down toward Eli, but Alex speaks as he pulls me up. "He can't get to you without pulling you back down, princess."

I turn to glare at Alex as he sets me on my feet on the concrete at the edge of the pool, hands on my upper arms. I'm having trouble focusing on his face, but I hear Eli say, "Let her sleep in the guest room. You're fucking drunk, man."

Alex smiles at me but I think he's talking to Eli when he says, "I'll take her to the guest room, but she's not fucking sleeping." Those words don't make sense to drunk me, but I don't have time to ponder them as he picks me up, tossing me over his shoulder. I hang upside down, trying not to throw up as I close my eyes tight, Alex's hands holding me firmly.

I hear Eli swear under his breath, but Alex starts moving with me and I have to work very, very hard to keep whatever it is I managed to eat today inside my stomach as he walks inside the house, water dripping wet from the both of us.

"Yo, she looks like she's gonna puke!" someone calls from inside the kitchen.

Alex slaps my ass. "Better not, princess," he mutters, and then we're going up the stairs, but I keep my eyes closed, dangling limply over Alex's back like a doll.

I want to go to sleep.

My body is so fucking tired.

My heart is working overtime.

My head is spinning.

And if Alex doesn't set me down, right now, I'm going to puke.

My eyes fly open, hand coming to my mouth, stomach convulsing.

But then he does exactly that.

He sets me down, soaking wet, in the middle of a big bed covered in a white comforter.

The guest room bed.

Alex stands in front of me, appraising me. I vaguely

register an open, empty closet at Alex's back, the fan spinning overhead that makes me shiver. I wrap my arms around myself, notice there's a dim light on behind me, but mainly, I'm just staring at Alex, dripping water all over the dark wooden floors.

"You feelin' okay, princess?" he asks me, eyes flashing like he hopes I'm not.

I bury my head in my hands, shifting on the bed. It's soaked beneath me, and I'm distantly aware that if the mattress gets wet, they'll have to replace it but it's kind of hard to think about furniture with the way my heart is pounding so fucking hard and my head is hurting and—

"Get out." My thoughts are interrupted by another voice.

I look up, dropping my hands as Eli comes into the room, pointing to the door he just walked in through. He's glaring at Alex, his jaw clenched.

Alex cocks his head, adjusts his dick through his swim trunks and I notice, not for the first time, it's…big.

How it could possibly be that big when it's cold in here and we're both soaked and there's a fan.

"You're drunk," Eli says, like he did at the pool. "You're going to regret this."

I force my gaze from Alex's dick to Eli's face. Eli doesn't anger easily, I don't think. Truth be told, I haven't spent much time with him, even though he's Alex's best friend. They're opposites in so many ways.

Hot. Cold. Loud. Quiet. Light… Dark.

Alex laughs softly, then glances at me. He runs a hand through his disheveled hair. "We're not quite done yet."

Eli's eyes narrow into slits. He's still dressed, but he's dripping water everywhere too. He doesn't say anything though. He just stares at Alex like he—I don't know, actually.

Eli is always hard to read. Now is no different.

Alex turns to look at me, a contemplative expression on his face. He scrubs his hand over his jaw. "This isn't your problem, E," he says, and his words are a little slurred, too. "She's a fucking whore. She fucking sucked Jamal's dick." There's real anger in his sloppy words, and I feel my chest grow hot with shame.

But Eli still doesn't say anything. He's not looking at Alex anymore. He's looking at me.

My stomach churns. I slide down the bed, knowing I'm leaving a wet puddle behind me. My feet hit the floor and I stand on shaky legs, wrapping my arms back around myself.

"Yeah," I mumble, trying to take a deep breath. Willing my heart to slow down. "I'm just gonna go." I don't know where. Maybe I can walk this high-gone-wrong off. Maybe I can call my mom. Maybe I can…

Alex's laugh cuts me off. He glances at Eli, who looks tense by the door, his hands fisted by his sides, dark hair falling over his brow.

"I don't think so, Zara." Alex's dark eyes are on me and he's looking at me like I'm his next fucking meal.

I shake my head, shivering in my bikini as I step toward the door that Eli's standing in front of.

"My girlfriend is a slut, but she's hot, huh?" Alex presses. "Her skin is so fucking pale I can practically see her veins, and her ass is kind of small, but her pussy is really fucking tight." He blows out a breath as I stare at Eli, and Eli stares back at me. Alex keeps going: "It's a shame she's a druggie fucking whore, but I guess that means we can use her—"

"Bye," I mumble, heading straight for the door, arms still wrapped around myself.

Alex moves so fast, I don't even know he's behind me until he yanks me backward, his hand knotted in my hair, the braids having come undone sometime in the past hour since we fought in his room. Has it been an hour?

What time is it?

I don't fucking know.

I stumble, my feet nearly slipping on the wet floor, but I

catch myself, arms shooting out by my sides as I spin around to stare at him.

He lets go of my hair, but the room is spinning too fast and my breath catches in my throat from the way my heart is pumping so hard in my chest, claiming all of my oxygen.

Alex smiles at me, cocking his head. "You're not just drunk, princess. You're high on something. And it's not just the molly, is it? Whose dick are you gonna suck to fix that now, huh?"

My eyes widen and I open my mouth to say something, but nothing comes out. My heart is still stuttering in my chest, and I press a hand over it, willing it to calm down.

I need to leave.

I turn and run toward the door, but shocking me, Eli tosses me back, right into Alex's arms. Eli shuts the door and Alex holds me tight. I open my mouth to scream but Eli is there, clamping a hand over my mouth, both of them on either side of me.

"Eli…" His name is a plea on my mouth, muffled and low, and I'm not even sure I said it out loud. *What is he doing? Is he going to hurt me, too?*

"We don't want to hurt you, baby." Alex's voice echoes my thoughts, his breath against my cheek. "We wanna make you feel good."

I shake my head, eyes pleading with Eli's green ones. *Don't do this.* And I thought he was… I thought he was fucking around with Rihanna Martinson? Why is he even here?

He stares at me a second then looks up at Alex.

"This isn't a good idea." The words are almost detached from what he's saying. Like he knows it's not a good idea, but he doesn't really care.

Even still, relief makes me sag in Alex's arms. But his grip only tightens.

He laughs coolly. "Come on, Eli. I know you wanna fuck

my girlfriend. You think I haven't seen you staring at her? Checking her out when she's in the pool?"

My face flushes. *Has he?* I never noticed.

Eli drops his hand from my mouth, and he swallows, looking back at me.

I feel Alex's cock against my back. His warm, wet skin against mine.

Eli steps back, his eyes hard as he looks at Alex. "I think you've done enough."

"Let. Me. Go!" I try to elbow Alex, but he just tightens his hold on me, not letting go.

"Your heart is racing," he says softly. "You're shaking. Shh, just relax. I won't hurt you, Zara."

"You said that about the pool—"

"I didn't hurt you then, did I, baby?"

Panic rises, a sour taste in my mouth. My fingers are shaking, my knees trembling. There's a dull roar in my ears and I'm worried I'm going to have a fucking stroke and these boys aren't going to help me. They're going to… "You're going to kill me."

"Don't be fucking stupid." Alex loosens his hold on me for a moment, shifts behind me. Before I can think to spring free, he holds up a white, oblong pill in front of me. I have no idea where the fuck he got it from, but I. *Need. It.*

"This is what you want isn't it, Princess?"

I don't take my eyes off the pill, resisting the urge to grab it. No. *No.* "You think you can…you think you can blackmail me into fucking you again with fucking—"

"You want it?"

I can't breathe. The panic is bubbling up in my chest, my vision blurring, making me see double the Xanax Alex is holding out in front of me, taunting me like I'm a dog and he's got a treat.

I see Eli, eyes flicking from me to Alex.

I still in Alex's arms, no longer fighting.

"Tell Eli you want it," he instructs me.

Eli doesn't say a word. He just stares at me.

"Zara. If you want me to help you, tell Eli you want it. Be a good little slut."

I lock eyes with Eli. His jaw is clenched, and I can see he's breathing hard. "Eli." My voice is hoarse. "I…"

"Alex." But Eli's voice doesn't sound angry. It sounds…strained.

"I want it!" I shriek, my face growing hot at the shrillness of my own voice, the desperation in it.

Eli doesn't move.

Alex brings the pill to my lips, rubbing it over them softly. "You want it now, princess?"

"I'm not your—"

He pushes the pill past my lips. I taste the bitterness of it on my tongue and he spins me around, hands around my waist, our nearly naked bodies brushing up against one another.

"Swallow it."

I want to spit it out onto the floor to spite him. But I know what it is. I know what it'll do for me right now. It could be fake, but I doubt it.

I swallow, grimacing as I do.

"Good girl," Alex says. He pulls me closer, pressing me against his wet body. "You're gonna feel good soon."

I shut out Eli behind me, don't think about him. About this. "I don't want to—"

"I won't hurt you."

I can't think. I feel Eli's hands on me.

Both of their hands are all over me.

"You tried to drown me," I tell Alex, my words slurred.

"You kind of deserved it. And besides, I didn't, Zara. If I had wanted to, I would have. But I didn't. And now, you're gonna feel good with us, yeah?"

My eyes flutter closed. The panic is subsiding. I know the Xanax hasn't kicked in yet, but I also know it's coming.

And taking alcohol with Xanax is basically like roofying yourself. Not to mention the molly and the Addie and... *What the fuck have I done?*

"Did you have fun, princess?" Alex asks me.

I force myself to open my eyes. "I'm not a..." I trail off, my tongue leaden as Alex skims his hands up and down my sides. Then he spins me around abruptly.

I'm looking at Eli. He's so close to me, but he takes a small step back, like he's taking us both in, me and Alex.

Eli has always had such nice eyes.

And his lips. They're so damn full.

I want them on my mouth.

I try to tell him that but then Alex buries *his* mouth against my neck as he hooks his thumbs through the waistband of my bikini and pulls it down.

"Step out of these for me, baby."

I wrap my arms around myself, shivering.

Eli frowns, then closes the space between us. "She's cold," he says quietly as I do as Alex says.

My gaze holds Eli's green one and he comes closer. So close we're nearly touching. My teeth are chattering as Alex unties my bikini at my neck, then my back, pushing it off my body. He grabs my wrists, uncrosses my arms from my chest and Eli's eyes dip lower, to my pebbled nipples. I think about them against his shirt in the living room, before he grabbed that guy by the throat.

"I-I'm f-freezing," I say through my chattering teeth.

Eli reaches out his hand. I suck in a breath as he brushes his thumb over one nipple, then the other. He palms my breast and squeezes, stepping closer.

I almost close my eyes. I almost lean into his touch.

He's touching me.

He's touching me and it feels so good.

"You won't be cold soon." And then he shoves me backward, into Alex's arms.

Alex laughs, his chest rumbling against my back as he yanks me up, onto the bed. He spins me around, positions my legs so I'm straddling him.

And he's completely naked, his hard cock against my bare pussy.

"You still with us, princess?" he taunts me, curling my fingers around his cock.

I look down, my mouth hanging open. I've seen it so many times, but I never get over the fact that it's so...big. And perfect and straight and thick and...

I want my mouth on it.

And not just that. I think about Eli behind me, watching.

"Yeah," I manage to say out loud to Alex, "yes. I'm still with you." I swallow, still staring down at Alex in my hand. "And I want you." I bite my lip, my stomach fluttering. "And him."

Without waiting to see his reaction, I brace myself with one hand on Alex's shoulder and try to ease back off his lap. But someone's fingers in my hair jerks my head back, stopping me, and then Eli's eyes are looking into mine, upside down.

"Careful with her, Eli. You know I like this one," Alex warns.

A slow smile curves on Eli's lips as he leans down close to me, and I gasp against his mouth as Alex brushes the head of his dick against my clit.

"I'm not careful, *princess*," Eli murmurs against my mouth, mocking Alex's nickname for me. He pushes my head up and Alex's fingers curl around my throat as he jerks me up and pulls me down on top of him.

He lies on his back, then his hands are on my bare hips, his cock between us.

"Fuck me, Zara."

I glance over my shoulder to find Eli pulling his shirt off.

His olive skin is fucking gorgeous, his six-pack defined and that fucking V. Alex grabs me by the throat again, jerking my head around so I'm looking at him again.

My brain feels fuzzy, everything around me spinning in slow motion.

And fuck, didn't Alex just try to drown me?

Didn't he flash my—

"*Now*, Zara. I don't want to wait all fucking night."

I shift my hips, stroke Alex's cock and he groans, biting his lip as he stares at me. I position myself over him and slowly start to lower myself onto him, but Eli's hands come to either side of my shoulder and he shoves me down just as I feel the bed dip.

I wince, falling forward, my hands on Alex's chest as his length nearly fucking impales me and it stings as I adjust to the size of him.

Alex is always rough, and I guess it runs in the fucking house.

But Alex surprises me as he frowns at Eli. "Fuck, easy, man."

Eli doesn't say anything.

As Alex helps me ride him, his cock hitting so far back I swear I can feel it in my stomach, Eli's mouth comes to my ear. "You ready, baby girl?"

Baby girl.

No one has ever called me that before.

When Alex isn't calling me a "druggie whore", he sticks with "princess".

But "baby girl" does things to me. It makes my stomach flip, my thighs clench.

Eli's hands go to my ass but then his fingers trail lower.

Alex stiffens as Eli's finger slides in beside his cock, and I wince as they both stretch me, the sensation new.

I stop riding Alex, my thighs shaking as I hover over him.

A strange thought occurs to me, like a cloud breezing

through my hazy mind. I have scars on my thighs. And Alex has never noticed.

Will Eli see them?

Before I can think about it too much, the thought drifts away.

My eyes flutter closed as Eli's chest brushes against my back and he tries to push another finger inside of me. But Alex is so big and…

This is happening too fast.

This is not a good idea. I didn't mean for *this* to happen. I meant to piss Alex off by coming here. Convince him that breaking up with me was a stupid idea. But I didn't mean to fuck him and his roommate at the same time.

But the Xannie and the alcohol and the Addie are making my head spin. My face feels numb, and as Eli works another finger into my pussy, already full but still dripping wet, Alex's voice cuts through my high.

"Stop, man. She's nodding off."

Eli laughs, his breath against my neck. He doesn't stop.

"She's fucking nodding off!" Alex says again, sounding panicked.

"This was your idea," Eli says quietly, still speaking against my skin. He feels so good. Everything is so tight and so full and so…

His hand comes to my throat as he jerks me back against him. "And you're still here, aren't you, baby girl?" His voice is so low, I don't even know if Alex heard him.

I arch my neck, but my mouth feels so dry, I don't know what to say or how to say it and—

"Eli." Alex's voice is laced with warning.

Eli's fingers thrust harder inside of me and I wince with his movements. It doesn't feel good anymore.

"Stop." Alex's voice is a growl. He wraps his arms around my waist and lifts me off him, pulling me to his chest. Eli's fingers seem to rip out of me, like he curled them up so it would hurt when Alex hauled me off them.

Alex's chest is warm and his arms lock around me as he sits up, cradling me to him. "This was a bad idea."

The bed shifts but I can't open my eyes. They're so fucking heavy.

Alex's grip tightens around me.

"Why the sudden change of heart?" Eli asks softly, his words venomous. "You having flashbacks?" I don't know what the hell he's talking about, but I can't really find it in me to care. My body feels so pleasant like this. Pleasant and warm against Alex and I don't want to move.

"I made a mistake," Alex says. He sounds strangely nervous.

Eli doesn't say anything.

Alex's arms tighten around me so much it actually hurts. He shifts on the bed, removes one arm only long enough to pull the covers over me.

"I'll sleep with her. Go fuck Rihanna."

My stomach churns for some reason with those words but even still…I can't move.

"You just tried to drown her. Blackmailed her with Xanax to get her to fuck us, and now you don't wanna go through with it?" Eli's voice is still low, as it always is. Still clinical, like he's just laying out all the facts with no attachment to the outcome.

"You're fucking around with Rihanna. Why do you care?"

Eli is silent, then I hear someone pounding on the door. A high-pitched scream.

Alex laughs, and it rumbles against my body. I don't open my eyes. I'm drifting off into darkness and it feels good.

But I guess someone opens the door and a girl is screaming. "What the fuck are you doing? You fucking asshole, what the fuck?!"

"Get out, Rihanna. Don't call me names," Eli's voice. Edging on impatience.

"No, don't you—"

There's another scream and something that sounds like a door slamming against a wall and footsteps coming close and Alex tenses with me still in his arms.

"You fucking bitch!" That same high-pitched voice, closer now.

"If you touch her, I swear to God, Rihanna, I'll fucking drown you in my pool." That's Alex's voice. His arms are tight around me, and he's not yelling but he sounds so...mad.

More footsteps. Some scuffling. A door slamming shut. More screaming, but it's distant.

I tremble in his arms, and it's completely involuntary. I don't even know why it's happening.

Alex holds me tighter. He presses a kiss to the top of my head. "I'm so sorry." His voice is a hoarse whisper.

Is he really sorry?

"I'm so sorry, I'm so...I'm sorry, Zara."

I hold him tighter, my arms around his neck.

"It's okay, princess." He kisses the side of my face. "Go to sleep, yeah?"

Yeah. Like I could stop myself.

But his words echo in my head. "I'll fucking drown you in my pool."

Alex already tried to drown *me*.

He pulled down my top.

He's an asshole.

I can't even manage a nod to his words, but despite all the shit he did, I still think it back. *Yeah.*

2

Zara

WHEN I WAKE UP, Alex is snoring softly beside me.

It's still dark outside, but I blink a few times, make out the time on the alarm clock beside the bed.

It's four in the morning.

My head is pounding, my throat feels like sandpaper.

What the fuck happened last night?

My hand goes to my chest and I stifle down a scream as I realize I'm fucking naked. It's not that I've never woken up naked beside Alex but we...

Fuck.

I can't really see Alex in the dark, but when I slowly move away from him, I realize he's naked, too.

Did we have sex last night? Did we make up?

I try to remember, but everything is so damn blurry. *Not again.*

This shit has happened one too many times the past three years. I bite back a groan, slowly slide off the bed and plant my feet on the floor.

My hair is damp, and I taste chlorine in my throat.

The fucking pool.

I feel something against my toes and squat down, grasping for it. It's my…clothes. What I was wearing before I stripped down to my bikini in Alex's room. Before we got into that fight and he tried to kick me out.

I feel my hand out blindly, the room so damn dark, and find my tank to, too, and in the back pocket of my jeans is my phone.

I use the flashlight on it to quickly get dressed.

Big thanks to the MVP who brought over my shit.

When I'm dressed, the jeans feeling very bizarre against my bare ass, I walk out the door, realizing with a jolt we're in the guest bedroom. Alex is still snoring behind me as I pull the door to and stand out in the hall, listening.

It's silent in this house. So different from all the people and the noise and the music last night.

Speaking of… *what the hell happened last night?*

I blow out a breath, consider pulling my phone out of my pocket and going through all the missed notifications I saw back in that bedroom but decide against it. I don't really want to know what bullshit I pulled after all those stimulants and all that alcohol.

Alex fed me Xanax.

I almost fucked him *and* Eli.

Jesus. I've barely even spoken a string of words to Eli since I've known him.

I need a glass of water.

I use my flashlight to head toward the stairs at the opposite end of the hall, then put my phone back in my pocket, once again ignoring the notifications. I creep down the stairs, see people passed out in the living room, on the couch, the floor. One dude is slumped in a seated position at the bottom of the steps, right by the front door, his head at a very uncomfortable angle against his shoulder.

Kylie drove me last night, but I can walk back to our apartment. It's not that far.

First, I need water because every step makes my head light up in pain.

Various levels of snoring fill the living room as I walk down the hall, and I smell alcohol and something sour.

Probably vomit.

The kitchen is a wreck.

There are tipped over bottles and plastic cups all over the island in the center of the room, more covering nearly every inch of the countertops. There's a brown puddle on the floor in the dining room adjacent to the kitchen, and there's someone sleeping *on* the table. Some dude on his stomach with his arms spread wide, like he's cuddling the fucking table.

Thankfully, no one is sleeping in the kitchen.

My bare feet crunch on something as I head toward the stainless-steel fridge, desperate for water. I pause, looking down.

Ritz crackers, and the empty box of them is strewn a few feet away. Damn. Someone was hungry.

I keep walking toward the fridge, my head pounding with every step.

But the pain doesn't stop unwanted thoughts from whirring.

I tried to make up with Alex. We fought. He tried to kick me out. I went downstairs and danced on the coffee table instead.

Alex came over. He was drunk. He hardly ever gets drunk because when he does, he acts like a complete dick.

He pulled down my top, someone tried to touch, me and Eli was there.

Fuck. *Alex flashed my tits.*

The thought is almost enough to make me run out of here, my stomach churning. If there's a video and my mom fucking sees it, I am so screwed.

Fuck, fuck, fuck.

I glance out the window over the sink—also filled with cups and bowls and something that looks like ramen noodles sticking to the faucet—and catch sight of the serene in-ground pool, illuminated by lights flush with the concrete.

The pool.

My blood runs cold, my fingers around the handle of the fridge as my eyes remain fixed on the pool, thinking about what happened last night.

Some of the lounge chairs are turned over, there are a few beach towels lying around the concrete.

Alex almost drowned me in that pool.

The calm surface seems to reflect the still-dark sky, but there are lights beneath the water and... *What the fuck is that?*

I bring my hand to my mouth, dropping my hold on the door of the fridge.

There's no one around the edge of the pool but there's...

Oh my God.

My limbs feel numb as I take a hesitant step toward the window.

No.

That's not...

I force myself to walk toward the sliding glass door for a better view. A different angle. A way to make this all make sense.

My fingers press against the cool glass and my chest tightens as I rest my forehead against the door, blinking.

Because I must still be drunk. I'm still fucked up. There's no fucking way.

I hear something move behind me.

Before I can scream, a hand comes over my mouth and a voice whispers in my ear, "There's a body in the pool, *baby girl.*"

3

Alex

HAVING a corpse at the bottom of your pool really dampens the party mood, and having the cops in my face, *again*, really annoys the shit out of me. They've been on my ass since last year, and then again a few weeks ago after that fucking game that got me suspended. It's not enough that they've tried to ruin my football career, my reputation—which wasn't great to begin with—and made my father's entire megachurch congregation pray for my soul on a weekly basis, now, they suspect me of murder.

Fantastic.

But regardless of what they think happened here, they've got no evidence to support their theory that someone drowned Rihanna Martinson. Besides, I know for a fact toxicology reports will show that her blood alcohol content will reveal she was a couple of milliliters away from being made of more vodka than blood.

Still. It's a fucking hassle, on top of all the shit I've got to deal with when it comes to Zara.

My father already had a lawyer sent to the station where

they brought me in for interrogation. I answered their stupid questions and walked out free in a matter of hours, which is more than I can say for last fall. That took a hell of a lot longer, and Eli's dad had to come bail me out of that shit.

I open the door of my black Jeep, parked behind the Falls Creek police station, and just as I slide in, my phone vibrates in my back pocket.

I pull it out, roll my eyes but answer it, holding it up to my ear, resting my head against the seat.

"What, Dad?"

"I'd think you'd sound a little more grateful considering I just saved your ass—"

Pastors shouldn't say "ass". Instead of telling him that, I interrupt him with, "I didn't do it." I've said that half a dozen times already this morning and it's not even seven a.m.

"I'm not saying you did, son, but we both know you're going to be the prime suspect because it was your house—"

"It's Eli's house." I live in it, but Eli's father, Eric, put it in Eli's name.

My dad sighs on the other end. "Eric called. Eli's name is already cleared."

Of course his name is already cleared. Eli is the fucking golden boy at Caven University.

It's not like I want him to get arrested but damn. Everyone thinks he's so damn smart and so damn responsible and it all rings in my ears, "Eli's dad is a lawyer," "and "Eli wins championships," and "Eli controls his temper and Eli has a bright future."

Yeah, well, Eli almost fucked my girl last night. And last year, we almost did the same shit with a different girl. I'm pretty sure Eli isn't as good as everyone thinks he is.

But I wouldn't actually know.

He's been my roommate for the past three years but some days, I don't think I really know the guy at all.

"My name is cleared, too," I tell my dad. "You know how

Rihanna is." I swallow hard, sitting up straighter in my seat as I stare at the grey police building in front of me. "Was," I amend, my voice low.

My dad is quiet on the line and for a second I wonder if we got disconnected. I pull my phone away from my ear, glance at the screen. Nope. He's still there.

"Dad?" I hate the way it comes out. Like I want him to be here or some shit. I don't want that. I haven't wanted my dad to be there for me since I was fifteen and everything went to shit.

Before that, I dealt with the fighting. My mother flinging accusations his way of cheating and being an asshole. Calling him a hypocrite, a liar.

He might've worked for "the Lord", but he was God to me. Throwing the football with me every single day at the beach. Taking me to practice, signing me up for camps. Watching the game with me every Sunday during the season.

I took his side every time she started screaming at him.

But then he fucked everything up.

"Yeah, son?" he asks in answer to my plea, his voice heavy. Full of exhaustion. As if he feels the past six years weighing on his shoulders, too.

I close my eyes, swallowing hard.

Rihanna is dead.

I say it out loud for the first time. "Rihanna is dead."

He sighs. "I know. I'll need to reach out to her parents later today, after they've had time to..." He just trails off. Time to what? Process it? That their twenty-year-old daughter was found dead in a pool after a back-to-school party, right after she started her senior year?

Yeah. Being a pastor sounds like it would blow. Dad's church is on the coast, a two-hour drive from here, but he knows Rihanna's family because I'm on the team and Rihanna was the cheerleading captain.

I mean, I'm just barely on the team, since I've got to sit the next few games out for breaking Nate's nose—he deserved it.

I blow out a breath, thinking of Rihanna.

I didn't know her well. Like most everyone else, she preferred Eli to me. Girls always thinking they can get him to open up, or some shit.

Eli doesn't even play fucking football.

"Is Eli okay?" my dad asks me.

I don't fucking know. Eli doesn't talk about shit like his feelings. Before the cops had me follow them down here, he was sitting in the wreck of a living room, silent, drinking a glass of my orange juice, as if girls who sucked his dick were found dead in a pool every morning.

My stomach flips, a lump forming in my throat.

"Son…" My dad's voice sounds strained. "Was Zara there?"

I tense in my seat. Dad doesn't like Zara. He thinks she's a bad influence. He's not wrong, but it's not really his fucking business. I don't know why it matters, anyway, except… I do know.

The thing about having a dad overly involved in your sport is that he hears shit he shouldn't. Things that would be better off kept from your parents.

And he knows I caught Zara sucking Jamal's dick last week.

I clear my throat. "Yeah, but we weren't… Not for me," I lie to him, not wanting to deal with this shit. I don't know what's going on with me and Zara anyway. "I don't want to talk about her." I start the Jeep, put my seatbelt on with one hand. "How's Mom?" I ask, changing the subject to one my dad doesn't want to talk about.

There's a pause and I realize I'm holding my breath, waiting.

Finally, he just says, "She's fine." Which means she's probably not fine at all. Probably pissed as hell at me, or in a fucking Xanax-induced sleep, which is why she isn't on the call. I can't even blame her.

I think my dad and I have just been one big ass disappointment after another to her.

"Great, well, I'll talk to you later."

"Wish you were going to be at service this morning," my dad says quietly.

Anger blooms in my chest, and I clench my jaw for a second. "Right. Well. I'll be down fall weekend for the beach party, if we still decide to throw it. I'll stop by then." I press my foot on the brake and put the car in reverse to pull out of my parking spot. "Talk to you later, Dad."

"Love you, Alex."

I end the call, toss the phone in the passenger seat and pull out of my spot, turning up the music playing through my speakers.

FEEL NOTHING by The Plot In You.

Rihanna probably fell in that pool all on her own. She probably didn't need any help drowning herself, as drunk as she was. Her friends saw her downing shots back-to-back after she saw Eli and me with Zara. She's always been a little fucking dramatic. She should've known Eli doesn't date. He was into her pussy. Not her.

But the last person to see her alive was me, and Eli himself.

Zara, though.

She didn't see shit.

4

Zara

WHEN THE ALARM on my phone goes off, my first instinct is to throw it across the fucking room.

So, I do.

Unfortunately, it keeps going off, some techno beat that usually gets me pepped up, but this morning just makes me want to scream.

I groan, flinging my covers off and stumbling over to the wall I threw the phone against, picking it up and silencing it as I rub my eyes with my fist. I've got one hour until class starts and the last thing I want to do is set foot out of this room.

The past three days have gone by in a haze of cops, questions, accusations, and fending off frantic messages from my mother. Not to mention the other texts from concerned citizens sending me links to the short video clip that's spread around campus like wildfire. The one of my fucking ex flashing my tits in his house.

In light of a dead girl at the bottom of his pool, it would seem my tits would be the least of anyone's concern. However, I've seen them on my phone screen more times than I'd like to count in the past three days, so apparently, people are as equally fascinated with nudity as they are death.

There's a knock on my bedroom door and I tense, opening my mouth to tell Kylie that I'm fine, but the door bursts open anyway because I didn't have the sense to lock it after I got back from my dealer, Jax's, house last night.

Kylie stares at me, looking a little dumbfounded, one hand still on the knob.

I arch a brow. "Yes?"

She opens her mouth. Closes it. Clears her throat and looks at the floor. She's in loose linen pants and a white T-shirt. Her pajamas. Her silky black hair is in a topknot, and she tucks a stray lock of it behind her ear before she looks up and meets my gaze again. Kylie Jones is like five feet tall and about as wide as my pinky finger.

She's as quiet as she looks like she'd be, which is why I'm surprised she's at my door right now. I know her even less than I know Rihanna Martinson, the dead cheerleader, as she's come to be known by now, despite the fact we've lived together since spring, when Mom agreed to let me get an apartment at Caven after the ECU-Narcan-rehab incident.

Kylie and I interact daily, but we don't *connect*.

Which is entirely my fault. I'm usually too high to do things like connect.

"I didn't think you'd be up," Kylie admits.

I would take it personally, but since I've been doped up on benzos for approximately seventy-two hours, she's got a point. I figured skipping two days of classes was okay, since I was the one that found Rihanna's body in the pool.

My stomach churns. I don't want to think about it.

"Surprise." I throw up my hands, phone in one. I've got more messages from numbers I don't know, which is not very surprising at this point. It seems my phone number spread around campus as fast as my tit video. I deleted all of my social media accounts and the apps on my phone, but people are still really into those tits.

I know it'll die down. At least, that's what I tell myself. Nudes get leaked every other week in college. It's not a big deal. But then again, I found the fucking body, and Alex Cardi was the one that flashed my boobs. Also, I'm still considered a source of fascination around Caven because I was dating their quarterback. And probably *also* because I was transferred straight from rehab, and people love a good overdose/rehab story.

I finished half a semester in the spring, and fall classes have been in session for three weeks now, but it seems still the only thing people really know about me is my love of drugs and Alex.

I'm not so sure about the last one anymore though.

Now I'm at the center of the death of the cheerleading captain.

Super.

But at least I'm not the only one. There were dozens of people at that party, and as fascinated as people might be with me, Alex and Eli are much more interesting. People know them. Respect them. Wanna fuck them.

The gossip around them should eclipse me.

Plus, a girl died for fuck's sake. They should hold pep rallies and memorial services for her and leave me the fuck alone.

Or take their concerns about my tits and the pool up with Alex.

The last I saw of him, I was in the passenger seat of Kylie's car after she, very kindly, came to pick me up when I was done talking to the cops. Alex was getting into his Jeep to follow an officer to the police station.

Eli had already left. He's the one that called the cops after he came up behind me in the kitchen.

I haven't spoken to either of them since then. Maybe I

should reach out to Eli, considering Rihanna was all over his ass at the party and maybe he's upset about it or something, but I can't do it.

We weren't friends, and despite what went down with us Saturday night—the fuzzy memory thankfully, or not, having come back—he wouldn't expect me to reach out.

Not to mention Eli wasn't dating her. They were just fucking around, I guess. I don't know. Eli never talks about women. Or anything. Not to me.

Besides, it's a little late to reach out now. Three days, and no arrests have been made. Toxicology results aren't in yet, but it seems the consensus is that Rihanna Martinson fell into that pool alone, and drowned because she was drunk off her ass.

Eli was asleep in his bed, his alibi vouched for by another girl that was at the party, because his dick was in her mouth most of the early morning hours so I've heard.

Lovely.

Alex, of course, was in the guest bed with me. My statement wasn't great, and I had to admit that I'd drank the night before even though I'm only twenty. They let that shit go since I wasn't drunk when they were talking to me, although if they'd given me a breathalyzer, I'm pretty sure they'd have found that I actually was, and of course, I didn't tell them about the drugs. Mine or Alex's.

I didn't need my mom breathing down my neck more than she has been since the Narcan incident. I didn't even tell her I was at the party. She's too spooked as it is that a girl died there.

No need for her to get all bent out of shape about my presence there too. She threatens to bring a drug test to my apartment every other week as it is. Thankfully, as long as I visit her often enough and behave myself, she never shows up. Thank fuck for that. It's probably because she's a little busy with her soon-to-be fourth husband.

But when I moved into this apartment, she made sure to tell little Kylie Jones that I was in recovery and Kylie should keep an eye out for me.

Kylie wants to be a pharmacist, and she's an overeager kiss ass, so she was more than happy to agree to be my babysitter.

"How was your weekend?" I clear my throat. "Week?" I amend my statement, trying to avoid any awkward conversation about my tit video or the rumors going around about me, Alex, and Eli, like how we were the last people to see Rihanna.

That last rumor isn't true.

I didn't see shit after Alex pulled me into his arms and kicked Eli out. I mean, no offense to fucking Rihanna, rest in peace, but I had nothing to do with what happened to her.

But I do remember her screaming at me, presumably because she was fucking around with Eli and I was fucking around with him.

And I remember Alex's words to her. "If you touch her, I swear to God Rihanna, I'll fucking drown you in my pool."

I start to make my bed after tossing my phone on my nightstand, pushing Alex's words from my mind as a chill slides down my spine. Yeah, no. Not gonna think about that.

I yank up the white sheet, then my pale green comforter. Kylie is still in my doorway, shifting from foot to foot, awkward as hell. I don't know who she hangs out with or what exactly she knows about last weekend, but she doesn't party. She at least knows about Rihanna though. Caven isn't a huge university, and despite her appearance, Kylie does not live under a rock. Besides, she dropped me off and picked me up from the crime scene.

Not to mention I've been skipping classes.

I guess that's why she's standing there.

"It was okay," Kylie finally answers me as I throw the pillows on the bed and open my curtains, looking down at the woods that edge our apartment complex. It's a nice, sunny day outside already.

I hate it.

I turn back to Kylie and nod. I'm in black booty shorts and a white tank and really should shower but I guess braids will do for today. My bleached white hair probably needs as little time as possible under a blow dryer anyway. More dry shampoo will do the trick.

But what I really care about more than the state of my hair is getting to the tampon box under my bathroom sink. Can't really do that with Kylie standing in my doorway though.

"How are you?" she asks, rubbing her hand up her arm as she watches me. I pick my phone up from the nightstand but don't look at it.

"Great," I lie.

She frowns, her thick, dark brows pulling together. "Zara, you don't have to keep things from me, you know. If you're feeling upset about—"

"I didn't even know Rihanna." Which is the truth. And what I did know of her, I didn't fucking like. She kissed Alex after practice last week in the name of being a "good cheerleader", or whatever bullshit he mumbled to me when I lost my shit on him.

Fuck her.

God, I'm going to hell.

"Yeah, but even besides that... I've heard some things. And uh...seen some things," Kylie continues.

I cross my arms, clench my phone tight in one hand. My usually rather eloquent roommate is stumbling over her words and it's making me uncomfortable. And angry.

"What are you really asking me, Kylie?"

Like most people, despite my mother's warning, I think Kylie believes that rehab is a cure for druggies, and I'm all fine. So, I don't think she's asking me about drugs.

Which is good because I'm not talking about them. But I don't want to talk about what it is I know she's about to bring up either.

She takes a deep breath, wringing her hands together as she leans against my doorway. "Are you still with Alex?" There's a note of anger in her words, which is unusual coming from her. Kylie doesn't really get angry, so I kind of feel a little sistership with her in this moment, knowing she probably saw that video and she's probably pissed on my behalf, but still, it's not really her business.

I roll my eyes. "So what if I am?" I counter.

She looks concerned. "I saw the video, Zara," she confirms. "Everyone has probably seen the video." She bites her tongue a second, waiting for me to say something but when I don't, she adds, "You didn't look like you were enjoying it."

I laugh out loud, dropping my hands by my sides. "Yeah? Well I saw the video too. Good thing there were so many damn people there live and in person, because it's kind of hard to make out the details of my nipples, huh?" I've seen a few of the videos, but only one really captures the heart-warming moment.

And it's blurry, and bodies are in the way, so whatever.

Kylie's cheeks flush pink but she doesn't drop my gaze. "Tell me you aren't with him. You know he's a complete jerk anyway."

It's not breaking news to me that she thinks that. She warned me about him when we started dating in the spring, telling me he had a bad temper. Was a loudmouth. Obnoxious. All the things you could expect from a preacher's kid gone wild.

He is all of those things.

But I need someone like that. Not that it matters.

I blow out a breath and break the news to her, "No, we aren't together. But not because of the video."

Kylie's mouth hangs open and she shakes her head, about to say something when I beat her to it.

"It's because I cheated on him," I admit, feeling my stomach clench as I do. "Last week." I shrug, turn away from her and step into my bathroom, setting my phone on the counter and glancing in the mirror.

God, what a mess.

I lick my finger and start rubbing away the eyeliner from under my eyes. Then I hear Kylie step into the bedroom, and she comes to stand in the doorway of my bathroom.

"You, what?" she croaks.

I glance at her big brown eyes in the mirror. "I cheated on him," I tell her again, more slowly this time.

She chews on her lip as I part my hair, going to work on one section, twisting it into braids.

"Oh. Wow…" she finally says. "I'm uh… *Why?*" she asks, shaking her head, her brows furrowed together.

I laugh a little, still braiding my hair and meeting her gaze again in the mirror. "You just pointed out that he's a jerk, right?"

She just keeps staring at me blankly. She's dating a pre-med kid, Ian. A nice, quiet guy that she's head over heels for. I think the whole concept of cheating is so foreign to Kylie that she probably wants to kick me out of the apartment right now so I don't contaminate her with my slutty ways.

"He let Rihanna Martinson kiss him after practice last week, so I sucked another guy off." I grab a small elastic from the counter of my bathroom, fasten my braid, and go to work on the other side.

Alex loves when I wear my hair in braids.

I hope I see him before my philosophy seminar.

"Zara!" Kylie gasps, a hand over her poor little heart. "That's… that's terrible."

I shrug. "Well, Rihanna is dead now, so——"

"No," she interrupts me, her voice rising an octave. "It's terrible that you... that you..."

"Sucked another guy's dick?" I supply, since she seems to be choking on the words. Every pun intended.

Her light brown skin goes pale and she looks like she might faint. "Yeah. That."

I finish braiding my hair, flick both ends over my shoulders and grab my toothbrush, wet it under the sink, and squeeze on toothpaste and start brushing.

I shrug and shake my head, but don't say anything until I'm done brushing, spitting in the sink and wiping my hand over the back of my mouth.

"Yeah, well." I turn to face her after I set the brush down. "No one ever said I was a good person, huh, Kylie?" I pat her awkwardly on the back and walk out of the bathroom, across my room, to my little walk-in closet.

"Gah, Zara. That's... wow," I hear her mumbling, and I don't even know if she's talking to me or herself at this point.

I pull a cream-colored tank from a hanger, grab my pale blue jeans, then my white bralette that's hanging on the back of the closet door. I start to change in the closet, and Kylie keeps talking, not really ready to give this up yet, apparently.

She clears her throat first, then says, "People have been saying the police are ruling out murder. About Rihanna."

I roll my eyes, unseen by her. "Yeah, they have to. They're the police," I call back to her from the closet.

"Yeah..." she trails off, but I know she's not done, because Kylie is a curious girl. It's one of the things that I like about her. She's super into science, which I hate, and she doesn't party, which I don't get, but she asks a lot of questions about a lot of things. Sometimes that's annoying as hell, but some- times it makes for interesting conversations. Like the time she drilled Ian about his past sexual partners at the dining room table.

Ian's face was beet red as he shoved his glasses up his nose and looked down at his hands.

Kylie was seemingly oblivious to his embarrassment. She just really wanted to know.

"You don't think anyone hurt her, do you?" she continues.

I straighten my top and walk out of the closet. "Like who?"

She shrugs, leaning against the doorway to the bathroom. "I mean, I wasn't there, but... I don't know. Alex didn't really have a problem pulling down your top in front of all of those people and, you know, he's got a bad temper."

I wince, remembering the time I threw a glass cup at the wall in the living room, in the middle of one of our fights. It shattered into pieces and Alex took the blame when Kylie came out of her room, horrified.

He's not the only one with a bad temper.

We're like fire and gasoline.

"Kylie. He didn't kill Rihanna. He was with me all night." Yeah, he's a hot head but the idea of Alex killing anyone is kind of hilarious. I push past Kylie back into the bathroom and grab my Chapstick from the counter. As I roll it over my lips, a sharp sting makes me wince. I lean in closer to the mirror, pulling up my top lip.

There's a small cut, angry and red.

From where Alex pried my mouth open with a tequila bottle.

I force myself not to look at Kylie because I'm not about to explain what happened in that kitchen. And then the pool.

Shit.

Maybe the idea of Alex killing someone isn't that funny after all.

I put down the Chapstick and pick up my eyeliner.

"You know he broke that guy's nose on the field," Kylie adds, as if she's building evidence against Alex.

"I know," I snap back. "I was there. But he didn't kill

anyone, Kylie. You sure you wanna be a pharmacist? I think you'd make a good detective."

She blows out a breath behind me as I concentrate on my liner. "Honestly, I'm just glad you two broke up," she continues. "He's not good for you."

I snort, shaking my head but not saying anything as I lean back from the mirror, pick up my mascara.

I'm not good for *him*.

I finish up my makeup, bat my eyes a few times and toss my mascara on the counter in the corner with my other products.

I glance over my shoulder and smile at Kylie. "Thanks, Ky."

She winces, and I remember belatedly she doesn't really like when I call her that. But she just says, "Of course. I already knew he was an asshole. I just wanted to make sure you're... okay."

The bathroom feels crowded and hot suddenly, and my skin itches, but I manage to say, "Thank you." It hasn't really sunk in, to be honest. Me and Alex aren't together.

I'm not even sure I believe it.

Kylie nods. "Wanna meet me at Oasis after your class? My first one isn't until ten."

"I have ethics after philosophy, but I'm free for lunch?" I don't want to meet anyone for lunch, truth be told, but it might be nice to not eat alone today. Me and Alex usually ate together.

God, there's a lump in my throat when I think about not eating with him, but I shove it down deep. We aren't over yet.

I know we're not.

Kylie smiles at me in the mirror and then, thankfully, walks out of my bathroom.

As soon as she does, I shut the door and lock it, exhaling with relief.

I squat down, open up the cabinet under my sink and

reach past the self-tanner, Q-tips, and box of razor blades for the blue tampon box at the back. I dig my hand around in it and my fingers curl around a little baggie.

Score.

I keep some of my stash in shoe boxes in my closet, but these are the magic pills. I take one of the red and blue capsules out of the bag and dry swallow it down. This is the closest thing I've ever taken to having a real personality. It helps me fake that shit. I try not to take many of them because they're just so damn good, and expensive as hell.

I went a little overboard on Saturday with all the drugs, but I'm better now. I just need this one. I'm fine.

I close the baggie, toss it back into the tampon box and shut the cabinet, standing to my feet and smiling at myself in the mirror.

See? I am not the same person that went into rehab. I'm better. I think of my future self.

pre-rehab Zara would never think of leaving future Zara a baggie to take the edge off.

And future self has arrived, ready to take on the first day back to classes after that little…mess up. Fully prepared to look everyone in the eye who saw Alex Cardi flash my tits at a party that ended with a dead girl in the pool.

5

Zara

I'M HEADED TO KIVETT, walking across the quad, my head held high and a smile on my face from the Vyvanse. I've got my fingers clenched around my green backpack. The sun is out. The fountain in the center of the quad is clear and sparkling, and while there are papers with Rihanna's face on them and the date and time of her candlelit vigil taped to the light poles around Caven's well-manicured campus, I'm feeling good.

No one has said shit to my face about the video, and most people seem too caught up in their own lives to give a damn about me anyway. The joys of college.

I'm about to turn off the brick walkway to head up the steep stairs to Kivett Hall when someone calls my name at my back.

I straighten my spine, bite back my smile.

I know that voice so well.

Tightening my fingers on my backpack straps, I turn around.

Alex is staring right at me, his brow furrowed, hands in the pockets of his grey pants. The sun is behind him, catching the lighter brown shades of his hair. But I'm standing in his shadow, and I can see the worry in his eyes.

Behind him, Eli Addison is looking at me with a strange expression on his face. Like we share a secret, the way his eyes are narrowed in on mine, but there's a slight curve to his lips. Almost as if he's smirking at me.

I know they go to the gym together in the mornings, and they're both business majors and have a class together, which is why he's here, I guess.

Alex steps closer to me, blocking my view of Eli.

I turn my gaze back to him, smiling. "Hi, baby."

He swallows and looks down at his shoes. "You haven't answered any of my texts, Za."

I step even closer, until there's little distance between us and I can smell him. He smells like fall. It's my favorite season. "Sorry," I tell him, trying to mean it. But since I've been sleeping hard the past few days, I'm not all that sorry. "I was just, you know, trying to process everything."

"There's a body in the pool, baby girl." Those words echo in my head, and I'm glad I can't see Eli right now.

Alex nods once, like he understands. His brow is still furrowed, but he finally looks back up to meet my eye. "I was worried about you."

I put my hand on his arm, beneath his white t-shirt and he seems to relax a little. "How are you?"

He chews the inside of his mouth a second before he says, "It's weird. But I'm fine." He shakes his head, and then his hand snakes around my waist, jerking me toward his warm body. He leans down close to me, his fingers splayed against my shirt. "Hey, I just—I'm sorry about this past weekend. About the flashing, and..." He shakes his head and takes another deep breath. "That wasn't cool."

I put my hand against his chest, feeling warmth spreading in my own with his words. "I'm sorry too, Alex."

I watch his throat bob as he swallows and then he straightens, letting his arm fall from my waist. I drop my hand, missing his warmth already. I want to ask him so many things. I want to ask if we're okay. If he really is done with me. If we took all of this too far.

But he takes a step back and I see Eli again. Alex turns to glare at him, and Eli steps forward, his dark green eyes locked on mine. He's got a messenger bag over his shoulder, a blue Caven Wrestling hoodie beneath it.

"We okay?" he asks me in that lilting, quiet voice. I'm not so sure the question is sincere. His lips kind of turn up into a smile and Alex is still glaring at him. I assume Alex put him up to this.

My vagina kind of hurts when I think of Eli curling his fingers up when Alex pulled me off of them.

I bite my tongue, holding back my wince. "Yeah, it's fine," I tell Eli.

His eyes rake up and down my body and I think about him standing in front of me over the weekend. Think about his hands around that guy's throat.

I take a step back, looking at Alex again. "Want to meet later?"

Alex runs his hand through his hair, and it's a sexy, disheveled mess like always. "I have practice later, and a marketing paper due tomorrow." He shrugs, dropping his hand. "Tomorrow?"

My chest deflates at that. I guess he hasn't really forgiven me. I can't blame him. *Don't leave me.*

I don't say that. I don't beg.

"Right. Tomorrow." I turn on my heel and head up the steps to Kivett.

6

Zara

THURSDAY MORNING before my abnormal psych class, and Mom is on one again. I'm meeting Alex for lunch today and I do not want to deal with her shit. She's berating me for not picking up the phone and calling her all week.

"I'm serious, Zara, if you're using again—"

"I'm not, Mom, damn." I shift the phone to my other ear, propping it up with my shoulder while I reach for the baggie in my shoebox at the back of my closet. "Just relax. I'll be home for the brunch thing. One week, right? Sunday?" I pull the white pill out of the bag, swallow it dry while my mom sighs heavily on the other end of the phone. I crinkle the baggie in my hand and stand to my feet, my head spinning a little as I do.

I close my eyes for a second, letting my blood pressure adjust.

"Yes, not this Sunday but the next. And it's not a brunch thing, Zara. It's Cory's first introduction to some of the family and our engagement party, and I want it to go well."

I roll my eyes, the slight bitterness of the drug lingering on my tongue as I walk out of the closet heading toward the bathroom. I toss the baggie in the trash while Mom rants and raves about this very important party.

I don't need to remind Mom this is her fourth fucking engagement party for her fourth fucking husband. Probably should just stop having those parties altogether.

"Yeah, yeah. I'll be there. I'm sure Cory will do great. Such a charmer, that guy."

I've never heard Cory string together more than three words at a time.

My mom exhales loudly, and I yank the phone away from my ear to protect myself from the staticky sound. She's saying something but I'm rubbing eyeliner from beneath my eyes in the mirror, leaving a trail of black shadows under the red rim of my lower lash line, barely listening.

I mean, do I look like a druggie?

I guess. But I also look like another exhausted college kid, and I'm starting to think both of those people look the same.

Mom is yammering away about something in my ear, but I'm not paying attention. I do not give a fuck about this party. I only answered her call because I wanted to test the waters, make sure she hadn't seen the video of my tits.

Apparently not, because all she can think about is my soon-to-be new stepdad, Cory.

So sweet.

"Yeah, great, Mom. Gotta go. Love you." I end the call, slip my phone into my back pocket.

I grip the edge of the porcelain sink, lean in closer.

My blue-green eyes are red, my pupils little more than pinpricks which means I probably should cut back on the Addie, but too late for that now.

Whatever.

I needed to be at my peppiest to deal with Alex today. And

as if right on cue, my phone buzzes in my back pocket in the vibration pattern I assigned to him.

My heart thumps in my chest as I pull it out and read his text.

Alex: **Meet me at eleven**, he confirms. **I miss you.**

I smile to myself. I knew he'd come back.

7

Eli

I SKIPPED CLASSES MONDAY. Considering I was dealing
with the cops and answering questions about just how
involved Rihanna and I were all day Sunday, it seemed like
the right thing to do.

But I've gone the past three days. Today is Friday and
Fridays I don't have class, but I do have wrestling practice.
And before that, I have to deal with something else.

My phone vibrates in my pocket as I head to the 370Z,
sliding in the driver's side.

I start the car, pull out my phone and check my messages.
There's a fuck load, because everyone wants to make sure I'm
okay, since Zara and I found Rihanna's body in the pool. I
personally want everyone to fuck off, but that's not really how
society works. I respond to a few of my teammates. Coach let
me skip wrestling practice all week, but I'm going back this
afternoon, deal with all the questions that'll no doubt come
my way.

When I'm done answering those messages, I open up a
new screen.

To Zara.

Aside from seeing her Wednesday with Alex, we haven't spoken since Sunday morning, when I was calling 911 as she stared out at Rihanna's body, which had already sunk to the bottom of the pool.

It was kind of eerie, Rihanna's brown hair fanned out around her face, limbs loose by her sides.

Zara was silent. I'd put my hand over her mouth thinking she was going to scream, and maybe she was, but she hadn't. She'd just jumped in my arms, clinging to me.

Me: **You wanna talk?**

Finding a dead body in a pool at your ex's house can't be fun. She looked paler than usual when I saw her Wednesday, and her and Alex aren't back together yet.

Someone should check on her.

I shoot off the text, turn up the stereo in my car. *Let Me Down* by Lil Blanket and that psychopath Landon Tewers. I stare at my phone, waiting for those three little dots. We've never texted each other. I have her number because since she's been dating my roommate, that shit just kind of happens, and I assume she has mine.

But maybe she doesn't.

Maybe that little secret of hers is one I should just stuff down deep and stop thinking about. Maybe this isn't going to work how I thought it might. Truth be told, I thought Cardi would be done with her by now.

Or I thought *she'd* be done with *him.*

I know he doesn't know her secret. If he did, he'd lose his shit.

And I know too, that they're probably still banging. They didn't see me, but I saw them in the cafeteria together yesterday at lunch.

She was picking at a salad.

He had his elbows on the table, staring at her and she was shaking her head as she stared at the food she wouldn't eat.

She never eats much.

I don't know if they made up. He hasn't talked about it except to tell me they aren't together again. He hasn't been around much either. I know he's got practice, and he's probably been fucking her, or someone else, but I don't really care if he's fucking her.

In fact, thinking about it gets my dick hard. I've had to hear it all summer. I'm used to it now.

My phone vibrates, and I see she's texted me back.

Zara: **Is something wrong?**

I roll my eyes. Me: **Just thought you might be a little spooked.**

She doesn't take long to reply.

Zara: **You need a shoulder to cry on, Eli? Find someone else.**

But she put a little laughing emoji at the end to help soften the blow. I can't help smiling to myself. She's such a bitch.

Me: **I'm picking up someone from your apartment complex for practice. I'll come by for a sec.**

It's bullshit of course, but I needed to give her something that makes sense.

I toss my phone in the center console and pull out of the driveway, glancing at Alex's black Jeep as I do. I wonder if he knows that I remember what he last said to Rihanna. I wonder if he knows I didn't tell the cops, because if I did, he would've been in some shit.

I wonder why the fuck he said it anyway. He got all protective over Za at the end, like he actually gave a shit about her. I'm sure it was because he was drunk. He doesn't know her like he thinks he does.

He thinks she's just some stupid whore, and maybe she is, but she's something else too.

She's got some nasty habits and he doesn't even know about all of them.

He probably doesn't know either, that the girls with the worst habits have the sharpest teeth.

And that girl could take a bite out of fucking glass and never bleed.

It's how I know she'd be able to handle someone like *me*.

8

Zara

"WHAT DO you want to talk about?" I don't wait for an answer, spinning around and heading back down the hall toward the kitchen.

I open the cabinet over the oven as Eli walks in and closes the door behind him. I grab two shot glasses and a bottle of tequila. I'm fresh out of lime, but I'm also fresh out of fucks to give so I pour two shots, pick them both up and turn to face Eli as I shoot both of them back, one right after the other.

Kylie is already off for the weekend, gone to visit her parents in Angier, and therefore I have no shame about getting wasted at two in the afternoon on a Friday. My classes are done for the day, my professors weren't too hard on me this week considering what happened, and tomorrow is Rihanna's funeral, so everyone has been very… somber.

Even people that didn't know her. I'd argue especially people that didn't know her, but whatever.

And Alex is playing the victim too, like he's torn up about the cheerleader he didn't give a damn about. Since he's being a shady asshole, we haven't spoken since lunch yesterday. He said he needed time to "think" about being with me.

God, he's fucking annoying.

I slam down the shot glasses and cock my head toward Eli.

He's been to my apartment before with Alex to pick me up for a party, but it occurs to me that this is the first time he's been here without Alex.

The realization makes my heart pick up speed. Especially as I flash back to Saturday night, my bare breasts against his shirt as he stood in front of me while Alex fucked with me in the living room.

It feels a little hot in here suddenly, even though I've got the windows open.

Eli is in a black t-shirt that shows off his broad shoulders, the veins prominent in his biceps. He's got a full sleeve on one arm, tattoos that bleed onto his hand and a few of his fingers.

He scrubs that hand over his face, and I see his five o'clock shadow. I prefer it to the clean-shaven look. He's hot as hell and either the tequila is going straight to my brain, or his coconut-citrus scent is making me high, or maybe I'm just insane because I kinda want to fuck him right now on this counter.

Not a good idea, Zara. If I did that, I'm sure Alex would never forgive me.

"I just want to make sure you're okay," he tells me, quite seriously. His voice is lilting, and when we first met at his and Alex's house, I thought for sure he was European or some shit. He is technically, considering his mother is from Greece, but he's actually just from Raleigh. He only went to school at Caven because his uncle owns an auto body shop in Raleigh, and Eli is obsessed with cars.

It's one of the very few things I know about him, aside from what everyone else does. He's a wrestler, he's smart, and quiet. The son of a wealthy lawyer. Has tattoos on his hands specifically so he couldn't become a lawyer.

Okay. That last part I made up, but I wouldn't be surprised.

"Are you shitting me?" I ask him, shaking my head and resting my palms against the kitchen counter at my back. For an on-campus apartment, this place is pretty nice. Hardwood floors, marble counters. It's small, the living room is straight across from the kitchen, Kylie's room is off from the living room and mine down a tiny hallway. But we each get our own attached bathrooms, and I can have lots of sex in here without worrying about dorm rules.

Eli takes a step closer to me and I feel warmth flood my veins.

I imagine what sex with Eli would be like. What it was almost like, before Alex stopped it.

"No, Zara. I know you like to pretend you're above it all but—"

"But the girl that died was the same bitch that was trying to suck your cock at the party, so if one of us isn't okay, shouldn't that be you, Eli?"

He slides his hands into his white sweats, bites his tongue as he averts his eyes. He's got long, dark lashes and with those fucking full lips of his, I swear to God he is the envy of every girl getting filler and lash extensions, everywhere.

It's getting hotter in here.

I'm breaking out into a sweat, and I think about asking him to leave.

He sighs. "I barely knew her," he tells me, meeting my gaze again. He takes another step forward and I instinctively try to take one back, but the counter is there, and I've got nowhere to go.

I cross my arms over my chest.

He stares at me for a long moment and it's as if all the air has gone out of the room. I can't breathe.

Then he places his hands on either side of me, on the kitchen counter.

I smell that coconut and citrus scent and resist the urge to inhale deeply. To touch him. To run my hands over his shoulders, up his throat. To press my lips to his.

Not a good idea.

This is not *a good idea.*

He leans down close to me, his eyes searching mine. "You're not upset about it? I know you have feelings, baby girl."

A shiver slides down my spine at those words.

I swallow, hating the way he's making me feel everything right now. "Why are you even here, Eli? You need to leave."

He smiles, his eyes flashing. "That's not what you want."

"I'm with Alex. I'm not... We don't even—"

He grabs my waist, his hands wrapping around my sides as he pulls me close to him, cutting off my words. I plant my hands on his chest as I look up at him, my breath coming out in a rush. "Are you with him, Zara?"

I shake my head, my heart beating a nervous rhythm in my chest. My mouth goes dry. I'm not really sure what the hell is going on here. Eli has never flirted with me. He's barely even spoken to me.

And yeah, maybe I've fantasized about fucking him a few times because he's hot as shit and he was unattainable and—

No.

Alex will never forgive me for this.

"What do you want?" I ask him, a little breathless. I wonder if he wants to finish what we started Saturday night.

He's staring at my mouth and I wonder if he's going to try to kiss me, but instead he just asks, "What happened to your mouth, baby girl?" He brings one hand to my lips, running his finger across my top one.

I flinch, the cut from that tequila bottle still healing.

"Eli—"

"Did Alex do that?" He drops his hand from my mouth, and his fingers dig into my sides, the thin material of my tank top suddenly too much for me. I want his hands on me. I want him to yank down my shorts, spin me around and fuck me against this counter.

I am insane.

"Eli," I whisper, his name shaky from my lips. "What are you doing?"

He pulls me closer to his hard body. I can feel his cock throbbing against me, between us. I want to touch him there, but I don't. Instead, I grab his arms, feel his muscles beneath my fingers.

"He hurt you." It's not a question.

"I don't know what you think is happening here, Eli, but—"

"Was he really in bed with you all night, Zara?" he whispers, pressing harder against me, the counter digging into my back. "Do you know that for a fact?"

My mouth drops open, alarm bells ringing in my head. "Are you trying to fuck over your own best friend right now? Is that what this is?"

The corners of his mouth pull up into a smile. "I've watched you the past six months, you know that? I've watched you fight with him. Heard you fuck him. I've watched him hurt you."

His dick is throbbing against me and I'm panting being this close to him, our bodies pressed together.

But I can't do this.

Eli is insane. Alex hasn't hurt me. Not anymore than I've hurt him.

I don't know what he thinks he came here for, but we can't. This isn't right. "I don't know what's going on with you two, but I'm not—"

"Has he ever once really seen you, Zara?"

"What—"

"Because I have," he interrupts me, bringing his mouth closer to mine. I can feel his words when he speaks, smell the way his breath is like cotton candy, tempting me with his sweetness. But he isn't sweet, and clearly, he's crazy. I don't know what he's talking about. "I've seen you," he continues. "I know who you really are."

He leans in closer, his lips touching mine.

I stiffen in his arms. *No, no, no.*

I don't say it, though. I don't say it.

"Remember that night you two fought about his dad? About how Pastor Cardi didn't want you to see his son anymore?"

We fought about that all the time. Alex wanted me to act more respectable, and dress "modestly" for his games. He wanted me to "stop fucking doing drugs" so his father might actually accept me.

It was a constant source of tension, among other things.

But I know. I know which night Eli is talking about. I know, and it makes my heart skip a beat, my stomach flipping.

He trails his fingers under the waistband of my shorts, running his tattooed hand over a scar right there, on my hip.

He knows.

"Because I do," he tells me. "I know."

I didn't think anyone else was home. I thought Eli was with his dad or out or…

Shame makes my stomach churn.

But he doesn't let me feel it. He doesn't let me feel it for more than one second before he licks along the seam of my mouth, and I part my lips.

Let him in.

He groans against me, as if he's been waiting for this for a long time.

How long? I want to ask him. *How long have you been waiting for me? All this time? Six whole fucking months? Why did you never say anything?*

But I don't get a chance to ask anything.

He breaks away, leaving me breathless, then lifts the hem

of my tank top. I raise my arms up as he pulls it off over my head and drops it on the floor. He bends his head down, dropping his mouth on my nipple, his hands trailing down my waist.

"I've fucking seen these all week," he says, speaking against my skin. I grab the counter to keep myself upright, gasping. "I've fucking seen these in so many fucking videos. Alex's hands all over you." He licks a line across my chest, taking my other nipple in his mouth as I throw my head back, closing my eyes, reveling in the way he shoves his hands down my shorts.

"Did you like it?" I ask him, wrapping my arms around his neck as he picks me up and sets me on the counter, swiping his hand over the shot glasses and the bottle of tequila, sending it all crashing to the floor.

He parts my knees, his fingers running up my thighs as he sucks on my neck. My nails dig into his back, but his shirt is still on, and his pants, and I want him naked. I reach for his cock, rubbing my palm over it, feeling how thick and hard he is for me.

How long? Has he just been waiting for us to break up?

"Shut up," he tells me instead of answering my question. He hooks his fingers through the waistband of my hot pink panties, and I throw my arms around his neck and raise up, letting him pull the material down, past my knees, past my bare feet and dropping them on the floor.

He steps back, and I reluctantly let go of him, my hands coming to the cool counter as he assesses me, his eyes raking up and down my naked body.

Maybe he wants to stop. Maybe he realizes this is bad. *This is bad.* We can't do this. We can't.

"We can't do this," I blurt out as he stares at me. "I don't know why you're even here, but we can't do this, Eli." I cross my arms over my chest, cross my legs, too. "You need to leave."

"You know, Zara, it's not a good look. Being with someone that treats you like shit." He steps closer, reaching out his hand, and I flinch but he just brushes his thumb across my hip. The scar he saw me leave there.

My face feels hot, my chest, too.

"That doesn't notice where you really hurt."

I don't know what to say. I can only stare at him. But then he takes a step back and for one wild moment, I want to grab him, beg him to stay. I don't want to be alone.

But I don't beg.

And I don't fuck my ex's best friends.

"I have to go to practice." He glances at the clock on the stove behind me. "What are you doing tonight?"

I scoff, and even though I don't want to say it, I still do. "Nothing with you."

He stares at me a long moment, his expression unreadable. Then he shrugs. "All right." He steps toward the door, then stops, his back to me. My heart soars, wondering stupidly if he'll stay. If we'll actually do this after all.

But all he says is, "Those scars are beautiful, baby girl."

And without another word, without an explanation, he just walks out, closing the door softly behind him, leaving me naked and alone in my kitchen.

I glance down at my thighs.

I look over the pale white lines in the thickest part of my skin.

He saw them.

He saw them.

9

Zara

WHAT THE FUCK JUST HAPPENED?

Does he really know?

Did he really see me that night?

What else does he know about me?

It's not like I keep many secrets. My bullshit is out in the open, for everyone to see.

Absentmindedly, I trail my finger along my bare hip, my clothes still in a heap on the kitchen floor. I glance down, see the pale white scars.

Alex has never even noticed them.

Maybe he thought they were stretch marks and wanted to be polite.

I laugh out loud in the quiet of my apartment at the idea. Alex is a lot of things, but he is not polite.

Fuck.

I wonder if Eli will tell him he came by. He said he had wrestling practice now, but the way he just walked out like that, not giving a shit that I didn't tell him what I was doing tonight… He doesn't care. He just wanted to fuck me. I think he just wanted to because he didn't get to finish over the weekend.

I've been watching you the past six months.

Or maybe he's just crazy.

He probably won't tell Alex, I assure myself. Besides, I stopped it. I stopped it, and nothing really happened. He won't tell Alex, and me and Alex will be fine. Things are looking up anyway, even if he needs "space". Lunch yesterday wasn't all bad. Besides, we've weathered storms just like this before.

Okay. Maybe not just like this. He's never seen me on my knees sucking another guy's dick like he did last week but it wasn't exactly a secret that I'm not the faithful type. I told him when we first hooked up that I'd cheated on all my exes.

Although I hadn't with him. Up until that bullshit with Rihanna.

I glance down at the bottle of tequila on the floor.

Might as well enjoy the weekend.

I take a few more shots.

Throw back an Adderall.

And then I pull out my phone.

Since I deleted all of my social media accounts, all I've got are messages from my mother, reminding me, again, of her bullshit engagement party next weekend, to which I don't respond, a message from one of my friends back at ECU asking me if I want to drive down for a party tomorrow night, which I can't because I don't have a fucking car, and one from Alex. My fingers are shaky until I open the message. *What if Eli told him already?*

But all it says is: **What are you doing?**

I exhale a sigh of relief, but then glare at the words on the screen.

I fucking hate "What are you doing" texts and he knows it. If he wants to fuck me, he should just say it.

I chew my nail—a disgusting habit but probably my least

bad one—and close my eyes a second. Should I tell him Eli came over?

Should I tell Eli not to ever do that again?

But what if I want him to do it again?

And what if Alex asks me to come over and Eli gets home and it's all weird and shit?

But maybe Alex doesn't even want to hang out. Maybe he's still feeling bad about the video of my tits, or maybe he's creeped out at the idea of spending Friday night alone in his house after Rihanna was found there, or maybe he just wants to humiliate me some more. Maybe he's upset he's missing the away game, or any number of scenarios.

I don't know.

Maybe he's having another party.

I'm always down for free drinks—and more importantly, drugs—but I've got a guilty conscience and if I get wasted with him, what if I tell him what happened with Eli and then he gets mad that I didn't tell him before?

Fuck.

But then again, I don't relish the idea of spending my next few weekends alone. It's why I like Alex so much. He's always doing something. And he always wants to bring me along. He's fun.

Not shit. You? I reply.

The tequila is *really* getting to my head now and I bypass the tiny kitchen table that serves as a divider between our kitchen and living room and sink down into the couch Mom's boss gave us after she moved from one mansion to the next. Real estate is apparently a good business in North Carolina right now.

I kick my feet up on the arm of the couch and hold my phone over my face, staring at my screen, waiting for Alex to reply.

A small voice in the back of my head asks me what the fuck I'm doing. Alex and Eli are best friends.

This could end very badly.

I should just tell Alex now. It wasn't my fault anyway. I stopped it.

I should tell him.

But I'm not going to.

I'm fucking stupid.

I rub my thumb over my inner thigh, still naked as I sit on the couch. I think about the razor blades under the sink.

I think about how easy it would be.

No. I won't do that. It's been a few weeks since the last time. The one Eli hinted at. My body feels flushed when I think about him watching me then.

So, I don't.

I push it from my mind. It's a habit from when I was a teenager. It doesn't really affect me now.

Nope.

I'm fine.

While I wait for Alex's reply, I thumb through my contacts, and my dealer's name, Jax, scrolls past the screen. I scroll back up, debate a second, and then shoot off a quick text to Jax in the event Alex doesn't actually want to see me.

I can't be alone.

Not tonight.

Jax takes no time to reply: **Come over at 7. I've got some good shit.**

He always has good shit, but I just send a smiley face back and throw down my phone. Fuck Alex. I don't want to get involved in that shit anyway. Not tonight. I need some space too, fucker.

Now I've got to take a shower and get some damn clothes on before I head over to Jax's to get all the way fucked up.

10

Zara

A LITTLE BREATHLESS, my black strappy heels dangling from my fingers, I finally make it the three miles to Jax's house a few minutes past seven. He lives in Shadow Lakes, which is a neighborhood known for its wild parties, edging Caven's campus. This is where I first met Alex.

I push him from my mind. I know he won't be here. He was only at Jax's party that night back in March because he was picking up some pot for a friend.

I met Jax through a mutual friend that goes to ECU, and he's saved my life since that stint in rehab, which incidentally was the same time Mom sold my car. My mother, and other responsible adults might disagree with that assessment, but I'm clearly not a responsible adult.

I slide my shoes back on, run the back of my hand over my brow and take a deep breath.

My heart is pumping at the thought of what Jax has in store for me tonight, and probably from the three-mile walk in the September heat, but I'm stoked I'm here before anyone else. I didn't take anything save for that tequila and the Addie

I did earlier. I don't want any other drugs to fuck with what Jax has.

I flick my braids over my shoulder and straighten my hot pink crop top.

Now that I'm here, walking up his driveway, I realize it's actually a little cool outside, a slight breeze making the little hairs on my arms stand on end, wicking against the sweat slick on my skin.

The heels of my shoes click on the pavement as I head up to his white, ranch-style home situated at the end of the cul-de-sac. Perfect for parties.

Jax has a well-tended flower garden which makes me laugh a little, but over the summer, I learned it's one of his hobbies. Go fucking figure.

I reach out to ring the doorbell but he's already pulling open the door, a big smile on his face and a beer in his hand. I smell tobacco and weed as he opens the screen door for me and I step inside, hugging him back as he throws one arm around me.

He shuts the door behind me, and I glance around his tidy living room; grey carpets and a flat-screen TV mounted on the wall across from black leather couches. I spin around and find him looking me up and down, nodding his approval.

"Like the leather," he says, pointing at my mini skirt. Yeah, that was a bitch to walk in. He seems to realize that's exactly what I just did because he narrows his blue eyes and says, "Wait. Did you fucking walk here?"

I nod once, throwing up my hands. "Yep. Sure did."

"Why didn't you tell me? I could've picked you up."

I glance at the beer in his hand, see his red-rimmed eyes. But I don't call him out on it. Driving a little drunk and a little high is probably nothing to Jax. I don't point out that he should know I don't have a car. I just shrug. "I don't know," I tell him honestly. I kind of like to walk. Back in high school, I'd go for runs at the park in Monkey Junction—where I grew up, and where Mom still lives, the next town over—all the time. Before my little problem started.

"Well, you look good," he tells me, nodding.

I laugh, shaking my head. "Good. Let's hope whoever I end up fucking tonight thinks so, too."

He scratches his neck, takes a pull from his beer as he saunters into the kitchen. "Oh, come on, Za," he says, his voice lazy as always as he opens the fridge and peers inside. "Don't be fucking around too much. Not good for your soul. Besides, Alex is probably still drooling over your ass."

He knows we broke up, because aside from Kylie, he's the only real friend I have. And unlike Kylie, he doesn't really give a damn I cheated on Alex.

He thinks Alex is a dick anyway. Which he is.

I don't say any of that though. I don't really want to talk about Alex, especially with whatever the hell it was that happened with Eli.

Instead, I just laugh out loud, flop down on the black leather couch and cross my legs at the ankle as I slouch down, fingers drumming against my bare skin beneath my crop top.

"Who you inviting?" I ask, changing the subject.

Jax pulls a baggie out of the fridge and I perk up but make myself stay seated.

His mention of Alex aside, I'm just relieved he hasn't asked about the dead girl. Every time I close my eyes, I can see the eerie way her brown hair was just floating in tendrils around her head in the water.

I don't want to think about it. Talk about it. Or, remember it. I didn't really know her, and what I did know, I didn't like, but seeing a corpse is kind of unsettling.

"You know. Just some people from around. None of those bullshit Caven athletes, don't you worry. People I work with." I almost laugh out loud at that. He's a dealer, and that's it. But looking around his house, it looks like that's really all he needs to be. "Who knows who'll end up showing up?" He sets his beer down on the counter in his kitchen, grabs a spoon from a drawer and comes into the living room, sitting right on the floor in front of his coffee table.

He sets the spoon and the bag which is full of white powder on the table and grabs his phone from the back pocket of his jeans. He scrolls through it a second and then *Problem$* by Somber floods some hidden speakers, the bass thudding.

I like this beat.

I sit up, start dancing with my hands up, eyes closed, a smirk on my face, and I hear him laugh.

"Hey," he says after a minute, and I pause my stupid dance moves, dropping my hands, and look at him as he scoops out half a teaspoon full of whatever is in that bag, "did you know that dead girl?" He sets down the spoon, pulls out his wallet, thumbs free a card.

Damn, it seems I can't get away from her.

"Rihanna?" I shake my head. "Nah." Technically true. "I was at the party though, when she was...you know." I wrinkle my nose at the memory, wondering if Jax knows about the tit video. If he does, he's probably too much of a gentleman to say anything about it. I walked by during the week to pick some shit up and he didn't mention it then, so hopefully he won't now.

He's cutting the powder into a thin line with his card, but he pauses at my words, looks up, his blue eyes on mine. "No shit?"

I scoot to the edge of the couch, knees together, elbows propped up on them. "No shit," I confirm. "I found her."

His eyes widen a fraction. He's always pretty high, so I don't think he can actually open his eyes any more than that. "You all right?" he asks, blinking, then turning back to his lines.

I eye them, my mouth going dry and excitement making my heart flutter, but I keep myself contained. I don't even know what it is yet. Not fine enough to be coke, not really grainy enough for ketamine.

"Yeah, I'm good," I tell him honestly. I actually wish I felt a little more at her death, but I didn't fucking like her and I didn't really fucking know her.

Jax doesn't judge though. He just nods once and says, "Let it be a lesson, Za. Don't get fucked up around pools."

I laugh, shaking my head. "Shut up."

The corners of his mouth pull up in a smile and when his lines are nice and straight, he picks his head up and looks toward me, putting the card back into his wallet. "You ready?"

I rub my hands together, lower myself onto the floor and cross one leg over the other so I'm not all spread out in front of Jax. I'm pretty sure he's not at all interested in me. He's never made a move and I know he sees some chick that he's always off and on again with. Either way, he seems to see me as strictly a friend and the feeling is mutual. It's good to be friends with your dealer. They won't sell you shit laced with fentanyl or jack up the prices for no damn reason.

And they let you try shit for free, like right now.

"What is it?" I ask, holding back, but my palms are sweaty. I'm ready to get fucked up before any of the people he invited come over.

He scratches his neck again and smiles. "I'd rather not say yet."

I give him the look. What kind of bullshit is that? Even I'm not that stupid. Or willing, I don't think.

He laughs, swatting away my concern with a lazy flick of his hand. "Nah, nothing crazy. It's kinda like K, kinda like coke. You get that kinda spacey feeling but like, a little hype too."

My eyes widen. "A dissociative and a stimulant? Count me the fuck in." *See Kylie, I could be a pharmacist too.*

He smiles, rolling his eyes. "Knew you'd be down." Then

he pulls his wallet out of his pocket, tightly rolls up a twenty and hands it to me. "You can take 'em all."

He doesn't need to tell me twice. The lines are gone in no time.

And it tastes like shit, dripping down the back of my throat. I can't help the snorting sound I make, coughing and rubbing the back of my hand over my nose

"What the fuck?" I say, the taste like a mix of chemicals and tar. I swallow as Jax gets up, taking the rolled up twenty and spoon back into the kitchen. "Need to work on your taste testing," I call out to him, massaging my throat. "Shit tastes terrible."

He laughs and comes back into the living room with an unopened sports drink. I twist off the cap, gulp the red liquid down until I can't taste whatever the fuck I just snorted.

I massage my throat again, then twist the cap on the bottle. I can't feel shit yet, but I'm just glad that taste is out of the back of my throat. The drip is awful.

Jax lights up a cigarette, sitting back down on the floor at the table, beside me. He pulls the ashtray in the center of the table closer to him. "That bad?" he asks after he exhales a cloud of smoke.

I cough, making a show of it. "That bad," I tell him truthfully. I drum my fingers on the table. "But I don't taste it now. That drink works wonders." I nod toward the half-empty bottle on the table between us. "How long 'til I start feeling…" I trail off, because I can see the smoke from Jax's cigarette in the air in front of me and it looks green.

I blink, and it's back to white and grey but I blink again and it's green, almost shimmering. The music, the table, Jax himself, they're all in the background of what I'm seeing.

I lift my hand to touch the smoke and my hand feels heavy. I catch sight of it, and it seems like it's not quite mine. But that's my black polish and the freckle on the back of my hand. But it still looks like it belongs to someone else.

I clamp my fingers around my wrist, holding my hand up, and it looks like my hands are just holding themselves. Detached from me.

Jax laughs. "Yeah. Not long."

I drop my hands and turn to stare at him.

He's watching me with mild amusement. "You all right?"

I nod, staring at his mouth. When he spoke, it wasn't with that same lazy drawl. It was musical.

"Say it again." I clamp a hand over my mouth. My voice is music too.

He laughs. "You all right?" He smiles, then asks, "You wanna put on the music?" His words seem to float in the air. "Might help you out."

I smile at him and nod slowly, then reach for my phone, tucked into my bra. My fingers seem like they belong to someone else, but strangely enough, they do what I will them to do.

They move with my thoughts.

My fingers move with my thoughts. Holy shit.

Distracting me from music and the insanity of that revelation, I've got a text from Alex. Asking if he could come over. Then several more after that.

Alex: **Come on, Zara. Don't be fucking shady.**

Alex: **I've had a long day.**

Alex: **I just want to talk.**

A grin spreads across my face, and I wonder what my smile looks like. For a moment, I wish I could just pluck it off my head, hold it up like a Mr. Potato Head smile and look at it.

I ask Jax what his address is because I highly doubt Alex remembers this house, and the numbers and words he shoots back are full of soft, lilting music.

Lilting.

That reminds me of Eli.

But this isn't Eli.

This is Alex Cardi.

I say his name out loud and Jax snorts. "Your ex, the great, beloved, champion quarterback asshole?" He laughs again. "Damn, Za. Get off his dick."

I don't let his words jar me. My fingers are already flying across the keyboard on my phone of their own accord with Jax's address and then: **Come find me.**

I open my music app, put on *IKnowI'mNotAHero* by The Virus and Antidote, then put my phone down on the table and meet Jax's eyes.

He frowns at me. "I've been meaning to tell you. I heard he got into some trouble last year at some house party," Jax says. He shrugs. "Almost got caught up in a rape scandal."

I know this should be disturbing news to me, but I can't really feel it. "Rape?" I mouth the word and it explodes with music, coming out like a musical refrain with an echo. Kind of disturbing, such a nasty word sounding so magical.

Jax raises a brow. "Yeah. I don't know the details. Just some gossip or shit. You good with sleeping with him or should I make sure he stays off you since you two broke up?"

I see he's shuffling a deck of cards on the table. I have no idea where they came from. Maybe out of thin fucking air. The cigarette is in the ash tray. I don't remember watching him put it out.

I think about his question, and I can't stop the slow grin spreading on my face as I think about Alex and Eli both almost fucking me.

"I'm good," I answer him. It comes out like "goooOoooo-Ooood" and I giggle, my hand over my mouth.

I think I need to ask him about this rape, but I don't really want to. It kind of just floats away into the back of my mind. Instead, I lift my hands in front of my face, twisting and twirling my fingers. Jax keeps shuffling the cards and then I notice my phone light up like a Christmas tree.

A Christmas tree.

Mom always put a white one up every year, dragged her husband (whichever number) to a little decoration party with me as the sullen stepdaughter. Her husbands have all been pretty decent to me—save for my own father, who I have very few memories of and get a birthday card once a year from and nothing more—but one of them really hated Christmas. He refused to decorate, and Mom called him Scrooge as he pouted in a corner while we hung the ornaments.

I laugh out loud at that random memory as I read the text from Alex.

Be there soon, princess.

My heart flutters with those words.

"He's so tall," I say out loud.

Jax starts dealing the cards between us, even though I have no idea what he's trying to play.

"Yeah, fucker is huge," he says.

I giggle again.

11

Alex

BY THE TIME I make it to the house, there are half a dozen cars in the driveway and more parked on the curb.

I back the Jeep into the next available space on the side of the street and when I get out, I can hear the bass from inside the house, but I can't quite tell what's playing.

I glance at my phone after I lock the Jeep. I've only been here once before. The night I met Zara at some party here. I was just trying to buy weed from the dude who lives here. I know him, but not well.

All I do know is that he better not have his hands on my girl when I walk into that house.

I rub my palms on my pants, walking up to the front door. I can't stand to be in this subdivision longer than necessary. I want to get in and get out. This is where all the shit went down last fall, when my life almost went to shit because me and Eli made a stupid decision.

But I don't particularly want to think about it, so I put it out of my mind.

I have several texts from Zara.

Her: **Hurry up, handsome.**
Her: **I can see the music!!**
Her: **Where r u?**

Clearly, she's drunk off her ass. It's amazing, how I want to kill her and save her all at the same time. I'm not sure which I'll end up doing tonight.

Sighing, I shove the phone in my back pocket and knock on the door.

It swings open almost immediately, and a woman that isn't Zara grins at me, a plastic cup in her hand. I don't know who she is, and she looks older than a typical college student. She's got curly brown hair and a heavily lipsticked smile.

"Welcome, partner," she says, clearly drunk, and steps back to let me inside.

I nod, not returning her smile.

Still Be Friends by G-Eazy is playing. There are tons of people in this little house, packed in tight, and the smell of tobacco and marijuana assaults my senses.

Someone tries to put a drink into my hand, but I don't take it, pushing past them.

It doesn't take me long to find Zara.

She's on top of the coffee table, twirling round and round, her arms spread wide. She's wearing a black mini skirt and a hot pink, short top that shows off her pale, taut stomach, heels accentuating her slim legs. Her head is tilted back, her long, white-blonde braids down her back.

People are standing around the table clapping and cheering as she spins faster and faster.

One dude with short, bleached-blonde hair and a cartoon character on his shirt isn't clapping, and he's watching Zara like a hawk. *Jax.* Where everyone else is chatting to each other, rubbing shoulders and laughing as they clap, Jax only has eyes for her. I can't really read his expression, but I'm happy to see his eyes are on her face, not her body.

He seems to actually give a fuck about her. Ironic, because

I'm pretty sure she gets all of her drugs from him. One day, I'll need to do something about this dude.

But that day is not today. I just want to get my girl and get out of here.

I look back at Zara's long and lean body, sexy as hell, the muscles in her pale thighs flexing as she spins. She has scars, just under that miniskirt.

I don't know what they're from. One night, I trailed my fingers over them in the dark when she was naked in my bed. She rolled over, out of my grasp. I've never asked her about them.

I'm not sure I want to know about that kind of pain, when she's still clearly in so much.

She's humming, I realize as I get closer, shouldering my way through her enraptured audience. A few people look up at me, someone whistles, but I ignore them, my eyes on her.

The dude with the cartoon shirt is beside me and he says, without taking his eyes off Zara, "Hey, Alex." He says it loud enough for me to hear over all the people in here and the music blasting, but not loud enough to draw attention. Although being the tallest fucker in this room does that all on its own.

I can't really read his tone, so I just say, "Jax," with a head nod.

I glance at him before I turn back to Zara. She has her eyes closed, and the table isn't high enough to give anyone a view of underneath her skirt. But still, I don't like all these people staring at her. I don't know what the hell she's on, but I want to pick her up off the fucking table and take her back to my Jeep. Something tells me Jax won't let me do that without causing a problem.

He's short and stocky though. I could easily take him. Still, I'd rather not cause another scene just yet. Watching Rihanna's sobbing family tomorrow morning at the funeral will be enough of a scene to last me a lifetime. Thinking of it makes my fists clench, dread twisting my stomach into knots.

Goddammit, why couldn't she have died in someone else's fucking pool?

"She's been asking about you," Jax says.

I cock a brow. Zara is still spinning, rolling her hips and laughing, her eyes still closed as people clap around us. "Is that right?"

He laughs a little. "Yeah. I don't know what's going on with you two but be careful with her."

I nod, feeling uncomfortable. She must've told him we broke up. I don't really like that, and I can't help wondering if she told him why. I don't want him thinking of her mouth on someone else's dick. "I plan to be." *I think.*

"Good." Then he puts two fingers in his mouth and whistles, loudly. It pierces the air, quieting everyone for a moment. Zara comes to a stop, swaying a little because she's probably dizzy as fuck, but her eyes lock onto Jax.

He jerks his head toward me, even though, considering I'm like a foot taller than him, he shouldn't have actually had to point me out.

But Zara's big blue-green eyes flick to me and then she squeals like a kid, clapping her hands and bouncing on her toes.

Without warning, she jumps into my arms and I catch her as she wraps her legs around me, squeezing me with her thighs.

I stumble back a step and everyone around us cheers as she kisses both of my cheeks.

I can feel her heart racing as she squeezes her arms around my neck, her chest pressed against mine.

"You're here!"

I meet Jax's eyes, asking him with mine what the fuck is going on. Za and I have spoken during the week but nothing great. She's pissed at me about the party, I'm pissed at her for having another guy's dick in her mouth, and I knew she was probably fucked up since she gave me this address in the first place. Which made me think I needed to get to her all the more.

But now she's jumping into my arms? I didn't think this would go *that* well.

Jax steps closer as the crowd disperses, some people dancing around the table, others drifting into the kitchen, some stacked on top of each other on the couch, making out and shit.

"She's on something," Jax tells me in my ear. "A new drug. Like K and coke."

I rear my head back, my eyes narrowed. "Who gave it to her?"

He frowns. "I did. She wanted it."

"Yessss!" Zara whisper-yells in my ear, making me flinch. "It is SO GOOD, Alex!" She kisses my cheek again.

Okay. So maybe it is good.

Her legs squeeze me tighter, and I keep her close, one hand under her ass to hold her up, the other around her back.

"It'll probably wear off in a couple of hours, and she'll crash," Jax continues, like he's a doctor or some shit, telling me the side effects. "Make sure she stays hydrated and sleeps well after it wears off, aiight?" He claps me on the back which I don't really care for.

"I'm taking her out of here," I inform him.

His fingers dig into my back.

I spin around to face him, hefting Zara up as she's momentarily quiet, her head resting on my shoulder.

"Don't fuck with her," Jax tells me. "If you do, I'll fuck you up."

Considering the dude is shorter even than Zara, I want to tell him he's fucking nuts, but he seems like he gives a shit about her so I just nod, not wanting to start anything. "All right. Thanks."

"Tell her to text me in the morning, will you?" He nods toward her. "She's got her phone in her bra."

I arch a brow, suddenly regretting everyone that got to see her tits at my fucking house and how I'm a dumbass for making it happen. But some girl is tugging on Jax's shoulder and he turns around, effectively dismissing me.

Thank God. I gotta get this guilt under control. She's the slut.

"I'm taking us out of here, Zara," I tell her, my mouth against her ear so she can hear me.

She wiggles in my arms, picking her head up off my shoulder and cupping my face with her hands. I stop walking toward the door as she stares at me. Her pupils are wide, obscuring most of the blue-green of her irises, but she focuses on my eyes, then presses a soft kiss to the tip of my nose.

Her lips are so soft, plump, and heart shaped.

And she smells damn good, like coffee and flowers.

"You are so beautiful," she tells me, still holding my face.

Despite myself, despite knowing she's all fucked up, despite the eerie way her eyes look, I can't help my smile.

"So are you, princess," I tell her.

She lays her head back on my shoulder and I carry her out of the door.

12

Eli

WHEN SHE COMES DOWN AT JUST after three in the morning on Saturday, she doesn't know I'm sitting at the dining room table, just off from the kitchen with a perfect view of the fridge. A perfect view of her ass, too, the bottom half of it visible beneath the oversized white t-shirt she's wearing. One I know doesn't belong to her.

Obviously, she didn't tell Alex I came over, or he would've asked me about it.

What a sneaky little bitch.

Her white hair is wavy and messy down her back, and when she opens the fridge, the soft light illuminates her pale, tired face. She yawns, covering her hand with her mouth as she stares into the fridge for a long moment, one hand on the door, propping it open.

I take in the shape of her firm calves, her bare feet. She has pink, chipped polish on her toes. Her pebbled nipples are barely visible beneath Alex's shirt that's dwarfing her. Those heart shaped lips, and that pale, slender neck.

I steal another look at the bottom curve of her ass,

wondering if right now, Alex's cum is dripping down her inner thigh.

I shift quietly in my seat at the table, the lights off in the dining room. No one around to see me as I adjust my dick, bite my lip.

Alex is a fucking idiot, letting her out like this, after what happened to Rihanna. In a few hours, I suppose I'll have to see Rihanna pumped full of embalming fluid at the funeral, if I go. Maybe that'll be a good reminder to Alex to be more careful.

Maybe I can give him a reminder sooner.

Zara keeps staring into the fridge with a vacant expression on her face.

I run my palms down my thighs as I watch her until I can't just watch anymore. I stand to my feet, letting my chair legs scrape against the wooden floor.

She turns her head, but otherwise doesn't move.

Even her expression doesn't change. She stares into the dark and I don't know if she sees me or not, but I feel a little unsettled with the way she's looking at me. Like she can see all of my secrets. I guess, more than anyone else, she can.

Because she's fucked up, too.

I take a step, the wooden floor cold on my bare feet.

I slide my hands into the pockets of my sweats, the only thing I'm wearing.

She still doesn't move.

"Zara?" I whisper her name, not wanting to wake Alex up. He'll ruin this for me, and I'm sure he already got his anyway. Now it's my turn to finish what he didn't let me. And if she's full of his cum, even better.

She tilts her head, a lock of white-blonde hair hanging over one of her eyes, but she doesn't say a word. Her expression is vacant, and as I step closer, until I'm right beside the fridge door and I can see that her pupils are blown, I realize she's not staring at me.

She's staring through me.

I flick my gaze to the sliding glass door beyond her. The lit pool. The calm surface of the water. I think of Rihanna's body beneath the surface. Zara staring out at her, her hand pressed against the glass.

A faint chill makes its way down my spine and I almost want to run.

When I look back at Zara's pale face, those high cheekbones, those empty eyes, "Zara!" I snap, wanting to shake her. The cool air from the fridge is still running out between us, and I know any second it's going to start dinging with the alarm that signals it's been left open.

I close it, knocking her arm out of the way.

She backs up, her movements clumsy, her steps awkward. She slumps against the island in the kitchen and I move toward her, the light from the fridge gone, leaving us only the light from the full moon outside.

Her hands grip the ledge of the island, her eyes on me, but still unseeing.

I reach for her waist, pressing my fingers gently against her, Alex's shirt beneath my touch. I want to run my hand up her thigh. I want to feel if he's been here. Inside of her.

I want to touch her scars.

But I don't.

I step closer, my bare chest against her shirt, my eyes searching for some sign of life in hers.

What is she on?

Whatever it is, I could give her more.

I could take her higher.

I press my brow to hers.

"Zara."

She doesn't say anything.

"Baby girl," I try again. She hasn't said it, but I think she loves when I call her that. Right now, though, she's just limp in my arms and her breath smells like alcohol. My heart is thudding in my chest and I want to know what she's on and I want to know where she's been and what she did, if she fucked Alex, and I can't—

I can't stop it.

My hand trails down over her hip bone, to her bare thigh, and then back up, under *his* shirt.

I try to stop myself. For one single second, I try.

I know Alex thinks I have a lot of self-control. He thinks, between the two of us, I'm the good one.

That's because he doesn't fucking know me.

Zara's skin is soft beneath my fingers and I stare into her eyes as I touch her. She's like a beautiful little robot, quiet and compliant against me. Unwilling or unable to stop me.

And if she's not going to, I'm certainly not going to stop myself.

I trail two fingers up her inner thigh, loving the way her muscles quiver beneath my light touch. Even if her mind is temporarily gone, carried off by whatever she got into tonight, her body is responding to me.

Her thigh isn't damp. I trail higher, brushing my fingers against her smooth, bare pussy. She trembles a little against me, and I feel her chest brush mine as she takes a breath.

I run my fingers up her slit, parting her lips, circling her clit with the pad of my fingers.

I hear her sharp intake of breath, and she shifts her hold on the kitchen island to my shoulders, digging her nails in.

I lock eyes with her.

She blinks.

I move lower, feel the slickness of her against my skin. I want to do more. I want to go further. I've watched for so long.

"Eli," she whispers, and my chest tightens.

"Zara." I lean back to take in her face.

She bites her lip. She's awake. She's conscious.

Her fingers are still on my bare shoulder, and she stands

up on her tiptoes, trying to get me closer. Trying to get me inside of her.

"You want me?" I ask her in the dark.

"Yes," she sighs, angling herself toward my fingers. "Yes."

"Tell me."

"I want—" She moans as I circle her clit again. "I want you," she finally manages to say.

"Yeah?" I taunt her, loving the way she's begging me with her body, rocking her hips forward as I touch her. Her lips part, a soft moan from her mouth making my blood heat. "You want me? Or do you want Alex?"

She gasps, taking a deep, shuddering breath. "You, Eli, you."

I keep touching her, then slip down my sweats and my boxers, pumping my dick. I'm so fucking hard and I am dying to fuck her but she's not really—I don't know if she really wants me. And when I fuck her, I want her to know.

I stroke myself as I rub her, but she's still on her tiptoes, and she lets go of one shoulder, shoves my hand down.

"You want me inside of you?" I whisper, still pumping my dick, the tip brushing up against Alex's shirt on her body.

She nods, biting her lip, her eyes on mine.

I push two fingers into her, loving the way she parts for me, tightens around me. And with only that shirt on and nothing else between us, I can smell her. She smells so damn good. So fucking clean.

"Eli," she moans, bucking her hips against my fingers, her hands behind her now on the counter to keep her upright. "Fuck, Eli."

"Are you my good little whore?"

She nods, another low moan coming out of those soft, pink lips.

"Touch yourself," I tell her, leaning close, my words against her ear. "You don't fucking deserve it, but I want you to come at the same time I do."

Obediently, she moves one hand from the counter to her swollen clit, rubbing herself with two fingers as I finger her, still stroking my cock. I want her to touch me. God, I want her to touch me, but I want to watch her touch herself more.

"Don't stop," I command her, "don't stop until you come all over my hand, baby girl."

She closes her eyes, and I know she's getting close. I can feel it. I can feel her, so tight and hot against my skin. She rubs herself faster, and I see her pink clit beneath her fingers.

I'm going to come.

I'm going to come all over Alex's shirt.

And when she gasps my name, her walls so tight and hot and wet around my fingers, I do just that. I can't hold back my groan as I finish, making a mess on her.

"Eli," she gasps, her eyes still closed tight, her chest rising and falling, my fingers still inside of her, still coated in her wetness.

She's still got her fingers on her clit, too, and I rub my dick against her shirt, pumping myself one last time, making sure it's all out.

I keep my fingers inside of her until she opens her eyes.

And then I slowly slide them out while she watches me. I bring them to my mouth, sucking her off me.

She trails her hand up, away from her swollen pussy, to the mess I made on her shirt. She dips her fingers into it, and then she tastes me, too, not looking away from my eyes.

Just as I lean in, wanting her mouth all over me, wanting to taste me from her lips, I hear something upstairs.

A creaking.

The sound of Alex's floorboards beneath his feet. I don't sleep much; I know all of the sounds in this house.

Zara's eyes flick up to the ceiling, her mouth open, her fingers on her tongue.

I wait, tense, hoping he'll just use the bathroom and go

back to sleep. But I know better. He's going to be looking for her.

And he does.

His footsteps pause, as if he might be confused, and then they head toward his door.

I kiss Zara's ear, her startled breath against my cheek. "It's okay, baby girl. Get some water." I reach between us, running my finger up her slit one last time, loving the way she shivers. Loving the way she's still so fucking wet. "I'll hide out until he takes you back up." I trail my hand over her thigh, her scars, just as I hear Alex come to the top of the stairs.

"Eli," Zara whispers, and it sounds pleading. Like she wants me to stay.

"Shh, baby. Have a good night." I kiss her again, and then I pull away, rubbing my index finger and my thumb together, the sticky wetness making me hard all over again.

I pull up my pants, and slink back into the dining room just as Alex comes down the stairs.

"Zara?" he calls, his voice soft.

I can see her from where I'm standing, but they won't be able to see me.

I see her drop her fingers from her mouth, tuck her hair behind her ear. She opens the fridge, and I see she's nervous in how she moves, her foot sliding up against her opposite calf.

She grabs a bottle of water, twists off the cap just as Alex comes to stand in the kitchen.

"Zara?" he asks again. He's in shorts and nothing else. From this angle, I see both of them, staring at each other.

I glance down at the hem of her shirt. *His* shirt. If he steps closer, if he touches her, he'll get my cum all over him.

I hold my breath, waiting, leaning against the wall in the dining room.

"Are you okay, princess?"

She tips back the bottle of water, the plastic crinkling as

she drinks. Then she sets it on the counter at her side, nodding.

I see her glance in the dark my way, but I know she can't see me.

Still, I slip my hand into my pants, rub my wet fingers up and down my hard cock, watching them.

Alex steps closer. "You scared me," he says quietly.

Then *she* reaches up, wraps her arms around his neck. Her shirt rides up, showing off the bottom curve of her ass. He grabs it, squeezing.

I bite my lip, stroking myself faster. Harder.

And then he says, "What's on your shirt?" as he steps back, dropping his hand from her ass.

She grabs it in her fist, covering the wet spot. "Water," she lies, her voice husky. "I spilled water."

Alex laughs a little, rubbing her arm. "Come on, clumsy. Let's get you back to bed." Then he throws his arm around her shoulder, and together, they walk out of the kitchen. But just as they disappear from view, she twists under his arm and glances back at me.

"Scared, princess?" Alex whispers.

I just catch sight of her smile before they disappear down the hall. "No. Not with you."

Bitch.

13

Zara

WAKING UP IS HARD.

I can *feel* the exhaustion in my bones and prying my eyelids open takes way more time than the half a second it should. I taste something strange in the back of my throat, like...

Whatever the hell Jax gave me last night that I snorted up my fucking nose.

I sit up in a bed that isn't mine, scoot back against the padded headboard behind me. I blink a few times, the light streaming in from the half-open curtains too bright for my sensitive eyes. I take in the familiar room that my brain is having trouble placing right now; hardwood floors, a desk against one wall, doors on either side of it.

A framed photo of some pro football player catching a ball in the endzone.

Alex.

This is Alex's room.

Get it fucking together, Zara.

I pull up the sheets to my chin and fist my hands in the shirt I'm wearing.

The shirt I'm wearing.

I yank the covers down, hold out the white t-shirt of Alex's I'm in. It feels rough in a spot at the hem, rough because...

Eli.

My chest tightens, panic making that taste in my mouth turn sour as I draw my knees into my chest, yank the covers back up.

Fuck.

Fuck.

Eli.

I think about his fingers inside of me. His lips against my ear. How he told me to touch myself.

I clench my thighs together and close my eyes a second, lost in the memory. Fuck. Alex could have seen. Alex could have seen and then we would be so fucked. What the fuck am I doing?

I run a hand over my hair and take a breath to pull myself together. Then I open my eyes, feel around under the covers of the king-size bed for my phone. I lift the sheets up, peer over the edge of the bed onto the dark wooden floors, then the night-stand, on my right, and the one on the opposite side of the bed.

Nothing.

An alarm clock, the end of a charger and nothing.

Aside from the football picture, I've always thought Alex's room felt impersonal somehow.

Except, no—

Is that a fucking Bible?

On the opposite nightstand, beside the alarm clock and the charger, a black, leather-bound Bible.

That's new.

I mean, I know Alex's dad is a pastor, but Alex has never mentioned God to me.

Jesus Christ.

I push thoughts of Alex and Christ from my mind and press the heel of my hand against my eyes, thinking about last night. There are gaps in my memory, which is no surprise. I was with Jax, and I snorted the line of the K-coke miracle drug, and everything was great. I was dancing on the table and Jax kept giving me water and I was sweaty, and my heart was racing, and I felt so…alive. The very opposite of what I'm feeling right now.

Right now, I feel heavy.

I need something to help me out with that, and since I have no clothes on, don't see them anywhere in Alex's room, and have no clue where my phone is, it's going to take me a minute to figure out how to get back home and get to my stash.

Alex.

I keep my eyes closed, fingers threaded through my hair, trying to piece it all together. He was at Jax's. Did I call him? I must have, because he wouldn't have come otherwise.

He said he needed space. Time to think.

Clearly not that much time.

And Eli.

I remember Eli.

But I don't remember getting to him. I don't remember getting out of this bed. I try to think through everything. Through Alex carrying me inside. Stripping me down. Putting the shirt over my head, muttering about how we needed to talk in the morning.

Then I got up, because I was thirsty, and besides that, every time I closed my eyes, stars exploded behind them. I couldn't lay down, couldn't stay still. I went downstairs, and Eli was there.

Eli was there and he touched me and God, I wanted him.

I wanted him.

I groan, pressing my fist to my mouth.

Fuck.

Alex will kill me. If he knew, he'd fucking kill me.

And then, what happened after that?

It's like grabbing at straws, it's right there. I can feel it, see it. But I don't know how I got from the kitchen to here. Another gap.

And then another thought intrudes on me trying to piece this together.

I pick my head up, nearly crick my neck turning to look at the alarm clock. It's one of those with the day and date in a little box in the corner. *Shit.* Rihanna's funeral is today.

I am definitely not going but I don't want to be here and see if Alex and Eli are. Fuck that shit.

Before I can decide to fuck it all and steal some clothes from Alex, the door flies open and then slams shut, making me flinch and yank the covers up higher.

Alex's entire body stiffens when he sees me, his eyes narrowing into slits, his jaw clenching, hands fisting by his sides. It's unfortunate he's so pissed off because without a shirt on, wearing low slung, black basketball shorts, he looks damn good.

"Get dressed," he barks, turning away from me and yanking open the door opposite the bed. His closet door.

He ducks under the doorway, storming inside.

Literally ducking.

He needs a bigger house with bigger doorframes and vaulted ceilings in every damn room.

I watch his back muscles shift as he rips a black t-shirt off a hanger and throws it at me without looking back. He yanks a pair of sweatpants off from the space above the racks and throws that at me too. I catch them before they smack me in the face.

He turns back toward me, shuts the closet door at his back. I see his nostrils flare.

I grab everything he threw at me and hold it close to my chest. Clear my throat.

"Um. Do you want to tell me why you look like you're about to drown me right now?" I almost wince as I ask the question, thinking belatedly about Rihanna Martinson.

And then, Eli.

God, Alex doesn't know. He can't know. He has to be pissed about something else because if he knows, that means it's really over and I need him. I need something stable in my life. I need a distraction.

He can't know.

But he really does look like he could strangle me right about now, no pool required.

"Are you fucking joking?"

I clench and unclench my fists, resisting the urge to bite my nails. He can't know. If he did, there's no way he would be this calm. There's just no fucking way.

But the comedown from whatever it is Jax gave me last night is already making me feel like shit, and compounded with whatever Alex is flipping out about right now, I feel sick with nerves.

I'm not about to ask any questions that could hang me before I know what his deal is though. I pull off the dirty shirt, pull on the clean one, trying to hide my body as much as I can because he's still staring at me like he wants me dead. I swing my legs over the side of the bed, thankful Alex is a big ass freak of nature and his giant t-shirt hits at my thighs.

I put on his sweats, use the drawstring to cinch them as well as I can. Then I steel my spine, facing him with my hands on my hips. It can't be about Eli, and if it isn't about Eli then I don't have anything to feel guilty about.

God, where the fuck is Eli?

I hope he isn't here. I hope he doesn't make this any more awkward than it's going to be.

Gathering up all of my courage, which is in short supply at

the moment considering I fucked around with my ex's best friend and he has no idea, I keep my tone even as I demand, "Either tell me what happened or please give me a ride home."

He laughs but it dies quickly, and then he steps closer to me, leaning down to get in my face. "Do you remember what you did last night? After we got back here? After I took you home from a party that you might've gotten gang raped at?" His voice is low, but I can sense his rage, and it makes my stomach twist up in knots. He's usually so loud and obnoxious; when he's all quiet and shit it's a little unnerving.

But he cannot know.

No way. He would've torn this house apart. Probably set the mattress on fire with me in it.

I need water. I need to go home. I need to get the fuck out of here.

But I do not need Alex fucking Cardi in my face talking about a potential rape of all things.

Because I remember. I remember what Jax said.

"No, but you wanna tell me why people say you might be a fucking rapist yourself?" I step back, his eyes narrowing into two coal-black slits. The flecks of amber are gone, almost as if his anger has swallowed them whole. "I didn't think so. Until you're ready to have that conversation, get out of my face with all this shit. I went to Jax's for the drugs, I went back here with you because you—"

"Because I *what?*" he snarls, stepping closer again.

I swallow, still tasting that vile drug drip taste in the back of my throat. Crossing my arms, I look down at the floor, not wanting to admit it. Not wanting to tell him exactly why I don't want to be without him. Even if I do stupid shit. Even if I fucking blew Jamal Clint.

Even if I just fucked around with his best friend.

It's stupid. Idiotic.

I can't say it.

I don't say it.

Because you make me feel safe.

I'm an idiot.

I shake my head, meet his gaze again. "Nothing. You said you needed space, I'll give it to you, okay? Just, take me home. Go to Rihanna's fucking funeral. Let one of her grieving friends suck your dick—"

He shoves me.

He actually fucking shoves me.

I sink down onto his bed, losing my balance, and before I can jump back up, he steps between my legs and grabs my wrists, pinning them down by my sides.

"Get off me," I snarl.

His eyes are blank. Dark and dead and he's breathing hard, his bare chest rising and falling with each inhale and exhale and I think about what Jax said. I think about watching Alex break Nate's nose. The blood pouring down his face. How he swept me up in his arms right after without a care.

I think about him forcing that bottle into my mouth. Jumping with me into the pool when he knew I wouldn't be able to swim.

He tightens his hold on my wrist.

I don't know if I'm afraid. I'm not sure if I think he'll hurt me. But maybe I'm just used to treating people like shit and being treated like shit. Maybe that's the comedown talking because everything feels kind of heavy and sad and some weird part of me wants to fold myself into Alex's arms even though he's not looking at me right now like he wants to hug me. Unless a hug constitutes squeezing someone so hard, they choke to death.

"What did you do last night, Zara? What did you fucking do?"

I suck in a breath, swallow a few times. My throat feels tight, but I keep reminding myself this room would be torn to pieces if he knew.

He doesn't know.

"What are you talking about?" I hate how my voice turns up at the end of that question, hate how his eyes flash when I ask it.

I hate how he smirks at me. "You don't remember." It isn't a question.

"Alex." I swallow, try to push up, but he yanks my arms down, keeping me on his bed. "I have to go." I try to find a reason I need to go and come up with, "My mom—"

"Your mom know you were snorting shit up your nose last night? Think I should tell her about that, huh? Maybe I'll go with you to the engagement party and make an announcement, what do you think?"

I furrow my brow, feeling suddenly clammy, my palms sweaty as I grip his sheets. "How do you even know I was snorting—"

"Your good friend Jax told me."

"Shit," I swear under my breath, going with this deflection. If he's pissed about me doing drugs, that's okay. I can live with that. I'm sure Alex asked him what the fuck I was on and Jax, being a fucking drug dealer, didn't think shit about it. I shake my head. "It doesn't matter. That was really none of your business. But speaking of moms, if yours needs a reputable dealer for all that Xanax she's doing, Jax is definitely her guy."

I know it's a low blow. I know I shouldn't have said it. I used a secret he shared with me against him. A moment where I met his family and knew his mom had a problem. And I know, I know it's wrong, but I can talk drugs all day long.

Eli, though, I can't.

Alex lets go of my wrists and digs his fingers into my thighs, pressing his weight into me as he leans in, his breath against my mouth. "Don't ever talk about my fucking mother. I—"

"Fine," I snap. "I won't talk about your mother, but I am not your problem, Alex——"

"You are." He presses his forehead to mine, his fingers tightening painfully around my thighs. "You *are* my problem, Zara. It's why you're in my bed. It's why I picked you up last night." I watch him swallow, watch him close his eyes. And for a moment, I feel guilty about something besides Eli.

I feel guilty about all the drugs and last night and even texting him in the first place. I feel guilty for trying—and failing—to hide my problem even from him. For lying to my mother. I feel guilty about all of it.

"Why did you take your shirt off in front of my best friend last night?" he asks me, catching me completely off guard.

What?

What the actual fuck?

I'm so genuinely confused, all I can manage is a, "What the fuck are you talking about?" Despite the fact I didn't do what he said, I feel my cheeks grow warm, and I'm so glad his eyes are closed.

Just keep them closed. Just keep them closed.

"Eli said you went downstairs, and he was there, and you… God, what did you do, Za?" His voice is hoarse, his words quiet, and his eyes, they're squeezed shut, like he's anticipating what I might tell him. What I might say.

Eli fucking lied. He lied to him. We got away with it, and he screwed it all up.

"I didn't, I don't know what you——"

"Tell me the truth, Zara." Alex's voice is still strained, his eyes still closed.

And I want to tell him. For one wild second, I want to tell Alex. I want to tell him that Eli is a fucking liar. That something is wrong with his best friend. Eli Addison is not right. He's full of shit, and I didn't fucking flash him, he fingered me.

I want to tell him, but I can't do it.

I'm not that brave. Eli put me in this position, and he knows it. He fucking knows it.

I'm going to kill him.

The only thing I can do is deny it. "I don't know what you're—"

Alex's eyes fly open and he grabs my throat, his brow still pressed to mine. "Stop fucking lying to me, Za! Stop fucking lying!" He's breathing hard, his eyes locked onto mine. "I am so fucking sick of your bullshit!" But his voice breaks on those last words.

And there's more than anger there.

He's scared.

He's scared for me.

"Alex…"

His grip on my throat loosens and he slides his hand down to my shoulder, then up through my hair, his fingers grazing my scalp. The little hairs on the back of my neck stand on end and he steps closer to me, between my thighs.

I lift my hands, run them over his back, feeling the strength in his muscles. His warm, smooth skin. He's so familiar to me. His body is so…mine.

"Don't lie to me, Zara. I can't do this with you if you lie to me."

I swallow, wanting to hide under these sheets. Wanting to run out of this room to disappear from his life. I think about him seeing me with Jamal. I think about how he carried me out of that house without saying a word after he beat the shit out of Jamal.

I think about how he took me home, still not speaking.

I think about everything he's done for me.

Everything I've done to him.

"I—"

"Do you remember?" he asks me, his fingers still massaging my scalp, his breath on my mouth. He smells like toothpaste. Different from Eli, from that cotton candy scent his mouth seems to have.

Don't think about Eli.

"Do you remember?" Alex asks again. "He said you took your shirt off. He said you tried to kiss him. He said you… Fuck, Zara. If you don't even remember…" His expression is one of anguish, his brow furrowed, jaw tight, lips pulled down. "Baby, if you don't even remember, you could've…"

"I don't," I lie to him, my lip trembling, and not from sadness. Not from the reason he thinks. My drug problem isn't a problem. I'm fine. It's everything else that's a mess. And Eli is going to fucking die. He's essentially blackmailed me into this shit. "I don't remember. I'm so sorry, Alex, I don't. I must've been out of it. I'm so fucking sorry."

"I think you should come to the funeral," he tells me quietly. "I think you need to know what could happen to you, Zara. I don't want anything bad…" He trails off, takes a shaky breath in. "I don't want anything bad to happen to you." His fingers are still in my hair, and he's got one arm around my back.

My mouth is so dry, my heart racing. I don't know what to say, I don't know what to do. Something bad is happening to me, I want to tell him. I'm the bad thing. Happening to my fucking self.

But saving me from doing anything at all, there's a soft knock at the door.

I flinch, and Alex drops his hand from my hair but keeps his other arm thrown around my back as he turns to face the door. "Come in," he calls softly.

No, please don't.

My stomach flutters as I watch the silver knob to Alex's door turn. I hold my breath as Eli Addison steps through the doorway, his tattooed hand clenched around the knob.

His eyes go to me first, and I can't breathe.

I can't breathe.

I want to kill him.

Alex's arm tightens around me, his fingers curling around my shoulder.

Eli must notice the subtle movement, or else he's done torturing me, because he looks up to meet Alex's gaze. "You want a ride?" He's in a black t-shirt, grey shorts. There are shadows under his green eyes, and I wonder if he's always up like he was last night.

I wonder if he ever sleeps. I wonder if he's actually insane. I wonder if I am.

I wonder when I can talk to him. When I can rip his fucking head off and tell him we are never doing that again. It was a mistake, and he's a fucking bastard.

I have no idea why he lied. Maybe he's just bored? I don't know, but I do know he doesn't know me. Not like he seems to think he does. And if he thinks I'm going to let him get away with that shit, fuck that.

"Nah," Alex says, leaning against me as he sinks onto the bed. "I've got to take Zara to her place so she can get some clothes."

Eli's eyes find mine again. I open my mouth to tell Alex I'm not going to the funeral. It's not my place to be there. I don't want to go.

But nothing comes out as Eli stares at me, the corners of his mouth lifting, like he thinks my paralysis is funny.

"Oh?" he says in his quiet voice. He lets go of the door-knob, crosses his arms and leans against the frame. "You're coming? I didn't know you and Rihanna were close."

Dick.

Alex looks to me.

My mouth is still open, but all I can think about is Eli fingering me last night against the kitchen island.

My face heats with the memory. This bastard.

"She wasn't," Alex finally answers for me, "but she's coming with me."

Eli arches a brow, focusing on Alex. "I didn't know you two were so close either."

"Whatever, man. My dad will be there. I've got to go."

His dad will be there? Yeah. I'm not going.

Eli nods. "See you there." Then he pulls the door closed without looking at me again and I hear him walk down the hallway, toward the stairs.

I exhale, my heart fluttering in my chest.

"You okay?" Alex asks me.

I clear my throat, shift on the bed and slide off, ducking out of his arms. He stands too, facing me, his hands in his pockets. "Alex, I'm so sorry. I didn't—"

"I know, Zara," he says through gritted teeth. "I know you don't know. I know you would never really do that." He says it like he's not sure. Like he's trying to convince himself.

"I'm not actually..." I clear my throat again. "I'm not actually feeling well. I'm going to um, I'm going to stay home."

Alex's brows flick up. "I don't think you should."

My temper rises alongside my hunger, my thirst, and my general irritation with being in this house, so far from my drugs, and with two boys that I've fucked with, one I've fucked over. "I want to stay home. I don't want to go."

Alex shakes his head, scrubs a hand over his face. "What is with you?" he asks, exasperated. "Why are you fucking like this?" He gestures toward me, as if this is just...me.

I don't know. I don't know why I'm like this. I don't know what's wrong with me. I don't even have a bad childhood to blame this shit on. I don't have a horror story. I'm all fucked up, and I don't know why, and I want to go home. I want to go to my room and crawl under my sheets and not think about Alex or Eli or why I'm like this.

"I just don't feel good."

He takes a step toward me. "Zara. Talk to me. What's wrong?"

I cross my arms over my chest, wanting to bury under his clothes that I'm wearing. Disappear and hide. "Alex."

He takes another step. "Yeah?"

"Jax said something about you last night."

Now it's his turn to squirm. His turn to look uncomfortable. *Guilty.*

"What did he say?"

I didn't really mean to bring this up. I didn't mean to talk about this right now. Before a funeral. While I'm coming down from whatever I snorted last night. I didn't mean to but, "He said that you…" I wrap my arms tighter around myself, looking down at the floor. "He said you hurt someone."

I can't bring myself to say it. That horrible word that sounded so musical last night coming out of my mouth. *Rape.*

Alex doesn't say anything for a long moment. He's silent, and I keep staring at the floor, waiting. The more time passes without him saying anything, the worse this will get. The more guilty he seems.

"Hurt someone?" he finally asks, a beat too late. "Hurt someone how?" There's an underlying edge of anger in his tone.

I rub my hand over my throat, one arm still wrapped around myself. "I don't know." My voice is a faint whisper, and I'm lying, but I can't say it. I just can't say it.

He takes another step toward me and reaches out his hand.

I take it with shaky fingers. He pulls me into his chest, wraps his arms around me, and I lay my head against his shoulder.

"Did you?" I ask him. "Did you hurt someone, Alex?"

He takes a deep breath. I feel his lungs expand and then deflate against me. He holds me tighter, his dark and woodsy scent enveloping me in familiarity. I think he's just going to deny it, but instead he asks, "If I did, would you still want me?"

I close my eyes, holding onto him tightly. "You still want me, right? After everything I've done?"

He doesn't say anything for a long moment. Hell, maybe he doesn't want me. Maybe he just feels bad. Maybe he only picked me up last night because he's got so much guilt. So much guilt about so many things.

"Did you do it?" I press. I didn't mean to talk about it, but now I want to know. Now I need to know.

"It was just…" He trails off, and I hear him swallow. Then he tries again: "It was just a big mess, Za. It was just a misunderstanding. I didn't hurt anyone, okay?" He holds me closer, tighter, his body pressed up against every inch of mine. "I didn't hurt anyone. Do you believe me?"

No.

"Yes."

He seems to relax in my arms. I don't believe him, but I'm full of shit. I'm so full of shit, it seems wrong to judge him. I don't know what happened. I don't want to know. I don't want to know, because then I'll have to do something about it, and I don't want to. I don't want to do anything about it.

Alex is my lifeline right now.

Alex is the only constant.

He pulls back from me, holding me by my arms. "I love you."

My heart flips. Can I say it back? Do I mean it anymore? Did I ever mean it? I look down at the floor again. "Look, Alex, I know you think I'm some druggie loser—"

"I don't think that."

"—but I'm trying, okay? I'm sorry for everything, but I'm… I'm trying." I press my fist to my mouth, swallowing back the tightness in my throat. Forcing back the tears that I feel pricking behind my eyes because I'm not actually trying, and I am a druggie loser but he can't leave me now. Not yet. Not now.

"I know, baby." He presses his lips to my forehead. "I know."

He's lying, just like me.

There's no truth between us. I don't know if there ever was.

And this fucking comedown is making me feel like absolute shit.

"We're going to your apartment," he says, his lips moving against my skin, his body pressed close to mine. "You're going to get dressed. You aren't going to take any drugs, and I'm going to take you to that funeral, because if you don't stop fucking around, if you don't try harder, Zara, that's going to be you in that casket."

I don't say anything at all. I just think of the scars on my thighs. The ones Eli saw. The ones Alex has never noticed.

Maybe a casket wouldn't be so bad, actually.

14

Zara

THE FUNERAL SUCKS.

The only good thing about it is Alex's dad couldn't come. Got caught up in some personal shit, Alex said.

Whatever.

The entire cheerleading squad is here and every single one of them threw shade my way when I showed up on Alex's arm. I've never really fit in with them, so it's not unexpected. Regardless, I throw it back by smirking at them, but that's probably more because I'm high on Vyvanse and has little to do with any mean-spirited intent on my part.

I'm dressed in a long black skirt, a modest—for me anyway—black tank, and huge sunglasses over my eyes so no one sees my pinprick pupils.

But apparently, I wore the wrong color because everything here is in shades of blue and orange. Caven colors. Alex is wearing a blue tux and so is fucking Eli.

He watched over his shoulder, from the front row, as Alex and I walked through the small church, his face a careful mask of disinterest. My knees trembled as Alex and I made our way into a pew.

All I could think about is that I don't like sharing a secret with Eli. It makes me feel physically ill.

And watching him dab at his eyes, making a show of mourning for Rihanna like he didn't tell me just yesterday that he barely knew her? I can't believe it took me this long to notice he was crazy. I should've paid better attention.

Right now, gathered around the gravesite, behind a sea of people that turned out for Rihanna, I see Eli offering her mother a literal shoulder to cry on. She's dabbing at her eyes and howling. Beside her, a man whom I assume is Rihanna's father is stoic, his hands clasped in front of him, shades over his eyes too.

Everyone is either crying, trying not to cry, or dabbing at their fake tears with tissues.

I'm hot and sweaty under the September sun and I want to push Alex into that open grave for making me come here. If he expected me to learn something out of this, he's going to be sorely disappointed. The only thing I've learned is that his roommate is insane, and I didn't need this funeral to tell me that. Him showing up at my apartment yesterday was proof enough.

Eli rubs Mrs. Martinson's back, and then glances over his shoulder, his gaze on me. I swear to God I see a small smirk pull on his lips and now I want to kill him too.

But I wait.

I'm not that great at it, admittedly, but for this, I can do it.

And after the first spray of dirt is thrown on the casket and everyone is bawling their eyes out and Mrs. Martinson buries her head in fucking Eli Addison's shoulder because he's such a model student, such a quiet, smart guy that cared for her daughter, a guy that's so distraught like everyone else over her death, he glances at me one more time to make sure I'm seeing it. And I am. Which is why I turn to Alex, stand on my tip toes, and press my mouth to his, clutching at his chest.

He's surprised, and for a second he just stands there, not kissing me back, probably shocked by my PDA at a funeral, as if he doesn't know I don't have morals. But no one is behind us, and he finally opens his mouth, lets me twirl my tongue around his, and we have our first cemetery kiss while Eli watches.

Fuck you, Eli.

15

Alex

ZARA WANTS TO GO HOME.

I don't really want her to. I don't know what she'll get into by herself, but she makes it pretty clear she doesn't want me to stay with her, and I guess we aren't technically back together. I mean, she's definitely mine, and I'm not fucking around with anyone else yet, but still. We're technically broken up.

She doesn't even kiss me goodbye as she slides out of the Jeep. She just waves without looking as she walks down the sidewalk, then up the exposed stairway to the second floor of her apartment complex. I keep staring after her, long after she's shut the door behind her.

She seemed so distracted today.

And then, last night. When Eli told me what happened, right before I'd found her in the kitchen and he'd gone up to his room, apparently. *Goddammit.*

She doesn't even remember.

She stripped for my best friend and she doesn't even fucking remember.

I close my eyes, my fingers clenched on the steering wheel.

And then my phone starts to ring through the speakers of my car.

I open my eyes and answer the call, holding my breath until the line connects.

For a few seconds, there's just silence and then I ask, "Mom?"

I hate that my voice is rough, kind of broken. I hate that my entire body is tense as I stare at the steering wheel, waiting for her to say something. Wondering if her calling me was an accident.

It wouldn't be the first time she's pocket dialed me.

"Alex!" she says in a false-cheerful voice.

That almost hurts worse. It makes my heart sink, hearing her pretend. Hearing her as the shell of the mother she used to be.

I flex my fingers against the wheel, lean my head back and close my eyes. I want to go upstairs, to Zara's apartment. I want to fall into her arms. I want to tell her I'm scared. I want to tell her I don't want her to become my mother.

I want to tell her I think she already has.

"How are you, son?"

I swallow down the anger. "I'm good, Mom. Dad said that he couldn't make it because—"

She laughs, cutting me off. There's no humor in her laugh. No amusement whatsoever. Just cold, bitter anger. "What did Dad say?" But she doesn't let me finish. "I'll tell you what really happened, because I'm sure he didn't. There were more pictures today, posted on the church website, right in the comments section under Dad's latest blog post." Her voice takes on a hard edge, and I can imagine her jaw locked, her narrowed eyes. I can imagine her rage. I can imagine how much she hates him. "Right under the latest post about keeping the fucking spark alive in your marriage."

I hate it for her. I fucking hate it for her.

I slam my fist against the wheel, but don't say anything.

She's not done ranting. But if she's ranting, it means she's not using. Not right now. Probably later. Probably as soon as I get off the phone with her, and I'd sit in this fucking Jeep all night long if it meant I could keep her talking. If it meant she'd fall asleep on the line with me. If it meant she wouldn't slip into a Xanax-induced coma.

"I confronted him of course, and he lied. Of course."

Of course.

"Mom, I'm so—"

"Don't ever do this, Alex, do you hear me?" Her tone changes. It's not hard anymore. Not so angry. It's…pleading. "Don't do this to any girl. Even if it's Zara. Dad said Zara was at the party, with Rihanna…" She trails off. "Screw what your dad says about her. Don't do this to her."

Obviously, Dad didn't tell Mom what Zara did with Jamal Clint. Probably better that way.

I glance up at the windows on the second floor of Zara's apartment. I wish I could see inside. I wish I could always be with her. I wish I could save her.

"Mom, I wouldn't—"

"Don't wreck her world because some newer, younger, shinier toy comes into your life. Do you understand me, Alex Christian?"

I rub my hand over my heart. "I understand, Mom."

But… *What if she doesn't want me? What if she pushes me away? What if she's like you? What if she leaves me for something new? Something…shinier?*

"I know you've made some mistakes, Alex, and I know you've got to sit the next three games out, son, but don't you dare let those things make you bitter. Don't you dare allow the world's hurt to make you into someone that hurts other people."

I think about that bottle of tequila. Forcing it down Zara's throat. I think about the videos going around about her. I think about pulling her into the pool. I was drunk, and stupid, and angry, but I had no right. I had no fucking right.

I think about last fall. Another party. Another girl. Another mistake.

The police. The accusations.

The girl left Caven. She left. Why didn't Eli and I have to leave?

Because Eli's dad is a lawyer. Because my family has money. Because that girl was no one.

That girl was just like Zara.

"Okay, Mom. I won't. I'm so sorry, Mom, I—"

"It's not your fault. It's your father's."

Are you going to leave him? "I'm sorry, Mom."

She sighs on the other line, and I can imagine her glancing at the orange tinted prescription bottle. I can imagine her fighting it. I can imagine when it all started. When the rumors of Dad cheating on her were in full force and I didn't believe it. I didn't fucking believe it, because Dad is a pastor and he wouldn't.

And then I went into the pool shed while Mom was away with some friends. I'd come home early from school, wanting to spend the weekend with my dad before he was engulfed with church on Sunday. I'd come home one hour early on a Friday, and he was fucking some girl in that shed.

"I've got to go," she tells me abruptly. I don't know where Dad is, or what she's doing, what room she's in. I know why she hasn't left though. She gave up everything for him. Her career, her home state, her family. Her life. She moved and gave up everything and now they have money and they have prestige and where would she go? And if she leaves, a divorced man can't lead the church.

More than that, she doesn't want to adjust her lifestyle. Even if it's just getting manicures and popping pills and being talked about around town. It's her life now.

"I've got to go, but I'll talk to you soon, okay? Come see us when you can." I can hear that faint hint of excitement in her words that don't mesh with what she's saying. And I know she's given in again. I know as soon as she ends this call, she'll be tossing back a handful of pills.

I know it, but there's nothing I can do.

Dad can't lead a megachurch if his wife is in rehab either, so they give each other their vices and no one says shit about it, until it comes to a head and they fight. They fight and they scream and in the end, they stay together because no one else would want them.

I look up at Zara's window again.

"Okay, Mom."

"I love you, Alex."

I swallow down the lump in my throat. "I love you too, Mom."

▼

SUNDAY NIGHT, AFTER SPENDING MOST OF SATURDAY IN BED, I'm outside on the back deck when Eli walks outside with a beer in his hand.

He slides the door closed behind him, sits down on the couch across from me. The sun is set, the tiki torches lit, the underwater lights glowing in the calm surface of the pool.

I turn to glance at him. He's watching the water, a Caven U wrestling hoodie on over his gym shorts. The circles under his eyes are pretty bad, and I wonder if he's actually more freaked out about Rihanna's death than he's let on.

Either that, or something else must really be eating at him.

"You see her parents today?" I ask him, breaking the silence.

He'd told me he was stopping by Rihanna's parents' house to offer more condolences, see if they needed anything. I'm sure he didn't do it out of the goodness of his heart, but then again, maybe it's finally sinking in that yesterday, he helped bury a girl who sucked his dick. They never dated, but they fucked around on and off the past few months. I'm not sure if they were actually friends or anything, but I guess you get used to someone's lips being around your cock.

He doesn't look at me. He's got his elbows on his knees, and he takes a drink from his beer and then shrugs. "Yeah." He doesn't offer anything else.

I nod, looking back at the water. I've got one arm around the back of the couch, my feet flat on the deck. I don't look at him when I ask, "Anything you wanna talk about?"

Silence rings out, and I wonder if he's going to answer me. I don't usually ask questions like that, but he's just seemed even more quiet than usual. I wonder if he's shook about the whole Zara thing.

I know it wasn't his fault. She's just...like that.

"Not really," he finally answers me. "You?"

I curl my fingers around the fabric of the couch, squeezing. There's a lot I want to talk about. I want to talk about my mom. I want to talk about Zara. I want to talk about what happened last weekend, at the party. Both with Rihanna and Zara. I want to talk about last fall, too. I want him to tell me that I'm not a bad person. That I just fucked up.

Instead I just say, "Nah. I've got an exam tomorrow I should probably study for." But I don't get up.

"What class?" he asks, but his voice is just so detached. I know he doesn't really care. I don't know if Eli cares about anything.

I glance at him, see his side profile as he stares at the pool. See the clock and skull on his hand, the roses and filigree that trail up his arm, underneath his wrestling hoodie. I think about the controlled way he wrestles, no emotion or outbursts or slipups. When he circles his opponent, he waits until the right time to make a move, and when he strikes, it's always for a takedown. Our schedules conflict sometimes, with wrestling and football, but I've seen a couple of his matches, and I've seen videos of the others.

He's good.

He wrestles like he lives, quietly, with control. I wonder what it would be like for that control to slip.

It almost did last fall.

And then last weekend, I stopped him.

"Just a sociology course, it'll be easy enough."

He turns to look at me and arches a brow. "Sociology, huh?"

I nod, flex my fingers and rest them on my thigh.

"You applied to law schools yet?" he asks me.

I bite the inside of my cheek, turn to stare at the pool. "No."

"Deadline is probably soon for some of them?"

I nod once, scrub a hand over my jaw. "Yep."

"Having second thoughts?" he presses with a hint of amusement.

I still don't look at him when I shrug, bouncing my fist on my thigh. "I don't know. Not really, because what else would I do?" I'm good at sports, but I'm not professional football-level good. I can admit that. Besides that, I don't really want to play for a league. I've thought about opening up a gym, but that seems like a waste of a business, pre-law major. And if I go to law school, my parents will be proud, Dad won't ride my ass about going into fucking ministry, and hell, maybe I can do some good in the world.

Probably not. But maybe.

I see Eli shake his head out of the corner of my eye. Tip his beer up, then bring it back down, resting it on his knee. "There's a lot you can do."

"Why are you even here, anyway?" I ask him, suddenly angry as I turn to glare at him. His father owns the biggest law firm in the state. He's got family money. What the fuck he's doing at Caven when he doesn't want to do shit but work on cars is beyond me. During the summer, he helps his uncle out at his auto body shop, and the only thing I've ever seen him act the slightest bit excited about is when he swaps out his car for a new one, which happens like every six months. "Why not just start working?"

He doesn't look at all affronted by my questions. He cocks his head, as if he's thinking. "Why not be here?" he finally counters.

I roll my eyes, but I grudgingly see his point, I guess. He likes to wrestle; he did it in high school. He got a free ride here, so it's not touching any of his family money. The first night we spent in a dorm together, after we were assigned to be roommates, we got high and he told me he wanted the whole college experience so that when he got older, he wouldn't feel like he missed out on anything.

He wanted to be as bad as he could be, he told me. He wanted to fuck everything up. And when he graduated, he'd put everything back together again.

He also told me, that same night, that his mom was a bitch and he never wanted to have kids. If you didn't have any, he said, you couldn't hurt them.

I figured out his mother left him and his father when he was younger. We've never discussed it since.

Catching me off guard, he asks, "What's up with you and Zara?"

My limbs feel heavy with his words because I don't know the answer to his question. And I wish I did. I know I should let her go. I know she fucked me over. I know she cheated on me, and humiliated me, and I know I should hate her for it.

But I don't.

I just don't.

Just like as much as I want my mother to be free of my dad, I also know it's probably best if she doesn't leave. Because if she does, who will be there for her? Who will make sure she doesn't OD? Who will take care of her?

I can't stop picturing Zara's blue-green eyes. Her arms around me when I picked her up at Jax's. *You are so beautiful.* How her hair feels in my hands. That coffee-and-flower scent that she wafts around her wherever she goes. How my sheets still smell like her, and I kind of hope they never stop.

I know she hurt me.

I know I need to cut her off.

I can't.

"I don't know," I finally answer Eli, looking down at my hands. "Honestly, I just don't know."

He's quiet for a moment, and then he says, "You need to stay away from her, man."

I tense, clenching my fists, but I don't look up. I know he's just being my friend. He's just saying what's best for me.

"Girls fucking line up to suck your dick. Forget Zara."

I can't help but laugh, even though I'm definitely not in a playful mood. "I don't know, after Rihanna, they might all be scared of her."

I look up and meet his dark gaze. He furrows his brow. "You think she had something to do with Rihanna?"

I shake my head, stare up at the stars above us. "Nah, I'm just fucking around. Guess it's not funny."

He laughs. "Not yet. Maybe a few more days." Then he asks, "I'm not trying to start anything, but why are you still fucking with her? After what she did?" And it's amazing, because he really doesn't sound like he's trying to start anything. He's just asking. Clinically. Curiously. He wants to know.

I keep looking up at the stars. "You really wanna know, man?"

"That's why I'm asking."

"She's addicting," I tell him. I dip my head down and he turns to look at me, his dark green eyes locked on mine. "All of her fuck ups, and even the way she gets a little out of control, she's just addicting."

"Do you love her?" It's a fast question, straightforward. It surprises me, coming from Eli. He doesn't really talk about girls, and we definitely don't talk about love.

"Yeah, I think so."

He nods, as if he expected I'd say as much. He gestures toward me with his beer. "You know she's not okay. You know she's still using. And you can't breathe for her too. She'll pull you down in that grave and bury you with her." He takes another pull from his beer. "She'll fuck you up, Alex. You won't save her. She'll just destroy you."

16

Zara

ONE IN THE morning on Monday, and I can't sleep. Sunday,
I did fuck-all. Ended up chugging cough syrup in the middle
of the day, and now I'm reaping the consequences.

I turn on my side to grab my phone from my nightstand.

I still haven't confronted Eli about his bullshit. Alex and I
have texted since he dropped me off here Saturday, and I told
him again I was sorry, but I'm not that sorry.

I'm fucking pissed.

I know Eli is probably sleeping, although I'm not sure he
does sleep, but I can't help it. I've been thinking about his bullshit nonstop, just waiting for him to tell Alex. Or to blackmail
me to meet him or some shit.

But he's just ignored me.

Me: **What the fuck is wrong with you?**

I send off the message, not really expecting a reply. I lay
on my back, holding my phone over my head under the
covers.

I wish Alex was here.

I wish I could be honest with him.

I wish I could tell him Eli is fucked up.

Instead, I just scroll through some pictures of us. My legs wrapped around him at the beach, his mom behind the camera. I have the biggest smile on my face, and I wasn't even high that day. He's pretending to bite my cheek, his hands under my ass. He looks happy too. I can see that dimple in his cheek, even with his teeth bared against my skin.

There's another picture of me, coming up out of the water at his parents' pool that night they were away. I'm naked, but he took the photo carefully, so you can't tell.

If only he'd been that careful last fucking weekend.

Before I can thumb through the next picture, I get a text from Eli. My heart flutters in my chest, my stomach in knots. I take a breath before I open it.

Eli: **Miss me, baby girl?**

This asshole.

Before I can compose myself, I just let my fingers fly over my screen.

Me: **Why would you do that? Why would you fucking lie like that?**

This time, I don't go back to pictures of Alex. I just wait, because almost immediately, I see Eli is typing.

Him: **He's not good for you.**

And then, a second later, before I can think of what to say, he adds: **Take a picture of your scars. I want to see them.**

I roll my eyes, squeezing said thighs together before I reply.

Me: **Fuck you.**

I bite my cheek as I wait for his response. I don't have to wait long.

Him: **How's your roomie, Zara?**

I frown at my screen, brow furrowed. My arms are getting tired of holding my phone up so I shift onto my side, still perplexed. I don't know if he even knows Kylie, and she is asleep in her room. I saw her when I came out for an apple earlier in the day.

Before I can ask him what the fuck he's talking about he says, **You know her and Alex are close?**

I laugh out loud. That's hilarious. Alex has been over a lot, and him and Kylie barely exchange three words to each other. They are definitely not close. Besides, I think about all those questions Kylie asked me about Alex. How she always said he was a dick.

Me: **Yeah. Funny. Fool me once...**

Eli's reply is almost instant.

Him: **I lied to him. I'm not going to lie to you.**

I bite my lip, frowning. He's obviously full of shit. Dude is crazy. He's just insane. He tried to start shit between me and Alex by making up some shit about me flashing him, so there's no way this is true. Kylie isn't Alex's type. Alex is definitely not Kylie's type.

How close? I ask, giving in. If he wants to talk shit, I'll see how far he can go.

He starts typing, then stops, then starts and stops all over again. My heart is pounding in my chest and I pull down my covers, glancing at my closed bedroom door. Kylie would not go there. Alex wouldn't either. Between the two of us, I'm the cheater.

Alex is arrogant, and a dick, but he's not a cheater.

I snatch my phone back up when I see Eli's text finally come through.

Eli: **How does it feel being with someone who wants to control the fuck out of you?**

I roll my eyes in the dark.

Me: **That's not an answer, Eli Addison.**

Despite how annoyed I am, I can't help smiling as I type out his first and last name. *Don't be stupid, Zara.* But fuck, I can't seem to stop.

Eli: **Oh, I like when you say my name.**

I slam my phone down on my mattress, biting my lip to stifle my laughter. He is so weird. I pick my phone back up to ask him about Kylie and Alex again, but he's already texted me again.

Eli: **What's your middle name?**

I'm momentarily distracted from the Kylie bullshit.

Me: **You're my number one stalker. Shouldn't you know?** And then, because I'm clearly stupid, I add, **What's yours?**

He replies instantly.

Him: **Adonis.**

And right after that.

Him: **You're cute, you know that, Zara Rose?**

I place a hand over my heart, willing it to chill out.

Me: **How did you know that?**

I find myself holding my breath while I wait for his response. There are a lot of red flags here. Eli is not a good guy. Not just that, but he lives with Alex. For all I know, they both could be fucking me over right now.

Even if they're not, this won't end well for me. They'll probably get over me, go back to being bros. But they'll forget all about me, and I'll be alone, and I can't do that. I can't fucking do it.

The internet has everything, he responds.

Yeah, maybe so, but even still, whether he's a real stalker or just good at searching online, I know what I need to say next.

Me: **We shouldn't do this.**

I send it before I can psyche myself out of it, but I'm still staring at my phone, waiting for those three little dots to let me know he's replying. Maybe to tell me he agrees or to say we'll put this behind us. Or even to tell me he's sorry for fucking me over.

But he doesn't say any of that. Instead, he replies with, **Do you want to stop?**

My heart is hammering so hard in my chest I feel like I might have a heart attack. *Do I want to stop?* I don't know.

Before I can answer, another text comes in, and it makes my stomach flip, every nerve in my body tingling.

Him: **I don't like it when he hurts you.**

My hand is sweaty on my phone, one hand flat against the mattress. I don't know what to say. I just keep staring at it until the screen dims and then goes black.

I don't like it when he hurts you.

I close my eyes, but then the screen lights back up and I see it beyond my lids. Taking a deep breath, I force my eyes open and read the next message.

Him: **I know you hurt him too. Do you think you'll always be like that? What if you found the right person?**

I should put my phone away. Every text I send is just more damning than the last, and Alex might've forgiven me for the bullshit Eli lied about, but if he were to see these texts, he definitely wouldn't.

Then again, Eli would be fucking himself, too. He can't lie about this.

I don't know, I reply. **I just want to experience everything**, I admit.

Me: **And then...then I'll be good.**

He doesn't start typing for so long, I think he's gone to sleep. I think I should probably do that too considering I have class in the morning, but just as I'm about to plug my phone back into charge, he sends me another text.

Him: **You already are so good, baby girl.**

17

Zara

"HOW WAS CLASS?" Kylie asks me on Monday, tucking a lock of dark hair behind her ear and bringing the straw from her mango smoothie to her lips. "You look worried," she adds before she takes a drink.

I throw my green backpack into the booth at Oasis, one of the little on-campus cafes. The walls are all painted Caven orange, and the place smells faintly of mildew, so it's not my favorite, but Kylie wanted to meet for lunch today.

I had philosophy and ethics this morning, and I'm pretty sure I bombed my ancient Greek philosophy exam.

I ended up taking an Adderall to study after Eli went to sleep last night.

Instead, I stayed up until the sun rose reading Marcus Aurelius' *Meditations*, which one would think would help me with the exam. Except he was Roman. Not Greek.

I slouch down in the booth as Kylie sips her smoothie, staring and waiting for me to answer her question. For a second, I think about asking her about Alex. About what Eli said. But I know Eli is just trying to start shit.

Still, thinking about him makes me feel all…warm.

Ugh.

"I think I just failed an exam," I admit to Kylie, trying to push thoughts of Eli from my mind.

She quirks a brow and pulls her smoothie away from her mouth as she swallows it down. "Oh, no. That's not good. What was it on?"

Considering I know Kylie is taking shit like organic chem, I don't really want to tell her. But I do anyway: "Ancient Greek philosophy. I studied the wrong thing." Kind of true. I knew Aurelius wouldn't be on the exam, but I'm not about to tell her I stayed up all night texting my ex's best friend, then ended up high in my bedroom reading *Meditations*.

I shrug, blow out a breath. "Anyway, it's okay. I'll live."

"How's your GPA?" she asks me, which seems like a personal question, but I realize, if my GPA was decent, it wouldn't be.

Still. I clear my throat and sit up a little straighter, looking over her head at the checkout counter of Oasis, watching the lady at the register add whipped cream to an iced coffee. Fuck, I want that. But I've got to ration out the money Mom sends me. I can't be spending it all willy-nilly on things like iced coffee when I've got things like illegal drugs to buy.

"It's okay," I answer Kylie, meeting her gaze. "Yours? You applying to pharm schools yet?"

She wraps her small hands around her plastic cup, grinning. I've noticed talking about her future as a pharmacist gets her super excited. I wish I felt like that about something.

"Yeah, I've sent out a few applications already, but I hope I get into Caven's program. Ian has already been accepted to the med school," she gushes, her cheeks turning the slightest bit pink.

God, I wish I felt that way about someone too.

As if on cue, my phone vibrates in the back pocket of my jeans and I know that pattern. Kylie keeps going on about how great Caven's pharmacy program is while I lean over and grab my phone, glancing at the screen.

Yep. Alex.

Him: **I want to see you.**

Him: **Tonight.**

Him: **Now.**

Him: **You can't just kiss a guy at a funeral and then ghost him. That's pretty macabre.**

I laugh a little out loud at that and then realize, belatedly, that Kylie is still going on about pharmacy schools because she trips over her words and I look up, embarrassed that I wasn't listening.

But she's staring at my phone with a smirk. "You and Alex made up?" she asks me, seemingly uncaring that I missed half of what she was saying. Her brow is furrowed, and she looks a little uneasy asking about him.

Again, I think about Eli's text.

Glancing down at my screen, I wonder what to say to Alex. Maybe I should confront him and Kylie both. Or I could just tell her about what's going on with Eli.

Yeah, no. Never mind. I can't tell her that if she's already talking to Alex behind my back. Besides, she probably still hasn't gotten over the fact that I told her I blew another guy.

I clear my throat, flip my phone over, leaving Alex on read. Well, not literally. My read receipts are turned off because I'm not a psychopath.

"No, no," I tell her, drumming my chipped black nails on the table. I'll have to fix that shit tonight, when I'll probably be alone and drunk watching *You*, or some other disturbing shit. As if my life isn't bizarre enough. "It's uh, just a dude from my philosophy class." Wow. I'm turning into a full-blown liar.

Kylie waggles her brows at me. "Care to share?" she asks me, then takes another sip of her smoothie.

I feel myself blushing, but obviously not because of the non-existent guy I just made up. And I kind of do want to share. I sort of want to talk about Alex Cardi, just like I want to talk about Eli Addison. I want to tell her that something is seriously wrong with me. I wish I could tell her I'm having a hard time staying on top of my drug use again, and that I'm so scared I'll end up alone for the rest of my life, mostly because of my own poor decision-making skills.

I wave my hand, shaking my head. "No, it's nothing, really."

She doesn't look like she believes me, but she lets it go, and she even does me a favor and changes the subject. Glancing down at my nails tapping again against the table she asks, "You gonna eat anything?"

Eat? The thought kind of startles me, but I guess it is lunchtime. I haven't had an appetite in days, between all the Adderall and the Xanax or cough syrup to knock me out when it gets too late.

The idea of eating right now is an unpleasant one. My mouth is dry, and I'm pretty sure food would taste like ash.

I shake my head raking my hand through my hair. Which needs washing.

"Oh, no. I'm not hungry."

Kylie takes a slurp of her smoothie, but she's eyeing me suspiciously. I don't like it. I squirm a little in my seat and then realize that makes me look guilty as hell. My next anxious instinct is to pick up my phone and beg Alex to come save me, but that would make me look weak. Instead, I reach for a subject change.

"How long have you and Ian been dating?"

This is, apparently, the right thing to ask. They were together before I moved into the apartment, and I never bothered to ask because I'm a selfish bitch.

Kylie grins so hard *my* face hurts, just watching it. Her fingers flex against the plastic of her smoothie cup, and she ducks her chin, laughing a little.

It's amusing and kind of annoying at the same time.

Annoying only because I'm fucking jealous. If anyone knows anything about me at all, it's for that stupid video, and the fact that I'm Alex Cardi's girlfriend.

Basically, I'm the tit girl.

It's college, of course, so no one really cares all that much about who you are if you aren't at the top of the totem pole, but still. Kylie Jones is definitely not the tit girl, even though hers are much bigger than mine, even on her small frame. She's the future pharmacist girl. The smart girl.

Ian's girl. More like, he's Kylie's boy.

"Since the end of last year," she tells me, still cheesin' like a fool. She props her chin on her hand and bats her lashes. "He asked me to be his girlfriend under a Christmas tree."

That makes me think of my mother which is kind of heart-warming and obnoxious all at once. Jealous. "Oh, wow. Like, an outdoor one or a fake or…?"

She laughs, clamps a hand over her mouth then speaks through her fingers. "My parents' tree. He asked them first. If he could date me."

My eyes almost bug out of my head. "Wow. That's uh… That's something." *That's disturbing.*

She is smiling so hard I swear she's going to split her cute round face in two. "Yeah, it's my favorite holiday and he knew my dad would want to be asked, so," she shrugs, "he asked them, then me." Her voice kind of goes up at the ends, like a squeak.

If Alex had asked my mother before he dated me, I would have punched him. If my mom had believed for half a second, I needed *her* permission to date someone, I might've punched her, too.

God, I'm a bitch.

But I can also recognize when another girl is genuinely happy, and Kylie is definitely that. "I'm happy for you," I tell her, and I do actually mean it. I just wish I had that. Not the parental permission thing because that's much too southern for me, and I'm a fucking Southerner, but the happiness part.

Alex makes me happy.

He also pisses me off.

I'm sure the feeling is entirely mutual.

"Yeah, he's the best," Kylie gushes, still riding high in her little love bubble. Whatever Eli was insinuating last night, he's full of it. Ian is a nice guy. He's got blonde hair and glasses and a boyish face, and he seems perfect for Kylie.

Maybe that's the problem.

Maybe there's no one that's perfect for me because I'm a fucking freak. And not just in the sexy way. Mainly, in fact, in the unsexy way.

Kylie cocks her head, holds up one finger like she's listening for something. It's pretty quiet in Oasis. Kind of too early for the lunch rush, so this place is nearly empty. I don't know what the fuck she's trying to hear.

Then she grins again, and I hear it.

A ringtone coming from her pink backpack.

Bella's Lullaby from the Twilight soundtrack.

"That's Ian!" she says excitedly. She pulls the phone out of the front pocket of her backpack and swipes to answer the call.

This is my cue to leave.

I stand to my feet after I slide out of the booth, grabbing my backpack. "See you tonight," I tell her, and she finger waves to me, caught up in the bliss of young, non-fucked up love.

Must be fucking nice.

18

Eli

WEDNESDAY NIGHT, I'm walking out of the gym from practice, duffel bag slung over my shoulder when I feel my phone vibrate in my pocket. I hear the guys behind me talking, and someone asks if I want to grab dinner.

I ignore them, walking toward the fountain outside of the gym as I pull my phone out.

Zara's name flashes on the screen. Since late Sunday night, or early Monday morning, I guess, we haven't texted. I know she met Alex for lunch on Tuesday because he told me about it last night. But he said he's not really ready to trust her again.

If it's up to me, he won't, ever again.

It's dark outside already, kind of cool for mid-September, and as I unlock my phone, I feel a chill run through my body, wicking the sweat from practice away.

Her: **Tell me about Kylie and Alex.**

I smile at my screen. So maybe she wants to try to trust me now. I shrug off my bag, setting it on the concrete ledge of the fountain.

Me: **What do you want to know?**

She replies immediately, and I wonder what she's doing. I want to see her and Alex went to the bar with Dwight for wing night.

Would she come over, if I asked her?

She's probably pissed I lied to Alex, but I don't care. I've been waiting for her for too fucking long. I don't want to wait anymore.

Her: **Everything.**

I glance up at the night sky, see the stars overhead. I don't know how long we'd have before Alex got back. Practice was later than usual tonight because the wrestling room was being used for some other shit, but it's only like eight now.

Alex probably won't be back until after midnight.

Me: **Let me pick you up.**

I stare at my screen in the dark, waiting. She starts to type, then stops. Then starts again.

Her: **Are you going to get me in trouble again, Eli Adonis?**

I smile in the dark, biting my cheek. My mom used to call me that.

Me: **No. I promise.**

Her: **I don't trust you. Pick me up anyway.**

And then, right after that text, **I want to experience everything, remember?**

19

Zara

I'M SITTING with my feet in the pool beside Eli, both of us on a shared towel. He's got his feet in too. He told me to bring my swimsuit and since I'm already being fucking stupid, it seemed silly not to.

I knew Alex was out with Dwight, so for at least a few more hours, we'll be alone.

I told Eli I had to be gone before Alex came.

I grab the red Solo cup on the blanket between us and finish the tequila soda before putting the cup back down.

"Want another one?" Eli asks beside me, turning to face me.

I meet his eyes in the dim light around the pool. The water is cold, and the night is kind of chilly too. It's not really warm enough for us to be sitting in our swimsuits, but I don't really want Eli to put his shirt back on, so I'm not complaining. Besides, the alcohol will warm me up soon.

"I shouldn't," I tell Eli, smiling a little as he grins at me.

He cocks his head. "You shouldn't be here either and yet here you are." He shrugs, the muscles in his shoulders flexing as he does. "Why not be a little more bad?" His words are a whisper, and there's like a foot of space between us, but it doesn't stop a chill from going down my spine. I clench my thighs together and hope he doesn't notice.

His eyes never leave mine.

"Okay, fine. But not until you tell me what you know about Alex and Kylie. And why the fuck you lied to Alex about me flashing you." I know I should be madder, but when he grins at my reply, I can't help but laugh a little too.

He's leaning against his palms, but he moves his fingers closer to mine, his thumb brushing against my wrist, his eyes still on mine.

"Alex told Kylie to keep an eye on you," he says quietly.

My stomach churns.

"She sends him weekly reports."

I snatch my hand away from him and sit up straighter, twisting to stare at him. "Eli, do not fuck with me. Are you lying right now?"

He sits up too, bringing his feet in, flat on the towel as he wraps his arms around his knees. "I told you. I'm not lying to you."

"But you fucking lied to Alex about—"

He puts his hand on my thigh, cutting off my words. His thumb strokes the scars, just under the edge of my bikini.

I shiver at his touch but don't dare move.

"Yeah. I lied to him. I'm not lying to you."

"But why?" I ask him, my voice hoarse as he keeps moving his thumb back and forth across my bare skin. I feel warmth spooling in my core, my insides turning to liquid. "Why did you lie to him? He was pissed at me."

"He's always pissed at you, baby girl."

I hold his gaze a second, then turn to look out at the pool. He keeps his hand on my thigh, still running his thumb back and forth across my skin.

"Do you think he cares?" I ask without looking at him. "Is

that why he asked Kylie to look after me?" I hate the rough edge to my voice, but I can't help it.

Alex has been lying to me.

Or at the very least, he's been keeping things from me. And Kylie? Fuck her. She was bullshitting me about Alex being a jerk. Or maybe she really thinks he is, but she fucking lied to me too.

Eli is quiet a moment, and his thumb moves closer to the edge of my bikini. The warmth under my skin is growing and I want to turn toward him, with his fingers higher, inside of me again.

But I need to hear this too.

"Probably," he answers me. "But wouldn't you rather know?"

I nod in the dark. "Yeah," I admit, and his thumb grazes just under the thin material of my swimsuit. My next words are a little breathless. "I would want to know."

Eli picks the red cup up with his free hand, moves it to his other side. I don't dare move as he comes closer to me, his thigh brushing mine, his shoulder bumping against my arm. I can smell him, and his scent does things to me.

I press my thighs closer together, kicking my feet a little in the cold water of the pool.

"Why did you start?" he asks me quietly. His thumb slips under my swimsuit, and it's hard to breathe. "Why did you start cutting?"

I bite my lip, still staring at the water.

I know he's waiting for some tragedy and it makes my face burn with shame. I don't have a tragedy. If that's what he thinks we have in common, we don't.

He shifts even closer, moves his hand, and pulls at the string of my bikini bottom until it comes undone. He slides his hand under the material, cupping me.

I turn toward him, and his eyes are on mine.

"Tell me, Zara. Why did you start hurting yourself?"

I stare at his mouth, his full lips, imagining them on my skin when I answer him. "I was lonely."

He bites his lip, and runs his middle finger down my slit, parting my lips.

I suck in a breath and I see his lips pull up into a smile.

"Were you?" he asks me softly, leaning in closer. He puts his mouth on my shoulder, kissing me.

I nod, still staring at his mouth, then parting my thighs wider, giving him better access.

He lifts his head. "That night, when you and Alex fought. Why did you do it then?" He pulls me apart with his fingers, massaging my clit with his middle finger.

I take a shaky breath in, glance behind him at the sliding glass doors. Any moment, Alex could walk out here. He could come home early. He could catch us. He would kill us.

"Look at me, baby girl," Eli commands me, sliding his finger lower.

I spread my thighs wider, wanting him inside of me.

He dips his finger down, and then he's right there, teasing me.

"I won't let him hurt you. Tell me." He flicks his gaze to my mouth as he circles my entrance. "Tell me why you did it that night and I'll reward you."

I want to touch him. I want to push him on his back and ride him. I want him inside of me. But I force myself to stay still. To do what he said. I hesitate, "I...I was just tired of feeling... unwanted." I whisper the last word. Think about Alex telling me that his father thought I was a whore. The words shouldn't have hurt, considering his dad really *is* a whore. But it still hurt to know Alex cared what his father said about me. And, he seemed to agree with him and what he thought about me.

It was painful, and so was remembering how it felt to know that my father didn't think of me at all.

"Did it make you feel better?" Eli asks, still teasing me. I shift my hips and I see a ghost of a smile on his lips. "When you cut yourself, did you feel better?"

I nod, whimpering.

"I love when you make that sound," he says, leaning closer. And then his mouth is on mine as he pushes his finger inside of me. I gasp into his mouth, his tongue twirling around mine as he fingers me. He pushes another finger into me, and I shift my hips, bucking against him.

He pulls back, his eyes on mine. I grab his thigh, squeezing the hard muscles below his swimsuit. I trail my hand up higher, palm his hard cock, running my hand along the length of it.

"I'm sorry," he says suddenly, fingering me slowly, teasingly. "I'm sorry for hurting you. The night at the party."

I remember how his fingers curled up inside of me. How it hurt when Alex pulled me off.

It's so different to this Eli now, being gentle and slow.

"Why?" I ask him, breathless. "Why did you do it?"

He kisses me again, licking the seam of my mouth as he pulls back. I rub my hand over his cock, wanting him inside of me so bad.

So fucking bad.

"I was pissed with Alex. It had nothing to do with you."

I want to ask why he was mad, but instead, something else comes out. "I like it rough."

He smiles in the dark. "Me too."

And then he pulls out of me, stands to his feet and offers me his hand.

I already miss the feel of him inside of me and I'm disoriented, throbbing between my thighs. "What are you—"

He doesn't wait for an answer. He grabs my arm and hauls me to my feet, my bikini barely hanging onto my hip. Before I can adjust it, he leads me to the shallow end of the pool.

My heart races, my skin crawling. "Eli…"

He glances back at me as we stand at the top of the steps. "You want to experience everything right?"

I bite my lip, my eyes flicking between the water and him. Slowly, I nod.

"Then let me hurt you. Just a little."

20

Eli

THE UNDERWATER LIGHTS in the pool and the moon overhead give me plenty of light to see by, so I catch the flicker of fear in her eyes as I lead her into the cold water.

"Eli," she says again, "what are you—"

"You trust me?"

She looks up from the water to stare at me, her aqua-green eyes wide. "I—"

I yank her in after me and the cold water nearly steals my breath. She yelps, throwing her arms around my shoulders and clinging to me like she's going to drown.

"What the hell are you—"

"A girl died in here, huh, Za?" I set her on the underwater steps at the entrance to the pool, the water to her waist. I sink down to my knees and she's still grabbing at me even though she's well above the two fucking feet of this part of the pool.

"Your girlfriend." Her words are bitter. It makes me laugh.

I part her knees, bring my thumbs to her inner thighs under the water. She's shivering, and she doesn't let go of me.

"She wasn't," I inform her. "But we're going to play a game."

"What kind of game?"

"A dangerous one." I rub the inside of her thighs, my thumbs teasing her but never getting close enough. She wiggles on the step of the pool, trying to get me closer as she bites her lip, watching me. "Take off your top."

She swallows, but reaches behind her to untie the string. She's so slow about it, I know she's fucking teasing me, but I don't care. I wait until it drops from her neck, and then she pulls the last knot free, behind her back.

The scrap of fabric falls away, floating off into the water. She keeps her eyes on me. "What're you going to do?" she asks me quietly. Trusting me. Waiting.

"I'm going to hold you under."

She sucks in a breath, her chest rising as she holds it, her nipples puckered with the cold of the water on her lower body, the open air of the night.

"And see if I can get you to come before you…" I smile at her, brushing my thumbs up higher.

She swallows, her eyes fluttering closed for one brief moment.

I remember when Alex stopped me, "She's nodding off. She's fucking nodding off."

But Alex isn't here, and she's looking at me again, waiting.

She's gonna do this.

I'm gonna do this.

It's a terrible idea, her being high and me being, well, me. And that's exactly why it's about to happen.

"Okay?" I ask her.

"This seems like a bad idea."

Very observant, this girl. "It is." I push my thumbs up higher and watch her squirm on the step, gripping the sleek metal handrail of the pool.

But she lets me touch her. Stares at me as if she's waiting.

I'm plenty good at waiting, but I'm kind of done with that tonight. There'll be more later, but for now, fuck it.

I stop touching her between her thighs, grab her by the throat and push her down, so the back of her head is submerged in water.

She takes a deep breath, her eyes wide, hands gripping the ledge of the stairs on either side of her as she floats horizontal on the second-to-last step.

"Take another breath," I tell her, still on my knees on the bottom of the steps.

She listens.

And then I push her under.

She's probably got about thirty, forty seconds before she needs to come up for air. I've been toying with her the past half hour, so I know she's ready. And with the fear, that panic bubbling up inside of her—her eyes are closed tight underwater, her hair floating white around her much like Rihanna's did—she's going to be close to the edge.

Fear always brings you closer.

I keep one hand on her throat, holding her down. I straddle her legs, keeping them down, too, and with my free hand I push two fingers into her, circle her clit with my thumb.

She's still grabbing onto the edge of the stairs, but under the water, she opens her eyes.

I'm leaned over her, sitting on her legs on the steps, but pinning her down with my other hand. I'm looking right at her face as I work my fingers in and out of her, under the water.

I add another finger, three inside of her as I stroke her, my hand cramping with the effort. Do I want her to die?

No.

That's why I have to work harder.

I do, her legs shaking under my body, but she tries to sit up. Using her hands to push her off the stairs, her chest thrusts against my hold on her but I'm not done. She's not done. I keep her down.

Her eyes are wide, bubbles coming from her mouth, popping at the surface. She's panicking, bucking underneath me, but her legs are still shaking, and I can feel her swelling against my fingers.

She's so close.

She's still scared though, thrashing under the water, more bubbles streaming from her mouth. She's freaking out, and if she keeps doing that, she won't finish.

Fuck.

I roll my eyes, pull my fingers out of her, grab her by the throat and haul her up to a seated position. She gasps for breath, grabbing my arm, trying to pry my fingers from her throat. Her nose is running, and she can barely breathe, her breaths short and shallow and so damn loud.

"Calm down."

She's staring at me like I'm a goddamn murderer, digging her nails into my forearm, scratching at my hand. I'll have claw marks over the clock and skull tattoo on my hand, and *shit*, the way she's digging those long nails in, I might be bleeding, too.

She manages to say my name, *"Eli,"* on a gasp as she tries in vain to pry me off her throat.

I grab her arm, too, and yank her into my lap as I turn to sit on the top step, her between my thighs.

I wrap an arm around her chest, pulling her back against me, wrapping my legs around her thighs so she can't get up.

"Calm down," I say against her ear. "Breathe. Trust me."

She's still gripping my forearm, but she's not scratching at me anymore. She tries to slow her breathing, and then she starts to shake in my arms. I can feel her pulse beneath my arm over her chest. It's erratic, wild and reckless just like her.

"You're okay," I tell her, my mouth against her ear.

If Alex walks out here, he might kill us both. I need her to calm the fuck down, because I need to get off and I want to get her off. And there's only so much time we have to do that.

"You're okay, baby girl."

She takes another deep breath, leaning back against me, still trembling.

"Don't hurt me," she tells me, her voice a ragged whisper. "Don't hurt me."

"I'm not," I promise her. "I won't."

"Don't hurt me, Eli." She's saying it again, over and over, like a chant or a mantra, like something to keep me from doing it. Like she's insane.

But she should know people don't do what you want just because you beg them.

I close my eyes, think about Mom leaving even though I begged. Think about when she walked out the door for the last time.

All the fighting was done.

All the arguments were done.

It was just me and Dad.

I think about when I was held under in a bathtub.

I think about what it was like, not being able to breathe. Knowing if I did, I'd die.

"Don't hurt me," she whispers again.

And it's only then I realize what she's doing. She doesn't think I'll hurt her.

This is part of the game.

"Eli, don't hurt—"

"Shut the fuck up." I wrap my arm around her throat, cutting off her words, my eyes flying open. She sucks in a breath, trying to squirm out of my grip, splashing in the shallow water. I glide my free hand down her stomach, and she freezes, not fighting me.

This is what she wants.

I inhale against her neck but all I can smell is fucking chlorine, not her usual dark scent. It kind of pisses me off. But I still kiss her, suck her skin between my teeth. She whimpers, trembling again in my arms.

I cup her between her thighs, then rub my fingers against her clit.

She gasps as I loosen my hold on her throat.

"You like that, baby girl?"

She murmurs, squirming a little on the steps, her ass brushing against my cock.

I rub her faster and she's panting, her heart pounding in her neck. I can feel it against my arm.

"Come for me, baby," I tell her. "I want you to come for me."

And then she grips my forearm, digging her nails in as she gasps, her thighs spread wide as I slip a finger into her as she comes, squeezing around me.

"That's it, baby girl." I kiss her neck again as she moans, arching into me. My cock is fucking aching, but I know we don't have much time left tonight. "Good girl," I whisper against her ear and she finally stops squirming, catching her breath in my arms.

Slowly, I slide my fingers out of her, then grab her face, twist her head around so she's looking up at me with wide eyes.

"I like you," I tell her, my lips moving over hers. "I like you a lot."

She doesn't answer me with words. Instead, she twists in my arms. "Move up," she tells me, her words ragged. "Move up to the top step." She grabs my cock through my swimsuit, her eyes still on mine.

I do as she says, coming to sit on the top step.

She's on her knees on the one below it, and she undoes the Velcro on my shorts. "Let me," she whispers in the dark.

I shift my hips, and she pulls my shorts down to my knees.

She grabs my cock, still keeping her eyes on mine, then she dips her head, taking me in her mouth.

And nothing has ever felt that fucking good.

I thread my fingers through her hair, thinking about her on her knees for Jamal. About Alex coming in and watching.

Alex will forgive her for that shit, because he thinks he's just biding his time, picking up her pieces until she's whole again. But he doesn't see what I see in her. She's not broken.

She's not looking for someone to save her.

She's looking for someone to drown with her.

21

Zara

"YOU GOING to the beach party next weekend?" Jax exhales a cloud of smoke on his front porch, the full moon directly in front of us, seeming to hover over Shadow Lakes' subdivision. I hear the thud of music from a few houses over, just a typical Friday night in Falls Creek.

Jax passes the joint to me and I inhale, closing my eyes at the tang of the sweet smoke in my mouth. I hold it, letting it heat up my lungs, and then exhale through my nose before I pass it back to Jax.

As the smoke dissipates in the air, I shrug. Who knows if Alex will want me to go? All summer, he talked my ear off about this little annual beach party him and Eli host, but he hasn't mentioned it lately.

We got dinner last night.

Wednesday night, I went home after I gave Eli head, and we saw Alex's Jeep pulling into their subdivision. I had to duck down in the seat.

I don't know how I'd go to a beach party with both of

them. It's all I could do last night eating with Alex not to think about Eli's fingers inside of me.

"You going?" I ask Jax, trying to clear my head.

"Nah," he answers me after he snubs out the joint in the glass ashtray at his side. "I wasn't invited. Besides, I don't really like the beach."

I turn to stare at him, shocked. "Really?"

He rubs his neck and laughs. "Yeah, really. Sharks and shit? No, thanks."

I rub my hands down my jeans, looking back up at the moon. "You know we all gotta die someday, right?" I ask him, kind of absentmindedly. As a teenager, it was something that drew me to philosophy, specifically Stoicism. The early Stoics did their best to accept whatever came their way and soldiered on despite their circumstances. Or at least, they tried. Death was one of those big things that was inevitable, and they made their peace with it, living while they could.

I'm not really sure how that shit will serve me when I graduate with a degree in fucking philosophy, but even if I end up in Jax's basement, I guess I'll be able to say I really lived life. Or, at least that's what I'll tell myself when I pass out in bed alone every night.

"I know, but I don't wanna die in the belly of a shark," Jax says with another laugh. "I ain't Jonah."

"You wouldn't be Jonah," I point out, still staring up at the moon. "Jonah was in a whale."

Jax cackles in amusement, slapping his knee. He must be high as hell because it really wasn't that funny. "You're a trip, Za."

"Something like that." I feel my phone vibrating in my pocket but ignore it. Kylie has gone home again, so it isn't her. Even if it was, I don't fucking trust her anymore so I'm not fucking texting her.

Could be Mom reminding me, for the millionth time,

about the engagement party this Sunday, like I could fucking forget. It isn't every day your mom gets engaged for the fourth time.

"Why'd you start selling drugs?" I ask Jax quietly, riding my high by staring at the moon as if looking at it long enough will shoot me right up onto its cheesy surface. I stifle my own laugh, because that wasn't very funny either.

I don't know why I asked Jax that, but it just kind of came out. Happens when you're high, I guess.

I can practically feel him shrug beside me. "I'm dyslexic. School was shit. I didn't really like the idea of working in an office, like Dad. Mom stayed at home and she tried to help me out but…" He pauses and I turn to look at him, see him looking down at his knees, his palms pressed together. "She didn't have a lot of patience. I think she wanted to be a house-wife." He snorts, shaking his head but not looking up. "Not a stay-at-home mom."

For some reason, that makes me sad, thinking Jax didn't feel wanted. But I don't say anything or move to touch him. I don't really know if he'd want any comfort anyway. He's prob-ably mostly over it.

Like I'm mostly over the fact my dad doesn't really give a damn about me.

"So, I started smoking pot in middle school. Then a buddy of mine's dad started growing it and in high school we start-ed…" He smiles, looking up at me. "We started distributing it for him," he tells me with that same smile on his face, his blue eyes bloodshot. He shrugs. "I dropped out of school in my junior year. I'd made enough money to buy this house a few years later." He looks really proud of that and it is something to be proud of, but even so, I still feel sad.

He lets out a breath and looks away from me, staring at the sky like I was. I wonder if he wants to go to the moon too.

"You ever wanna do anything else?" I ask him quietly,

wondering if someone will be asking me these questions in a few years. Will someone wonder what my future might've been, if I'd stopped doing drugs? Because despite what I keep telling myself, about not being an addict, my bank account is depleting and I've seriously considered offering to blow Jax in exchange for supply, so… Yeah. I wonder what college student I'll be talking to in the future, telling them all of my hopes and dreams that never came to be.

Jax sighs. "This is heavy, Za."

I laugh a little, run my hands through my hair. "Yeah, sorry, I don't know. Must be the full moon."

He nudges me with his shoulder, and I look over at him. "Don't be sorry," he tells me earnestly. "I don't think either one of us imagined being this when we grew up."

I look down at my hands. My bitten nails, chipped polish that I never fixed. At least Jax is making a living at this. I'm just fucking everything up, left and right.

"Anyway," he continues, before I can feel too down on myself, "I guess when I was a kid, I saw movies with men in suits, like bankers and shit. Saw those law shows on TV my mom always watched. I mean," he snorts, "I never wanted to be a lawyer. But I thought I'd grow up and wear a suit every day to work too. But then I realized most of those suits spent all day in an office and that didn't really sit right with me." He sighs. "When I fell into dealing, it just…well, to be honest, it just fit." He scrubs a hand over the back of his neck. "Just wish it was legal, ya know?"

I laugh a little, running my hand over my thigh. "Yeah, that'd be nice. If using paid the bills, that'd be cool too."

He doesn't laugh at that and my palms feel sweaty. "What do you want to do, Zara?" he asks me quietly. The way he phrases it, like I still have a chance, like I might *be* something, it makes my throat tight, pressure building behind my eyes.

I cough, pressing my fist to my mouth and staring up at the moon again, trying not to get too emotional over this shit. "I uh, well, you know I like philosophy, and—don't laugh, I know it's a useless degree—but I kind of thought it would be cool, if I ever…" my voice cracks and I take a deep breath.

Jax claps his hand over my shoulder in a friendly gesture, kneading my muscles.

I close my eyes, a little overwhelmed. "If I ever get over this, you know, if I don't drive my life completely into the ground, I'd help other people. Like not a therapist, because I hate therapists." I laugh a little and Jax's fingers dig in a little deeper. Not to hurt me, but to comfort me. I think about the therapist I went to when I was five. They let me play with blocks and assured me that my parents' divorce wasn't my fault.

A lot of good that did for the empty hole in my chest that my father had left.

"But I don't know. If I could be a speaker, or just a support system to someone. Using the whole Stoic bullshit about handling your own emotions. About getting over your own mental blocks that tell you that you just can't quit."

I open my eyes, turn to Jax, who still has his hand on my shoulder. "I'm probably just full of shit. Don't listen to me."

Jax doesn't laugh like I wish he would. He meets my gaze instead, his eyes watery and blue. "You're not full of shit. But to be honest, you're makin' me feel a little guilty about, you know, being your dealer and shit. If you really wanna stop, I can help out, you know? And you'll hate me for it." He drops his hand from my shoulder, scrubs it over his jaw. "God, you'll hate me, because I've done it before. And you'll scream at me and we won't be friends anymore, but if you want that help, I can do that for you."

My chest tightens with those words, and I can't look away from him. I can't look away from him and I know it's a genuine offer, just like I know I'd never be able to accept it. Maybe right now, when I'm high as hell and in the moment, but as soon as I needed something, I'd be back on his doorstep and I *would* hate him.

"Nah," I smile at him. "It's okay. It's not that bad." I turn again to the moon. "Not yet."

We're quiet for a long moment. I'm not sure how much time passes but I start to feel sleepy when my phone vibrates again in my pocket.

"Wanna get that?" Jax asks me lazily, like he doesn't really care either way but he's just making sure I know my phone is buzzing.

I lean to the side, pull it out of my back pocket. I've got several missed texts from Alex.

And one from Eli.

Jax must peer over at my screen because he says, "Oh nice. The rapist."

I laugh, flipping my phone over and turning to look at Jax. "Is he really though?"

Jax shrugs. "Probably not, but some bitch said he was."

"What happened?" I press. "Women don't usually cry rape unless it really happened." That's an actual fact. And I don't know if I want to know the whole story, but I know I need to get my head out of my ass and find out. A girl ended up dead at his house. He threw me on his kitchen counter and shoved a bottle in my mouth, hard enough to split my lip, just a few hours beforehand.

I need to stop being stupid.

But Jax just throws up his hands. "I dunno. Some wild party in this neighborhood and then some girl called the cops and said Alex and one of his friends tried to rape her and then prevented her from leaving the room. Apparently, they eventually let her go and she called the police."

My skin crawls thinking about that. *One of his friends?* And Alex is huge. He could easily stop a girl from leaving a room, and he could easily rape someone. At least physically. But I'm not so sure he'd actually do that. I mean, he was the one that put the brakes on the threesome.

"Who was the friend? Were they charged with anything?"

Jax shrugs again. "Dunno the dude's name, I only heard this secondhand. I don't fuck with most college boys. They're pussies. Anyway, girl probably got spooked. I don't even think she did a rape kit or whatever that shit's called. She transferred from Caven though."

My throat feels dry and I rub it with my hand, my phone vibrating again on my thigh. "What was her name?"

He cuts his eyes to me. "Oh, come on, Za. Don't go trying to track the poor girl down. Ask Alex about it yourself."

I did, I don't say.

"Besides that, honestly, I don't remember her name. I wasn't at the party, just heard it through the grapevine, and you know that shit is crawling with bugs."

I flick my brows up, impressed with that metaphor. Jax is a smart dude.

My phone buzzes again and I flip it back over, read Alex's texts. He's clearly drunk as fuck, because there are a lot of typos and question marks. That means I should probably stay far, far away, but…

I never can resist making a damn scene.

"What's he want?" Jax asks me.

"Wants me to come over."

A pause, and then, "Well, I'm going to bed soon. You wanna go? I'll drive you."

I glance up at Jax, see his squinty eyes. He's high as hell, but Eli and Alex's house is like, a thirty minute walk from here, and I'm high as hell, too.

"Yeah, but you got anything I can take before I go?"

Jax narrows his brows, no doubt thinking about the offer he just made me. "You sure that's a good idea?"

I shrug. "No," I say honestly, smiling. "But I'm sure they're having a party and this conversation with you was kind of a buzzkill."

He laughs, shaking his head. "All right, give me a sec." He stands to his feet and goes inside, and I tell Alex I'm on the way.

I open up Eli's text while I'm alone on Jax's steps. All it says is, **I want to see those scars, baby girl.**

22

Zara

I ASSUMED CONSIDERING Rihanna just died two weeks ago and her funeral was just last weekend, there wouldn't be an abundance of her friends at Alex and Eli's house.

I thought wrong.

The music is so fucking loud, I know no one would hear me knock, so I let myself inside. And as soon as I glance around, I see Eli Addison. Almost as if he's waiting for me, and he's positioned himself in the living room chair that faces the front door.

He's got a drink in his hand, and a girl on his lap.

My body flushes hot with anger that I know is completely unwarranted. I came here for Alex. I can't be mad.

I shouldn't be mad but I am. I stare at that girl for far longer than I should too.

I know for a fact that she was friends with Rihanna. Her name is Kaitlyn or Ashley or something like that. And right now, she doesn't seem to be thinking too much about her dead friend, the way she's got her legs splayed over Eli's lap as she smokes a joint, talking to another chick beside them on the couch.

He has his hand on her thigh, and he lifts his cup up to his mouth, keeping his eyes on me.

Before I can think about his text, about *him*, about how weird it is that we're both here, someone touches my arm.

I flinch, turning my head.

Alex.

"You came," he says, sounding pretty damned surprised. And more sober than I thought he'd be, which is good.

I swallow, push Eli from my mind even though I can feel his eyes on me as I look up at Alex.

"You didn't think I would?"

Surprisingly, he looks nervous, and on a giant like Alex, it's cute. He rubs his arm with the opposite hand, grinning, flashing that one dimple in his tan face. "Nah, I didn't," he admits. He swallows, looking down at the floor.

I bump my hip against him, smiling. In the moment, a horrible thought occurs to me. I don't know if I'm doing all of this for Eli's reaction, or because I want to flirt with Alex. "You planning on flashing my tits again, Cardi?"

He meets my gaze, arching a brow. "I mean, only if it's in my room and we're alone."

I bite my tongue, flicking my eyes up and down his body. He's wearing black, fitted pants and a plain white tee. How such a simple outfit could look so damn sexy, I don't know. This reminds me of when we first met. When I first fell for him. Before all the fighting and the shitty thing I did to ruin us.

This is—dare I say it—fun.

"I thought you needed space," I remind him, but I keep my tone light. I don't want to fight, and since he doesn't really seem drunk, tonight could be peaceful between us.

His jaw clenches and I see his hands curl into fists. I

wonder if he's thinking about Jamal. I wonder if I should've reminded him of my bullshit. I wonder what he'd think if he knew just two nights ago Eli fingered me in their pool.

"I did," he admits. "But this week, I haven't been able to stop thinking about you, Zara. And after lunch yesterday I just I needed to see you again."

My heart skips a beat in my chest. I try to play it off. "You just wanna fuck me, huh?"

This seems to settle him. He runs a hand through his thick hair and flashes me a lopsided smile. "If I'm allowed to."

I laugh a little. Force myself not to think about Eli. "Get me a drink and we'll see." I can't tell if he's already been drinking, but he doesn't look messed up. Then again, I probably don't either. Before I left Jax's house, I used some eyedrops he had on hand, wiped away my smeared eyeliner— Jax told me I wear too much, I told him to shut the fuck up— and took a shot of vodka before I used Jax's mouthwash.

I'm just in skinny jeans and a cream-colored tank top, platform boots on my feet, but I know I look good.

Not because my own eyes told me, but because Alex still seems nervous and I can feel Eli's eyes on me.

"Yes ma'am," Alex tells me and turns to walk down the hall.

But he holds out his hand.

I glance at Eli before I take it.

He's still watching me, but his hand has moved further up the cheerleader's thigh and she's spread her legs wider on his lap. I wonder if she'd let him hold her underwater while he fingered her.

Motherfucker.

I take Alex's hand as I stare right back at him.

The kitchen is thankfully empty, but I'm shocked as shit to see people swimming in the pool past those sliding glass doors, like not shit happened just two weeks ago. Like a girl isn't dead. Like her body wasn't just floating at the bottom of that pool.

Don't think about it.

"You okay?" Alex asks me and I realize I closed my eyes.

I spring them open, pushing the memory of Rihanna away. I don't know why it bothers me so much right now. I didn't know her. I didn't like what I knew about her. But for some reason it just pulls at me. Along with Alex's word to her before she left the room with Eli. And Jax's warning. Alex's confession, "It was just a big mess, Za. It was just…a misunderstanding. I didn't hurt anyone, okay?"

"Yeah," I answer Alex, forcing a fake smile on my face as I look at all the bottles of alcohol on the island in the kitchen. Try not to think about him shoving me against it. That tequila bottle. The cut between my lips. "What're you gonna make for me?"

He's standing beside me and I realize he isn't moving, his big ass hands resting on the marble of the island.

I turn to look up at him.

I don't like what I see.

Something that looks far too much like pity. It makes me squirm.

"What?" I ask him, unable to help myself.

His dark brown eyes soften, and this is the kindest look he's ever directed toward me. I liked it better when he was being an asshole. I'm about to tell him so when he just says, "You found a dead body the morning after a wild party." His tone is so straightforward, I don't interrupt him even though I feel all itchy and hot and I'm dying to grab the closest bottle and start chugging it. "It's okay to be weirded out by it."

I glance at the pool again. I see her again.

I hear Eli behind me. "There's a body in the pool, baby girl."

"Did you at least have it professionally cleaned?" I ask

instead of mentioning any of that shit. Instead of thinking of Eli pushing me under in it or what we did together.

I meet Alex's gaze, but he's still staring at me with a mixture of pity and something like desire. But for what? Why did he really invite me here? Is this where we have our pivotal relationship talk? Is this where I confide in him like I did Jax?

I don't want to do that.

I'm here to get stupid drunk. Maybe piss Eli off. Or turn him on.

I don't want to bond with Alex over Rihanna's dead body.

Finally, he just shakes his head. "Yeah, we did. You want to get in again? I could help you out. Like last time."

I shoot him a glare.

He holds up his hands, all innocence. "Okay, okay. You're right. We'll save it for later when you're drunk and will definitely drown."

I just stare at him, equally horrified and amused. He really is a dick but that's one of the things I like about him. I'm not exactly a good person, either. "I'm not sure if you're joking or not."

He shrugs, slips his hands into his pockets. "Me neither."

I scoff, rolling my eyes. "Where's your posse? Why are you alone right now? Aren't there girls dying to suck your dick or dudes waiting for you to flash another girl's tits so they can make a video? Why'd you have to invite your ex over, huh?" I turn away from him, not really wanting an answer, and grab a cup from the stack of them, flip it over and fill it with about two shots worth of tequila.

At least, I think it's two shots, but Alex whistles.

Ignoring all my questions, he just says, "Careful, Zara. I think we've all learned the key to pool safety is staying sober."

"Too late for that," I mutter, grabbing the seltzer water and pouring it in. When it fizzes to my satisfaction, I cap that shit and then hold the cup to my lips, turning to Alex.

He meets my gaze.

Something in his eyes makes me lower the cup. "What?"

"What you said," he muses, his eyes gleaming. I see the amber flecks in them again and I feel myself getting stupid from how hot he is. Why does he have to be so fine? Why are quarterbacks always hot anyway? It's like some trick God pulled to make cocky athletes even cockier.

And why do they always do bad shit?

"About girls waiting to suck my dick," he continues.

I force myself to drink, even though I am interested in hearing where the hell he's going with this. Did he just invite me back tonight to hurt me like I hurt him? Maybe this was all just a big setup and I was stupid enough to fall for it.

"Would you mind?" he asks me.

I nearly spit out the tequila in my mouth. But instead, I swallow, hard, blinking up at him. "Excuse me?"

He shrugs. "If I went upstairs right now to get my dick sucked, would you mind?" His eyes flick upward with his words, and instead of immediately lashing out at him like I want to, I try to imagine it. He jerks his head back, indicating the pool. "There's a pretty hot redhead out there right now that I know for a fact would jump at the chance."

I narrow my eyes at him. I know the redhead. Her name is Molly, and I know that she and Alex used to fuck around. But that was before me. "Be my fucking guest."

Who am I to stop him?

I think about Eli's fingers inside of me. About his hand on my scars.

"I'm serious," Alex says, interrupting my thoughts. "I gotta get off somehow, and you don't have a good track record recently of helping me out."

My mouth drops open. "Are you fucking kidding me?"

"Answer the question. Think about it if you have to."

I want to throw this cup in his face, just like I did two weeks ago in front of Dwight. I want to slap him. I want to tell him he's an idiot, and that if he's trying to make me jealous it's fucking working.

But maybe this was his roundabout way of working on us.

So, I do what he said.

I think about it.

If he walked upstairs right now with Molly trailing after him, and she got down on her knees and wrapped her lips around his cock, would I care?

Do I care that Rihanna's friend is probably gonna do the same to Eli?

I don't know.

Alex, though?

Same answer.

"I think the more important part of my question was about flashing girls' tits, to be honest," I tell him, avoiding telling him anything. I tip back my cup, finish the rest of the tequila and soda water. It's not the best thing in the world but it's not the worst either. I set my empty cup down and cross my arms, turning to stare at Alex.

He leans against the island, cocking his head. "You don't really seem that upset by it," he says plainly.

"That my tits are probably on everyone's phone in this house right now?" I counter, shrugging. I see his jaw clench and it's a little satisfying. "Not really." That's mostly true. Worse things have happened to college girls. Like ending up dead at the bottom of a pool.

I hop up on the counter, feeling a little dizzy as the bottles slide behind me, dangerously close to the ledge.

I cross my legs at the ankle, watching Alex. "But it seems to bother you, handsome."

I can tell he tries to fight it, but a small smile pulls on his lips. "Does it?"

I roll my eyes, looking away from him for a moment. "Why'd you do it? Two weeks ago, you wanted to kill me, wanted to kick me out and be done with me. Then you needed space. Now you're inviting me to your house, talking to me alone. What's going on with us, Alex?"

"Two weeks ago, I was fucking pissed at you."

I turn back to look at him. Before I left Jax's house, Jax gave me MDMA. It usually takes about half an hour to kick in for me, and I wonder if that's how long it's been since I left his house because as I stare at Alex staring at me, I just want to taste him.

I want to kiss him.

I want to wrap my legs around him and forget I ever messed around with Eli. Technically, it's not cheating. Technically, Alex had broken up with me. Technically, we still aren't back together. I'm in the clear. Eli is in the clear. Technically, we're okay.

"But I really did miss you and I know you were really fucked up that night and…" He takes a deep breath and I love the way his shoulders move as he inhales. Exhales. Love the veins in his biceps beneath that white t-shirt. Love the one in his neck, too. "I don't know, Zara. I think we could just, you know, make this work. If we really tried this time." He meets my gaze. "I've never met anyone like you. You're fun and I don't just mean when you're drunk. You're always fun to me. And I know you love me even if you do some fucked up shit." He glances at the island I'm sitting on, and says, "And even if I do some fucked up shit. I don't want anyone else to have you."

My mouth goes dry.

I feel a jolt of something warm in my chest at his words, but I push back on it. It's just because I'm high. It's just because I'm drunk. Technicalities where Eli are concerned won't count, because Eli is his fucking best friend.

If Alex knew the truth, he'd never forgive me.

God, my throat feels like sandpaper.

Speaking of… "I need water," I blurt out, meaning it. Alcohol and MDMA can dehydrate you fast as fuck, and I feel myself rolling. That's the only explanation I have for the warm feelings that seem to be filling my brain. My whole fucking body for that matter.

Alex narrows his eyes. "You need water? After all that, you need fucking water?" I hear the note of anger in his words. That's the Alex I know.

I just nod, and almost as if someone took ear plugs out of my ears, I hear the music playing throughout the house. Like my Alex-goggles are momentarily fading.

Thank fuck.

I start swaying to *Overdose* by KAIBA, and Alex just watches me.

I smile at him, but he doesn't smile back.

"Water?" I remind him, hopping off the counter and walking up to him, wrapping my arms around his broad back, rubbing my hands up and down his muscles, slipping underneath his shirt.

He's stiff beneath my hands but I know he'll melt soon. Shit, if he doesn't, at least I will.

"What are you on, princess?" he asks me, his voice quiet. I can't really read his tone, and I can't stand still either, the music making me sway against him.

I think about Kylie. About what Eli said. How they're both conspiring against me to find out exactly what I'm on. But I don't want to talk about that shit right now.

That's my secret with Eli anyway.

I smile up at Alex. "You," I tell him.

A small smile pulls at his lips.

Someone walks in from the pool outside, dripping water on the floor. She closes the door behind her and looks up at Alex, without sparing a glance at me, running her fingers through her red fucking hair.

Molly Bachman.

Her hair is long, down to her very large tits, barely hidden beneath her emerald green bikini. She eyes Alex up and down, but I've got my arms around him and she has yet to pay any attention to that shit.

"Hi," she says to Alex, still ignoring me. She tugs up the straps on the bottoms of her swimsuit, making them sit high on her curvy hips. "You coming out or what?" Her voice is husky. Pretty damn sexy, actually.

I dig my nails into Alex's back.

He's just looking at her, and I'm still all over him. If he doesn't say something, I might offer to fuck them both.

Molly is hot, even if she doesn't want to look my way. Even if she doesn't like that I'm the more recent ex.

Alex clears his throat, and then he rests an arm around my back.

Molly's eyes narrow.

"I'm good," he tells her.

"Didn't she fuck around with Jamal?" she asks, in a tone full of false innocence, still without looking at me.

Alex's arm tightens around me. "Watch your fucking mouth or leave, Molly."

She rolls her eyes, biting her tongue, clearly upset with that answer. Then she mutters something under her breath that I can't hear, thankfully, and goes back outside, slamming the door shut a little harder than necessary.

Alex looks down at me. "So? What do you think? If she sucks my dick, you gonna be mad?"

I shrug, smiling up at him. "Can I suck it too?"

He cocks a brow, definitely surprised. Our failed threesome with Eli was the closest we ever got to consensual sharing. He clears his throat again and he can't hold back his smile either. "You're dirty, princess."

"You have no idea."

The smile dims a little. "Yeah, I'm not sure I wanna know. Forget it. I think you'd want to get back at me after that. And you've already done enough of that shit to last me a lifetime. Fuck that." He pulls out of my reach, grimacing.

"Alex, come on, don't—"

"Don't what?" he asks me, clearly pissed.

He shouldn't have asked me to come here. I shouldn't have agreed to come here. He rounds on me, stepping closer. My back hits the kitchen island and he cages me in, hands on either side of me as he leans down close. "Did you fuck Jax, too, huh? You fucking him for drugs?" He runs a hand through my hair, yanking my head back, his mouth over mine. "I guess the better question probably is who aren't you fucking, Za?"

"Alex, don't do this." I can't fight back. Not because I literally can't, but with the drugs in my system, I just don't want to. I want a truce. I want to just relax. I just want to chill with him. "Alex, please."

His fingers only tighten in my hair as he runs his mouth over mine, but then he sighs, pulls away, letting me go and running a hand through his hair. "Look, I'm gonna get you some water," he tells me. Then he leans down close again, wraps his strong arms around me, jerking me away from the island and molding my body to his. He presses his lips to my ear. "And then I'm gonna take you upstairs."

I feel my body heat up with his words. I can feel them against my skin. I'm almost humming with the safety I feel, right here in his arms.

I know Alex isn't bad. I know he isn't the asshole he pretends to be. He's something else entirely. He's good. He's pure. He isn't a criminal. He didn't hurt anyone.

"And I'm going to fuck you good, princess, and you're going to show me just how big of a whore you really are." He presses a kiss to my neck and then pulls away, out of my arms. I feel his absence with the sudden rush of cold where his body was against me, but I lean against the counter, watching him, his words echoing in my head.

I start swaying again to the music and as he pulls a glass from the cabinet, opens the fridge and gets water from the big pitcher inside, I can't stop thinking about it. How good he is. And then I can't stop the question that comes out of my mouth either, all fast and quick like if I don't get it out in a rush, I won't have the nerve to ask it at all.

"Alex, what happened at that party? With that girl?"

I see him tense, his back muscles knotting up under his shirt as he flips off the spout for the water pitcher.

For a moment, he doesn't move. He only says, "What party and what girl?" with an edge to his voice.

I think about wrapping my arms around him. Turning him around. Kissing his gorgeous mouth.

I don't answer him though. We both know what party.

He closes the fridge door, turns to face me and extends his hand, offering me the full glass of water.

I take it greedily, gulping down the ice-cold liquid, humming as I do. Halfway through, I tell him what I know to be true: "You didn't hurt her. You didn't hurt anyone."

"How do you know?"

I eye him over the rim of my cup but drink again.

"How do you know I didn't hurt her?" he clarifies.

I keep drinking, unable to stop even if I wanted to. It's just so damn good. Or maybe I don't want this conversation. Maybe I've lost my nerve all over again.

Finally, I finish the water and exhale my contentment, setting the glass on the island at my back.

I turn back to face him. I watch him staring at me as I sway back and forth, unable and unwilling to stop. The music is just flowing through me and it's as if it's a part of me. I can't stay still.

"You're too good," I tell him.

He crosses his arms over his chest. "I almost drowned you."

"I know." I twirl around, bringing my hands up in the air as I dance.

"I'm the reason that video exists."

I drop down low, turning back to face him. "I know."

He comes closer, but doesn't reach for me and I don't stop dancing. This time, though, I grind up on him, my ass against his cock, which is already hard.

"I almost broke your teeth with a bottle."

I glance over my shoulder, my eyes connecting with his. "I know."

He still doesn't touch me, but I see his gaze darken. I feel him growing harder against my ass, and I don't stop grinding against him.

When I feel like I can't take it anymore, when I feel like if he doesn't put his hands on me, I might explode, he grabs my hips, yanks me back against him. His arms come around my front, caging my back against his chest, hands splayed around my torso.

"You're fucking perfect, you know that?" he says against my ear.

Some people come into the kitchen, staring at us as they head outside to the pool. We don't pay them any mind.

I rest my head against Alex's chest, my eyes closed. I feel so warm and safe in his arms, it's like I'm under a blanket of pure love.

I know, somewhere deep down, that's just the molly talking, but it doesn't change the feeling.

"You are," I tell him.

He laughs against my ear, runs his lips against my neck. I shiver, my core tightening with his mouth on me. I want nothing more than to go upstairs and fuck him. Let him fuck me. Take turns exploring each other.

"I'm not even close, princess," he tells me and my heart almost aches with those words because they're not true.

I tell him that, my eyes still closed as I drown in the feel of him against me.

He sighs, his breath against my neck. "You're mine, you know that?"

I think about Eli. This bad secret between us. I don't want to, and I definitely shouldn't say it, but I feel like maybe it would be best. Maybe if I just came clean to Alex, maybe if we just told each other our worst secrets, we could start over. We could start over and we could be like this, always. We wouldn't fight or scream or yell, but we would be good for one another.

"I do bad things," I tell him, testing the water, pressing further back against him, still swaying in his arms.

He tenses but holds me tighter. "I know."

"Do you?" I counter, my words a whisper.

"Yes." His every breath makes my nerves light up, and that warm, peaceful feeling in my chest expands.

I raise my arms up, wrap them around his neck. He runs his hands up my shirt and the feel of his warm skin on mine lights a fire in my core.

"Take me upstairs."

His fingers dig into my skin. "Zara, what are you on this time?"

"Take me upstairs," I say again, more urgent this time. "Take me upstairs, Alex, please." I can feel his erection against my back, but I need it touching me, no clothes between us. I want him in my mouth, his hands all over my bare skin, completely naked with him inside of me.

I want him again. Always.

He takes a deep breath. I feel his chest rising and falling behind me, hear his indecision in the sound against my ear. But finally, as I keep swaying against him, feeling as if it's just us at this party, no one else, not even Eli, he says, "Okay."

And then I spin in his arms, eyes flying open, and he picks me up. I wrap my legs around him, cup his face in my hands and kiss his lips. His grip on my thighs tightens and he kisses me back, opening his mouth for me.

It's intoxicating, this kiss. I almost don't want to go upstairs. I almost want to love him right here, right in this kitchen. But he breaks away from our kiss and I lay my head against his shoulder as he carries me down the hall. There's a lot of noise coming from the living room. I hear people shouting his name and someone whistling, but the music is really loud, too, and I focus on that, swaying in his arms as he carries me up.

I don't think about Eli. Don't look for him.

Alex takes me down the hall, toward his room. He shoulders open the door, kicks it closed behind us.

He sets me on my feet but keeps an arm around my shoulders as he slides up the dimmer on the lights, a soft, dim glow barely illuminating the room.

His bed—decked in Caven-blue—is opposite a flat screen TV mounted on the wall, and angled beside his bed is a loveseat, but otherwise, the room is clean and empty.

I glance at his nightstand.

The Bible is still there.

Alex steps toward me, his hands moving down to my hips as he stares at me, blowing out a breath. "I'm glad I got you away from everyone," he says, his voice rough.

I smile at him, gripping his biceps. "You can invite some people up here if you—"

He puts his hand over my mouth, startling me. "I'm not like you," he informs me, taking another step toward me, forcing me to concede one. My mouth is dry again and I think maybe I should have had more water but it's a little late for that now.

Besides, when my legs bump up against the bed, all I want to do is tell Alex to lie down on it so I can ride him. So I can make him feel good, because he deserves it. We deserve it.

"I don't want to share," he keeps talking, his warm hand still clamped over my mouth. "I'm not going to. Ever again."

I stroke my hand lightly up his forearm and he lets his hand slide down over my lips, to my throat, resting it there gently. "No sharing," I lie to him.

He smirks at me, his eyes trailing down over my chest and his hand following. He cups my breast over my tank top. "No sharing?" he repeats, gaze finding mine again.

I bite my lip and nod, slipping my hands under his shirt. He's all hard muscle and sharp lines but his skin is so fucking smooth. I want it on mine.

"Zara," he says, my name a whisper on his lips. "Are you sure you're not going to regret this? Your eyes…" He trails off, staring into my eyes.

I know they must be dilated right now, but I know what I want.

"I'm not going to regret it. I know what I'm doing." It's true. I do. MDMA doesn't impair judgement in the way the shots of tequila I chugged down will. It just makes everything better.

He still looks unsure, and I can't help but think it again. *He didn't hurt that girl.* I need to find her. I need to know what happened. I need to ask her. Maybe someone hurt her, but him? I don't think so.

Either way, I know he won't hurt me right now.

He's not even moving. He's just staring at me with this pained expression on his face like he's torn between fucking the shit out of me or running the fuck away.

I vote for the former.

I grab his shirt and pull him, spinning us. He moves with me, amusement flickering in his eyes. When I get him where I want him—his back to the bed—I plant both hands on his chest and shove him.

He sinks down onto the mattress, in a seated position, trying to bite back a smile but he can't quite do it.

"God, I've fucking missed this." His hands come to my thighs but he's still staring into my eyes.

"Take off your shirt," I tell him.

He flicks up his brows. "Commanding, huh?"

I grab his wrists, make him drop his hands from my thighs

as I take a step back and then let go of him. I want to pounce on him. I want to feel him everywhere. But right now, I want to watch him take off his shirt.

I cross my arms, still swaying slightly even though the music is just the sound of the bass up here. I want to change that. I know there are wireless speakers in his bedroom, we always had something playing when we were fucking around in here.

Did Eli listen, then? He said he heard us, and he saw me...

I push him from my mind. Not because I don't like thinking about him, but because if I think about him too much, I'll go find him and bring him up here and I'm positive Alex doesn't want that.

And right now?

I want to give Alex everything he wants.

He crosses his arms, lifts his shirt over his head. I swear to God my mouth starts watering when he drops his white shirt onto the floor, rests his hands on his thighs and stares at me, almost defiantly.

I find every freckle over his long, lean torso, his abs still visible and defined even though he's sitting down. Those veins in his biceps are like another fucking drug, and even though I meant to make him strip down completely, I can't stop myself.

I kick off my socks and shoes, unbutton my jeans, tug them down my thighs. I go to slide my fingers under my bright green lace panties, but Alex reaches for my wrist, stopping me.

He doesn't wait for permission anymore, doesn't ask me if I want it.

Instead, he holds my gaze while he leans forward and uses his teeth to pull down my underwear, his mouth scraping against my skin. His thumb pulls down the other side until the lace just falls to the floor and I step out of it as Alex sits back, watching, one hand still on my thigh.

I wonder why he never noticed my scars.

Now's not the time to ask. I don't want him to notice. I didn't want Eli to, either.

Eli seems to have a habit of noticing things he shouldn't.

"Your turn," I tell Alex, smiling brightly as he takes in every inch of my skin from the waist down.

His touch lingers, but slowly, he slides his hand away from me, reaching for his belt. He undoes it and flicks open the button of his pants.

But he's moving too slowly for me.

I stand between his legs, yank down the zipper.

He adjusts his position, letting me pull down his pants and his boxers, to his knees.

I can't get any further than that before my hand is wrapped around his dick, and I lean over, my mouth on the head of his cock. He tastes so fucking good, so fucking hard and soft at once, my fingers barely touching, circled around him.

I stroke him while I suck on the tip and he groans, his fingers in my hair.

"Fuck, Zara." He doesn't move his hips, just lets me suck him how I want to, and in this moment, I've never wanted to do anything more.

I try to deep throat him, which has always been a fucking challenge. And just as I think it's too much, just as I think I'm going to choke on him, he shoves my head down and my eyes water as he hits the back of my throat.

I try to jerk my head back up, but his grip tightens in my hair.

I dig my nails into his thigh, and he hisses but still doesn't let me go. I'm gagging on him, but no sounds are coming out. Everything seems to be going gray, saliva dripping from my mouth to the base of his cock.

My stomach tightens.

He's done this before, but I can't quite shake the feeling

that maybe he's paying me back for Jamal. Maybe we aren't done with that little standoff. Maybe I'm a fucking idiot.

But then, when everything starts to turn black around the edges, he lifts my head up by my hair, all the way off him. Drool spills down my chin as I lick my lips and he stares at me, a conceited little smirk on his face.

"You're so perfect," he tells me. He caresses the back of my head and my eyes flutter closed.

He's perfect.

Alex.

He's not bad.

He's good.

He runs his thumb over my swollen lips. The gesture is almost tender.

He's so good.

"Now get up here and ride my dick, princess," he commands me, one hand curling around the base of his cock.

He doesn't need to tell me twice.

I stand to my feet, spin around.

He runs his hands up and down my sides. "I think I'm going to like this," he whispers against my spine.

I brace myself on his forearm, reaching between us to grab his cock and position him underneath me. He helps me get both feet up, my knees on the bed as I kneel over him.

Slowly, I lower myself down, feeling the sting of his width as he enters me, and I stretch around him.

"You're so fucking tight, princess," he whispers, gathering my hair in his hand, pulling it away from my neck as he kisses my shoulder.

I wince, but I want him all.

Every inch of him.

Fisting my hands in his sheets, I lower myself all the way down.

"*Alex,*" I moan his name even before I start fucking him.

He kisses my back again, then lets go of my hair, his hands dropping to my sides.

"Fuck me, Zara," he tells me, grabbing my waist and helping me do just that. "And make it good, because last time I didn't get to fucking finish."

My thighs burn as I bounce on his cock, his hands helping guide me. It's so fucking worth it. I tilt my head up, close my eyes. The feel of my hair grazing my low back makes me flush with confidence. The feel of Alex stretching me, filling me, the sound of his rapid breaths, his low groans makes me feel sexy.

I run my hands through my hair, close my eyes as I focus on the feel of him inside of me.

Sex has never felt this good.

I'm going to come, and I don't even need to touch myself.

I'm going to fucking come all over his cock and he's going to finish inside of me and in the moment, that's all I want.

Maybe that's all I've ever wanted. Maybe I'm just really high, but I don't care.

I don't care.

I can't stop the moan that escapes my lips, and I don't want to.

"Fuck, baby," Alex says. "You feel so good. You sound so fucking good."

I moan louder, all of my nerves tight and taut and ready for me to just fucking explode. I feel so safe here in his lap, with him inside of me, his hands on my hips as I ride him.

And just as I'm about to throw my head back, just as his brow comes to my shoulder, his groans telling me *he's* almost there, too, I see the doorknob to his room twist.

So slowly.

So slowly that maybe it isn't really turning. Maybe the door isn't really being pushed open, just as Alex is moaning my name, just as I feel him tightening inside of me, maybe that isn't—

All the air leaves my lungs, and the door *does* open, just a crack, and Eli's eyes connect with mine.

But I can't stop it.

I can't stop it, and I'm coming all over Alex as I hold Eli's gaze, until I can't. Until I have to close my eyes, Alex's hands on my breasts as we slow, panting. Breathing. Feeling.

And when I open my eyes again, the door is closed, and Eli is gone.

23

Eli

KAITLYN'S FINGERS trail down my chest, her mouth against my neck as I stare up at the dark ceiling of my room, one hand on my stomach, the other by my side.

The music is so loud downstairs, there's no way I'm going to be able to sleep. But even if it was quiet, I can't stop thinking about her.

It's impossible to stop fucking thinking about her.

Wednesday night, after we got each other off, I wanted to beg her to stay. I wanted her to stay in bed with me. Sleep with me. I wanted her all over me.

Fuck what Alex thought.

He doesn't deserve her. He's lied to her. Kept things from her. He doesn't even know her. Not like I do.

I fist my hands by my sides.

"Get off me."

Kaitlyn stiffens, her lips still on my throat, her fingers still grazing my chest. I can feel where every inch of her body connects with every inch of mine and I can't stand it.

I need her to get off me.

She sucks in a breath. "What?" She sounds offended.

I don't bother repeating myself. I sit up abruptly and she crawls backward on the bed, holding up the white sheet to cover her chest as if I didn't just fuck her sixty seconds ago.

I don't bother looking at her as she stumbles off the bed, picking her clothes up from my floor. It's dark in here anyway. Not much to look at.

I run my hand through my hair, lean my head against the headboard at my back as Kaitlyn huffs and stomps around as she gets dressed, clearly pissed.

I was surprised she came up to my room with me so easily. She's not a cheerleader, but I thought she and Rihanna were friends. They were always hanging out with each other at the house on the weekends. Shows how much I know about the inner workings of girls.

I close my eyes, and Mom's eyes flash in my mind.

Green.

They were so green.

Looking up at them through the bath water, they were brighter than usual. Things are usually murky underwater. Dim. But not her eyes. Not then.

This is why I don't fucking sleep.

I open my eyes to clear the memory.

"Have a great night, Eli," Kaitlyn snarls at me, but she doesn't open the door.

I wish she'd open the damn door.

"Yeah. You too."

She sighs again. Loudly. "I thought Alex was the asshole."

I think about Alex shoving Zara onto the kitchen counter. I think about him pushing that bottle between her teeth. I think about how I wanted to break it over his head.

My thoughts shift to last fall.

How he got hammered because his dad cheated on his mom, again. I think about how he followed that girl upstairs.

"He is," I assure Kaitlyn. "Close the door on your way out."

That does the trick. I watch as she storms out, slamming the door so hard the white model Trans Am on my nightstand slides into a glass of water, making a high-pitched sound that makes my skin crawl.

I stretch out my hand, without looking, to steady it and my fingers curl around the cool metal car. I rise to my feet and head to my desk on the opposite side of the room from my bed. I sit down, flip on the little black lamp, and tap the keyboard on my laptop.

The browser is already open, cars for sale in Falls Creek on my screen.

I grab my noise-cancelling headphones and slip those on, turn up *Feel You Out*, and start scrolling through cars, first checking out an old Corolla that would be a good daily if I wanted to spare the 370Z a few miles.

But I'm not really seeing the dark green paint, gone pale from the sun. I only just notice the rust on the side of the driver's door. I'm barely paying attention.

All I can see is her face as she came on Alex's dick.

I press my thumb to my mouth and bite the skin hard enough to bleed. The taste of iron fills my mouth, and I think about her blood. I wonder if she'd let me lick it from her thigh.

I wonder what it tastes like.

Sweeter than mine.

That's all I know. It's definitely sweeter than mine.

24

Zara

WHEN I OPEN MY EYES, I'm standing up.

I'm standing up, and for a second, I can't move. I'm paralyzed, and everything is dark and it's so quiet. It's so fucking quiet that I don't know where I am. I'm not in Alex's house.

This can't be his house.

This is not a party.

This is like hell.

I sense something looming in the shadows, something coming closer, the hairs on the back of my neck standing on end. Something is going to get me, and I can't move. I can't scream. I can barely even *breathe*.

I want to clamp a hand over my mouth.

I want to turn around. I want to scream.

Run.

It's getting closer and everything is so dark and so quiet except this *thing*.

"Zara. Zara, wake up."

I flinch, my eyes flying open, and I stumble back into

someone's warm body. I open my mouth to scream, but a hand comes over my mouth.

"Shh," a voice says in my ear. "Shh, baby girl. It's me. It's Eli."

Slowly, like binoculars coming into focus, I see the room, and it isn't Alex's. It isn't the one I fell asleep in.

It's bigger, and it's shrouded in shadows. There's a bed in front of me, a desk to my left with a dimly lit laptop screen. *Is that a car?*

There's a door between the wall of the desk and the bed and I think it's to a bathroom. I think I see white tile beyond it. And the floor beneath my feet is cold.

But Eli's hand over my mouth is so warm.

With another little jolt, I realize his body is pressed against every inch of mine.

I open my mouth to speak and he must know I'm not going to scream because he drags his hand over my lips, my chin, down my throat, then brushes back my hair off my shoulder.

The words I was going to speak are stolen from me. Hijacked by the feel of him.

I'm in a tank top, and he slides his finger under one strap, pulling it down. His mouth touches my skin, warm and wet and so soft. His other arm is wrapped around me, fingers digging into my waist as he holds me to him.

"Why did you come here?" he asks me. I can feel his every breath against me.

I realize I've been holding my own breath and I exhale, slowly, trying to will my pulse to calm. My head to clear.

Why did *I come here?*

He drags his bottom lip over my shoulder, toward my neck. I tilt my head to the side, giving him better access. I shouldn't…

"Talk to me, Zara. Why did you come here?" His mouth trails up my neck, just underneath my ear.

"I don't—I don't know."

He slides the hand on my waist lower, his fingers gliding under the material of my tank top until his skin is on mine and I feel a fire light in my core. It's hard to stay standing, hard not to sway here in his arms.

"What did I…I don't remember—"

He kisses that hollow behind my ear, and I can't think. I can't do anything but feel him. His mouth, his fingers on my skin. His erection against my back. He's so hard.

He's so hard for me.

"You don't remember?" he teases me, his voice low but rough. Playful but…not.

I don't remember. I fell asleep with Alex, after we…after Eli saw… "You watched us."

He nuzzles his nose just below my ear. "I watched *you*," he says, and I can feel those words against my skin.

I clench my thighs together, wishing I was wearing something besides Alex's boxers, far too big, barely hanging on as it is. And if Eli just brushed his fingers a little lower, grazed the waistband, he could send them floating to the floor with barely a touch.

But I want that, too.

I want him.

"Why?" I gasp as he walks us forward, until the front of my thighs are against the side of his bed. "Why did you watch?"

He slides his hand down my abdomen, slipping it under the loose boxer shorts. I should stop him. I should tell him no. I should get out of this room and tiptoe back to Alex's room.

I should do a lot of things I'm not doing.

How did I even get here?

I try to reach for something. Something to put distance between us as he runs his teeth over my shoulder, his hand reaching lower down my shorts.

"S-shouldn't that *bother* you?" I whisper into the dark. "Watching us?"

He pauses, his hand still on my low belly, his mouth momentarily gone from my skin. Then he laughs, a throaty sound. He kisses my neck with an open mouth, and I shiver at the warmth of him in this cold room. "Oh, Zara." He laughs again. "You can fuck him all you want, baby girl. I couldn't care less about that. In fact, it turns me on, thinking about his cum inside of you right now." He brushes his hand lower down my shorts, until his fingers graze my inner thigh. "Keep it up."

God, what is wrong with you?

Fuck, what is wrong with *me?*

"You don't mean that, Eli," I whisper, wanting it to be true. "You don't mean that."

"You don't want me to share you?"

"I don't know."

"I thought you wanted to experience everything, Zara. And that's what I want for you. Everything."

I bite my lip, gripping the sheets of his bed in front of me. "How did I get in here?" I shake my head, trying to remember. "I don't remember walking in here."

He's quiet a moment, only the sound of my own pulse in my ears. The feel of his breath against my skin. His fingers calloused and rough, igniting a fire within me. But I have to think over it. I have to breathe through it. I need to know.

"You really don't remember?" This time his question isn't teasing. It's curious.

"No," I whisper into the dark.

He kisses me again, on the curve of my shoulder, and even though I don't remember wanting my brain to do it, my head leans back against him, resting against his chest, my throat exposed.

Surprising me, he pulls his hand from my shorts and wraps his arm tighter around me. "You walked in."

I blink into the darkness, and then I laugh. He seems to stiffen behind me, like he doesn't know what to make of it.

But I can't stop it. I'm laughing, gripping his sheets, him tense at my back.

"Do you mind telling me what the fuck is so funny?" he asks quietly, and it makes me laugh a little more.

His hand goes up to my throat, clamping down around me.

I stop laughing. "Eli…no fucking shit I walked in here."

He's silent a moment, then he sighs, his hand loosening around my throat.

And then he lets me go. He just…steps back, and I have to tighten my grip on the bed in front of me to keep my balance. The absence of him is so disorienting.

I spin around, see him running both hands through his hair, the glow of his laptop screen behind him.

That is a car, I realize.

"You need to go back to Alex's room," he says, turning his back to me, his hands fisted in his hair. His shoulders are so broad, and I can see his biceps, the dark stains of tattoos on his arm, trailing down to his hand. I can't make out the art in the darkness, but I can see it there.

Almost like a reminder.

Eli is cold.

"Okay," I tell him, my voice rough, my own hand at my throat. "Sorry for…" I trail off. I don't know what I'm sorry for. I don't know if I *am* sorry.

He doesn't look at me.

I take a step toward the door, the floor creaking softly beneath my feet.

"It's not the first time," he says, catching me off guard.

I freeze, staring straight ahead, at the door. My mouth opens to ask him what he's talking about, but nothing comes out. I think because I know.

"Remember that night, against the counter. You came down to the kitchen."

My chest is tight. My hands clench into fists, and I feel a shiver start down my spine, trail to my knees, making them tremble. And I hold my breath. I hold my breath as I wait for him to say it. To say what I don't want to know.

But he doesn't say anything.

He's silent.

"You can stay," he adds quietly. "If you want. You can stay."

"Why do you want me?" I ask him instead, not wanting to talk about sleepwalking. "Is this just a game to you, Eli? What are we fucking doing?"

More silence. I want to turn around and face him. I want to ask him if it hurts, knowing I fucked Alex. I want to ask him what he wants from me.

But it's his turn to speak. Not mine.

Yet when he does, I almost wish he hadn't. I almost wish I had kept my fucking mouth shut.

"Why do *you* want me, Zara?"

Shame washes over me in a hot, uncomfortable wave, replacing the fear. The dread. The shiver. My hands feel clammy, my heart is racing too fast. Uncomfortably fast. *I need water.* That's probably why I came here. That's probably what I was looking for.

Water.

"Why do you want me, Zara?"

Because I can't have you? Because you're taboo? My ex's best friend? Because you see me? Because you pulled me out of the very same pool you held me down in?

I shake my head, crossing my arms over my chest. I need to get back to Alex's room. I need to let this shit go.

I take another step, but then Eli says, so softly I almost don't hear it over the creak of the floor and the pounding of my own heart, "Wait."

I turn to face him. I watch him grab a glass of water from his nightstand, beside a model car, a flash of white in the dark room.

He closes the space between us and hands me the water. I just stare at it for a moment, and he says, "MDMA is dehydrating. It also disturbs sleep, if you do too much of it." He sounds like he's memorized a PSA pamphlet or something. "It can make you sleepwalk."

I glare up at him, still not taking the water. Dread tightens my stomach again like a closed fist squeezing my guts. "Are you suggesting that I have a problem?"

From the light of his laptop screen, I see the corner of his mouth curve up into a lopsided smile. "We both know you have a problem. I'm just giving you information."

I glare up at him a moment longer then turn on my heel, leaving him and his stupid fucking water.

25

Alex

I PICK up the bottle by the neck, slam it against the sliding glass door. It shatters into a thousand pieces, the sound soothing my rage, splintering the quiet of the morning.

There are people passed out in my living room, some idiot naked and drunk on a pool chair. Zara is still in bed and I want all these people out of my fucking house. All of them except her.

Fuck.

I run my hands through my hair and hear someone padding down the hall from the living room. I whirl around, glaring at a guy I vaguely recognize as someone on the fucking wrestling team.

His eyes go wide as he stares at the shattered vodka bottle on the floor.

He scrubs his hand over his face, blinking, as if he thinks he might still be fucking drunk or still asleep.

Slowly, his eyes slide to my face.

"You okay, man?" he asks me cautiously, taking a small step back.

I glare at him in answer.

I see him swallow. He doesn't have a shirt on, his jeans unbuttoned. All I can think about is my fucking father. His jeans shoved down to his ankles while he plowed into that woman in the pool house.

I was fucking fifteen.

I'm twenty-one now and he still hasn't fucking stopped.

I close my eyes, hands still fisted in my hair, willing it to stop. The memory. The anger. The hatred. The distance between us now.

What he did to my mother.

"Hey, Alex, you need anything—"

My eyes snap open. "Get out of my fucking house."

The guy nods. Backs away slowly. "Are you sure you don't need—"

"Get. Out!" I point to the door at his back, in case he doesn't fucking know where it is.

"Shit," I hear someone whisper from the living room. "Alex is fucking trippin'."

And then it isn't just the kid without the shirt leaving. It's a fucking mass exodus from mine and Eli's house. I turn my back to everyone getting their shit together and leaving, and I pick up a bottle of tequila, ready to fling it at the door, too, when someone grabs my elbow.

"Alex."

A lump forms in my throat at the sound of her voice. I shrug out of her grip and take a step back, lowering the bottle by my side before I turn to face her.

Her eyes are bleary, tinged with red, some of that fucking excessive eyeliner she wears smeared all over her face. She's dressed in the same clothes she wore last night, not my clothes. She's even got her shoes on.

"You can't leave," I tell her, confused. "You can't leave right now."

She glances at the bottle in my hand, her eyes going to the

shards of glass behind me, at the sliding glass door. "I've got to go," she says, clutching her phone in her hand. "What…happened?"

I curl my fingers tighter around the bottle, half-expecting it to burst into pieces. But I'm not that strong. If I was, I'd have found a way to tell Mom before she found out the hard way.

I slam the bottle on the counter, grip the edge of it with both hands, hanging my head. I was out of bed before Zara, which is no surprise. She sleeps a fuck load in the morning after she tosses and turns all night.

I slipped out of bed and intended to come down and clean up. To cook breakfast. To have a nice fucking day. But I got the email from Dad to his congregation, just like everyone else. I didn't even get my own email, nor did he have the decency to warn me beforehand. Instead, he let me read it in his blubbering, half-assed apology, proclaiming that it wasn't what it looked like.

Zara's hand rubbing my back brings me back to the present. "Alex," she says softly, "what's wrong?"

"It's my fucking Dad." She doesn't know everything. She doesn't know how I saw him. How I caught him the first time, before people started paying attention. Before Pastor Cardi became a local celebrity and a big fucking dumbass at the same time. Before he started being more brazen about his mistresses, seemingly uncaring that everyone in Grove Beach has a fucking cellphone and could snap a photo at any time.

Zara doesn't know all of it. She and my father already dislike each other. I didn't want to add more fuel to the fire.

But she knows enough.

Her hand stills on my back. I wonder if she's thinking of saying something snarky. I wonder if she's about to piss me off even more.

But surprising me, all she says is, "I'm sorry."

I glance over my shoulder and meet her blue-green eyes. I think of my mother's own deep chestnut eyes. I think of her curled up under the sheets of her fucking oversized bed. I think of coming home from school to a silent home. Of tiptoeing up to her bedroom. Of watching her slight form move up and down under the sheets confirming that she was still alive. The relief I felt knowing the prescription bottle that dwindled far too quickly every day on the nightstand hadn't yet killed her.

I think of her trying to fake it every Sunday, smiling and standing beside my father in the church that looks more like a mall than a house of God.

I would never do that. I would never fucking do that to Zara, and yet all this bullshit started because Rihanna fucking Martinson kissed me on the cheek after practice one day, and Zara is immature and childish.

She's already doped up on pills half the time she's awake and she doesn't even have shit to deal with like my mom does.

I want to step out of her touch. I want to scream at her too. But I don't yell at her, because I don't want to push her away. Not really. I just want her to wake the fuck up and realize that, just like my mother, she's on a collision course to an early grave.

I straighten and she drops her hand.

For a moment, I feel guilty. For the video that's going around, and the pool shit and all of it. For a moment, I feel fucking bad about that and everything else I've done to fuck with the women in my life.

But the moment passes. Quickly.

I was drunk then. It's not an excuse, but I was drunk, and...

It doesn't fucking matter.

"Where are you going?" I ask her instead. "Where do you need to be?"

She twirls a lock of hair between her fingers, shaking her head and looking at the floor. "It doesn't matter. I was going to…I was going to walk anyway. I'm sorry about your dad and—"

I run my hand through my hair again. "Just fucking answer me. Where do you need to—"

"Her mom's engagement party," Eli says, coming up behind her and brushing past us both without sparing a glance at the glass all over the floor. He walks over to the fridge, opens it up.

Her mouth falls open.

I turn to stare at Eli. He's not wearing a shirt, his black hair is disheveled and he's just staring into the fridge like something is going to float out and pour down his throat.

"What—" I start to say.

"Yeah," Zara interrupts quickly, swallowing hard. She's looking at the floor again. "Mom's having that stupid—"

"Shit, I forgot that was today." I scrub a hand over my face. I should remember. Zara sent me a calendar invite one night while Eli, she, and I were in the living room. Eli was on his phone, silent as usual. I made a shitty joke about Zara's mom, and the fourth fucking husband. I didn't even know Eli was listening.

He's still staring into the fridge.

Zara's eyes are flicking from me to him and the silence in the kitchen is weird. I clear my throat. "I'll take you," I tell Zara, and she wrinkles her brow. Like she doesn't want me to take her.

She shakes her head. "You should be there for your mom," she says softly.

"It's okay, I'll just go down after. I don't want you to have to go by yourself." I know she's pissed with her mom as is about this fourth engagement shit. I know she doesn't want to go alone. She never really wants to do anything alone.

She glances at the glass on the floor. "No, you really don't need to—"

"Fuck, Zara, just let me fucking take you." I walk toward

her and it looks almost like she flinches. *What the fuck?* "I need to get out of this house anyway," I tell her, my voice lower. "I don't want to deal with my parents' bullshit."

She swallows hard, then looks up at me. "You need to deal with your mom. She's probably hurting right now."

Eli clears his throat and we both turn to look at him. The fridge door is still open, but he looks at me when he says, "I can go with her."

I start to tell him that that's completely fucking unnecessary, but Zara speaks first.

"Thanks," she says quietly.

Eli holds my gaze.

I'm torn, because I know Mom will need me. Even if she doesn't want me to come down, she'll want to talk. And if she doesn't talk, she'll be using, and I don't want that.

I clench my hands into fists and turn to Zara. "Are you sure? Look, Za, I really don't——"

She wraps her arms around my neck, pressing her body to mine.

Out of the corner of my eye, I see Eli is still watching us.

"I'm sure," she tells me, her voice low. "I'll be okay with Eli. Take care of your mom."

26

Zara

ELI'S CAR smells just like him, mixed with leather.

It's really clean, and I feel dirty sitting in it. Knowing I fucked Alex last night. Knowing I'm wearing the same clothes I was in yesterday.

But as Eli pulls out of his driveway, he grabs my hand, threading his fingers through mine without looking at me.

I glance at him out of the corner of my eye, warm butterflies tumbling in my stomach. His side profile is so hot, a straight nose, the slight scruff on his strong jawline. And his fucking lips.

I press my thighs together, force myself to look straight ahead.

"Thank you for taking me," I say quietly, the music a low noise in the background. I can make it out though. It's Falling Apart, by CVLTE.

Eli squeezes my hand. "I wanted to be alone with you."

I feel my stomach flip at those words. "Eli," I whisper after a moment as he pulls into my apartment complex, the drive

27

Zara

I'M LATE.

By two minutes, which is fantastic because people are already there, crowded around the private room reserved for Mom and Cory. It means Mom can't blow up at me just yet and if I leave early with Eli, she'll have to get me on the phone.

But it seems like Eli Addison helps soften her anger anyway. She has no idea he's Alex's roommate, and besides that, she's only met Alex once before, over the summer when I was blitzed out of my mind and she had no idea. The whole exchange lasted five minutes or less, a run-in at the grocery store where Alex was buying me wine.

She was pretty mad I hadn't told her I was dating someone. I lied to her and told her I wasn't. I don't need them to talk. It's enough that Alex is using Kylie to keep tabs on me. I don't need her talking to Alex too.

Mom's big blue eyes light up when she sees Eli though, which is a relief. The pressure is no longer on me. Mom pulls him in for a hug, which is a little comical, I get my height from my father and she looks like a child in his arms, and she admonishes me for not mentioning I was bringing my "boyfriend". She said she would've had a place setting for him.

I glance around at the private room of Crate & Egg. It's a high-end brunch spot just outside of Monkey Junction, but place settings definitely aren't fucking necessary.

"He's just a friend," I tell her quickly as Eli laughs softly to himself, slipping his hands into his pockets. "We're just, uh… we just met for coffee this morning," I add awkwardly. Despite myself, I almost laugh, too. Like, why the hell would I bring a friend to meet my future new stepdad?

"Well, *friend* of my daughter, it's nice to meet you."

Eli flashes her a grin and I think about him holding me underwater on Wednesday night. I think about his forearm against my throat. "You, too, ma'am."

Oh, wow. There's that Eli charm. "Where's Cory?" I ask Mom quickly, looking around the room for him before she can question Eli about our non-friendship. I can't think straight enough for questions.

My body is sore from sex with Alex I guess, and I'm feeling pretty fucking low after last night's high, but I'm here. That's what matters. I made it, and clearly, Mom doesn't suspect me of using anything right now even though I swallowed an Adderall at the apartment in my bathroom while I changed.

Even Eli doesn't know that.

I spot one of my cousins, Jessica, across the room, eyeing the pale pink cake on the banquet table. She looks up and offers me a little wave, her eyes going from me to Eli and back again, brows waggling. I roll my eyes with a smile and look away.

Many of the people here are Mom's coworkers, a couple who I assume must be Cory's parents because the man has his same sad brown eyes and the woman has his rather large nose.

It occurs to me that this is a little elaborate for an informal engagement party from two people who have been married before and have already met the family more or less, but then Mom holds up her hand, wiggling her slender, manicured fingers and I see why this is happening.

Jesus Christ.

There's the diamond engagement ring that Cory gave her two months ago, but there's another ring, too.

A fucking wedding band.

They're already married.

What the fuck?

"What the fuck?" I can't stop the words from tumbling out.

Beside me, Eli brushes his arm against mine casually in a sort of silent warning, I guess, but I don't give a shit. He doesn't know my mom. He probably doesn't really understand what's happening right now, so I spell it out for him, refusing to take my mom's hand.

"When did you get married? I thought this was an engagement party. A chance for everyone to meet Cory, *before* you went and married him?" The chatter of voices at my back has grown quieter, and Mom glances nervously over my shoulder, fiddling with the neck of her pale pink satin shirt, to match her stupid *wedding* cake.

"Zara, I told you to come early specifically so—"

But I don't let her finish. "You couldn't have told me before today?"

Mom swallows, twirls her necklace between her fingers.

My stomach churns. "You lied to me!" Mom getting married a fourth time was bullshit enough, but this shit… "You fucking kept this from me!"

"Sorry, Miss…?" Eli says quickly and then trails off, uncertain if Mom shares my last name. Ha. I have my father's last name. That was three husbands ago, apparently.

Mom swallows again, glances up at Eli and brushes her

pale blonde hair over one shoulder. It's just past shoulder-length and beautiful, just like Mom herself. She's got the same pale skin as me, but her eyes are bigger, a lighter shade of blue, and she's petite and well put together and I'm not surprised at all that she keeps convincing men to marry her but for fuck's sake.

She fucking lied.

"Mrs. Rushing."

My gut clenches. Cory's last name. Of course.

"Unbelievable," I mutter, not done with this. She lied to me. And yeah, sure, I lie to her too but I'm the fucking kid. I shake my head, run my hand over the bun I threw my messy hair into. "This has got to be bad for business, huh, Mom? Always changing your name on the real estate billboards?"

"I'm sorry, Mrs. Rushing," Eli continues, ignoring me, "but last night I kept your daughter out too late." He averts his eyes, making a good show of his bullshit apology. "That's why we were running late. Congratulations on your marriage."

Mom looks from me to him warily as I hear someone call her name from behind us. "Zoe! Oh my gosh, Cory just told me!"

"I'm sorry, Zara," Mom whispers quickly, smoothing down her blouse and looking over my shoulder again at whoever the hell it is that's rushing over here, her heels clicking on the linoleum floor. "I wanted to tell you this morning." Mom pastes a smile on her face. "I thought you'd be happy for me." And then she pushes past me and I turn to see her get thrown into a bear hug by a large lady with curly highlighted hair and a glass of champagne in one hand.

My cousin Jessica is still by the cake, and I see her grab a small plate and a fork. I wonder how long it'll take her to dive into it. If she can hold off until after Mom makes this stupid fucking wedding announcement. Jessica is always the first in line to eat free food.

Today, I kind of hope she destroys that fucking cake.

It would serve my mother right.

I want to get out of here.

I don't even know why I came in the first place.

I turn to Eli, who is quiet at my side. People are hovering around the banquet table as waiters in white set down plates of scrambled eggs, French toast, and a bowl of what is probably spiked punch.

"I'm ready to leave," I announce. I look down at my ballet flats, eager to grab the pill I shoved in there before I left the bathroom.

I glance up at Eli, into those green eyes, and I'm thinking back to last night. To him in the doorway. To me, waking up in his room.

To how he set down a glass of water on the island, right in front of me, before he went upstairs to change.

To how *he* remembered today was my mother's fucking engagement party.

He offers me a small smile, glancing over my head at the party. Music starts to play, *Die for Me* by Post Malone and wow. Just fucking wow.

"Your mom is a bitch."

I stare at him, shocked.

He shrugs. "That was shitty."

I take a deep breath. My irritation is climbing, and while I know maybe I should eat something or have some water, I stalk away from him and head straight to the enormous plastic punch bowl.

Beside me, a waiter puts down a plate of deviled eggs.

"There alcohol in this?" I ask the guy, pointing at the bowl.

He glances at me, straightens, and smiles. "Yes. Coconut liqueur, spiced rum, and—"

I don't wait for him to finish before I grab a plastic cup from the stack of them and scoop it directly into the punch, filling my cup up to the brim. The waiter stares at me, dumb-founded, his eyes darting to the black scoop in the punch.

Yeah. I don't have time for a damn scoop.

I tip the contents of the cup down my throat. It's sicken-ingly sweet, but I can taste the alcohol in it, and I wipe my hand over my mouth when I finish, then go to dip it back in.

But a hand on my arm stops me.

"Hey, let's get out of here," Eli says softly in my ear.

I try to shrug his arm off, but his grip tightens. I can feel the calluses on his hand. I think about that car on his computer screen. The model car beside his bed. I think about his hands on me. The water he tried to give me.

"Alcohol is legal."

"I know. But don't you want to get drunk somewhere else?"

He lets my arm go. I spin around, clutching my cup in my hand.

"We've got all day," he says quietly. "Alex texted me. He left for the coast. He'll probably be there all week, until the party next weekend."

All day.

All week.

My mouth goes dry. This is it. This week we can figure this out. He reaches his hand out to take my cup.

I let him, and he sets it on the buffet table. Then he holds his hand out to me. "Let's go?"

I reach for his hand and nod. "Okay." I hiccup, brushing my other hand over my lips to try and cover it. A blush creeps onto my cheeks and Eli laughs, his beautiful lips and the husky sound of his laughter distracting my thoughts for a second.

He steps closer to me, tucks a lock of hair behind my ear. "Don't be embarrassed." He leans in close, kisses my mouth lightly then pulls back. "With me, you never need to be embarrassed."

As we cross the room together, hand-in-hand, Jessica gives

me a little wave and I see she's got icing on her fork and is shoving it into her mouth with no shame.

I know she's doing drugs, too, from shit my mom has told me, but it's probably just pot, which might explain why she couldn't get her fork away from the cake. Either way, I give her a wave back with my free hand, and once again, she looks at Eli and this time, she gives me a thumbs up.

I laugh, shaking my head, and the way Eli's fingers squeeze mine lightly, I know he saw it too.

Mom and Cory are talking to one of her co-workers that I can't remember the name of, and I'm about to walk out without a word. That, however, is apparently not acceptable, because Mom does a double take as she sees I'm headed out the door with Eli, and then, out of the corner of my eye, as we walk out, I see both Cory and her bustling over.

The door closes behind us, shutting the noise and them out. We're standing in a little hallway at the back of the restaurant, secluded and alone.

"Should we wait for them?" Eli asks me, his warm hand still in mine.

But before I can decide what to do, the door bursts open and Mom and Cory come pouring out, skidding to a stop in front of us.

Cory's sad brown eyes are wide, and he runs a hand over his thin hair. He's wearing a golf shirt, pale pink like Mom's shirt and the stupid cake, and I see his golden wedding band on his stubby finger.

Mom surpasses him in looks but considering he's a nuclear engineer—and he's got the small little glasses on his face to prove it—I don't think she minds much. It's his money she wants to join with hers, not their hands in holy matrimony.

"Where are you going?" she asks me, trying to keep her voice polite because Eli is by my side, still holding my hand. She catches sight of it and clears her throat, but before she can say another word, Eli interrupts.

"Sorry, Ms. Rushing," he glances at Cory who swallows nervously, "but Zara isn't feeling well."

I want to twist around and glare at him because I don't give a damn if my mom knows I'm bailing. In fact, I want her to know. That's the whole fucking point. But if Eli's lie will get us out of here faster, then fine.

I twist my face into a grimace and clutch my stomach with my free hand, looking at Cory because he's the weakest link. "Stomach bug." I flash Mom a tight smile.

My mom shoots daggers my way while Cory covers his mouth with his fist and coughs, then slides his hands back into his khaki pants, his little belly straining against the brown belt around his waist. He's a little taller than Mom, which means he's a lot shorter than me, and Eli, well Eli could fit three Corys into his frame.

That thought is morbid enough to make me laugh—thanks, punch—and I quickly cover my mouth with my hand.

I think Mom must assume I'm about to blow chunks because she takes a step back, her golden strappy sandals clicking on the floor. God forbid I vomit all over her at her wedding party.

The thought is amusing.

"Well, Zara," Cory says, adjusting his glasses, "if you aren't feeling well, then please do rest up and—"

"No!" my mom protests, shaking her head and cutting off Cory's words. "This is our *wedding*—"

"When did you get married?" Eli asks politely, my hand still over my mouth to keep up the charade.

Mom's words die on her tongue as she turns to look at Eli, and it seems like she's trying very hard to keep her expression polite. When she meets Eli's green eyes, it becomes a little easier for her. I can see the way she's affected by him. I am, too, and I imagine most women are.

It's probably why he gets so many girls without any effort at all.

I think about him sleeping with Rihanna's friend last night and I genuinely *do* feel queasy.

"Yesterday," my mom answers him with a tight smile, smoothing down her shirt again. And again, Cory adjusts his glasses. Their nervous tells.

I squeeze Eli's hand a little harder, and he returns the pressure, but doesn't look at me.

"Congratulations," he offers, and he sounds sincere. Wow, he's such a good bullshitter. "I'm just going to get Zara home, and I am sorry we have to leave early, Ms. Rushing." He nods to Cory, correctly assuming his last name when he adds, "Mr. Rushing."

Cory looks mighty pleased with himself. "I'm sorry you aren't feeling well, Zara," he says, then looks to my mom and puts a hand on her shoulder.

My mother moves away from his touch and sighs, but she's glaring at me. "Feel better, Zara."

Cory turns to go but Mom hangs back and then she says, "I'm sorry, Zara." She looks up at Eli. "Take care of her," she nearly whispers.

Eli's fingers tighten in mine. "Of course, Mrs. Rushing."

All I can manage is an eye roll.

28

Zara

AS SOON AS we get back inside Eli's car, I turn to stare at him. "Take me for a drink now, please."

He laughs, reaching for his seatbelt. But before he puts it on, his phone rings through the Bluetooth in his car.

I see a string of numbers flashing on the center screen, an area code I recognize as Raleigh.

He presses a button on the steering wheel, answering the call with a quick glance toward me.

"Dad," he says, turning to gaze out the window. His tone is unreadable. I have no idea if he's happy to hear from his dad or not.

It doesn't take long to find out.

"Eli," his dad breathes his name out like a sigh of relief. I stare at his clenched jaw, his white knuckles on the steering wheel.

He doesn't say anything.

"I sent a few texts," his dad continues, sounding nervous. I thought he was a lawyer. I didn't think lawyers got nervous.

Eli still doesn't respond.

His dad sighs on the other end. A sigh I know too well, because I've heard it from my mother enough times to recognize just what it means. *I'm tired of your shit but I'm your parent so I'm going to keep trying here.*

"I was just calling to remind you of your appointment tomorrow."

I glance at Eli. He's still staring out the window. But finally, he says something. "Got it."

"It's important you go, Eli, you've missed the last two and Dr. Shaw is—"

"I said I got it." Eli's voice is quiet, as it always is, but it sounds almost venomous.

I stare straight ahead, try to tune them out. Giving them some kind of privacy. I have the distinct feeling I shouldn't be listening to this conversation.

I look at the brick walls of Crate & Egg. I imagine my own mother inside, flaunting around with her new nuclear engineer husband, imagining their combined wealth and her temporary rush of happiness.

We're all addicted to something. Drugs just happen to be illegal.

"Are you feeling okay?" Eli's father asks, bringing me back to this car.

"Goodbye, Dad."

The call ends.

Eli doesn't look at me.

He puts the car in gear, and then drives off, turning the music up loud.

Into the Dark by Point North fills the interior of the car and as we head toward my apartment.

I'm not sure what he's addicted to, but I have this strange feeling that if it were me, that might not be a good thing at all.

29

Zara

I SPEND Sunday night curled up in bed, knocked out from two doses of NyQuil.

Kylie came home sometime late last night. I heard her knocking on my door but rolled over and jammed a pillow over my head. I'm not ready to confront her on her bullshit.

I didn't hear from Eli after he dropped me off, apparently wanting to be alone after that phone call I probably shouldn't have overheard.

Monday and Tuesday pass in a blur, but a decent one. I didn't bomb my philosophy exam after all. I made a nice, healthy "C."

Wednesday morning, I wake up to several missed calls from my mother. I don't call her back, but she's sent a few texts too, probably knowing I wouldn't answer.

Probably because she's called all week, and I haven't fucking answered.

Mom: **We need to talk.**

Mom: **I'm sorry, Zara, it was a rushed thing. Let me explain.**

Mom: **Zara Rose, if you don't call me back, I will CUT OFF YOUR PHONE**

I laugh out loud at that one because it's bullshit. If she cuts off my phone, then she can't reach me at all. I ignore all her texts too, and then I see I've got one from Eli, and one from Alex.

Alex has been at the coast with his parents, keeping me up to date every day. But I guess he's back because he said, **I miss you, baby. Are you coming to the beach with me this weekend?**

And Eli's text says, **Come this weekend. I won't make it weird.**

My mouth turns dry.

He won't make it weird? What happened to "I like you a lot?" Does he expect me to go with Alex, and we'll just act like nothing has happened? Is he bullshitting me? Is this a test? Why hasn't he been in touch all week?

I don't reply to him.

Instead, I sit up in bed and rub my temples, dreading my eight o'clock philosophy seminar. I've got an abnormal psych test tomorrow I really need to study for, although I really don't want to.

I don't want to learn about why people are fucked up. I am one of those people, and I've realized the "why" doesn't fucking matter.

Knowing the root cause doesn't change the disease where my mind is concerned.

Knowing Alex's dad is a cheater and that's why he was such a dick to me doesn't change the fact that he was a dick. Knowing that, according to Alex, Eli's mom left him when he was a teenager doesn't change the fact that he's all messed up. Knowing I have daddy issues doesn't change the fact that I'm going to fuck anyone who wants me because it makes me feel loved.

I snatch my phone up from the bed and throw it across the room. It's becoming a habit.

Fuck this shit.

I'm not going to class.

I scrub a hand over my face, feeling really fucking low and debating going to Jax's house. He's the only person I know that might be down to have a party on a Wednesday morning but then again, he's probably not up yet.

And before I can decide if texting Eli back and telling him to meet me here so we can work this shit out or not is a good idea, my door creaks open and I tense, digging my nails into my palms.

"Hi," Kylie says, staring at me with her wide brown eyes. She's dressed in a pink collared pajama shirt and matching pants, her glossy black hair sleek and straight over her shoulders, like she just flat ironed it but didn't bother getting dressed yet.

I don't even know why she gets up so early. Her first class isn't until ten. I want to ask her what the fuck she wants, and why the fuck she was talking to my boyfriend behind my back while pretending to hate him, but I don't say any of that.

It's too early for that shit.

"Hi," I answer her, my voice groggy. I finished the rest of the NyQuil last night. Mom is transferring money to my account Friday, so I'll be able to get more then, but then again, maybe she won't since I refuse to answer her calls.

Guess I'll have to get over myself and do that, in the interest of having money.

I could just get a job but I don't really want to. A wave of self-loathing washes over me as I look at Kylie, tiny and cute and put together even in her damn eighty-year-old grandma pajamas. She's got her shit figured out. She's going to pharmacy school. Ian is going to med school. They'll have heaps of money in a few years and I'll have, what?

Probably even more self-loathing.

She'll forget about the girl she agreed to babysit and I'll probably OD in Jax's living room and ruin his life by racking him with guilt, too.

"Are you okay?" Kylie asks in her soft voice, edging her way into my room with her hands clasped in front of her.

I stare at her a second, my eyes narrowed. I think about telling her the truth for an entire minute: *No, I'm not okay. I think I'm actually an addict again, but I refuse to go back to rehab. I think I want to fuck my ex's best friend. I also want to get really fucking high right now, but my dealer is probably asleep and he's the only person who might consider getting high with me on a Wednesday morning. Oh, and my mother got married for the fourth fucking time, in secret, and my father is doing God-knows-what on the other side of the country, so I'm just biding my time for his yearly Christmas card that he doesn't even write anything in except his stupid, shitty name. And you're a fucking liar and I want you to get the fuck out of my room.*

"Yes," I lie to Kylie.

She doesn't buy it, I can tell in the way she squints her eyes just a fraction, but she, unlike me, isn't rude, so she doesn't say anything.

She wrings her hands and I kind of want to break them.

"You want to get dinner tonight?" Kylie asks me.

No. For a long moment, I contemplate saying it. I contemplate telling her to go fuck herself. But instead, what comes out of my mouth is, "Yeah, that'd be great."

I need to do something tonight and getting high probably isn't ideal. My boundaries are all blurred and the schedule that I clung to in order to make sure I wasn't really an addict is all fucked up. Maybe dinner with Kylie will be enlightening. Maybe I'll find a way to absorb some of her perfection. Maybe I'll scream at her and ask her why the fuck she's talking to Alex.

Maybe I just won't feel fucking alone.

"Really?" she asks me, startled. Like she expected me to say no.

Fair, I guess. I smile at her, trying to make myself feel it. Trying to make it real. "Really."

▼

I SHOVEL THE PEAS FROM THE CAN AROUND ON MY PLATE, listening to Kylie talk about her mom. I don't have much of an appetite for conversation or for dinner, and I keep looking down the hall to my right, to my closed bedroom door. I found a new bottle of cough syrup in a shoebox. I must've hidden it from myself because post-rehab Zara is smart.

And as soon as I make it through this dinner, I'm going to chug it.

Fuck Kylie and fuck Alex. It somehow feels better, spiting her right under her nose instead of yelling at her.

I smile and nod at Kylie as she keeps talking, but she furrows her dark brows and I quickly realize this isn't a part of the conversation I should be smiling and nodding at.

I look down at my plate, frowning at the porkchop she cooked. It looks good enough, but my mouth is dry, and I know chewing it will be like trying to force down ash. I need to lay off the fucking Adderall.

"Anyway," Kylie continues after she wipes her mouth with a napkin and then sets it back in her lap—yep, perfect, that girl—"they're going to have to sell their house." She picks up her fork and knife, slices off another bite of meat but of course she doesn't put it in her mouth yet because she's still talking, and Kylie Jones doesn't talk with a mouthful of food.

"She's having trouble getting around without a cane. The pain is getting a little much, too, so her doctor prescribed her some…" She trails off and I look up at her, wondering why.

She looks kind of apologetic, lowering her eyes and shaking her head. "Sorry," she says a little awkwardly.

"For what?" I ask, confused, scraping my fork against my plate, jostling some peas around.

Kylie blows out a breath, looking past my shoulder. "About the, you know, my mom's pain medication, I didn't mean to…" She can't get a full sentence out and I have no idea what she's fucking talking about.

Until I do.

My face flushes red, but I think its second-hand embarrassment for her. I'm glad in that moment that I don't have food in my mouth because if I did, I might've choked on it.

"Wait, wait, wait," I say, shaking my head, a bite to my tone. "You think that talking about your mom's prescription pain pills will, what exactly? Make me salivate and I'll lose my shit?" I laugh, sitting back in the rickety chair that's half in the kitchen and half in the living room. I drop my fork with a clatter. "It doesn't work that way, Kylie."

I see her squirm in her chair, taking the porkchop into her mouth and chewing furiously. Her olive skin is flushed pink.

Good. I hope she is fucking embarrassed.

I swallow, take a sip of water from my glass and set it back on the table, trying to keep my hands from shaking, from anger or too much Adderall, I'm not sure.

Meanwhile, I could hear a fucking marijuana leaf drop in here, it's grown so quiet.

"Look Kylie, your parents' house is safe and shit." I shrug. "I promise not to go up inside and rob the place, all right? Downers aren't really my thing anyway."

I watch her finish chewing her food, then she sets down her fork, hands in her lap, over her napkin. She arches a brow. "Really?" She seems very surprised by that statement. I take in her pigtails, smooth skin, and the pink cardigan she's wearing —even though it's technically still summer for another day, and definitely still hot outside—and realize that as much as she might know about the technical aspect of drugs from her pre-pharm work, she probably doesn't know shit about drug abuse. The heart of it, anyway.

Alex picked the wrong girl to spy on me because fuck the science.

Addicts are not fucking thinking about the science when they snort their first line or inject their first bag.

"I thought your mom said naloxone saved your life—"

"It was a precaution," I interrupt, waving her concern away. "I wouldn't have died." I clench my fists on the table and look down at my full plate. "At least, I don't think I would have," I mutter to my peas. "Anyway, that was an exception, which is probably why the Oxy hit me so hard anyway. I did Xanax sometimes, but that's about it when it comes to downers."

I click my jaw, thinking about the upper I did today to make it through this dinner. Double my usual dose because my usual dose isn't fucking working. I know what that means. I know I need to taper off, take something else in the meantime, let my tolerance die down. But Kylie wanted this dinner and I didn't want to drown myself in cough syrup yet—shit, guess that's a downer, too.

I don't mention it.

"So, what did you like to do?" Kylie asks me, her hands still in her lap. Surprising me, she doesn't sound the least bit judgmental.

I wonder if she's asking for Alex's sake. I wonder if they've been texting behind my back. I wonder when I'm going to confront him about that shit. I wonder if I have a right to, considering what I'm doing.

Whatever. Hopefully she will report back. Hopefully it'll keep him up all night, thinking about me still doing all of this shit.

"Uppers. Adderall, Vyvanse. Ecstasy. Cocaine, every now and then, but that was seriously addicting." I laugh, because it sounds funny, coming from an addict. It's true though. Coke just hits different. "Shit that made me more social."

There's silence that stretches between us for a moment,

and I hope she feels awkward, but to be honest, it doesn't seem like she does.

It kind of seems like my roommate is just absorbing this admission I gave her, and I'm waiting to see what she's going to do with it as I stare down at my ripped jeans, my hands twisted together.

"So, you don't really like going to parties, then?" Her tone is light, curious.

I shrug, swallow down a sudden lump in my throat that makes me want to get up, put my dishes away, and run to my room. "I do, but just not the way I usually am." I realize that doesn't make much sense, so I clear my throat and add, "I'm lame without drugs." I look up and meet her gaze. "I'm awkward and shit so I take—*took*—things to get pumped up. To want to be around people. Otherwise, I'd just sit in my room all day and stare at the ceiling." Like I've basically been doing for the past three days.

Otherwise, I wouldn't have ever met a guy like Alex Cardi, star football player and hot jock. Otherwise, I would've never had the balls to let Eli fuck with me. I would've never had anyone in my life.

I wouldn't have done anything like that if I was just…me.

I would have even fewer friends than I do now.

I'd be a fucking hermit.

Kylie is regarding me with an interesting mix of detachment and sympathy. It's like she's trying to figure me out through a clinical context, but she also feels something for me because unlike myself, she's not a shell of a human being.

"I don't think you're awkward," she finally settles on, picking up her fork and knife again, glancing at the small piece of porkchop left on her plate.

That's because I'm still on drugs. But I'm not trying to be taken out of school again or have my funds cut off from Mom *or* have Alex beat down our door, so I just manage a half-smile and say, "Thanks."

She sighs, a lock of her shiny black hair fluttering as she does, and then she drops her utensils on the table and pierces me with her big brown eyes.

I feel my stomach jump into my throat. *Does she know? Is this dinner just a big trick for her to drop a bomb? To tell me any second my mom is going to walk through that door and drag me out of here? Or maybe Alex? Maybe this is what it all comes down to.*

Fuck.

I force myself to sit still. But if Mom comes in here, I will run the fuck out and I will live on the streets before I go back to rehab and become a freak again.

No fucking way.

"I'm kind of weird too," Kylie finally says, and I just stare at her, my mouth falling open. Her face flushes pink again, and she shrugs, hands flat on the table as she sits up a little straighter. She's like eight inches shorter than me but she looks pretty damn regal like that, as if she's just owning who she is. "I actually take an antidepressant," she admits. "Have for years."

I get the sense she doesn't tell everyone this and for some reason—maybe because I just assumed she didn't have any secrets worth hiding—I'm hanging onto her every word.

"I was always withdrawn," she continues, looking down at her hands. "My teachers thought I was just shy." She laughs a little, but there's no humor in it. "And smart." She shakes her head ruefully. "Shy and smart." She smiles at me when she lifts her head, but it's a bitter kind of smile. "My parents, faithful churchgoers and kind of oblivious to *life,*" she throws up her hand with that last word, "just enrolled me in more after-school programs. Placed me in 'gifted' classes." She says gifted like it's a disease. "It just made things worse because then I was forced to interact more, and I hated it."

Ah. She's an introvert. The thought is startling, because of the amount of times she's come into my room without asking. I

It's why she left. It's why she almost killed me.

"I can't just let that go," Alex continues.

I think about him slamming her against the kitchen island, the bottles that scattered around her body. I think about his hand on her chest as he opened the tequila bottle with his teeth.

My eyes flick to his. "Did you let it go?" I ask him, my tone plain.

His brows shoot up. "What are you—"

"You caused a big fucking scene a few weeks ago, Alex." I shake my head and set down my glass on the counter. "Whatever, man. Do what you want. But don't expect her to be faithful to you if you aren't really together."

He snorts. "Well she wasn't when we were together, so what fucking difference does it make?"

I turn to look at him, his jaw clenched, brown eyes hard on mine. *You are a dumb fuck.* And this is exactly why I don't want to be a lawyer. They might be book smart, but when it comes to common sense, they're terrifyingly short on that shit. My dad is example number one.

"It doesn't. Do what you want." I start to head down the hall, but he calls my name at my back and I stop, waiting.

"You like her, Eli?"

Huh. Maybe he's not that dumb. Either way, I don't answer him. I just walk out, up the stairs, and to my room. I need a shower after wrestling practice today. I need to get Zara Henderson out of my head.

This is not going to end well for one of us. Logically, I know that. But the thing about logic is that it has no effect on the heart at all.

That's very clear with Alex. He doesn't understand her.

She just likes things.

She just wants to experience the world.

Like Mom did.

I could give her that freedom.

Alex would never be able to.

Still. *This isn't going to end well for one of us.*

fucking weirdo, because I do not want Alex to see my face right now.

"But what about everything that happened?" I don't really want to remind him of the Jamal incident. I don't want him to blow up about it again, but he's bringing this shit up. I need to test the waters. If he could forgive me for Jamal, maybe he could forgive me for Eli. Maybe this could work between us.

His large hand rests on my thigh. I tense beneath his touch and he only presses against my skin harder.

He still doesn't answer me, though.

"Alex," I whisper into the quiet of the car, "do you forgive me?"

His fingers dig into my thigh. "It's not your fault that the girl who fucked this all up is dead and the guy isn't."

I almost flinch at the words. At his callous tone. I mean, I didn't like Rihanna or know her either, but the way he says it, it's cavalier.

She fucking drowned in his pool. Maybe it's just the fact that I'm irritated because I'm not on drugs for once, or maybe it's just because I'm not high that it finally gets to me, his atti-tude about her death.

But it does.

At least Eli pretended to give a damn.

At least Eli acts like he has a heart.

I twist around to look at Alex, ripping my sunglasses off, knowing that my surge of anger is irrational, but I can't hold it back. "How can you say that?" I ask him, thinking back to that party. That girl that I don't know shit about. What he might have done to her. "How can you—why don't you fucking care?"

He stares at me a second too long and we almost run off the goddamn road.

"Alex!" I scream, and he yanks the steering wheel, nearly overcorrecting. But he straightens us out as my heart pounds way too fast in my chest. He keeps his eyes on the road, his jaw clenched, and he's not touching me anymore.

"Why the hell are you suddenly acting like you care about what happened to her? She died, like, a month ago, and you haven't given a single fuck."

My chest feels hot with his words, because they're true. Because I've spent the past three weeks in a drug-induced haze, like I've spent the past six months. The past three years, if I'm being honest with myself.

Because I've been so caught up in my own shit I haven't cared about Rihanna Martinson. About a girl drowning in a pool because she was so fucking drunk because she was so upset over a boy that didn't give a damn about her.

It happens all the time, girls dying over boys. Literally, figuratively, at their hands or not. It happens far too often, and no one cares. No one cares, and I wasn't an exception.

It could've been me.

Eli told me I've been sleepwalking. I know as much myself. *That could've been me in that pool.*

I don't say anything. I don't have anything to say.

"Whatever, Za. Don't act like you suddenly grew a fucking heart." He snorts. "It's just like you to fucking deflect. Rihanna kissed me on the goddamn cheek, and you sucked Jamal's dick."

As if I don't remember. I mean, it wasn't my finest moment. But it's what we do. We hurt each other. Get pissed. Do it again. Make up. It's a vicious cycle, but it's our entire relationship. So maybe I took it a little too far. It's not like the precedent hadn't been set early on.

And besides, Alex isn't an angel.

"What happened?" I ask him, keeping my tone even. This is why I'm really angry. Because I need to know. I deserve to know. But I stay calm, because if I start flying off the handle about this, he won't tell me. "What happened at that party? Tell me why people are saying you were involved in some sort of rape scandal. I want to hear the whole story."

He's oddly quiet for a long moment.

I don't like it.

But finally, he says, "I don't know."

I twist my hands in my lap, unease stealing through me. "You don't know?"

I hear him exhale, his eyes on the road as we drive through the night. "I was really drunk. I don't know."

"Oh, come on. You have to give me something more than that, Alex."

He sighs. "I went to a house party with Eli. I woke up with a black eye, busted knuckles, and a police officer in my face." I see him shrug, keeping both hands on the wheel. "Apparently, some girl I'd never met before in my life told the cops I was trying to, like, force myself on her, or some shit."

I hold my breath. Waiting.

"But she didn't press charges. She didn't—It went nowhere. She was as drunk as I was."

I think about how big Alex is. How it would be impossible for me to fight him off. "How did she get away?" I ask, finally exhaling. Inhaling. Trying to act normal. It was a mistake. It was a crazy night.

I've had my share of those.

"I don't know," he says again.

"Who was she?"

He shrugs again. "Weren't you listening? I said I'd never seen her before in my life. Some girl that went to Caven." He laughs, but it's bitter. "She doesn't anymore though," he adds quietly.

"Why?" I ask, my throat so dry, my question comes out rough.

"She transferred after that."

"You really don't know?" I ask him again, whispering in the car.

He's quiet a long moment and then he just says, "No. Eli was there, too. You should know that. Eli was there."

My skin crawls. "And he doesn't know anything?"

Alex doesn't answer me. At all. He just stares at the road, silent.

I don't press, and I don't know why. I think about Eli holding me under the water. About his fingers curling inside of me the night of the bad party. How he lied to Alex about me flashing him. But Eli isn't bad, is he?

I don't say anything, and we drive in silence for a long, long time, until Alex says, "I have to stop by my dad's before we get to the beach house."

I turn to glare at him, indicating I'm not fucking going inside his house, when he beats me to it. "You can wait in the car."

I'm not sure if I should be offended by that or relieved since I definitely wasn't going in anyway. Still, the way he says it, like he's dismissing me, hiding me. Whatever. I'm not his anyway.

32

Alex

DAD IS PISSED.

"You're back for the party? You should've just stayed. We need you here." His tone is even, his voice low, but I know him. He's staring at me from the doorway of the kitchen, leaning against it, one foot crossed over the other, hands in the pockets of his khaki pants. They're rolled up at the ankle, showing off his year-round tan.

He's got a white golf shirt on. This is his standard pastor uniform. Beachy, to help make him "one of the people." In this palatial house, nearly ten thousand square feet, French doors leading out from the kitchen to the inground, Olympic-sized pool at his back, it's unlikely my father remembers what it's like to be one of the people.

Grove Community has thousands of congregants year-round, a one-off in a beach town known for its tourist seasons. My father didn't exactly come from nothing, my grandfather had his hand in some Wall Street shit and all of that money passed down to his three sons. But this? The high ceilings, commercial stove, three full-time staff members and four-car garage? Yeah, I guess this all came down from God.

I also happen to know my parents are nearly drowning in debt and with this fucking divorce that is bound to be coming, it's all about to get really messy. But that's God and Preacher Cardi's problem, not mine.

"Sorry," I say, dropping down into a stool at the marble kitchen island. "Forgot I was here at your beck and call for your mistakes and not living my own life. My bad."

"You know after the latest scandal, I needed you here," he goes on, turning to track my movements, still leaning against the doorway. He runs a hand over his dark blonde hair, his blue eyes flashing.

I look like my mother's child.

Which reminds me. "I was here most of the week," I say through gritted teeth. "Besides, I didn't stop by for you. How is Mom? Any more bombs hit?" I clasp my hands together on the table, refusing to look away from him. We don't fight exactly, but this secret that's been between us since I was fifteen has put a considerable strain on any chance of a good relationship between us both. I guess now it's not really a secret.

I think of Mom this past week, sleeping most of the day away. I think of her wanting a divorce. She told me, a quiet confession one night.

My father doesn't know.

Just like he doesn't know about me and Zara.

I clench my fists on the table, thinking about her in my car right now.

She didn't come for me. I know that much. She came for an escape. For something to do. Not me. But I didn't want her to show up on someone else's arm, and besides that, I didn't want to be alone either. I need an escape, too.

And before she tries to escape my car, which would be just like her, I've got to make this shit quick.

Dad rolls his eyes. "This isn't that, Alex." He's in fucking denial.

"There were pictures, *Dad.*"

He grinds his teeth together, eyes narrowing. I see lines in his tan face and his eyes are a little red, too. Nothing like Zara's, but still. I guess he's been trying to drown his pain, too. Soon I'll have two parents who are addicts.

Lovely.

"Pictures of me helping a member in need?"

"You needed to take her to Saks to help her? Couldn't have a driver do that for you? Couldn't just make a donation—"

"Being the hands and feet of Jesus requires being the hands and feet, Alex. Not hiring paid servants to do the hard stuff for you."

I grit my teeth. He should tell that to the hired help that scrubs his fucking toilets. But there's no use fighting over this. Besides that, if Mom isn't here, I'm not staying long. Unbeknownst to my father, I've already contacted a lawyer and he's working with her in secret. I'm footing the bill with my own inheritance from my grandfather.

I unclasp my hands, make one into a fist that I knock softly on the island in the kitchen. "Where's Mom?" I'm not debating the hands and fucking feet of Jesus Christ with my father.

He shrugs. "She was upset you left."

I know that's bullshit. She was upset that she's still married to my dirtbag of a father. She's miserable that she spends most of her time in a Xanax-induced fog, so she doesn't have to deal with this shit he's brought upon us.

Besides, she already knows my dad and his love of Jesus haven't meant shit to me for a long time.

"Did you offer your congregation an explanation in person?" I ask him, feigning innocence. I read his stupid fucking newsletter.

"I gave them the truth." There's venom in that word.

"Right." We glare at each other a second and then he seems to deflate, as he sometimes does when the guilt weighs him down.

His shoulders sag, and he approaches the island, places both palms flat atop it. "I'm telling the truth, son."

I swallow down the lump in my throat. I hate when he does this almost as much as I hate when he lies to my and Mom's fucking face. I like his cool, detached tone better. The hint of anger lying beneath the surface, but dormant.

Something we have in common.

"Where's Mom?" I ask again, forcing back that emotion he stirs up. I need to get back to Zara.

"At the spa."

Little late for the goddamn spa. I wonder where she really is, but then again, the spa is her home away from home. I don't really blame her for wanting to hide out from Dad.

"How are you doing? With everything with Rihanna and—"

I wave away his concern. I spent most of the week with Mom, and I guess he's trying to take advantage of her not being here by forming some sort of connection between us. Fuck that. "I'm fine. I told you, I didn't really know her. Nice of you to come to the funeral, by the way."

His eyes narrow. "I tried to get away but—"

"Don't finish that." I don't want to hear his bullshit anymore.

He glares at me and I glare right back.

He takes a breath, hangs his head. He's not looking at me when he says, "I would think you of all people would understand that sometimes honest men make mistakes."

His words are a fucking cheap shot and I know he knows it. That's why he can't pick up his head and look at me right now. He's a pussy.

"I never said I was an honest person."

He looks up at that, a scowl on his weathered face. "Son, we both know——"

I stand to my feet, the chair scratching along the floor as I step back, throwing up my hands. "What do we know, Dad, hmm?" I ask him. I drop my hands, but don't drop his gaze. "What do we really know? For all I know, I did hurt that girl. You ever fucking think about——"

"She knew you were popular, well-liked, and wealthy, Alex. Don't you dare think that she——"

"Fuck that," I tell my father, clenching my fists. "I didn't know her from shit. I'd never seen her before in my life. You think she actually scoped me out, tempted me to that empty room and then cried rape so she could, what, exactly? Get paid off?"

My father raises a brow. "Well, she did, didn't she?"

I bite my tongue, taking a deep breath in. Out. This is why I play football. For a fucking outlet for this temper. One more week and I'm back on the field.

One more fucking week.

"Are you still messing around with that girl from rehab?" my dad continues, as if he doesn't know her name.

I freeze, holding my breath this time as I stare at my father.

"Zara?" he prompts me, pretending to remember, and asking me as if I don't know it. As if I don't have her body memorized. Burned in my brain. He rubs his hands together and I see his stupid gold wedding band gleam under the lights strung in the high ceiling. "Don't you think you need to take a break from girls?" He levels me with his gaze. "They've caused you nothing but trouble."

My heart is hammering in my fucking chest and I want to knock his teeth out, but I just stare at him.

"I only say that for your own good. Stay away from her."

"Don't talk about her," I say through gritted teeth. "Don't say another word about her."

He stares at me a long moment and then, changing the subject, he asks, "How's Eli's season going?" I know why he's really doing it. To spite me. To rub it in my face that I'm suspended for three games while Eli isn't.

Three games, over Zara.

But fuck it. I don't care. I'd do worse for her.

"Wrestling starts in October, *Dad*. Since Eli is the son you never had, you should know that." I shove my hands in my pockets. "I'm gonna go."

"Don't you want to stay and wait for your mom?"

"Can't," I lie. "I've got a sociology test I need to study for before the party tonight." Bullshit, and we both know it, but Dad doesn't argue.

Instead, there's a small smile on his haggard face. "Sociology, huh? You know that transitions well to pastoral care."

"Dad." I take a breath, clench my jaw a second. "We've been over this—"

"I know, I know." He holds up his hands in surrender. I see his pale gold wedding band again. Every time I do, it pisses me off even more. He might as well pawn that shit off. We both know it doesn't mean shit to him. "You don't want to go into ministry. You'll make a great lawyer anyway, Alex."

"Great. Glad you get it." I make to walk past him, but he claps a hand on my shoulder, and I freeze.

"But as good as your debate skills are, I need you to know that I'm telling the truth, son. I wouldn't do that to your mother. Not again."

Bullshit.

"Cool."

What a pointless fucking stop.

33

Zara

THERE ARE cars parked along the quiet road of the island. And it is an island, we took a whole damn bridge to get here. A secluded little part of Grove Beach full of enormous beach homes built up on white stilts to protect against potential hurricanes.

The smell of the sea through the windows in Alex's Jeep was enough to get my heart thrumming with anticipation, despite our stony ride of silence for the last half hour.

It's been a while since I've been to the coast. I used to go with Mom a lot when I was a kid, but then things got weird between us and we just stopped going.

That was about the time I started using.

Maybe things didn't get weird. *I got weird.*

Alex sits in silence after he pulls through the gravel drive, parking away from the grey and white house at our backs, all the outdoor lights on. It's a three-story house that looks even bigger on the stilts. I hear the music but can't quite make out what's playing, and right under the carport, in the side view mirror, I see Eli's black 370Z.

I think about that model car on his desk.

The one on his computer screen.

I imagine his hands on me at the pool.

My stomach flips as the memory plays in my head. And he's in this house. I wonder who he's with. There are over half a dozen cars here, and more along the road. Could be anyone.

Alex is silent, and he's made no move to get out. I get the distinct feeling he wishes he was anywhere else.

"Look, if you don't want to go—" I start to say, but he turns to glare at me in the dim light of the Jeep.

"We're here, aren't we?" he asks, his fingers still on the steering wheel.

I look out my window, stare at the trees lining the property. The moon overhead. "Didn't go well with your parents?"

"My mom wasn't home." It's an agitated growl, that voice, but it's an admission, too. It's why he's so upset.

"Where is she?" I don't look at him as I ask the question. I just keep staring at the window, which is rolled up now. And I remember looking out of another pane of glass. The one in Alex's kitchen. Seeing Rihanna Martinson floating in that pool.

"Fuck if I know." He opens his door.

I open mine, too, and we step out of the car, closing the doors behind us.

We meet at the back of the Jeep, and he grabs my hand, pulls me close to him. He's so hot to the touch, and his jaw is set even as he laces his fingers together behind my back, drawing me to him.

"Let's have fun tonight, yeah?" he asks me, his words at odds with how he looks, which is mainly pissed off. "Let's have fun tonight, and in the morning, we can work this out, okay?"

I swallow, averting my eyes for a second. Thinking about Eli.

God, if Alex fucking knew.

I look up, meet his eyes, force myself to nod anyway.

Then I jerk my head toward the trunk. My overnight bag is in there. And even though I told myself I wouldn't do it, there's some E in there I'm definitely going to take.

Alex stares at me a long moment, and then he lets go and opens the trunk. I shoulder my bag, and together, we head for the winding wooden deck that leads up to the door of the beach house.

34

Eli

I SEE her before she sees me.

I'm on the couch in the living room, my arm around Kaitlyn, a beer in my other hand. Dwight, Alex's friend, is sitting on the opposite end of the couch with his girl, Nadia, and at the table a few of my teammates and some girls are playing Jenga. It all goes to shit when I hear the blocks scatter and everyone laughs, one lone voice calling out, "Jenga!"

The lights are low, the music on, Kamaara, *Techno Thot!*, and I see her come up the stairs opposite the couch, arm in arm with Alex.

Who, as usual, looks pissed.

"Alex!" Dwight calls out, shrugging his arm off Nadia, who takes a drink from her cup. "You made it!"

Alex doesn't bother putting on a party face. He just flicks his brows up in acknowledgement of Dwight, then, arm still threaded through Zara's, he steers them both down a little hall to the left of the stairs, toward the kitchen.

They disappear beyond it, and Dwight rolls his eyes, turns to me. "What's buggin' him?"

Nadia shifts on the couch, curling into Dwight. She tucks a strand of long black hair behind her ear. "Alex is always buggin'."

Kaitlyn laughs into her cup.

I keep staring down the hall toward the kitchen, waiting for them to come out.

Kaitlyn shifts a little toward me, putting her hand on my thigh. I didn't invite her, but then again, I don't usually invite most people that come here. It's my dad's place, but more than out of respect for him, I just don't like most people. This shit is always Alex's idea.

"You got a light, E?" Dwight asks me, and I force myself to look away from the kitchen. I move my arm from around Kaitlyn, pull my black lighter out of my jean pocket and hand it to Dwight.

"Thanks, man."

I know he's not about to smoke a cigarette, and when he offers me a joint, I don't hesitate to take it. I don't drink that much, and I don't smoke that much, but some nights just call for it.

Like tonight.

With Zara being so close but so fucking far.

Finally, after I've already smoked half of Dwight's joint, Alex and Zara come walking back into the living room, and they take a seat on the couch across from mine.

Zara is wearing black, ripped shorts and a tight, white tank. Her sunglasses are pushed up on her head, and I imagine she left the rest of her shit in the room Alex usually stays in downstairs.

Her white hair is wavy and loose, kind of wild around her pale face. She's got a cup in her hand and she's done with her drink before Alex even takes a single pull of his beer.

While Alex and Dwight bullshit about next week's upcoming game, and Kaitlyn runs her fingers up and down my arm while Nadia plays on her phone, Zara just stares at the floor.

And I stare at her, but she refuses to meet my gaze. Even though she knows I'm looking at her. She has to know.

Abruptly, she stands to her feet, sets her empty cup on the table.

"Where's the bathroom?" she asks the room, raising her voice so she can be heard over the music. The guys and their girls at the table are playing another riveting round of Jenga, and Alex glances up at her but keeps talking to Dwight.

"Downstairs. To the right," I tell her.

She doesn't look up. She just tucks her hands into her pockets and nods, then walks away, practically scurrying for the stairs.

"Chick is weird," Kaitlyn mutters beside me, so quiet only I can hear her. "I don't know how Alex can stand to be in the same room with her after the shit she did."

I glance at Kaitlyn, my head feeling a little less heavy from the marijuana.

Kaitlyn is pretty, she's got long, dark blonde hair. Bright blue eyes. A fake tan. Her eyes are kind of freakishly big and her cheeks are kind of sunk in—nothing like Zara's round face —but she's got a fat ass and she gives good head.

She also happens to be a shallow bitch.

I stand to my feet, clear my throat. And I don't say anything as I step between Dwight and Alex's conversation, and head down the stairs into the darkness of the first level of Dad's beach house.

Mom and I used to come here a lot. Dad rarely did, he worked. And working was for men and entertaining me was for her.

Didn't work out so well for him when I turned thirteen, but I guess by then, she'd already done all the hard work.

The stairs creak with every step as I head downstairs, so it's not like I'm a ghost drifting through the house, but even so,

Zara fucking runs right into me as I step down onto the main floor.

I reach my hands out to steady her, and she's clutching my shirt, just above my biceps.

"Oh my God," she says, breathless. "Sorry, I..." She falters, maybe realizing it's me.

I can smell her. Flowers and fucking coffee, like she's a barista at a nursery. And her skin beneath my fingers...

Fuck, she feels good.

"What were you doing?" I ask her in the darkness. Light drifts down from the first floor, along with the music and the sounds of people talking, but it still feels like we're alone right here.

It's how we always meet.

Alone.

"I uh, I was just..." she chokes on her words, her fingers gripping my shirt so tight I can feel her knuckles brushing my skin.

"You were just what?" My hands are around her forearms, and there's less than a foot between us. Less than a foot and when I take a step, I'm so close I can hear her breathing.

I can hear her swallow.

"I should go upstairs."

"Oh yeah? Why's that?"

Silence.

Silence, save for everyone upstairs. Everyone I don't want to see. I wonder if she wants to see them. I wonder who she is, when she isn't playing this role.

"Alex is—"

I tighten my hold on her. "Fuck Alex."

"Eli, you don't—you don't even know me. This isn't a good idea. Not tonight."

I pull her closer to me, and her hands rise to my chest as she looks up at me, the breath startled from her pretty little mouth. "Does he know?" I wrap one arm around her back, using my other hand to brush a lock of hair behind her ear, trailing my fingers down to her neck, where I rest my hand against her collarbone. "Does he know about those scars, baby girl?"

In the dim light pouring in from upstairs, I see pink blooming on her cheeks. "Why are you so obsessed with—"

"With the ways you hurt?" I ask her, leaning down close, pressing my brow to hers.

She doesn't answer me, but I can feel her pulse beneath my hand on her collarbone, and it picks up speed.

Knowing that it's because of me...that *I'm* doing that to her...

"You saw me," she says, her voice rough, interrupting my thought. "You watched me that night. You watched me. But you didn't stop me—"

"Would you have wanted me to?" I tilt my head, angling my mouth over hers. I can smell her breath. It smells like alcohol and hard candy and I wonder what she did in that bathroom. I want to press my lips to hers. I want to feel her mouth crashing against mine.

"Eli, I don't think we should—"

I brush my hands down her side, skimming her waist, beneath her shirt. "Tell me to stop."

She doesn't say anything.

She doesn't move away, instead, she leans closer. It's such a subtle movement, if we were further from one another, I wouldn't have noticed it. But we're not, and her lips brush mine.

"We shouldn't—"

"Tell me to stop," I tell her again. "Tell me to stop and I will. I'm not like him."

"That night, you weren't going to stop." Her lips move against mine, and fuck, I want her.

My dick is aching with her being so close to me. All the blood has rushed from my head and all I want is her.

I fucking want her.

"That night it was Alex that stopped," her voice is little more than a whisper. "And you pushed me onto him. You pushed me and your fingers…"

I've already apologized for this shit. I don't want to talk about this again. And those very same fingers she's referring to dig into her skin. "What, baby girl? Tell me what I did."

Her hands are still on my shirt, but slowly, she uncurls her fist. She uncurls each smooth finger and she slides it under the sleeves of my t-shirt, and my chest tightens with her touch.

"You hurt me," she tells me in a whisper. A whisper that I feel against my mouth. "You hurt me, and you watched me hurt myself and you—"

"What the fuck are you doing?"

Alex's voice startles her.

I heard him coming.

She didn't.

She drops her hands, tries to back up, but my hands are on her waist and I'm not letting her go that easily.

I hear Alex take the last few steps at my back, but I still don't let her go.

"I…I was just—" she starts to say.

"Let go of her," Alex cuts her off.

I don't like his tone. "I don't think she wants me to."

He walks to stand beside us, glaring down at me. I can feel Zara's heart pounding a rhythm throughout her entire body. She's nearly shaking in my arms.

Is she that scared of him?

Or is she that scared of *me?*

"I don't give a fuck what she wants. Let go of her."

"Eli, please just—" she starts to say.

I drop my hands, take a step back from her. Not for his sake, but for hers. He's still glaring at me, and I can feel the tension between us. Not just me and Alex.

Between the three of us.

We have unfinished business. And he might hate it. He might hate what he invited me in on, because he doesn't want to see someone else fuck her, but I don't have that problem.

I don't have that fucking problem at all.

"Kaitlyn is waiting for you upstairs," he tells me, his jaw ticking, his eyes dark pools of black in the dim light. His hands are fisted by his side. "Might wanna get on that."

I don't say anything.

"Alex, we were just—"

He rounds on her. "Shut the fuck up."

She flinches, taking a step back. I don't know what she took in that bathroom—and I'm positive she took something —but it doesn't seem to be working too well for her right now. She seems paranoid. Like she's lost her fight or something.

"Back off. We bumped into each other at the bottom of the stairs," I tell Alex. "Leave her alone."

"I'm not with you," she tells him, making me second guess that shit about losing her fight after all. "I'm not fucking with you and if you didn't want me talking to your friends, you shouldn't have brought me to your stupid fucking beach party."

"Talking?" Alex mocks her, cocking his head and stepping closer, forcing her to step back in the little hallway just off from the bathroom. There's not much here, the stairs at my back, the front door to my right, past the bathroom, and behind Zara and Alex, there's a bedroom. "It didn't really look like you were talking to me." He glances my way. "You wanna finish this?" he asks her, dragging his gaze up and down her body. "You wanna finish what we started the night Rihanna died, huh? Have a little memorial with the three of us?"

She doesn't answer him.

"Because if you do," he says, leaning down close to her, and I see, for the first time, he's got a beer in his hand. Different from the first one he drank. I would know, because this one is *mine*. "If you do, we can." He holds up the beer, shaking the bottle a little. "I think I've had just enough of this to want to share you tonight, Za." And he doesn't wait for an answer.

He threads his fingers through her hair, leans down close, and kisses her. She's frozen for a moment, and I see her eyes. I see the gleam in them as she looks to me, and then, holding my gaze, she kisses him back.

I have this very, very fleeting urge to snap his fucking neck.

But then she moans.

And the urge is gone.

He crowds her against the wall, puts his hand on her throat and shoves down her top, taking her breast in his mouth.

I don't like his hand on her throat.

I don't like that shit at all.

But her eyes are still on mine and even as his mouth covers her nipple, her fingers threading through his hair, she doesn't stop looking at me. She doesn't stop fucking looking at me.

I can't stay away. Not anymore.

I close the space between us, and I don't care what Alex is doing. I don't fucking care because I know she wants to kiss me, and when I'm close enough to, I angle my head, my body to the side of hers, and she kisses me.

She kisses me, and my hand comes above Alex's, circling her throat. She moans into my mouth, one hand still in Alex's hair, but the other comes to my face. She's pinned against the wall between the two of us, and I don't know if I can wait. I don't know if I can fucking wait to get to a bed and I kind of don't care.

But apparently, Alex does.

35

Zara

"NOT HERE," Alex says, his voice hoarse as he straightens, whispering over my mouth. Beside me, Eli's pulled away, but my hand is still on his face and he turns his head, runs his lip over my palm.

Alex steps back, glances at Eli.

I wait for him to stop this.

I wait for him to stop it, but he just grabs my other hand, pulls me toward a closed door. I follow him, and Eli takes my hand from his mouth, and together, me between them, we stumble into a bedroom.

Eli closes the door. I hear the snick of the lock at my back, his hand still in mine.

There's a big bed in the center of the room, white plantation shutters closed in the window. There's a built-in bookcase beside the bed, lined with tall, thin books that I can't quite make out in the darkness of the room.

A closet is at my back, beside the door. There's one white nightstand beside the bed, a grey lamp off atop it. No alarm clock. Beneath my feet there's a white rug, but otherwise, it's hardwood floors like the rest of the house.

It smells like the ocean here. More than anywhere else in the house, I smell the salt of the sea in here

That, and Eli.

Coconut and citrus.

While Alex shucks his shirt off over his head, Eli pulls me toward him, his hands running up and down my body.

He kisses me, his mouth open, his tongue running along my teeth.

And then Alex is behind me, his hands coming around my waist, flicking open the button of my shorts, his mouth on my neck, kissing and sucking and biting.

My hands are on Eli's shoulders, and I want more from him. My tongue is in his mouth, his hands come to cup my face, like he might pull me away from Alex at my back. Like he wants to claim all my attention. Like this is what he's been waiting for the past six months, and he can't get enough.

Alex pulls down my underwear, and they hit the floor with my shorts.

I pull away from Eli, reluctantly, but I need his clothes off, too. I need to feel his skin against me like I can feel Alex's chest at my back.

"What are you doing?" Eli rasps, his hands coming down to either side of my neck. I hear a zipper behind me.

"Your clothes," I manage to say as Alex wraps his hands around my hips and jerks me back into him. I feel his cock, hard and thick against my low back. His hands trail lower, to the inside of my thighs.

Eli glances down, and I see a slight frown between his brow. I wonder if he's thinking about the scars. I wonder if he's thinking about the fact we've already done something just like this before.

"Do you like this?" Alex whispers in my ear, distracting me. His hands come up higher, fingers grazing against my pussy but not quite touching me where I want him. "Do you like being between us?"

Eli pulls his shirt off, and I watch him as Alex touches me. Watch him keep his gaze on me as he kicks off his shoes, unbuttons his pants. I watch him bite his lip, hook his thumb through his boxer briefs and pull them down, too.

He doesn't come closer while Alex grazes my slit with his fingers, still kissing my neck, my ear, my face, his cock growing hotter and harder at my back.

Eli wraps his fingers around the base of himself, his eyes dipping down to watch Alex touch me.

"Do you like being used like a whore, Zara?" Alex whispers, brushing his thumb over my clit, but only for a fleeting second.

I whimper, wanting more.

He laughs against my ear, stepping closer to me, forcing me to take a step forward.

Toward Eli.

Alex slides his thumb over the crease of my thigh. "Do you feel that?" he asks me. "Do you feel how wet you are, for both of us?"

I do feel it.

I feel it, but I want more. *So much more.*

Eli runs his thumb over the top of his cock, the thick head glistening with precum.

I want to taste it.

I want to taste him.

But he's still watching Alex touch me. He still wants to watch, even now. Even though he's a part of this, it turns him on to watch.

I shift my stance, parting my thighs wider and grabbing my breasts, pinching my nipples. I tilt my head back as Alex touches me, leaning against him as I give Eli a show.

Alex sucks on my neck as he runs his fingers down my slit, parting my lips for Eli to see me. The sensation of being so exposed to Eli like this, so vulnerable between them, it makes my knees shake.

All I want to do is fall onto the bed at Eli's back with the both of them. All I want to do is collapse into the feel of them both moving inside of me, but I want Eli to get what he wants too.

I reach my arms back, wrap them around Alex's neck behind me, my body pulled taut, elongated and *open.*

If Eli has really been watching me so long, I want him to see everything.

My eyes are closed as I drown in the feel of Alex behind me, of his mouth on my neck, of his hands between my thighs. He's so warm. So familiar. So *mine.*

I want Eli to see that. To see how Alex and I belong to each other. Not to tease him, but because that's what he wants to see, isn't it? That's the whole reason he has a thing for me in the first place.

Because I'm Alex's, and he can't have me.

If that's the kind of pain that gets him off, I want him to see all of it.

Because I want him to feel good too.

Alex groans against my neck, and his fingers dip lower. He pushes two into me and I moan his name as he wraps his other hand around my low belly, holding me in place as he fingers me.

"God, you're so wet, princess." He nips at my shoulder. "Is it because my best friend is watching?" He trails his tongue toward my spine. "Is it because he can see every fucking inch of you?" He fucks me harder with his fingers, the heel of his hand pressing against my clit. "Are you going to cum before we even get inside of you, huh?"

I think I am.

I press back against him, even though we're already as close as we could possibly be. "Yes," I gasp, "I'm going to——"

But there's movement in front of me and when I open my

eyes, Eli is there, holding my gaze. He grabs Alex's hand, and Alex lets him pull his fingers out of me.

I'm throbbing, missing the feel of Alex's palm against my swollen clit. Missing the feel of his fingers inside of me. I clench around nothing, I was so close.

So close.

Alex slides his fingers up my belly, letting me feel just how wet I am.

Eli's eyes lock on mine. "Alex," he says softly as Alex shifts his hips behind me, rubbing his cock against my back. "Do you want to fuck her in the ass?"

I still have my arms locked behind Alex's neck, my body still fully visible to Eli.

But he's not touching me. As close as we are, he's not touching me.

Alex is quiet a moment, his hands still on my belly. But then he says, "Nuh uh, I don't think I do," against my ear, and I shiver.

Eli steps closer. The head of his cock is against my stomach, right below Alex's hands on me. Eli doesn't take his eyes off of me. "Neither do I."

My stomach flips.

Eli steps closer, rolls my nipples between his fingers and I gasp, but don't move my arms from around Alex's neck.

My chest is heaving, my breasts feel heavy as Eli plays with them, but no one is touching me where I want them to. No one is helping my ache between my thighs.

"This isn't going to go how you think it's going to go, baby girl," Eli says softly.

My breath is loud, panting and labored as Eli pinches one of my nipples, palms the other. Gentle and rough. Hot and cold.

"Because both of us want to be inside your tight pussy."

Tight. He would only know if he'd been there.

For one heart-stopping moment, I wonder if he'll tell Alex.

I wonder if he'll tell him right now. I wonder if that was his plan all along.

But, still staring into my eyes, he just says, "Beg him."

I furrow my brow, confused and caught up in both of them surrounding me in this dark room, the music and voices still carrying on from above our heads.

"Beg him to share you."

Alex laughs and nuzzles his nose against my neck. "I like that idea."

I open my mouth, and Eli tugs on both nipples. Only a soft moan comes out and I almost stumble forward, but Alex pulls me close to him, and I don't dare lower my arms.

"Alex," I whisper. I'm desperate. Desperate to have them both inside of me. Desperate for Eli's cock to be lower, brushing up against my clit. I hold his gaze as I beg my ex. "Alex, please." I bite my lip and Eli's eyes dip to my mouth. I see the vein in his neck straining against his skin. "Alex, please let me."

Alex moves his hand, then brings his forearm against my throat. Now I don't have a choice. I can't move my hands from his neck. He's holding them back while he nearly chokes me.

I see Eli's eyes narrow.

"Zara," Alex says quietly, "I told you. I'm not fucking sharing you."

Eli's full lips turn into a smile. He palms one breast and the other he slaps, bringing his hand down. The sound is loud in the room and I flinch.

"Be careful with her." Alex's words are low, not wanting to ruin our game, but he's serious. I hear it in his tone.

Eli ignores him. "Beg more." His voice is so cold. "You're not trying nearly hard enough."

"Alex, *please.*"

Eli finally breaks my gaze. He looks at Alex, at my back.

"She's convincing," he says quietly, "and if she wants to be a whore, why not let her?"

Alex shifts his arm from around my throat, then tangles his fingers in my hair, yanking my head back, burning my scalp.

"There you go," Eli says in that same quiet voice. "You don't need to be careful. Treat her like the slut that she is."

"This is what you really want?" Alex snarls in my ear. "You want us both to fuck you?" Without waiting for an answer, he shoves me down, toward the floor, but his arm is still wrapped around me, so I don't fall. He goes down with me.

Eli moves out of the way, and I'm at his feet.

Alex's knee is in my back, my face pressed against the side of the cold, wooden floor.

"Fucking answer me."

I swallow down my nerves. Because I *do want it*.

"Yes," I whisper, my lips moving against the floor. "*Yes.*"

Alex's knee digs in harder against my spine and I wince. His fingers tighten in my hair as he leans over me, his mouth inches from mine. "You're a fucking whore, Zara. After tonight, I'm done with you."

My heart cracks with those words. Are they true? Is this still part of the game? Does he mean it? But I don't want to stop. Whatever this is, I don't want to end it.

Because I want them.

He moves his knee from my back and I almost exhale a sigh of relief. Maybe he'll actually *enjoy* this. Maybe it isn't a punishment.

But then he yanks me by my hair, forces me to my hands and knees.

"Arch your back."

I do, the column on my throat stretched taut as he holds my hair back. His hand goes to my inner thigh, and warmth heats up along my core, even as he spreads my legs wider, roughly.

Exposing me.

To him, *and* Eli.

He runs his hand over my pussy. "You're disgusting," he says to me, rubbing my own wetness over my thigh. "Fucking disgusting, princess. Don't move."

He pulls back, the absence of anyone's touch while I'm on my hands and knees nearly humiliating.

Eli moves to stand in front of me, but from this angle, I can't see his face.

"Get on the bed," he says.

"No," Alex counters, "you said it yourself. She's a fucking whore. She deserves to get fucked on the floor."

My heart is pounding erratically in my chest, my eyes on the floor. I'm torn between wanting to get up and end this and wanting them to hurry the fuck up because I'm still desperate for *someone's* touch.

Eli leans down, extends his hand to me.

I look up, meeting his eyes.

"She's *our* whore. Besides, you say the word like it's a bad thing." He looks past me as I take his hand. "She's about to make both of us feel really fucking good. Show some goddamn respect."

They're making my head spin, this hot and cold, good cop, bad cop shit. And the molly I took in the bathroom seems to be working its way into my head, because I don't care.

I just want them.

Eli pulls me to my feet and wraps a possessive arm around my back. "You ever done this before, baby girl?"

I shake my head, my palms on his chest as he holds me close, looking into my eyes. *Like he sees me.*

"She doesn't need a step-by-step manual," Alex growls behind me. "Hurry the fuck up."

Eli ignores him, brushing a lock of hair from my face, his fingers lingering on my throat as he stares down at me. "I'll lay down first. Get on top of me."

I nod, biting my lip as I stare at his. I want his mouth on me again. I want to feel him.

He leans in close, brushing his lips over my ear, sending a chill down my spine. "And just relax, baby girl. I'll take care of you."

And then he pulls me toward the bed.

Lets me go.

Just as he said he would, he lays down first, his hand behind his head, propped up on the pillow. With his other hand, he strokes his cock, his eyes on me, an arrogant smile playing around his mouth, his dark green eyes locked on mine.

And I know, as I crawl toward him, Alex watching me from behind, that he's not going to be as gentle as he just was.

That was a break from what he really wants.

A moment to reassure me.

Now, though...

Now he'll be back to rough hands and rougher words.

But it's Alex that speaks first, from behind me. "Hurry the fuck up." He slaps my ass. "Get on top of him."

Carefully, I climb over Eli, hands on either side of his head, knees beside his hips.

My tits are by his face.

He just keeps stroking himself, one hand behind his head. Still cocky. Arrogant. Back to being cold. This is what he wanted. *This is probably what he wanted all along.* "Spread your legs wider."

I adjust my knees, widening my stance, my fingers digging into the soft white sheets. I know Alex is there, behind us, watching. It's unnerving, knowing I'm exposed to him like this and he's not touching me. He's not close enough for me to feel him.

I feel Eli's cock brush against me, and I suck in a breath, remembering. Knowing this isn't the first time we've touched each other. But Alex thinks it is.

And I know Eli is thinking exactly that as he holds my

gaze and guides himself into me. I see the smirk on his face, the heat in his eyes. The way they crinkle just a little as he watches my face flush when he lifts his hips and pushes all the way into me.

He lifts his head. "Come closer. I want those in my mouth," he nods toward my breasts, swaying between us. I whimper, adjusting myself on him as I lean forward, my hands on the headboard behind him.

When he speaks next, his breath is on my skin. "For such a big fucking whore, you're still so damn tight."

He takes my nipple into his mouth, sucks hard, and then lets me go with a pop. "For now." He shifts his hips again and I can't hold back my moan as I bite my lip, Eli's hands going to my ass.

He pulls me apart, looks past me as he says, "Use her while you still can."

Alex wouldn't know. He wouldn't know that there's a warning laced in those words. "While you still can". Alex probably thinks that's because I won't be any good to him after this.

What he doesn't know is Eli doesn't care who I've been with. Eli doesn't give a fuck about things like that.

It's not just a warning to Alex.

It's to me.

My heart flips in my chest. I wonder if this is a bad idea. I want it, but what happens after this? What happens in the morning? What happens to me? Alex?

Alex doesn't say a word. I keep my eyes on Eli. Watch him watching Alex. See the stubble on his face. The curve of his Cupid's bow. The dusty rose color of his lips. Those long fucking lashes.

God, I want to ride him, but he's gripping my hips so hard, like he wants me to stay still. And then the bed shifts, and Eli looks back up at me. He runs his thumb over my hip bone, and I know what he's feeling.

I know he knows what he's doing. He doesn't smirk as Alex drops to his knees behind me. He doesn't tease me with his eyes or taunt me with cruel words. He just holds my gaze like he sees me.

Because he does.

And when Alex's cock brushes against me, and I suck in a sharp breath, Eli says, "It's okay, baby girl. Just relax," in such a quiet, soothing voice I just want to...I just want to sink into him. Sink against his chest and let him touch me and love me and—

"Arch your back more." Alex's voice. Cold and impassive. Like they've switched. Hot and cold, I don't know which one's which anymore.

But I do as Alex says.

His fingers come to either side of my lips, stretching me wider. And he can see everything. It's nothing he hasn't seen before but this way, like this...

Again, I think this might not be a good idea. This is incredibly fucking stupid. My mind is getting in the way of how I feel physically, ruining this for me. Like a hamster on a wheel, my brain keeps thinking of all the ways this might go wrong.

Fuck, I'm an idiot.

Eli keeps one hand on my ass and jerks my chin with the other, forcing me to look down at him. "Hey," he says softly as Alex puts a hand flat on my back and starts to press himself against me. "You're here. Right here. Don't think, Zara." He pulls my face down to him, so my lips are hovering above his. "Don't think," he repeats softly, and his words touch my mouth. "Just feel."

And then Alex is pushing into me and everything...burns. It's tight and uncomfortable and it hurts and...

"Just feel," Eli says again as I throw my head back, arching my neck and my back as Alex keeps pushing and pushing and just as I think my eyes are going to roll back in my head and I

might black out and I don't know if it's from pain or plea-
sure...he's in.

He's as far in as he's going to get, and his chest falls against
my back as he fucks me and Eli starts to move too,
beneath me.

Both of them are inside of me is nearly too much and I'm
too tight and too full and yet...

It's everything. It's fucking everything. Especially as Eli
trails his hand down my throat and reaches between us, his
fingers circling my clit. My inner muscles contract around
them and Alex groans against my neck, brushing my hair from
my back with one hand and gripping my side with the other.

"Fuck," he says against my skin. "Fuck you feel so good,
Za. You're so fucking tight. You're so fucking good."

They fuck me together, and Eli keeps circling my clit with
his fingers, he keeps gripping my ass with one hand. The three
of us are a sweaty, panting mess and Alex is still groaning and
I'm moaning so loud I know people can hear me.

Kaitlyn will hear me. Us.

I know it and I don't care.

I don't care.

When Alex's hand comes around my throat and his
tongue is against my ear and then he's actually all the way in,
all the way inside of me and Eli is too, I just don't care. I don't
fucking care.

I just want them. I just want this.

"Fuck, I love you," Alex pants against my ear. "I fucking—
I fucking love you," his words are groans, and his fingers
tighten around my throat as he fucks me harder and beneath
me, Eli pinches and pulls my nipples and he fucks me, too.
They're both moving so fast and so hard I almost feel as if
they're competing. As if they're trying to see who can break
me first.

And maybe I shouldn't be, but I'm turned on all the more
for it and when I feel myself getting close, they must feel it too.

Eli cups my face with his hand. "I like feeling him fuck you against me," he tells me as Alex does just that, every thrust driving me further against Eli. Eli's hand is still between us, still circling me and I'm so close. "I like feeling you nearly get fucking ripped apart."

God, I'm so close.

Eli likes it. Alex hates it. But Alex just told me he loves me. He just told me, so maybe he doesn't.

Maybe he likes this, too.

Maybe he likes what I like.

"Come on, baby," Alex says in my ear. His grip tightens on my throat so hard I'm no longer moaning because I'm no longer breathing. "Come for me. Come all over us for me. You're a nasty fucking whore, but you're my whore. *You're mine.*"

And then Eli's hand comes beside Alex's and they're both choking me, covering every inch of my throat. And everything is exploding in shades of grey and black behind my eyes and Eli's other hand is between my legs, his fingers slick and wet against my swollen clit.

Just like when Eli was holding me under, just like when he almost killed me that night, I'm dying for air, but I can't stop it. My body can't stop it. I clench around both of them, everything so tight and so full.

They keep their hands on my throat but loosen their grip and I'm moaning, my forehead against Eli's chest, slick with sweat, and his hand still between us.

And then Alex is tense against my back, grabbing at my neck, his teeth against my shoulder and I know he's coming, too. The both of us, together, all over Eli.

But Eli isn't done.

He brings his hand up, the reverberations of my orgasm still throbbing between my legs so that I don't even need anyone to touch me there. It's like I can still feel it. And I'm still gasping for air when Eli puts his fingers in his mouth, licking me off him.

I pick my head up, watching him, and behind me, Alex slowly slides out of me. My hands are on Eli's chest as I stare down at him still tasting me.

The bed dips and I don't know if Alex gets up, and I don't care either.

I can't stop staring at Eli. I'm still breathing hard, still caught up in the feeling of coming around both of them, I can't really think. I don't know what Eli wants now. I don't know how he wants to finish this but, he moves quickly.

One second I'm on top of him, gasping, and the next, he's flipped us both over and he's on top of me. For a crazy moment, I imagine him wrestling. I think about how fast he must be. How strong he is.

How hot he probably looks on the mat.

And then he's kissing me again, the taste of me on his lips, and all of those thoughts are gone. The only thing I can think of is now is the taste of him, the feel of him as he reaches between us and guides himself back into me.

I'm sore, and it hurts, and he doesn't go slow. He's hard and fast and rough and I whimper, and it isn't a good sound.

"Hey," Alex calls sharply from somewhere beyond the bed, somewhere I can't see. "Be fucking careful with her." I hear the restraint in his words. I know he doesn't want Eli to finish at all. I know Alex doesn't care about that, but Eli doesn't slow.

He's fast and rough and tears are pricking behind my eyes.

"Eli, slow down," I manage to say, my words shaky.

His hand comes to my throat. The sound of his hips connecting with mine is so loud and I wince with his every thrust.

I dig my nails into his chest, trying to push him off of me at the same time.

This hurts.

But I can't say anything. I can't say anything, because in the darkness, Eli is choking me. He's actually choking me.

What the fuck?

Panic, more than anger, engulfs me. What is he doing? Why is he doing it?

His thrusts shake the entire bed and everything is burning. It's burning and I'm still digging at his skin, trying to him hurt enough to slow down. But he doesn't. He doesn't slow.

"Fuck this," I hear Alex say quietly, and then he's there, his hands on Eli's shoulders, pulling him off of me. Out of me.

I sit up, pushing back against the headboard, bringing my knees to my chest, wrapping my arms around my legs.

Alex throws Eli toward the door. "The fuck is wrong with you?" His voice is a growl. I see he's got his pants on, but nothing else. "You were fucking hurting her!"

I take deep breaths, squeezing my thighs together, the pain between them like fire.

I hear Eli laugh in the dark. "Was I? I think she likes it rough."

Alex steps back from Eli, as if he struck him. He edges against the bed, obscuring my view of Eli by the door. "Get the fuck out," he says. "Get out of here."

Eli laughs again. "This is my dad's house. *You* get out."

I hear Alex breathing, deep inhales and exhales. I see his shoulders rise and fall.

My mind is spinning. My head hurts. Why did Eli do that? Why did he...

"Fine." Alex turns to me, offers me his hand. "Let's go, baby."

I shake my head. "Y-you can't drive," I whisper in the dark, but I take his hand anyway. He threads his fingers through mine. "You can't drive."

And I can't drive because I'm not just drunk, I'm tripping, and...

"I don't care. We'll walk. I'll carry you." Alex starts to pull me up off the bed.

But Eli laughs one more time and I feel the hairs on the back of my neck stand on end.

Alex hears something in that wicked laughter, too.

He stops trying to pull me to my feet, and turns to face Eli.

I hold my breath, knowing what he's going to say. Knowing it and hating it. Hating him.

"You said you wanted to experience everything, Zara," Eli says softly in the dark as Alex and I stare at him, Alex's fingers tightening around mine. "Isn't that right?"

No one says a word.

Even with the music and the people upstairs, no one says a thing.

I hear shuffling, and I imagine Eli getting dressed, even though I can't see him. I can't see him, and still no one speaks.

My heart is beating too fast in my chest. Too fast, and I can't breathe. I still can't breathe.

"Oh, now you've got nothing to say, baby girl?"

Alex's fingers tighten painfully around mine. His grip is so tight, his hands clammy. "What *the* fuck are you talking about?" he asks Eli in the dark.

I can almost hear Eli smiling.

No.

He wouldn't do this.

He wouldn't fucking do this.

"Ah, well, since she seems to be so shy now, I guess she won't mind if I say it for her." He blows out a breath. I screw up my eyes tight. "Just before I had my fingers inside of her at our house, she was just telling me how she wants to experience everything."

No one moves.

It feels like no one breathes.

No one says anything.

Does anything.

My pulse is so fast, the blood pumping so hard in my veins, I can feel it everywhere. Behind my eyes. In my head. In my hand, which, for now, is still in Alex's.

But that doesn't last long.

He lets go of me and stumbles away from the bed.

He doesn't look at me when he says, "What are you talking about?" And the scary part? He doesn't sound angry. He doesn't sound jealous either.

He sounds genuinely confused.

Maybe even hurt.

"No," I manage to say, my voice a croak. "Eli. No."

Alex still doesn't look at me.

"Yes, baby girl. Yes." He sighs again, and I can see him now. He is dressed, and he's got his hands in his pockets. He stares at me while he speaks to Alex. "She feels good, man. I know why you like her so much, even if she is a fucking slut."

I flinch, cover my hands over my eyes.

He's not doing this.

He's not really doing this.

"Her mouth." Eli groans. "She gives good head, too. Everything about her is just fucking tight and perfect and damn, when she comes, she's so wet, she's just gushing."

No. No. No.

"What are you fucking talking about?" Alex asks again, and this time, he's angry. This time, he turns toward me.

I drop my hands from my eyes, wrap my arms tighter around myself, wishing I could disappear. Wishing I could be somewhere else. Far, far away from here.

I shouldn't have come here.

"I don't know what—"

"Don't lie, baby girl," Eli cuts me off cruelly. "Don't you dare fucking lie now."

"What is he talking about?" Alex's voice grows louder. He steps closer to me, and I can feel it. His anger. It's like heat radiating off his body. "What the *fuck* is he talking about, Zara?"

I start rocking, my body in a ball. It's hard to focus and to think and the alcohol and the molly are making everything so much more difficult. So difficult.

"Don't leave me." That's all I can say. My voice is small and quiet, and I just want to leave. Just like Alex said. I want him to carry me out of here. I want to leave. "Don't leave me," I plead again. "Please don't leave me."

Alex steps closer. "What. The. *Fuck. Is he fucking talking about, Zara?*" He's screaming now and I just press tighter against the headboard.

Eli says nothing.

It suddenly dawns on me that he's enjoying this. That he likes *this.*

I try to swallow but my mouth is dry. My throat is tight. "Alex." The word is jagged. "Alex, please don't leave me. Can we go? Can we just go?"

Don't leave me here with him.

Alex grabs my face, tilting my chin up so I'm looking at him. "Tell me it isn't true."

I take a deep breath in. Out.

"Tell me it isn't true, princess." He's pleading now. He's begging me. "Tell me he's lying."

I want to. God, I want to. Tears stream down my face, hot and wet against my cheeks, running onto Alex's fingers, still gripping my chin.

"Zara." Alex sinks to his knees, dropping my face, his hands on my feet under the sheets. "Zara, please tell me it isn't true." He's so quiet, his words little more than a whisper, and he has his head bowed. His head is bowed over my feet.

My heart cracks in my chest.

Eli is still silent, watching all of this unfold.

"Don't leave me," I say again, sniffling. "Please don't leave me, Alex."

He's quiet, and then he pushes to his feet again, fisting his hair in his hands as he turns his back to me.

"You stupid, stupid fuck." The words are barely out of his mouth before he shoves Eli against the door of the room, and I swear I hear the wood splintering. "You stupid motherfucker," he says again, and he has both hands around Eli's throat. He slams his head against the door once, twice, the sound so loud, the crack of Eli's skull making me flinch each time. "What the fuck is wrong with you?"

"Alex," I say, his name hoarse from my mouth. I wipe the back of my hand over my eyes. "Alex, can we just go please?"

Alex slams Eli's head against the door again, but Eli just laughs. Like he doesn't care. Like he's a fucking psychopath.

But Alex laughs, too.

He steps back from Eli, letting him go, his hands up, letting him know he's done.

He turns to face me.

"Fuck you, Zara. I am fucking done. I'm fucking done with you. Fuck you. Find your own fucking way home."

And then he grabs his shirt from the floor and pulls it on. He steps to the door, grabs Eli by the collar, opens the door, and shoves Eli out before he follows, slamming the door so hard a book thuds to the floor from the built-in shelves.

I hold my breath, hoping he'll come back.

Hoping he'll at least take me home.

But he doesn't.

Minutes pass and he doesn't come back.

36

Eli

SHE BEGGED HIM.

She fucking begged him when I gave her an out.

She fucking begged like she really is a fucking whore.

Alex locked the door before he pushed me out, and then left without a word to anyone. I thought about breaking down the door to the room she was in, but *she fucking begged him.*

I went upstairs. Kaitlyn was in my face, demanding to know what the fuck I was thinking.

I left. Fuck her. Fuck Zara. Fuck Alex.

I left for my dad's house. A two hour drive I took in silence.

My father lives ten minutes from Caven's campus, but I never go home. He's usually traveling anyway for work, or else he's fucking some bitch he barely knows, and I don't want to hear that shit.

When I get here, early Saturday morning, he's gone.

I knew he would be. He's with his girl of the week. It's a little ironic, the one time I decide to come here, it's when he's gone. Maybe that's why I'm here.

I don't want to go to my house right now. I don't want to see Alex. I don't want to deal with that bullshit.

She fucking begged him.

I drop my bag by the door to Dad's huge, empty house. The spacious foyer is the size of a goddamn bedroom itself, a winding staircase to my right. His office is to the left, closed and probably locked.

Addisons always like to keep their secrets close.

If you let people in, they can hurt you.

It's a damn good thing I never let Zara in. She's obviously not who I thought she was. I guess I thought that night, the one when I watched her take a knife from the block, roll down her shorts and run it across her hip as she cried, I guess that night I saw something that wasn't really there.

Someone that wasn't really there.

Maybe all that time we spent together meant nothing to her.

Fucking bitch.

I head up the stairs, turn down the hall toward the double doors that lead to my room. Dad and I have our own suites, as I liked to think of them when I was younger. Mom had one, too, the one she shared with Dad.

But that was eight years ago.

She hasn't been back since she left, giving me a kiss on the forehead, squeezing my hands in hers.

I wrench open one of the doors to my room, flinging it back. It crashes against the wall, but I don't fucking care. My bed is before me, and on either side of it are two dark, wooden nightstands.

One is empty.

The other has a framed photograph.

I head straight for it, yank it up and stare at it as I do every single time I come in here.

A boy's face, with dark hair like mine but brighter eyes like my mother's, looks back at me.

Adonis.

His first name is my middle name. Almost like Mom was trying to replace her family completely when she went back to Greece.

Adonis is my half-brother that I've never met. Living a life that I was meant to live.

He stole her from me.

He fucking stole her from me.

I hurl the frame against the glass door that leads out to my balcony, and it shatters into pieces that fall to the hardwood floor.

It's not enough.

I run my hands through my hair, looking around this empty room. There's nothing else to fucking break. I don't really live here, I never did.

I went through the motions.

I took showers.

Did laundry.

Jerked off.

Fucked girls.

Ate in bed.

Stared at Adonis's photos that Mom sent every year with a letter wishing me well.

I didn't live, though.

I haven't done that for a long time.

So, there's nothing else to break.

There's my dresser, but it's empty. I took all my shit when I moved out.

I kick the dresser anyway, loving the pain that lights up from the tip of my foot to my thigh. I kick it again, the wood splintering.

It feels pretty damn good.

Imagining my father walking in on this makes it feel even better. He did it. He probably held her so tightly. He probably suffocated her. He never wanted to visit her family. Never wanted her out of his sight. It's why he made such an elaborate home office.

They were always together when he wasn't in the office.

I thought it was because they were happy.

Really, it was because she was trapped. He didn't let her live.

But I let Zara live. I let her do whatever she wanted.

And she begged *him*.

The one who doesn't let her do shit.

I kick the dresser again. And again. And again. And soon there's a hole in the bottom of it and my heart is pounding, sweat on the back of my neck.

I tip the whole fucking thing over and it splinters onto the floor, the sound ringing in my ears.

My chest is heaving, and I step back, up against the wall. I knock my head against it, close my eyes, my hands balled into fists.

Everything swims into focus then.

Everything I've done.

Everything I should have done.

The scene with Zara at the pool plays in my head. How I dove in to save her.

Then one with her between me and Alex that night Rihanna died.

I didn't really want to hurt her.

I just wanted her to learn a lesson. I just wanted her to know that he wasn't good for her. He's never been good for her.

He's never let her take a breath without him. Never let her live without him. Just like my father, with my mother.

It's why she held me under.

I know it's his fault.

He was too much for her. He was too controlling. Too demanding.

I would let Zara do anything she wanted, if she'd just *choose me.*

Instead of someone that wants to change her.

I've known Zara was a lost cause since I first met her. But I didn't care. I don't want to change her. I didn't want to change *for* her, either. We could be as fucked up as we wanted to be, together. I haven't gone to any of my appointments, for her. Because she would want me just how I am.

I slam my fist against the wall.

My kind of fucked up is the kind I can't tell anyone I know. But it's the kind she'd understand.

But she begged him. Even after he treated her like shit.

Maybe that's what she wants.

Maybe she wants someone to try and save her, after all. Save her with violence and threats and cruel words.

Someone to not accept her for the fucked-up mess that she is.

If that's what she fucking wants, I can give her that, too.

37

Zara

SEPTEMBER FADES INTO OCTOBER.

I see Alex sometimes around campus, laughing and joking with his friends. I see him at lunch when I meet Kylie. He looks my way sometimes, but he doesn't speak. Doesn't wave.

We haven't spoken since he left the beach house.

Dwight drove me home. Asked me about Alex. I didn't tell him anything.

I hear about Eli, but I guess our schedules don't line up because thankfully, I don't see him. I hear he's done really well at all of his matches. It's all I hear of him.

Praise.

He doesn't try to contact me.

I guess the game the three of us played really is over.

No one won after all.

Sometimes, I'll rub my thumb over my hip, and I'll remember it.

I remember his words from that time he came to my apartment, "Those scars are beautiful, baby girl. "

I guess I really was just a distraction for him. A game for him to play.

Now, Jax and Kylie and my professors are the extent of my social interactions, and I avoid the latter as much as possible. I go to class, slink out, do my work in an Adderall-induced haze, glug down cough syrup and go to sleep.

I'm responsible though. Wednesdays I don't take anything. Wednesdays are to reset.

Wednesdays are fucking trash.

I also try to get to the little park that edges campus every day. The weather is turning cool, and it's nice being outside for it.

A few of my old friends from ECU text me sometimes, asking me to come down for parties. I still don't have a car. Or a job. I still don't want to get one.

I'm doing a paper on Epictetus, a slave-turned-philosopher who said, "You cannot learn that which you think you already know," but I kind of wish I could hold a séance and ask him what happens when you don't think you know shit and you still don't learn a damn thing.

I don't know shit.

I'm not learning.

Seems like a good Stoic philosophy, always being open to wisdom because you know nothing. Turns out, though, it's not helpful in my everyday life. I don't think I'll ever learn.

Two Fridays before Halloween, I shoulder my bag after leaving a seminar on ancient Greek philosophy, hands jammed in the pockets of my black and white zebra-striped hoodie. A gift from my mother that I actually really love.

We're talking again, and she seems happy.

That's good, I guess. But I kind of just don't care about much of anything. The high I felt after that night with Eli and Alex before it all went to shit, it's long gone. And not even the drugs can get it back. But I keep doing them anyway, hopeful they'll spark something in me.

I've got my hood over my head as a light mist descends upon campus, and I'm not really paying any attention to where I'm going, just staring at my black wedged boots, when I almost walk right into a fucking light pole.

I lift my head up, startled and glancing around to make sure no one saw me. The campus is dead. It's four in the afternoon, which means most people are probably on their way to their parties or games—there's a home game tonight, based on all the Caven blue I saw around campus—and no one gives a shit about a girl almost walking into a pole anyway. I wonder if Alex is happy to be playing again.

I push him from my mind as I stare at the light pole, really seeing it for the first time.

There's a sheet of paper taped to it and I stare at it for far longer than I should.

It's Rihanna.

The photograph is black and white, but I know that long, shiny hair of hers is brown. I think her eyes were blue or maybe they were green, or maybe I really don't know at all. She's smiling, dressed in her blue and orange cheerleading uniform, kneeling on one knee with her pom poms in her hand.

There's some loopy type that just says, "Live life to the fullest!"

I want to rip the paper down, but that seems mean-spirited. I guess it is. I guess I am, but staring at her, alive, makes me think of her, dead, and that makes me feel uncomfortable.

Makes me think of Alex's words, too. "If you touch her, I swear to God, Rihanna, I'll fucking drown you in my pool."

Why didn't I tell the cops that? I don't know. I'm sure it doesn't matter. I'm sure he wouldn't hurt anyone.

He stopped Eli. That night, and the one at the beach. He stopped him.

And as far as I know, he and Eli still live together. They were able to push me aside and become bros again. Yeah.

Alex Christian Cardi is not the murdering type.

But sometimes I still get sent that video of him yanking down my bikini top, the gloating smile on his face, the way he bent his head down to my neck. My wide-eyed stare, like I didn't know what the hell was going on.

Mainly because I didn't.

I remember his words to me, too, before he pushed me in that pool, when I told him I was too drunk to swim. "Yeah, here's the thing, princess. You should've thought about that before you put Jamal's dick in your pretty little mouth."

Eli did way worse, but I don't think of him.

He was a distraction too.

I scuff my shoe against the brick walkway, still staring at that piece of paper. A girl died in a pool and I found her, and I feel nothing.

Maybe I think she got lucky, really.

Death is the easy way out.

If that Narcan hadn't been administered because a sober girl at the party I went to in the spring was paying attention, I would've gotten to taste it too. To drift off into a beautiful oblivion.

It would've been all over then. I'd have never met Alex or Eli. Never fucked up their worlds. Hell, maybe Rihanna might even still be alive.

My phone buzzes in my pocket, and I tear my eyes away from the picture.

I pull my phone out, glance at my text. There's an earlier message from Mom. I'm meeting her for dinner next week because I really want someone to buy me a dinner out and I really don't want to ask her for any more money lest she suspect I'm spending everything she sends me on drugs, which I am. And a text from Jax.

Him: **Wanna come over?**

I haven't partied with him in a while. I've been by, of course. Walked over. Had Kylie drive me over, telling her I had to pick up some notes for school, even though he doesn't fucking go to school.

All lies to get what I need, but I haven't spent any time with him.

Kylie is already gone for the weekend though, home to have dinner with her parents and Ian. I wonder if she still spies on me for Alex, but I have a feeling he doesn't care. I almost want to ask her, but it doesn't matter now.

None of it fucking matters.

I look back down at my phone.

What time? I ask Jax.

What am I going to do otherwise? Sit in my room and drink NyQuil until I fall asleep, or until my liver fails me.

Jax: **I'll pick you up in ten?**

I smile at my phone in the rain, the quiet campus serene around me.

Me: **Make it twenty.**

I shove my phone in my back pocket and book it to my apartment.

38

Zara

JAX and I are the first people there, and I'm glad.

He offers me a drink as soon as we step inside his kitchen, but just before he goes to pour the mixer in, Diet Coke, I shake my head.

"Nah. It's been a rough few weeks. Give me straight rum."

Jax eyes me with a little half-smile, scrubs his hand over the back of his neck and shrugs. "All right," he says lazily, capping the Diet Coke and tossing it back in the fridge.

While he's busy with that, I just help myself, pouring the rum until it fills up half the cup.

"Yo, chill," Jax says with a little laugh. "You don't wanna get sloppy."

I'm always fucking sloppy. Instead of saying that, I just tip back the cup and drink as much as I can stand before I feel like I might vomit. I slam the cup down, sloshing the contents inside as I wipe the back of my hand over my mouth.

Jax sips his own drink. A beer. He's much more responsible than I am. "So, you're really through with that quarterback cock suck?" he asks me calmly, leaning against the kitchen counter.

My stomach burns with the rum and it churns, too, with Jax's question. He doesn't know the truth, of course, because I suck at telling the truth. I shrug. "Yeah," I say, trying to keep the emotion out of my voice. "We're through."

Jax lifts up his beer in a 'cheers' motion, and I touch my cup to his and drink again. "Good." He swallows his beer. "Didn't like that guy."

I laugh a little, setting my cup back down. I'm already feeling a little tipsy, and I use the counter to hold me up. "You didn't even know him," I point out.

Jax shrugs, quirks his mouth to the side. "Yeah, well, fuck 'em anyway."

I burst into laughter and take another drink to hide my smile. Fuck it. I might as well finish the entire thing. I don't really like being awake much nowadays anyway. If I black out, Jax will put me in the spare bedroom and I'll just drift off into sleep. I finish it off, wincing a little as it burns down my throat, and then start spinning the empty cup on the counter.

"Jax," I start, swallowing and looking down at my black shoes, "you ever wanna be sober?"

At that moment, the door opens, and I glance over my shoulder as I feel the cool October air rush in.

A couple of guys lift their hands in greeting and I nod.

"Start up the music," Jax tells the guys. "Make yourself at home. There's pot on the table."

The guys give a thumbs up and shuffle off to the living room, closing the door before they do. One catches my eye. He's got dark blonde hair, dressed all in black. He looks a little older than me, and I'm positive he doesn't go to Caven. His eyes linger on me a moment before he finally follows his friend into the living room, disappearing from view.

Music starts up in there, but as I turn back to Jax, it kind of fades away. He's quiet a moment as he stares at me, and the strange silence is almost deafening, even though it isn't real. Even though the guys are talking in the living room and the music actually gets louder, it still feels silent.

I've noticed lately that most things are like that for me. Almost like I'm dissociating from myself.

I wonder if it's all the drugs. I wonder if I'm making myself schizophrenic or something. I wonder if I've just always been like this. I can't really remember.

"Nah," Jax finally says, sighing as he does. "I remember what being sober was like. I didn't feel good in my own skin."

I look up and return his small smile with one of my own. But the truth is, I still don't feel good in my own skin.

Right now, though, I feel a little wobbly.

Unsteady on my feet.

I grip the counter and Jax flicks his brows up. "You need something to eat?" he asks, still working on that first beer. Meanwhile, I've downed about half a dozen shots in about as many minutes.

I shake my head, smiling at him. "No. Who was that guy?" I ask instead, pointing my thumb over my shoulder, toward the living room. "With the blonde-ish hair?" My words are already slurred, and I laugh a little as Jax smiles slightly. "Who was he?"

Jax sighs, sets his beer down. He takes my hand in his. "Come on, I'll introduce you."

THE GUY'S NAME IS BEN, AND BEN OWNS A FARM. AN HONEST-to-God farm. He tells me so and I slap his knee, laughing on the couch beside him.

A few more people are here, some of them on the floor around the coffee table, playing cards and doing drugs. I see someone snort a line and my eyes instinctively find Jax, although my hand is still on Ben's thigh.

"Can I get a bump?" I ask Jax, who is on my other side. I

nod toward the table where the line has disappeared, but I know Jax has more.

Jax just shakes his head. "I think you're good for now, Za."

When he calls me that, I think of Alex and my throat feels tight.

I turn back to Ben, who is staring at me with big blue eyes. He's thirty, he told me. He's thirty, which is ten years older than me and I've never hooked up with someone that much older.

I tell him so.

He puts his hand over mine on his thigh. "Slow down, babe," he says with a small smile. "I don't think you're quite sober enough for all that."

The noise is loud around us and I know no one heard him reject me, but I don't like it. It makes my cheeks flush, and the water in the cup Jax gave me sloshes as I lean an arm through two people sitting at the table in front of me and set my cup down.

I turn back to face Ben, wrap my arm around his broad shoulders. He has a lot of stubble on his jaw, and there are faint lines under his blue eyes.

I'm just glad they're not brown. If he looked like Alex, I couldn't do this.

"I don't need to be sober to fuck around," I tell Ben, leaning in close to him, my words against his ear.

Jax clears his throat on my other side. "Hey, Za, I wanna show you something."

Ben looks past me, exchanging a look with Jax. I think they're talking about me, but I don't know what they're saying without words.

I don't like it.

But when Jax grabs my hand, I turn to him and let him pull me to my feet.

Maybe Jax will fuck me.

Carefully, he guides me through the crowded living room,

and then we disappear down a hall. I'm unsteady on my feet, leaning against Jax, linking my arm through his.

"You wanna sleep with me?" I mumble, resting my head against his shoulder. "Because you can, you know. I always thought you were hot."

Jax laughs, shaking his head a little as we come to a stop in front of his spare bedroom. "Did you now?" he asks, pushing open the door.

I nod, turn to kiss his cheek.

He lets me, and then he closes the door after we get inside the room.

I flop down on the bed, on my back, staring at the ceiling as it seems to spin overhead. Jax turns the lamp beside the bed on, and sits down beside me.

"Touch me," I whisper, eyes still on the ceiling. "Touch me, Jax."

Jax clears his throat. I glance at him, see his hands clasped together, wrists on his knees. "You're really drunk, Za. We're just going to relax, okay?"

My heart pounds out an uneven rhythm in my chest. "No. Touch me. Please." My voice is hoarse, and my words are slurred, but he knows what I said.

He knows.

I grab his hand when he doesn't do what I told him to, put it on my belly, where my shirt has ridden up.

His fingers are so warm.

They remind me of Alex.

I try to trail his hand lower, but he stops me. Just keeps his hand on my low belly.

"Zara," he says softly, turning toward me, keeping his hand right there, right under mine. "I think you need help."

I close my eyes and groan. "Not you, too," I say, annoyed. "Not you. You're my friend, Jax. You're my friend." I try to push his hand lower again, under the waistband of my jeans, but he keeps it firmly planted on my stomach.

I clench my thighs together, eyes still closed as I lie on the bed.

"I am your friend," he assures me, his voice low and soothing. "I am your friend. And tonight, I think you should just sleep this off, okay?"

I let go of his hand and drop my own by my side as I look at him again. His eyes are a dark blue. Like the ocean.

The ocean reminds me of Alex. And his dad. And his mom.

And how he left me.

"I miss him," I say suddenly.

Jax's eyes soften. "Who?" he asks quietly.

I stare at the ceiling again, my face flushing. "Alex," I admit. "I miss him."

Jax's hand moves just the slightest bit on my stomach, like he's reassuring me. "Do you?"

I nod without looking at him. "Yeah." I bite my lip. "I miss him so much."

A moment of silence, and then Jax says, "Where's your phone, babe?"

I pull it out of my back pocket, lifting my hips a little and secretly hoping Jax will move his hand down my pants, but he doesn't.

I hand Jax my phone, uncaring why he wants it.

He takes it, and I just keep staring at the ceiling. "Was Alex good to you?" Jax asks me.

My lower lip trembles. I nod again. "He was so good."

Jax sighs. "I did some digging for you."

My stomach clenches. I don't take my eyes off the ceiling.

"About that party." Jax blows out a breath, presses a little harder against my skin, but he's still so gentle. "I don't think it was him, Zara. I don't think he did the bad thing."

I feel tears well in my eyes. "Me neither, Jax. Me neither."

39

Zara

I'M GOING HOME.

In the middle of the night, or morning I guess, Jax is taking me home. Because I begged him. I begged him to let me sleep in my own bed. He fell asleep beside me, not touching me, and I woke up begging.

Because I need to get to my supply, and I know he won't give it to me.

Jax rolls down the windows of his Camaro, and I stick my arm out, letting the cool breeze blow against my skin. I don't think he's super happy to be driving me home at this time of night, but he's doing it.

"Whatcha gonna be for Halloween?" I ask him, laughing at my own question even though it isn't funny.

The fall air smells amazing; like woods and campfires and life, even though I don't think there's a single campfire happening along this stretch of the road right now. I can smell it anyway, the scents alive in my brain.

I love fall.

Mom used to love decorating for Halloween, too. She

made her husband-of-the-year join in with that, too. I think I should call her soon. I think next weekend, I won't cancel on her dinner like I usually do.

I think I'd like to see her soon. I miss her. I think I need someone now, and she's my mom after all.

I close my eyes, floating my fingers through the air as Jax drives on. But behind the blackness of my eyelids, I see Alex. I see his deep brown eyes, those flecks of amber.

My stomach churns.

I open my eyes just as Jax finally answers, "A drug dealer," in a flat tone.

I turn to stare at him, but I see the hint of a smile tugging on his lips.

I burst into laughter that rumbles through my chest and he joins in, one lazy hand on the wheel, his eyes half open as he drives.

"Really?" I ask him between fits of laughter. "Seriously?"

He shrugs. "Easy costume." He glances at me before his eyes go back to the road. "What about you?"

"A slut," I deadpan, watching him carefully.

He shakes his head, a little frown tugging on the corner of his mouth. "You're not a slut," he says quietly.

I roll my eyes, turn back to watch my fingers dancing on the wind out the window, barely visible in the darkness of the night.

"I am, but that's okay."

"You're not."

"Whatever."

I think about what Eli said, about the word 'whore'. You say the word like it's a bad thing.

Alex thought it was a bad thing.

Alex only ever wanted me.

Jax and I don't really talk much after that.

I stumble up to my apartment, head spinning with mostly

good things thanks to the fact that I'm still a little drunk, but a few bad ones, too.

Mainly watching Alex walk out without coming back.

Mainly thinking about Eli holding me underwater.

I let myself into the apartment, close the door at my back. It's quiet, and I think about blasting my music when I get to bed. I head toward my room, jangling my keys. When the drugs hit my system, I'll be fine. I'll be strong. I'll be brave and everything that happened all those weeks ago will be fine.

"Zara."

Kylie's voice shatters my invincibility. I come to a stop, halfway to my room. It's completely dark in the apartment, just the lights from the microwave and the time on the stove glowing green.

I turn my head in the direction of her voice, make out a shadow on the couch.

Fuck. I thought she was gone for the weekend. For the week, actually, because fall break starts Monday.

"Kylie, what are you—"

"Alex called me."

My stomach churns, my high dropping. I think about Eli. He wasn't lying. He wasn't fucking lying about that. "Why the fuck—"

"He told me where you've been. He wanted me to make sure you were okay."

How does he fucking know?

And then I think about Jax asking for my phone.

That mother fucker. They've all betrayed me.

Kylie clears her throat and I see her stand to her feet. "Zara, I think you need some help."

I drop my keys to the floor with a clatter and turn to face her fully. In the dark, it's easier to tell her exactly what I think about Alex fucking Cardi and her in my business. And her as a person, while I'm at it. If she isn't going to be on my side, then fuck her. I thought we were friends.

"Alex and I aren't together. I'm not his problem, and what I do isn't his business anymore." I take a step toward her. "Or yours, Kylie."

Silence.

I think I can hear her breathing. Or maybe that's me, I don't know.

And then she flicks on the light in the living room and I stumble back, shielding my eyes. Fuck, that's bright.

I blink a few times, lower my arm. Kylie has mascara streaked down her cheeks, a tissue balled up in her hand. I didn't even know she wore mascara. I have no idea why the fuck she's crying.

She's wearing fuzzy long pants and a hot pink t-shirt, which is so unlike her usual sensible, matching pajamas.

"Kylie?" My voice comes out as a croak. In the light, I almost regret what I said to her.

Almost.

I think about Alex and my heart aches. I remember him walking out. He had no right to leave me.

I clutch a hand to my chest.

Kylie's red-rimmed eyes track the movement and she sniffs, brushing the tissue over her nose. "Oh, Zara..." Her shoulders shake.

Alex's eyes.

His gorgeous eyes.

The way Eli set me up.

Eli fucked with my head and he set me up.

"Zara. What have you done?" Kylie asks.

I shake my head, shaking off the memory, too.

"Zara," Kylie sobs again, stepping toward me.

I take a step back. "No." I close my eyes and say it again, "No. I'm fucking fine."

Kylie comes closer. I can feel her in front of me. Hear her sniffle. "Zara. Alex said you..."

I clamp my hands over my ears. "I fucked them both." I

say it again, and again, and again. "I fucked them, I fucked them, I fucked them."

Kylie pulls me into a hug, and I drop my hands, sagging against her. This is the end of it.

Everything laid bare.

This is the end.

"It doesn't matter," I whisper into her shoulder as she holds me, the sweet scent of her raspberry-scented shampoo filling my nostrils. "It doesn't matter, it doesn't matter."

"Zara..."

"Alex can go fuck himself." My voice cracks, and I feel tears pricking behind my eyes, but I close them tight. No, no, no. He tried to drown me. He embarrassed me. He slipped a pill into my mouth.

He hurt me.

God, he hurt me so bad.

He almost made me think I deserved love. He almost made me love myself.

"Alex can fuck off," I whisper, letting the tears spill down my cheeks as Kylie tightens her grip on me. "He thinks I'm crazy. He thinks I'm a slut. He...he..."

"He cares about you." Kylie's voice is a whisper and I feel my heart ache at her words, but I shake my head against her shoulder. She doesn't know that. She warned me away from him. She doesn't know him. She doesn't know me, either. She has no idea.

"No. He hates...he hates me..."

"This isn't about him, Za," Kylie whispers, stroking my hair. "It's not about him."

I swallow down the lump in my throat.

"This isn't about Alex or Eli..."

He told her. That motherfucker told her.

I squeeze my eyes shut tighter, my chin trembling. "I don't understand..."

I hear the door to the apartment open. Cold air gusts in.

The door shuts.

I try to pull out of Kylie's grip as I open my eyes. Footsteps come closer.

"This isn't about them," Kylie says again, still holding me.

"This is about you, princess," Alex's quiet voice says from the dark hall.

"I'm so sorry," Kylie whispers, finally pulling back but not dropping her hands from my shoulders. "I'm so sorry but—"

"I'm not." Alex's dark gaze is locked on mine.

"You let him in here." The words are little more than a whisper.

Kylie squeezes my shoulder. "I'm sorry but—"

I lift my hands, knocking hers off me as I turn to face Alex. "You let him in here. You don't even know him! You let him—"

"Shut up, Zara. You sound like a fucking child," Alex snaps.

Kylie turns to glare at him, and a laugh bubbles up from my throat.

"Oh, you think that's bad?" I snort.

Alex takes a step toward me.

"Oh, Kylie. You have no fucking idea what Alex is like. You warned me about him yourself!"

"He said he wanted to help—"

Alex gets up in my face. "I *am* helping her," he cuts Kylie off. "You're not leaving here until I know you're fucking done with those pills, Zara. Until you get your shit together. Until I stop hearing how you're slipping out of your chair in class and you're walking around in a fucking fog and even your *dealer* is worried about you."

I laugh again, on the verge of hysterics. I wipe the back of my hand over my eyes and stand on my tiptoes. "And you think you're actually going to keep me here in my own fucking apartment? You're as dumb as you fucking look."

He looks like he wants to punch me in the face and I kind of want him to.

"Zara," says Kylie.

I turn to glare at her, pointing my finger in her face. "You fucking did this. You set me up. You backstabbing—"

Alex grabs my finger and yanks it down, twisting it as he does. Then he backs me up against the counter, dropping my hand and caging his hands on either side of me. "You're filthy, Zara. I'm fucking done with you. But I refuse to let you destroy yourself. I won't have that on my conscience."

I push against his chest. "What fucking conscience?"

He scrubs his hand over his jaw, places his hand back on the counter beside me. "Funny, Zara, considering last time I saw you, you were getting pumped full of my best friend's—"

"Enough!" Kylie snaps, coming to stand beside us and pushing Alex away from me. His jaw ticks but he doesn't break my gaze even as he drops his hands. "Just leave her alone, okay? Give me some time with her."

"I'm right fucking here. You don't need to talk about me like I'm—"

"Shut. The fuck. *Up!*"

I flinch, startled as I look up into Alex's eyes, his face a mask of fury.

"I'm not leaving you alone with anyone." He shoots a glare at Kylie whose eyes harden. I underestimated my roommate. She's tougher than I thought, which right now, is not good for me.

But it's Alex that keeps talking. "I'm not fucking leaving you until you've got your shit straightened out."

I laugh, rolling my eyes, trying to recover from momentary fear. "You gonna skip all your classes? Miss out on all your fucking football parties and your practice and your—"

"You might've forgotten, because you're too busy using your cunt as a Hoover, but fall break starts Monday, princess."

Kylie's face turns an alarming shade of red, but she

doesn't hesitate to jump to my defense. "If you're going to be staying in our apartment, you cannot talk to her like that!"

Alex smiles. It sends a chill down my spine. "You got it, Ms. Jones. I'll be sure to speak to her exactly how she deserves."

Kylie's voice shakes with fury when she says, "Alex, I'm leaving tomorrow. If you can't watch out for her like you claimed to want to, I'll take her with me, and you can——"

"I'm done with both of you." I turn to go, headed straight for the front door. I'm not a child. I'm not an addict. I'm fucking fine and these two assholes just want to blow my high.

Maybe I've got a small problem. But it's nothing I can't deal with myself. Fuck them both. Surely Alex has better things to do than babysit. I am not his problem. And he's pissed I fucked his roommate, but he has no right.

He has no fucking right to be mad.

Fuck him.

I don't want him.

I don't want anyone.

I just want to be alone.

I unlock the door and just as I'm about to pull it open, Alex slaps his hand against it. "You're not leaving, princess."

"I swear to God, I'll call the police if you don't let me——"

"Please do." He steps toward me, backing me into a corner by the door. "Please fucking do call the police, so they can see how drunk you are right now. So I can show them the shit you kept in a goddamn tampon box——"

I slap him.

I don't think, I just do it.

"You had no fucking right!" I slap him again. He works his jaw, turns back to face me, teeth clenched. "You had no fucking right to go through my shit! Do you know how much that shit costs——"

"If you start fucking your dealer, too, Za, you should get a pretty good discount, huh? Or is your pussy not that good anymore?"

Again, I raise my hand to slap him, and again, he lets me. My hand hurts, the sound echoes in the apartment and Kylie gasps somewhere behind Alex's big frame.

"Do it one more time," he tells me, his voice low. "I dare you."

"Zara, don't," Kylie says, pleading with me.

But I do. Or at least, I try to. The rage is blowing my fucking high. I'm ready to fucking scratch Alex Cardi's face off.

But he stops me.

He grabs my arm, forces me further against the wall, my head knocking against it, his grip on my arm painful. Kylie is calling his name, but he ignores her, getting in my face, his eyes dark pools of anger in the dim light spooling in from under the apartment door.

"I won't let you kill yourself. You don't deserve the fucking rest."

He pins my other arm up against the wall as I try to shove him away.

"Eli never gave a fuck about you, and goddamn, I wish I could say the same, but I *do*, Zara. I fucking do."

"That's not—"

"Eli doesn't love you. He's sick, just like you. But I fucking love you just as much as I hate you, and I won't let you get worse. Now," he leans his body against mine, and I hold my breath, "I'm staying here with you this entire week. You can make it easy, or you can make it hard. But if you try to leave without me, I'll fucking call your mom and she will cut you off. Do you understand?"

No.

I swallow down my anger, trying to work a different angle. Screaming at Alex won't get me what I want. It'll just make him louder. Worse.

He has no right to be mad but telling him that again won't help me now. And if he doesn't let me leave this apartment, if he really took all my shit I can't survive that.

I open my eyes and relax against the hold he has on me.

He relaxes too, but he's watching me suspiciously. Skeptically. I know he doesn't trust me any more than I trust him.

He doesn't step back and he doesn't let me go, but I didn't expect him to.

"It's not what you think," I finally say, keeping my tone even. I see his brow furrow, I see him ready to argue, so I keep going, my words quick but soft. "I'm not an addict. Not like you think." There's a sinking feeling in the pit of my stomach because what I'm saying is true and I don't want to give it to him. I don't want to feel this vulnerable, but I have to. I need to tell him some truths, so he'll leave me alone. So he won't fuck everything up for me. "I'm not addicted. I just...I just feel so weird and alone, and my brain is a fucking mess and the pills help me feel alive. But I know how to live without them." I swallow down that little lie and hope Alex does too. "I know how, I just thought I'd go out with a bang my senior year and then get my shit together." I laugh a little, because when I say it out loud, it does sound ridiculously stupid. "I realize that's not going to work."

He loosens his grip on me, but still doesn't let go completely.

"I don't...I don't want Eli."

His eyes narrow but he doesn't say anything.

"I never wanted him." My voice breaks.

"That was my fucking *best friend*," Alex seethes, as if I don't know. As if I don't see just how screwed up everything is. How screwed up Eli is. How screwed up I am. "How could you? *How fucking...could you?*" His voice breaks, his hold weakening. He presses his forehead to mine and I smell him, feel him. It's overwhelming, him being so close to me after so long we've had apart. "How the fuck could you, Zara?" His words are soft, broken.

I swallow down the lump in my throat. "I'm sorry. I'm sorry." But there's something more pressing, something more important. "I'm sorry but you can take the pills. You can take everything. There's even a stash in my shoebox that I'll—"

Alex pulls back, taking a deep breath, composing himself. "I already got it."

I fight down the flash of anger, and just take a deep breath instead. "Right, well, you can take it all. I'll stay here, in this apartment, but you don't need to give up your fall break to stay with me." I stare into his eyes, pleading. "I need to be alone. I need space to think. I could even go home, to see my mom."

He looks at me for a long moment, his face unreadable. He doesn't drop my gaze and I find it almost hard to keep my eyes on his. To not look away. To not cower, because I'm full of shit. But he can't see that. He doesn't know me like he thinks he does. If he thinks Eli is bad, he's got no fucking clue how I am.

Kylie doesn't know me either. We really just became friends, and that was all bullshit too, because I didn't tell her any truths and she kept shit from me.

"Yeah," Alex finally says, and I feel relief start to spread like a warm blanket over my limbs. He lets go of one of my arms, brushes his thumb over his lip and steps back, finally dropping my other arm. My knees feel weak with gratitude, that he bought the lie.

But then he slides his hands into the pockets of his sweats and says it again, "Yeah." He blows out a breath. "Here's the thing, princess. You're full of pretty words. But I know you're full of shit, too. I know, because this isn't my first fucking rodeo with girls like you." He reaches a hand from his pocket, strokes my cheek.

His fucking mother.

The touch is tender, despite his words.

It makes tears prick behind my eyes and I don't know why. I don't know if it's because I'm trapped or because of something else...

I don't know.

I just don't know.

"I can't promise you much after this, but I can promise I'm going to take care of you, princess." And then he presses his lips to my forehead. "And you're not leaving this apartment until you're better, because I will not fucking let you destroy your life."

I try to shove him away, but he grabs my arms.

I try to move, to pull myself free from his grip while Kylie watches, her hand over her mouth, silent.

"Let. Me. *Go!*" I scream at him, trying to get to the door. But he's so much stronger than me and he doesn't let go.

"Let me fucking go!" I scream again, at the top of my lungs. He spins me around, pulls my back to his chest and covers my mouth with his hand.

"Relax," he whispers in my ear. His voice is still so broken, it gives me pause. It's so broken and I hear the grief in his tone. "Just relax, princess. I'll take care of you. Just don't fight me, please. Please don't."

His words linger in my head long after he pulls me to bed. Long after I give up the fight for tonight. Long after Kylie leaves with a warning for Alex that if he hurts me, she'll call the police herself.

Long after he takes off my shoes and my clothes and offers me his own shirt. Long after he pulls my back against his chest and wraps his strong arms around me.

"Don't fight me. Please don't fight me."

40

Alex

I'VE GOT APPROXIMATELY a dozen missed texts from a dozen different numbers asking me what I'm doing for break. I put my phone on silent, open my music app, and then flip it over.

MANTRA by Saint Slumber plays alongside the sounds of frying bacon on the back burner as I scramble some eggs on Zara's stove.

I could've taken her to my house for the week. Eli was supposed to be away, for a wrestling tournament. But we haven't exactly been on speaking terms lately and I'm moving out at the end of the semester.

So, Zara's apartment it is.

It's nice anyway. Cozy, and shockingly, there were eggs and bacon in the fridge. Probably Kylie's, who seems to have her head on straight. I'll have to restock their food before I go back home.

I glance down the hall. The door to Zara's room is wide open, but I've got to step back into the living room to actually see her, the pan of eggs in my hand, spatula in the other. She's huddled up under her green comforter, a tendril of her white-blonde hair splayed against the grey pillow.

Relief washes over me, and I recognize the feeling as stupid. She's not better yet. Not even close.

I already confiscated all her shit. She even had a bag in the vent in her bathroom, but that's gone now, too.

After I got that call from Jax, of all fucking people last night.

My chest tightens.

I step back to the stove, slam the pan down a little harder than I meant to.

I don't want to think about last night. About what a fucking moron I am for doing this. For being here with her.

She's not my mother.

She's not my responsibility.

I turn off the burners on the stove, the bacon completely fried, which is exactly how I like it.

I run my hand through my hair and lean against the counter. The smell of bacon and eggs is second only to the scent of flowers and coffee that seems to permeate the air in this little apartment.

I try to think about how all of this happened, but it's like her scent is embedded in my brain and for some reason, she makes me fucking stupid. She makes it impossible to think.

God, I'm an idiot.

I should just call her mom. I should call the damn police. I should send Jax to prison. I should... I should do so many things besides what I'm doing right now. I'm in over my head, and I have no idea the extent of Zara's addiction, besides knowing she clearly has one. I've tried to be blind to it all these months, but I saw it.

I saw it, and I never did shit about it until it pissed me off.

I turn to the stove, grab a piece of bacon from the pan

and pop it in my mouth. I go to reach for another one, but I hear Zara's footsteps, and turn to see her coming to a halt at the end of the hall, staring at me.

Seeing her messy waves like a lion's mane around her face, her bleary eyes and those long, pale legs beneath my t-shirt, all thoughts of calling the cops or her mother or anyone at all vanish. I don't know why I'm so fucking weak for this girl but I am.

No. I do fucking know. It was right around the first time she was drunk out of her fucking mind. It was at my house, a party, and she was sitting on the couch, her eyes fluttering closed. Some of my teammates were sitting around her, and I just thought, *God, if they fucking touch her, I'll kill them.* There was something about her vulnerability in that moment...yeah. That shit softened me.

And her heart is so big. She pretends it isn't, but God, it is.

Her heart is big, and she cares about me, and her mind is sharp and when she isn't on drugs I fucking like her even more. Her quiet contemplation. Her obsession with fucking philosophy, of all goddamn things.

I like her more in the quiet. Not at the parties, but in the night, when she's against me. In the mornings, when it's just us.

I like that version of Zara so much more.

She needs me.

"Good morning, princess."

She crosses her arms over her chest and leans against the doorway, her bottom lip stuck out in a pout. She does not look like she thinks it's a 'good morning' at all. Behind me, my phone is still playing music and I reach my hand out and turn it down, pocketing my phone.

"You're still here," she finally says, her voice groggy with sleep.

I try not to take offense to that. "Yep."

She sighs, runs a hand over her face. I see her wince and I don't know why at first, but then I realize she hit her nose ring.

"You do that a lot," I tell her, tapping the side of my own nose.

Her pale cheeks bloom pink and she rolls her eyes, but there's a smile on her pretty mouth.

I jerk my chin toward the stove. "Come eat."

"I'm not hungry." She looks down at her bare feet, flexing her toes. They're painted pink but the polish is chipped.

I drum my fingers on the counter at my back. "It's only Saturday, princess. You've got a full week of me living here." I look around the little living room, knowing I've got my work cut out for me. Knowing I won't be able to keep her in here the full seven days. "Might as well start by having breakfast, don't you think?"

She chews on her lip, still flexing her toes. Even her goddamn toes are pretty. Which gives me an idea.

"Let's go get a pedicure."

She lifts her head to stare at me as if I've asked her to shoot up heroin.

I shrug. "Get dressed. I'll take you."

"You want to get a *pedicure?*" she asks me, skepticism laced in her tone.

"Aw, don't be sexist, princess. I keep my toes groomed, too. It's my favorite part of the off season," I admit. "Working out all those blisters."

"Did you paint your nails pink, too? Because if I'd have known…"

I cock my head and shrug. "Would that be a problem?"

She laughs a little, running a hand through her hair. "Alex Cardi, quarterback and jock asshole, got pink pedicures?"

All right, this has gone too far. "No, for your information, I did not." I grab another piece of bacon and throw it in my mouth, chewing and swallowing it down as I walk over to her.

She eyes me with suspicion, but when I throw an arm

around her shoulders, she doesn't scream or shove me off or back away. It seems as if she's already resigned to this shit.

I tug her close to me, loving her scent.

"You can get all the work done without the polish, you know? The nail people love it, too, even though my legs get cramped as hell in those massage chairs. They weren't built for pro athletes, apparently."

I pull her down the hall, toward her room. Reluctantly, she walks with me.

"You're not a pro athlete."

"Nope. I'll be something less flashy and more deviant. A *lawyer.*"

She looks up at me, twisting under my arm. "Lawyers shouldn't hang out with addicts."

"It's why I'm here to cure you, so when we're married and shit, I can go to work without worrying about you."

She tenses under my arm and my heart clenches, wondering why the fuck I said that. And what she's going to say to it.

She ducks under my arm and stands in front of me, eyes meeting mine. Even lined with red and smeared with her stupid eyeliner, the aqua blue and green of her eyes is mesmerizing.

"Alex." Her brow furrows as she stares up at me, sun streaming in through the window at her back. We're standing at the foot of her bed, the green comforter halfway on the floor from when she rolled out of bed a few minutes ago. "You don't have to do this."

I glance at the messy sheets, imagine they're still warm from her body. I think of how she felt against me all night.

"I do, though."

She puts her hands on her hips. "You don't. This isn't your problem."

I grit my teeth, curl my hands into fists. How many times do I have to tell her that she is exactly my problem?

"Zara. I'm not leaving. Not until you're better."

"That's not fair. This is my apartment. You have no fucking right to be here."

"Haven't you heard, beautiful? Life isn't fair."

She rolls her eyes. "Fuck you, Alex."

"Whatever." I turn away from her to head back into the kitchen. This isn't up for debate. I'm not leaving.

She grabs my arm though, yanks me around. "Don't be an asshole." I know she knows what she's doing because her eyes flash with that last word, and her pink lips turn up into a smile as she bats her lashes at me.

"Zara. Don't do this."

"I want you to leave. I'm not the only one with a problem, you know. That temper you've got? Fucking ridiculous. Why don't you work on yourself before you—"

I feel that temper rising. My body gets hot all over, my chest, especially. My pulse is flying, and I want to explode. "I'm not the one with the fucking problem, Zara!" I pull out of her grip, flinging her arm off me. "You are! You're the one getting high every damn day, you're the one fucking my best friend. You're the one with the fucking drug dealer who is worried about you!" I lean down close to her. "You are the addict. You are the fucking problem. I'm not fucking up my life. You fucking are!"

She's still gripping my arm, glaring up at me.

"Let go of me, Za."

She only squeezes my arm harder, her nails digging into my skin. She steps closer, until I can feel her body heat. Smell her scent. "Get the fuck out of my house."

I bite my tongue. "Let go of me."

She doesn't.

We both know I could shove her away if I wanted to, but I think she expects that, so I just slide my hands into the pockets of my shorts and glare at her.

"You don't want to let me into your brain, you clearly hate mine, so what the fuck are we doing?" she spits at me.

"Shut the fuck up and let me out of this fucking room."

She tips her head back and laughs and I want to wrap my fingers around her pale fucking throat. "I will," she says, dipping her chin down to glare at me, "as soon as you agree to leave." She lets go of me, and her words venomous when she says, "If you don't let me go, you see this fucking scar?" She pulls up my shirt she's wearing, points at those scars on her thighs. The ones I've been too scared to ask about. "If you don't leave, I'll tell everyone you did that. Now, get the fuck out."

"What the hell happened?" I ask her, because now is the time, above all others. Now is the fucking time, when she blackmails me with them. I take a step closer to her and see some of the defiance leave her eyes. She's tall, but I've got close to a fucking foot on her. "Tell me how you really got them."

She drops the shirt over her thighs. "You never noticed. You never fucking cared."

Stupid. For a smart girl, she can be so fucking stupid. "No." I grab her shirt—my shirt—and spin her around, so she's against the wall. Her breath leaves her in a rush and rage colors her face as she grabs my hand, but I don't let go of her. "Don't put that on me. I've cared about you from day fucking one. Way more than you ever cared about yourself. I've noticed everything about you. The scar on your thighs. The one on your hip." She gasps at that. "Now, you can tell me how you really got them, or you can keep that shit to yourself, but we aren't discussing me. I love you, Zara, and I always fucking have. That's not up for debate and neither is me leaving."

Roughly, I let her go and step back.

"And don't even think about running. I swear to God, Zara, if you do, your ass will be back in rehab so fucking fast you won't even know how the fuck it happened."

"Why would my mom trust you?" she spits at me, her eyes narrowed. "Why would she believe you over me?"

"I got Kylie to trust me, didn't I? Kylie fucking Jones, and I can guarantee you we do not have a damn thing in common. Don't test me, Zara. Don't fucking test me, because I'll come out on top every time."

41

Zara

I PACE around the living room, Alex is sitting at the table with his back to me, his feet propped up on the chair beside him, his phone in his hand.

Fucking asshole.

He's just a fucking asshole.

There's no more daylight outside of the open blinds in the living room, and I don't know how the fuck the day has passed like this, in fucking silent rage, but it sure as shit has. He made lunch, burgers without buns because we didn't have fucking bread, and frozen French fries. I ate none of it and ordered dinner. Chinese.

Didn't eat that either, even though the take-out bags are still on the kitchen table and it smells damn good.

But fuck him.

Fuck his food, too.

I took a shower, checked under the vent in the bathroom, but he stole my shit from there too. He has no idea how much money he's flushed down the fucking toilet, or wherever he put it. He doesn't care either, because the asshole doesn't work anyway and will never have to. He's made out of God money, which is almost hilarious.

I want to needle him about his parents and their divorce and the headlines in North Carolina's local news about his father having an affair with dozens of women, but I also don't want to listen to his stupid voice.

I know, logically, that part of my irritation stems from the fact I'm off Adderall for the first time in weeks, maybe even months. I glance at the fridge, think about opening the freezer and swigging down some coconut rum, but I know he'll start bitching about it and I don't have the energy to deal with him.

Speaking of energy, my fucking headache would probably go away if I drank coffee.

I march past him, flicking my braids over my shoulder and pulling out the coffee and the filter from the cabinet. I can feel his eyes on me, but I don't say shit as I fill up the machine, measure out the grounds.

But when he says, "It's a little late for coffee, don't you think?" just as I start brewing a few cups, I spin around to face him.

He's got a stupidly cocky smirk on his stupid face and I want to punch him.

"Fuck off." I know it's a lame retort, but I don't care. "Am I not allowed caffeine now, huh? I mean, I know that shit is a drug too, but it seems no one gives a shit about that!" I throw up my hands, just raging now. It has very little to do with Alex and a lot to do with the fact that I want some legal meth in my system.

Goddammit. I guess it's a good thing I didn't do real meth, but it's all the fucking same, isn't it? One just has the government's approval and the other they can't make money from, so they throw you in jail for cheating them.

I realize my hands are shaking and I curl them into fists, turn away from Alex, staring at the coffee pot. It's moving too fucking slow.

"Zara…"

I refuse to turn around. I don't want to see him or his pity.

I don't want him to see my fingers shaking, or to know what he's doing to me. What I've done to myself.

My throat feels tight, and I'm so fucking pissed and just so…exhausted. I just want to be alone. I don't want to think about this, or him, or Eli, or any of it.

"Just go, Alex," I whisper, brushing the warm tears from my face with the sleeve of the hoodie I'm wearing even though I'm sweating right now, and I just want to tear something apart. I want to throw the coffee pot against the wall. I want to cut this fucking sweatshirt off me. "Just go." I take a shaky breath, listening to the end of the brew cycle, inhaling the scent of the coffee, but keeping my eyes closed tight. "Please go."

He doesn't say anything, and I know he won't listen but it's for his own good. I don't know what's going to happen with his mom, but I'm not her and he can't fucking save me. I'm not her, and him pretending I am, pretending he can fix me, is just going to ruin us both.

He needs to leave.

"Alex, I can't do this!" I shriek, burying my head in my hands. "I can't do this and I'm so fucking sorry but I—"

He's behind me, his fingers circling around my arm, but I yank back from him.

"No!" My voice comes out nearly broken and I hate it. "Don't touch me! Just fucking go!"

He grabs me again and I try to fight against him, jerking in his grip and twisting my body in his arms to try and strike him. Hit him, kick him, whatever I can. But he's got his arms wrapped around mine, pinning them to my sides, and it seems he expends no energy at all as he pulls me away from the kitchen counter, then slides his leg underneath one of mine and pulls up, causing me to lose my balance.

We hit the floor together, a solid thud throughout the

whole apartment that I'm sure the people below us could hear but I don't give a fuck about that at all.

His legs stretch out on either side of mine as he sits behind me, wrapping his arms around mine, my knees, too. He tugs me into his chest, and I start shaking, wanting to pull away. Wanting to run out of this apartment, down the steps, far away from here. Maybe even into that pool Rihanna Martinson drowned in. Alex's pool. Eli's pool.

I want to know what it feels like to drown.

I want to know what it feels like to feel nothing at all.

"Shh," he whispers against my ear as I shake in his arms, burying my head against my own knees. His body is strong and warm and comforting behind me and I fucking hate it. I hate it because I don't deserve it. I don't deserve him, and everything he's doing for me. The way he's putting his life on hold for mine. Even after everything I've done, he's still here.

"Shh," he says again, holding me tighter, trying to stop my shaking. "It's okay, princess."

It isn't okay. It'll never be okay. I'm not okay. I'm not fine.

I'm *not fine.*

I can't stop the tears from rolling down my cheeks and I hate that they're here, in his arms. I hate it, because this isn't where I want to be.

This isn't where I want to be. I don't deserve it.

Alex has a good heart.

Sometimes I think I was born without one. Just like Eli.

42

Zara

"WE NEED MORE ORANGE JUICE," Alex informs me as I sit in the passenger seat of his Jeep. It's Wednesday, and I begged him to take me outside.

A week and a half until Halloween and the weather feels like fall. His windows are cracked as we sit in the parking lot of the empty grocery store—apparently, no one comes for a shop at nine in the morning on hump day.

"Uh huh," I tell him, glancing down at my fresh pink polish, wiggling my toes in my sandals. I refused to get a pedicure mostly because I wanted to refuse anything Alex wanted to do.

The past few days I've downed a few pots of coffee with half-and-half, and not much else, and I'm still a raging bitch. But I finally did let Alex paint my nails in bed last night, and he didn't do a horrible job at it, either.

It was almost amusing to watch him use a cotton ball to dab at my skin when he went off track.

He sighs, turning to look at me, his phone in his hands as

he makes a list of shit we need. "You said the orange juice was helping."

I pat my stomach beneath the tight black t-shirt I'm wearing over my fitted black sweats. "My waistline doesn't like the sugar."

His eyes nearly bug out of his head. "You're fucking with me, right?" He flicks his gaze over my body and despite my general irritation with fucking life, I feel my core tighten.

The past few nights he's slept on the couch.

I considered making a run for it, but decided against it. Mainly because I just don't have the energy. I'm fucking exhausted, even though I've done fuck-all.

"No, I am *not* fucking with you."

"You're a stick."

My mouth falls open. "That's... Wow, that's probably the rudest fucking thing you've said about me." Then I tilt my head to the side, tap my finger against my chin, pretending to think. "Oh, wait. No. That must've been when you called me a fucking cunt."

He rolls his eyes and shoves his phone into the pocket of his sweats.

"Let's go," he says, ignoring my comment. He reaches for the door handle but turns to stare at me when he realizes I'm not moving.

"What now, Zara?" he asks, irritation in his words.

I just stare at him for a long moment, looking at the amber in his dark eyes. "Why are you doing this?"

He frowns. "You need help."

"You're not doing this for me."

He flinches, but just keeps staring at me. I can practically feel the tension in the Jeep, despite the fact the windows are down, and I can hear traffic from the main road behind us. It feels like we're in a warpath in here beside each other, and every little misstep is like detonating a fucking bomb.

"You're doing this for her. And I'm not her, Alex."

He keeps staring at me, and I feel that irritation pricking again, just under my skin. I want to get out and slam the door and call my mom myself and tell her to pick me up. But I have no doubt Alex would be on her ass in a minute if I did that.

Finally, he just gets out without a word, slamming his door nearly as hard as I slam mine.

43

Zara

THINGS GET LESS tense that night.

We play Uno. I win. Three times in a row. Alex gets pissed, but he laughs too, and it just—shit, I don't know.

It feels good to see him laugh. To not be fighting with him. And as it gets later and the exhaustion wears on me, I invite him into my room. My bed.

And he comes.

"Why did you start?" he asks me after he's curled up around me, my back to his chest in the dark. There's an empty glass of orange juice on my nightstand, and I'm still feeling edgy and tired all at once, but I'm sober.

And Alex is here.

For the first time since he's been here, I'm kind of *happy* about it. My favorite times with him were when we weren't fighting. When we could just be together without the drama and the bullshit. That's what this feels like. Peaceful. I don't think I realized how much I craved that until now.

But at his question, I just close my eyes, tucking my hands under my pillow. I know what he's asking. "Because I was weird." That is, truly, the simplest explanation. The more in-depth one? I don't have the energy for that.

But his lips find my neck, just above the t-shirt of his that I'm wearing, and it sends chills down my spine, the good kind. And yeah, it makes my thighs clench together, and yeah, I want to turn around and kiss him, too, but more than that... more than that, that gentle touch makes me feel safe.

Just like he's always made me feel. Safe. Loved.

"You're not weird, princess," Alex says against my skin.

There's a pain in my chest, and I feel almost paralyzed. By guilt, maybe. Or grief for things that haven't even happened yet. All of this all might end. Because I'm not coming out of this clean.

"I am," I tell him, even though I know this kind of argument never works out well, so I quickly add, "It doesn't matter, anyway. Why I started."

His arms are locked around my torso and he squeezes me tightly. It feels so damn good, and I don't deserve it.

"You don't have to talk about it," he tells me, his breath on my skin. "But if you want to, I'm here."

God, I don't deserve you.

"It's just..." I trail off, trying to think about the reason for the first time. I mean, it's simple enough, really, but it's also so complicated. I snorted a hydrocodone through a dollar bill one night at my best friend's house, when I was fifteen. I'd only ever drank before that moment. I'd never even smoked pot.

My friend was older than me. Seventeen, but she was nice, and her mom was always gone, and boys loved her, and I wanted that.

So, when we had a sleepover, and she invited some guys over and they were all snorting shit and smoking pot and drinking, I did too.

Everything just kind of spiraled after that. My home life wasn't bad. Mom was a huge flirt and not very faithful, and I didn't talk to my dad, but I was taken care of. No one beat me. No one molested me. No one raped me. Even the older guys my friend had over, they were nice and respectful for the most part. I slept with one, eventually, when I was high, and it was good, and he treated me well.

"It's just I've always thought something was wrong with my brain. I was always awkward and shy, and people always said how quiet I was. Pretty, but quiet. I heard that so many times and it was annoying."

I know that probably doesn't make sense. I know Alex was probably waiting for some huge traumatic moment, but it wasn't like that.

"I wasn't comfortable in my own skin. I tried downers first." The hydrocodone became a little bit of a habit. "But then I discovered uppers." Adderall, specifically, which didn't seem so bad because it was legal, even if it wasn't legal for me. "And I was an entirely new person. I was shiny and loud and giddy and happy, and I wasn't anxious, and I could party and socialize like a normal fucking person, and boys liked me better for it."

And I wanted boys to like me. I wanted them to like me for the attention, because while Mom wasn't neglectful, she was gone a lot and my dad…well, he ended up leaving. Obviously, I have daddy issues, but I didn't recognize that then, and even if I had, I was a teenage girl. I was left alone a lot and I wanted attention. My stepfathers were decent human beings, but they were enamored with my mother and not so into the idea of being fathers at all.

"I went to the doctor, trying to get my own prescription for Adderall, but I didn't prepare for that visit well enough because they didn't diagnose me with ADHD. They diagnosed me with anxiety." I laugh a little, and Alex squeezes me tighter. I open my eyes, staring into the darkness of my room. "They prescribed me Xanax, which I found to be a great comedown for the Addie."

"Anyway, it all kind of got fucked up in spring." My throat tightens as I realize I never really talked about this with him. I made a joke about rehab, and that was all I ever said about it. I clear my throat, swallow down my nerves. "I overdosed at a party on fucking Vicodin. I wanted something different and the end of the semester, working toward my stupid philosophy degree had become stressful because I wasn't going to class and shit."

Alex kisses my neck again and I keep talking. "I probably didn't need the Narcan but one of my friends called 911 anyway, and they administered it and my friend called my mom and...well, here I am."

Alex's lips are warm and soft against my skin and I let my eyes flutter closed, falling into his warmth. Into his goodness.

"I'm glad you're here," he finally says. "It sucks it happened that way, but I'm glad you're here."

"Me too." The words come out without thought. I don't think about them at all. They're just true.

"You mean that?" Alex asks, hope in his words.

"Yeah. I mean it."

"What comes after this?" he asks next, and there's hope there, too, but something else in the way his words are so quiet. Lower than a whisper. Almost as if he's asking himself and not me, which might be the smarter thing to do because fuck if I know what comes next.

I turn in his arms so I'm facing him. From the moon shining through my curtains, I can make out his dark eyes, his beautiful mouth. The worry on his brow.

I trail one hand over his bicep, and his hand finds my waist, clamping down on it as if he can keep me forever. As if this week isn't just a fantasy. As if it's something real.

Is it real?

I don't know.

I don't have any idea what this shit is between us anymore.

"What do you think?" I ask him instead of saying any of those things.

He slides his hand under my shirt and it's so warm against my skin. I keep trailing my finger up the veins of his arm, the hard muscle beneath his soft skin.

"I think I want to keep you," he says with a faint trace of a smile. "I think I want to keep you and I think I don't ever want to let you go, Zara Rose."

There are so many things I could say. What about this? What about that? What about everything?

But I don't say any of them, because then he'd ask *me* questions, too, and I don't want to think about the answers. For one of the first times in my life, I just want this moment.

He moves his hand from under my shirt and cups my cheek instead. His hands are so big, it nearly covers my entire face which makes me smile. He brushes his thumb over my bottom lip.

"What do you think about that?" he asks me, and I stop skimming his arm with my fingers and instead rest my hand on his back, scooting closer to him in my bed.

"I think I like that idea a lot," I admit.

"Really?" He sounds surprised, and I guess I can't blame him.

"You really want me?" I counter. "After everything I did? Everything you know about me?"

He still has his thumb over my mouth, and he doesn't move away from me. He doesn't run, even though bringing up all the ways I've wronged him gives him every reason to.

He's not like Eli. He admitted as much to me before. He doesn't like to watch me with other guys. He doesn't want to share me. But he's seen all of that, seen me at my worst, and he still wants me? It's almost hard to fathom.

"Yeah," he says, his voice kind of hoarse. "I do." I hear him swallow, and he pushes his hand back, through my hair.

"Why are you so good to me after all the shit I've done?"

I hear him swallow. "I could ask the same of you." This time, *he* clears this throat. "I'm sorry too, you know. For how I always get so angry, and not sticking up for you with my dad. But fuck him, Zara." His eyes are shining in the dark. "I mean it. Fuck him, and fuck me, too. I promise I'm going to work on my own shit, too. I promise you, princess. I'm sorry for all of it." He takes a deep breath. "We've all made mistakes, Zara. It's called being human."

I laugh, shaking my head as he strokes my hair. "I think I've done a little more than make mistakes."

"Yeah, maybe." He smiles at me, his white teeth visible even in the dark. "But I see everything you could be. Everything you already are, even if you don't know it yet. I see more than what you want people to see, Zara. I see past your bullshit, and that's what I want. What you really are."

"What if you're wrong?" My mouth is dry, my stomach fluttering as I meet his gaze. "What if I'm not any of the good things you think you see? What if I'm just as wrong as I look?"

He smiles. "You don't look wrong. In fact," he bites his lip, eyes dipping down to my chest even though he can barely see me in the dark, under the covers, "you look really fucking right."

I roll my eyes, smiling despite myself. "You know what I mean. What if I'm just a druggie whore? What if I'm not going anywhere with my life? You know I'm a philosophy major. Like, what the—"

"Yeah," he interrupts me, "I never fucking asked. What is it you intended to do with that degree?" There's a teasing edge to his voice that makes me laugh.

The fact we never talked about these things, it's almost funny. Almost, but it's just how we are. Or were.

I shrug, and his hand goes from my hair to my back and he pulls me closer, rolling onto his back so my head is against his chest. I curl up around him, arm stretched over his torso as he keeps stroking my hair, gripping my arm with one hand.

"I just liked the idea of Stoicism," I admit. "A teacher touched on it in history class, back in high school. I liked the idea of focusing only on what we can control. Mainly, how we react to shit. And how life is short, how we can't count on a long one or even a good one." I shrug against him. "Obviously, I suck at applying any tenets of Stoicism to my own life, but I like the concept."

Alex laughs, his chest rumbling against me. "Okay, so, if you could do anything in the world, what would you do?"

"Drugs," I deadpan.

He tenses beneath me, his hand on my arm tightening.

I laugh, flicking his chest playfully. "I'm joking."

He exhales, like a lover putting up with my bullshit solely because he loves me.

"I'd like to help people, I guess. When I'm done helping myself. I'd like to help people who feel uncomfortable in their own skin feel a little better. Without drugs," I add quickly, in case he has any ideas on exactly what it is I want to do. I do not want to be a dealer like Jax. "I'd like to write a book about Stoicism one day, maybe even how addicts could apply the teachings to their own life. Obviously, I've got no idea how to do that because here I am with you right now but…" I trail off, drumming my fingers against his skin. "I don't know. I never gave much thought to my future, beyond the next party." It feels cathartic, like a release, having this conversation with him, like I did with Jax.

It feels good confiding in Alex, I realize.

He plays with my hair and breathes evenly beneath my arm. I wonder if he's going to fall asleep, or if he just doesn't know what to say. I start to wonder if I've shared too much. If this bonding we've done today is more than we should have. If I've fucked this up all the more.

"What do you want to do?" I ask him softly, not quite wanting to be alone yet. "I mean, I know you want to go to law school. But what is it you really want?" If he falls asleep and I don't, it'll feel that way. Like I'm alone. And as exhausted as my body feels, my mind is still wired.

"Yeah, well. I never told you but I don't actually want to go to law school."

I should be surprised, I guess, but I'm not. Alex flies off the handle too easily. He'd make a horrible lawyer.

"I want to open up a gym," he admits, his voice a whisper. "I've never told anyone that, but I want to open up a gym and I wouldn't mind running a camp too. For kids. Or maybe teenagers. Not something pretentious, like the shit I went to. Something for kids who might not be able to afford it. Kids with special needs, maybe, or shitty home lives. I don't know. Maybe that's just a pipe dream considering I'm not exactly an upstanding citizen." He laughs, but it's definitely lacking in humor. "Anyway, I just know that working out gives me an outlet, and I want kids to have that, too."

We're both quiet a moment. I could picture Alex doing that. He knows he has anger issues, knows he needs to work on them, and if he could help other people do the same, I think he'd be good at that. If he gets his shit under control like he said he will.

"Maybe we could open up a business together," he tells me, and my stomach drops. "We could have the gym, and you could counsel people in the wisdom of Stoicism, and I could run a camp in our backyard, because it'll be fucking huge. I like the outdoors far better than anything inside, and you'd learn to like it, too, if you don't already." He kisses me again, apparently unaware that I'm having a mini heart attack.

My limbs are all tingly and I kind of feel like I'm floating. The idea of him being with me past college, past this week even, is unfathomable. And I don't like it. People always leave.

"Too soon?" he asks me. His tone is light, but I hear the worry in it, too.

"No, it's just…" It's just you're going to leave me. No one

ever stays. Good marriages and never-ending romance don't exist. "I don't think you mean it."

He pauses his gentle strokes of my hair, just for a beat. "Why?"

People always leave. My dad. My mom, to all of her husbands. I can't recall a single friendship I've had that's lasted the test of time, or a move, or a major life event. Usually, it's my fault. I don't keep in touch. I'm not a victim in that regard, but still, that's life. That's how it happens for me.

"Your parents are not doing well," I point out. "Mine are divorced. My mom is on her fourth marriage."

His hand trails down over the nape of my neck, and again, he turns over, unsettling my comfortable position against his chest. Then we're lying on our sides, facing one another again, and he grabs my hand between us, his fingers threading through mine.

"We're not them." His voice is almost stern. "We don't have to repeat our parents' mistakes. I sure as shit will be nothing like my father. Or your father."

My heart feels heavy, and I feel tears prick behind my eyes, but I force them back.

"You think I'll leave you because he left you. You think you'll leave me because your mother leaves. But you're not like that, and I'm not like that."

"Alex," I say, my lip trembling, "I am exactly like that."

He shakes his head, squeezing my hand. "I told you, Zara. I see you. I see what you can't. You aren't like that. Not at your core. Not in your heart. You're so much more. You have scars, like we all do, and yeah, you're pretty damn chaotic and wild and kind of insane." He smiles, and I do too, even though my lip is still trembling. "But you are so beautiful, too. So fucking beautiful, inside and out. And you're funny and kind and your recklessness makes you interesting. And you deserve love, Zara. Whether you believe it or not, you deserve it."

I'm holding my breath as he leans in closer, his brow to mine.

"I see you. And I think you see me, too, yeah?"

I nod, biting my lip to hold back my tears. I do see him. He's nothing like the asshole jock he pretends to be. And I don't even know if he ever pretended to be that, or if his temper just gets the best of him sometimes like my loneliness and awkwardness and need to be loved gets the best of me.

"And call me crazy, which I know is usually your thing, but I'm pretty damn sure I'm falling in love with you all over again."

I can't breathe. He picks his head up, presses his warm, soft lips to mine. It's a gentle kiss, but when he runs his tongue over the seam of my mouth and I open for him, it changes. It's not rough or hard but it's possessive.

He lets go of my hand, pushes my shoulder so I'm lying on my back. Not breaking away from our kiss, he positions himself on top of me, hands on either side of my head, knees either side of my hips.

His tongue swirls around mine, and I slide my hands over his back, feeling his strength, his hot, smooth skin.

"Fuck that," he says against my mouth, pulling away for a second. "I know I'm falling in love with you. All fucking over again." He kisses me again, one hand going to the waistband of my shorts. He yanks them down and I move my hips to help him, pushing the material off with my foot when they get to my ankles.

He breaks away again, licks a line down the column of my throat as I arch my neck. He shoves up my shirt, biting at my stomach, running his hand over my breasts, first one, then the other.

And then he's between my thighs, lifting one leg over his shoulder, pushing my knee to the side with the other hand, spreading me wide.

"Alex," I murmur, running my fingers through his hair.

His breath is against my pussy. "Shh." His hand trails up from my knee to my inner thigh. And then he runs his tongue up my slit and I gasp. It's the first physical thing, aside from anger and frustration and exhaustion, that I've felt in days.

"You like that, princess?" he asks me, his words sending shivers down my spine.

I can only murmur my answer because he doesn't wait for one. Instead, he flicks his tongue over my clit, and then his hand leaves my thigh and he pushes two fingers inside of me. My grip on his hair tightens as he fingers me, licks me, fucking lavishes me.

I'm a bundle of pent-up energy and nerves, and he knows exactly what I need.

His tongue works me faster as I get closer, his fingers, too, and when I come, I cry out his name, yanking on his hair so hard, I'm surprised he doesn't complain but, in the moment, I don't really care.

He doesn't stop until I'm gasping, nearly begging him to let me breathe. My chest rises and falls rapidly, my heart pounding so fast I can hear it in my head.

He gives me one last, slow lick that makes me squirm, and then he's crawling over my body, pushing down his shorts and tossing them on the floor. I can feel his cock against my thigh as he cradles my head in his hands, boxing me in beneath him, in what seems like a protective way.

Or maybe I just think that because I feel a rush of gratitude toward him. I feel high off that orgasm.

"You ready, princess?" he asks me, kissing my mouth. I taste myself on him and it drives me fucking wild.

I nod, not wanting to break our kiss.

He reaches down between us, guides his thick cock to my wet entrance. Then he pushes into me and my toes curl. I wrap my legs around his back as he slides all the way in, groaning.

"Fuck," he says through gritted teeth, his mouth still

against mine as he thrusts slowly in and out of me. "You are so damn tight."

I drag my nails lightly down his back. "Or maybe you're just really, really big."

He pauses, staring down at me, brushing a lock of hair from my eyes. "You think so?"

I nod, biting my lip.

"And how do you feel about having my really, *really* big dick inside of you?" he teases me, pulling halfway out.

"I—"

I don't get to finish because then he slams it back into me and the words turn into a moan as I bury my head against his shoulder.

"Yeah?" he asks. "I didn't hear you, princess. What was that?"

I wrap my legs tighter around him, gasping as he thrusts into me again, filling me up. "I—I—"

He fucks me harder, one hand going to my throat as he pulls back from me to stare down at me. "You what, baby?" He doesn't choke me, but that possessive touch around my neck makes me wetter, and I clench my muscles around his cock, and this time, he's the one groaning.

"Goddamn," he says through clenched teeth. "If you keep doing that this is going to end a lot sooner than I'd like."

I smile up at him and he leans down, kissing me with an open mouth.

"I fucking love you, Zara," he says against my mouth, then he licks my lips, down my chin, his fingers still around my throat.

My mind is spinning, and I don't know what to say. I don't know if he meant it or if he's just feeling really good or… "I love you, too."

He pauses, his eyes wide as he pulls back to look at me.

"Yeah?"

"Yeah."

And then he thrusts into me again and I'm lost in a wave of sensation. Not just my body. My mind is wandering. Did I mean that?

Did he?

His eyes close tight as he comes inside of me, groaning my name.

He's breathing hard and my legs loosen around him, my knees falling to the side as he comes to rest on top of me, still inside of me. He's heavy, and I can hardly breathe, but he wraps his arms around my back, holding me so tight I don't care if I can breathe or not. I don't want him to let go of me.

Slowly, he lifts his hips and slides out of me.

"Did you mean it?" he asks me after a moment, rolling off me and pulling me to his chest again. The inside of my thighs are sticky and even though he did all the work, I'm a sweaty fucking mess.

"Did you?" I counter. "You said it first."

He laughs, his body vibrating beneath me. "Clever girl."

"Well," I ask, spent and finally exhausted in body and mind, ready to drift off into sleep right here in his arms, "did you?"

He sighs, contentment in the sound. "Yeah." He laughs again, a deep, boyish chuckle that makes me feel good all over. "I did."

I swallow down my emotions. Down what might happen in the morning. At the end of this week. Next week. Next semester. When we graduate. I swallow all of that shit down and live in the moment.

"Me too. I meant it too."

He holds me closer, tighter, and I close my eyes, sighing in his arms.

"I'll always take care of you, princess. Not just this week. Not just while you deal with this shit. Always."

I don't know if I believe him, but I don't know if I care, either. In the moment, it's enough.

44

Zara

OUR WEEK ENDS EARLY, and I know Alex is torn about it.

Yesterday, Thursday, we went to see a movie. Some stupid action shit with a bunch of car chases and spectacular crashes and a loosely developed plotline that I couldn't give a damn about. But Alex liked it, and I liked sharing popcorn and cookie dough bites with him in the nearly empty theater.

We spent the day having sex and drinking orange juice and eating more bacon—I'm fucking sick of bacon—and then we fell asleep tangled up in each other all over again.

But this morning, his mom called, and she needs him to come to a meeting with her lawyer over some shit with his dad. The divorce is messy, and his dad is pissed because a divorced preacher isn't one that can really lead a church. At least, that's what Pastor Cardi thinks.

Alex tried to resolve the issue over the phone, but his mom was insistent.

He comes out of the bathroom, towel-drying his hair, steam billowing out after him. His jaw is clenched, and I see that familiar anger in the hard lines of his face, the furrow of his brow. He turns back, throws the towel on the counter of the bathroom and stares at me, another towel wrapped around his waist.

His abs are truly a thing to behold. If I had to become addicted to a part of his body, it would either be those, or his dick. Probably his dick, which I can see the outline of even beneath his towel, even though I think he's not hard right now. Considering we had sex just this morning, before we brushed our teeth or rolled out of bed, I'm not surprised.

But just thinking about having sex with him again gets me all worked up and I know he has to go so I tear my eyes away from him, looking at the three empty glasses on my nightstand instead. They're sticky around the top with residue from the orange juice, and I'm grateful he bought a few cartons of it last night after the movie.

I don't know if there's science behind OJ helping with addiction, but damn, it seems to be helping me.

"Look, Za, seriously, you can come with me. It won't be a big deal."

I keep staring at the empty glasses, my legs swinging off the bed, my hands in my lap. "It's okay," I assure him. "I'm having dinner with my mom tonight anyway. If I feel crappy, I'll stay with her." I mean, fat fucking chance, but maybe.

"I just hate leaving you like this."

I cross my legs at the ankle. If he had told me that a few days ago, I would have laughed in his face. Maybe given him the middle finger to make my point. But now? I hate him leaving me like this too. Full of warm-fuzzy feelings that I haven't felt from something other than drugs in a long, long time. Part of me is worried that he's the new addiction. That despite our declarations of love, mine was only because I was feeling high from his orgasm, and his was only because…I don't know. Maybe he meant it.

But then again, maybe he didn't. Maybe we didn't mean what we said at all. Maybe we aren't ready to love yet.

But despite knowing that, it doesn't stop my heart from aching at the thought of him walking out of my apartment today.

He tilts my chin up, forcing my gaze from the orange juice glasses to his big brown eyes. "Princess."

I swallow past the dryness in my throat, try to smile up at him, but it feels like it comes out more like a grimace.

"Yeah?"

"You promise you'll be good?"

I don't know if he means "good" as in, I won't do drugs or "good" as in, I'll be okay. Either way, I nod, his fingers still under my chin. "I promise." I smile again, and this time it feels more real. He's so damn hot, it's kind of easy to fake that smile.

He leans down and kisses me, like we do it all the time. Like it's nothing. Like my lips belong to him. And even though it feels commonplace, because it is, it's become natural for us to touch that way, it still leaves me breathless, especially as he runs his thumb over my bottom lip before he drops his hand to get dressed.

Don't leave, don't leave, don't leave.

My mind is screaming it, but I won't say it. It's true that I do have dinner with Mom, and it's a beautiful fall day. I can go outside, for a walk or a hike. I can even call Kylie if I start feeling too low. I can call him too, if I need to. He's already told me as much.

But it doesn't make it hurt any less when he throws his arms around me and picks me up in the doorway of my apartment after he's all packed and ready and smelling so damn good.

It doesn't hurt any less when he says, "I love you, princess," against my ear and kisses my neck and doesn't put me down until he's squeezed the fucking breath out my lungs.

And I tell him I love him, too. And maybe I do. *Maybe I do, I remind myself.*

I watch him from the doorway as he walks down the steps, his gym bag over his shoulder. When he turns back to wave at me, my stomach flutters as he runs back over, kisses me again, slinging an arm around my neck.

And I laugh as he leaves, for real this time, and I laugh again when he honks the horn of his Jeep and tosses his hand out the window.

And then he's gone. And the darkness settles in again. The loneliness.

My phone is still in my drawer beside my bed and I need to charge it and get in touch with Mom, but I kind of don't want to because it would be so easy to thumb through my texts and shoot Jax one. He'd probably deny me and I can't take that.

I shut the door to the apartment, lock it, and head off down the hall to the shower. It still smells like Alex. My entire room does, and it makes my heart hurt.

It's so fucking stupid. He promised he'd be back as soon as he could. Probably tomorrow, he said. If not, definitely the day after.

Promises, promises.

I can't keep them, but that doesn't mean he has the same problem.

I decide to fuck the shower and sink into a bubble bath instead, closing my eyes as I lie back against the tile.

The sound of the water makes me feel at peace. I think about the waves of the ocean, without thinking about that shitty beach party. I think about what it would be like to live at the coast with Alex. Maybe we could even have an outdoor part of our gym. Maybe I could be an example to young girls. Maybe he could help boys from broken home, and we could save lives instead of destroying our own.

Maybe Eli Addison will be a distant memory and the horrible things he and I have done won't come back to haunt me.

I let myself dream, just for a little while. Because when I open my eyes again, it'll all slip away and the reality of who I am and what I've done will come back to crush me.

I'm not even sure Jesus Christ himself would truly forgive someone like me. And Alex doesn't have the heart of the son of God, so I know he definitely won't. No matter what he says, I don't think he meant it.

He can't love me.

I'm too broken for that.

It was nice though. While it lasted, it was nice.

45

Zara

"YOU LOOK GREAT," Mom tells me, picking at her salad. "Less...tired," she finishes with, eyeing me as she drops her fork, giving up. I don't blame her. It's a fucking garden salad without dressing. At a restaurant in Falls Creek, just a little bit away from Caven, known for its pulled pork.

I think she picked the wrong place to diet at. Of course, Mom doesn't need to diet. She just does. She always has.

I look at my own burger that I've taken two bites out of. But my orange juice is drained, and even though Mom looked at me like I was high when I ordered it, it was damn good.

I play with the paper napkin in my lap. "Thanks."

She leans back in the rickety wooden chair, tilting her head as she eyes me. Her big blue eyes are full of something like suspicion, and if she accuses me of being on drugs right now, I might throw this napkin to the damn floor and walk right out.

But she doesn't.

She accuses me of something worse.

"Zara Rose Henderson," she chides me, but there's something playful in her words. She leans forward, her hand on the table, and I see her wedding ring glinting in the lights overhead, the gold band etched with roses, pretty on her slender, manicured fingers. "Are you in love?"

My mouth falls open, and I ball the napkin up in my hand. *What the actual fuck?*

She smiles, small little wrinkles pulling at the crease of her eyes. She tosses back her shiny blonde hair, sitting up straighter and giving me a self-satisfied smirk. "I knew it. You are." She sighs, blinking at me. "Well, go on. Who is he? God knows you've had to deal with a whole hoard of men from me, so I think I should at least get the lucky guy's name." She shrugs her shoulders, the tan sleeves of her silk blouse bunching up a little as she does. "Is it that boy you brought to the engagement party?" She narrows her eyes. "The one with the tattoos?"

I feel sick just thinking about him. "I'm not in love," I manage to say, way too fucking late.

She stares at me, a scowl on her face. "Come on, Zara. Don't lie to me. I'm your mother." She smiles, and it's genuine for once which is kind of weird since it's directed at me. All I've done the past few years is disappoint her. Probably get in the way of her love life. "And obviously, I know a thing or two about love. Or how to fuck it up."

My eyes go wide, jaw dropping. She just made a self-deprecating joke. She just said the F word. Is this my mother? Has she always been like this and I was just too high to see it?

I laugh, shaking my head a little, relaxing into my seat.

The waitress comes bustling over, glancing at our still-full plates. "Still workin' on that?"

My mom doesn't break eye contact with me, as if she's willing this moment to stick. "Yes," she says curtly, and I hear the waitress kind of huff at my mother's tone—and probably the fact that my mother looks a little like a bitch—but she walks away without another word.

"I know," Mom says suddenly, tapping her nails on the wooden table. We're tucked into a table in the corner of the restaurant, far from the door—Mom insisted, so none of her clients would "recognize" her, which I had no words for—but she still leans in close to the table and whispers, "It's that really tall boy I saw you with at the grocery store. It's him, isn't it?"

I laugh a little, but I can't even manage a good denial. Despite the orange juice and the sex that I had and texting Alex and telling him I loved him, I'm still exhausted.

Or maybe all of those things are making me more exhausted, despite my mother's words about looking "less tired".

"He was hot, Zara," she says, leaning back in her seat. "Really tall, and really hot." She quirks her mouth to the side. "What was his name again?"

My cheeks are growing warm and I kind of want to start talking about him. I'm surprised she even remembers, but she's always been good at paying attention to me, even in her absences. But I'm glad she doesn't remember his name.

There's the article about him breaking that guy's nose on the field, and the shit about his dad in the papers. No, thanks.

Even though, between the two of us, *I'm* the fuck up, Mom wouldn't see it that way.

"It's not him, Mom," I lie, even though I'm desperate to gush about him. To talk about his thick hair and his dark eyes and God, he is so fucking tall. And how kind he is and what he wants to do with his life and how he's helping his mom and how he sounds kind of like a dick sometimes, but he actually has the most forgiving heart of anyone I've ever known.

Yeah. I want to say all that shit, but I don't say any of it. Besides, I still have to work out my own shit before I can think about having a stable, steady relationship with Alex Cardi. We might have said we loved each other, but that was in a sex-induced haze of lust.

I see you.

I hear his words in my head, and I can't stop the little smile on my lips. I avert my gaze from Mom, but she already saw it.

But then again.

Eli said those same words.

"Oh, hon," she says, her words a breathless sigh. "I wish you'd talk to me about him. Unless it was the tattooed boy. You can talk to me about him too though, you know?"

I flick my gaze up, my stomach twisting into knots thinking about Eli. Thinking about that night at the beach. But Mom must read something else in my expression because she says, "Zara, don't tell me you have feelings for him too."

"What?" I ask, taken aback. "No, I don't, I—"

"Two boys, Zara?"

My face flushes, and I feel uncomfortably warm even though I'm in jeans and a white tank top twisted into a knot, exposing the lower part of my waist. I pinch the thin material of my shirt between two fingers, fanning myself, and Mom grimaces.

"I'm sure only one of them really wants what's best for you. They can't both love you equally, Zara. And you probably can't love them both either." She sighs. "Two boys are trouble, hon. *Trust me.*"

"Mom, it's not like that."

She shrugs her narrow shoulders, tapping her nails again against the table beside her plate of salad. "I know things, Zara. It's why I'm the top agent in Monkey Junction."

I mean, I guess I can't argue with that stat, so I just keep quiet.

"Do they know each other?" she asks, quirking a brow.

"Mom, it isn't…" I trail off, glancing out the wooden blinds beside us. The sky has grown dark, and I take in the cars in the parking lot beyond the rocking chairs on the covered porch outside.

I blow out a steady breath, turn to face her again. I don't

love Eli. But I can't really tell her what happened between us, and Alex. I can't say all that shit. But I guess I could go about it in a roundabout way. See what she thinks of it all.

It wouldn't hurt to confide in Mom. Not everything, obviously, but getting a little advice couldn't hurt.

"Yeah," I tell her, straightening in my chair, elbows on the table, hands clasped together beside my barely touched burger. "They know each other."

"Are they friends?" she pries. There's no judgement in her eyes, and considering her marriage track record, I guess there wouldn't be.

"Yep." At least they used to be. Until me.

She shrugs. "Well, I might not know exactly what's going on, but speaking from experience, I can tell you this." She leans in closer and my heart pounds in my chest. "One of them doesn't want you, Zara. One of them only wants to see if he can take you away from the other. That's part of the appeal." She levels me with her gaze, and I feel her next words like an arrow to the heart. "Once he gets you, he'll drop you, and it'll hurt like hell when he does."

▼

Alex: **I miss you.**

Alex: **A lot.**

Alex: **You okay, princess?**

I've stared at Alex's texts for half an hour, thinking about Mom's words. I should've confided in her long before this shit show. I don't know what's going on with Eli and Alex because I didn't have the nerve to ask him, but I guess that's another thing we'll have to clear up when he gets back.

Me: **I'm good. Miss you too.**

I exhale deeply, about to toss my phone back in the drawer of my nightstand when another text comes in.

My stomach drops, and I sit up in bed, flinging my covers off.

It's from Eli.

Him: **Be there in ten.**

That was eight minutes ago.

Fuck.

Fuck, fuck, fuck.

For a second, I think about him fucking me so hard at the beach house, how he wouldn't stop. How he liked *really* hurting me.

I think about it, and cold fear washes over me. But I'm not that girl anymore. I'm not afraid. I'm going to deal with his ass once and for fucking all, and then I'll be done with him. I'll be done.

I sigh, looking down at what I'm wearing. I'm in short black shorts, a loose pink tank that barely covers my damn tits and considering I don't have a lot of those to begin with, that's saying something.

I open my closet door to grab a hoodie when I hear knocking at the door.

My phone starts vibrating in my hand. Eli is calling.

Shit, shit, *shit.*

I run a trembling hand through my wavy hair, taking a deep breath as my heart pounds a nervous rhythm in my chest.

It'll be okay.

I need to end this anyway.

It's not like he's going to fucking kill me or something. Eli might be crazy but he's not *actually* a psychopath, I tell myself like I might believe it.

My phone starts buzzing again, I toss it on the bed, and slam my closet door closed. Fuck the hoodie.

"I'm coming!" I call out as he starts beating on the door again. I glance out the open blinds in the living room. It's pitch-black outside. The clock on the stove says it's eleven.

And beside it, on the counter, are all of the liquor bottles I lined up earlier. Half a dozen.

I didn't take a single fucking sip. I was planning on throwing them out in the morning.

Instead of alcohol, I finished another carton of orange juice.

I'm different.

I'm stronger.

I can do this.

I get to the door just as Eli starts hammering away at it again. I bet he thinks I'm high.

Surprise, surprise. This might be one of our first sober conversations.

I unlock the door, throw it open, the cool October air rushing in.

He cocks his head at me, phone in his hand. Arching a dark brow, he glances behind me and asks, "You're alone?"

A shiver of something like fear runs through me at those words, and at the way he looks me up and down. The way my nipples harden with the cold and I want to cover myself and close the door and tell him I'm not doing this right now.

"I've missed you so much." He slips his hands into the pockets of his black hoodie. "I've been meaning to tell you... I'm so sorry."

I laugh, not moving from the doorway. "Thanks for the apology. But things are done between us. *We're done.* You're insane, and you lied to me, and you betrayed me." I jerk my chin, indicating the stairwell at his back. "We through now?"

He smiles at me and I feel my knees going weak, my heart pounding so hard in my chest.

Then he says, "I've got some more things to say," and he shoves past me, *hard*, checking me with his shoulder.

I don't move from the doorway, the door still open. "Eli." I hate the way my voice shakes. "Get out right now."

He doesn't even turn around to look at me. He just says,

"Close the fucking door, Zara, or this is going to get really messy." His words scare me.

My hands are trembling. I think about running. But then he says, "It'll only take a second, okay?" still without looking at me.

Just a second.

I can do a second, and then he'll be gone from my life for good.

Slowly, I shut the door. Lock it back.

When I turn around, he's right there. His eyes are on mine like he's looking for something, trying to read me. Maybe trying to see if I'm fucked up.

I offer him a small smile that I don't feel. My mind is racing, but I feel bold, too. Stronger. Now I'm facing the consequences of my own actions, which might be a first for me. This time though, there's no way out. There's no pill or shot or high to chase. This time, I've got to deal with this shit all by myself.

And I will. I'll deal with him.

"I've missed you," he says again. He reaches a hand out to my face and his touch feels electric, like it did that very first time he came alone to my apartment.

The memory makes my face heat and he must see it because he grabs my chin and tilts my head up when I try to avert my eyes.

I can smell him. That delicious coconut and citrus scent. It reminds me of the sea.

"What are you thinking?" he asks me.

I arch a brow, try to turn my head from his hand but he holds tighter. "About the last time I saw you," I admit. About how you hurt me. How you fucked me over.

"Are you still mad at me?" he asks, incredulous, like he doesn't believe it. Like he doesn't deserve my anger.

I grab his wrist, try to pry his hand off my face. He just

tightens his grip, painfully, and I dig my nails into his skin, trailing up over the tattoos on his hand.

"Let go of me."

He does. Shocking the shit out of me, he drops his hand and looks down and I exhale a silent sigh of relief. Maybe this won't go how I think it will. Maybe this will be much better. Maybe he came here to tell me he missed me, but he realizes we are not good together. That we need to cut each other off for good.

But instead of doing any of that, he grabs my arm, and yanks me into the kitchen, shoving me against the counter where my back hits a bottle of alcohol that slides into another, thankfully *not* falling to the floor.

He takes hold of both of my arms, leans down close, and I must be fucking paralyzed with nerves because aside from a small gasp that escaped my mouth when he shoved me in here, I say nothing. Do nothing.

"What's going on, Zara?" he asks me, the mint of his breath caressing my mouth. "You don't seem very happy to see me."

"I—"

He clamps his hand over my mouth, his eyes narrowing. "You've let this go a little far, huh, Za?"

"Eli." The word is muffled beneath his hand, and I hate that his name is shaky on my lips, but I hate that I let him in even more. I shouldn't have done this. He has the power to ruin me and we both know it.

He drops his hand from my mouth.

"Get off of me," I snarl at him.

He laughs, grips my arm tighter, but then, throwing me off again, he steps away, toward the door.

I back up, still against the counter but moving down, toward the fridge. Toward my room.

He doesn't move.

He's standing between me and the door and unless I want to jump out the window, he knows he has me trapped.

"What are you talking about? Going a little far?" If I run, if I try to attack him, he's just going to feed on my fear. Maybe I can talk my way out of this.

He smiles at me, that charming smile I've watched him flash dozens of times, never knowing he was actually a fucking monster.

"I admire your effort, baby girl, but I know you don't really want him. And now you let him stay the week with you? Let him try to sober you up?" There's real anger in those questions. It makes me feel physically sick. I didn't think he actually cared. I thought this was all a game. A game for a boy with strange tastes. But he's mad?

"I don't know what—"

"I think you should stop playing games now, Zara."

But now it's my turn to be angry. The rage flushes white hot through me, and that rush of irritation that I've felt all week comes back in full force. I push off the counter, turn fully to face him. His eyes light up with amusement because he wants this fight.

"You don't get to do this," I tell him, pointing his way. "You fucked this all up!"

He steps forward, but I don't falter, even as he cocks his head, his expression still full of amusement as he listens to me.

"You don't get to come back here after you fucking fucked me over. And besides, I'm fucking done with you. I am so done with you."

"You wanted me." His tone is plain, his words simple. "You still do."

I close my eyes tight, trying to think. To breathe. Dammit, I really want some more orange juice. Or, more than that, I want to chug down one of these damn bottles beside me.

"Come on, baby girl, this was the plan all along." His

voice is soothing and when I open my eyes, he's a foot from me.

I try to swallow down my rage, my confusion. My fear. "What the fuck are you talking about?"

He swipes his hand over the counter, sending all the bottles of alcohol I have lined up crashing to the floor, glass bursting into pieces. But he doesn't stop there. The glass crunches under his shoes as he steps toward me, yanking me by the collar of my shirt, my bare feet on the broken glass, sharp pain stinging under the arch of one foot. I whimper but he doesn't seem to care. He doesn't let go and he doesn't look down.

"I gave you space," he breathes down close to me. "I let you breathe. I let you...live. I didn't know all this time you wanted me to take it away from you."

I grab his hand, digging my nails into his skin. But he suddenly sweeps his leg behind mine, knocking me off my feet. I fall against the glass, shards digging into my back. My lip trembles, tears springing to my eyes as he kneels down, too, still fisting my shirt.

"I didn't know you wanted me to suffocate you, Zara. I didn't know you wanted me to kill you. Why didn't you just fucking ask?"

He leans down close, and my head is inches from the glass that's currently slicing into my back, only his grip on my tank top holding me up, and my own core muscles, straining.

"Now I know, Zara." He runs his tongue over my mouth. "Now I know, and I won't ever fucking forget it. You want to be treated like a stupid bitch without a brain?" He yanks me up until my forehead is pressed against his. "I can do that for you." He kisses me but I clamp my lips closed.

Fuck him.

"The thing about Alex, baby? He shows his crazy. But me? I like to hide mine. I like the fear in your eyes right now because you once thought I was something better. You once thought I was the good one." He laughs, pulling on my lip with his teeth. "With the three of us? There's no such thing." He lowers me down onto the glass, pinning me down with his hand on my chest. "You should've known better, Za."

The glass digs into my scalp, my back, my thighs. The pain is burning, stinging, sharp. "Let me up." My voice is little more than a whimper.

Eli laughs, pressing me further into the ground. "I don't think so, baby girl. Not yet. Not until you remember what it was like."

I frown, the pain momentarily numbed with my confusion. "Remember what what was like—"

"I know you're stupid but you're not that fucking stupid, Zara. Remember what it was like when I met you. What it was like when you were all over me and you wanted to do anything I asked. When you let me hold you down in that pool? When you agreed to this, Zara."

My stomach twists. The pain of the glass makes my eyes water. "But this is…this is all wrong, Eli. You know this is all wrong."

His hand shifts to my throat. "Yeah. You fucking knew that, too, huh? But you wanted to experience everything, didn't you, baby girl?"

"You fucked me over. You fucking fucked me over and—"

"I gave you an out."

"No. No. Fuck you. You have no right. No fucking right!" I try to scramble upright but glass lodges itself into my palm and I hiss between my teeth, Eli still pressing down on me.

"You think Alex is gonna treat you right, Za?" He switches his grip, jerking me up to my feet. My back is on fire, and I feel blood warm and wet on my palm. Eli's forest green eyes darken as he pulls me into him, glass crunching under his shoes, slicing into my feet. "You don't fucking know him like I do. And he doesn't know you."

"But I know you. I know you and I know you're a sick fuck, Eli Addison. Fuck you. Get out of my house."

"End things with him."

"No." My jaw clenches. "No. You're fucking sick, Eli. You're fucking sick and you need help——"

He slams me against the counter, then wraps both hands around my throat, fingers digging into my skin as he leans over me.

My heart is going to shoot out of my chest. Eli was always this quiet, simmering darkness. Always. It's why I was drawn to him. It's why I fucked with him in the first place.

But he was more than that. So much more.

He was *fucking insane.*

My mom's words echo in my head. "One of them doesn't want you, Zara."

"If you don't break up with him, I will kill you. He can't even stand watching someone else fuck you, Za. How's he going to put up with your bullshit?" His hands dig deeper into my throat, and my head starts to swim, brain desperate for oxygen. "Only I can do that, baby girl." He brushes his lips over mine. "But you know what? I kind of like you like this. Stealing your breath." He turns his cheek against my mouth. "I kind of like feeling nothing where your life should be."

I open my mouth, but nothing comes out. I dig my nails into his arms, and he laughs as he turns back to me.

I'm going to die.

He's going to kill me.

And in this moment, something occurs to me, and I don't know if it's a gift from God, right before I take my last breath, or if I really am stupid, but I can't stop the thought that blares in my head like a warning too late. *Rihanna Martinson didn't drown. He killed her. I don't know how or why or when, but he did it.*

I dig my nails in deep enough to draw blood, but his smile just widens.

"You gonna break up with him, baby girl?"

No. No I'm fucking not. But I'm not stupid. I'm not a stupid bitch. I nod my head.

He presses his nose to mine but doesn't let go. I feel myself sagging further against the counter, the blood leaving my head.

"And then you're gonna be mine to fuck, huh? Just mine?"

I nod again.

"Because no one else will fuck you like I can and you know that, don't you?"

My eyes flutter closed but I still nod.

"And you're never going to run from me again, right?"

Another weak nod.

He loosens his grip and I take a gulp of air, filling my lungs on a gasp. His fingers trail down my collar, splayed against my skin.

"You're so beautiful, baby girl."

I'm still taking in air, but the sting in my back, the cuts on my feet, it's shooting fire through my body.

"Eli," I say, my voice hoarse. "I need..."

His eyes rake over my body before coming back to rest on my face. "Me," he finishes, "you need me." His mouth lands on mine, his tongue sweeping past my lips.

"No," I whimper around his mouth, "it hurts..."

He pulls back, staring at me, and then a smile curves on his lips. He reaches into his hoodie pocket, letting go of me.

I exhale, but then he holds up a baggie with something off-white in it, and a lighter in one hand. He reaches into his other pocket, murmuring to himself.

"Ah. Yes." He pulls out a syringe. "I've got something to help you, baby girl. I just need a spoon."

My mouth goes dry as Eli opens up a drawer, slams it closed. Opens another one. He pulls out a spoon, grinning at me as he sets the syringe down on the counter.

"Eli..."

He ignores me, dumps some of the powder into the spoon,

his movements sure. Steady. He sets the spoon down, grabs the syringe and fills it halfway with water from the sink, drops it into the spoon.

"Eli. No." I step back, the blood seeming to freeze in my veins. He wouldn't.

And that can't be...

He flicks the lighter, heating the contents in the spoon to a liquid.

"Eli."

He just smiles wider, pulls something else from his pocket. A cotton ball.

He soaks up the heroin in the cotton, then plunges the syringe into the cotton, pulls it out and drops the cotton ball.

He turns to me, syringe in hand.

"No."

He wouldn't actually...

I take another step back. I'll never be able to run to the door before he gets there. I won't be able to stop him. Not by running away. Not by fighting back.

"Eli."

"Yeah, baby girl?" He advances toward me.

"No."

I back up into the wall that Kylie's room is on. But Kylie isn't home. And Alex is at the coast.

Eli grabs my arm.

"N-no." I try to snatch it back. "Why would you want me to—"

"I want to give you the best high, Zara. Better than those little pills you've been doing. This will be like ecstasy, and not the fucking club drug, baby." He yanks my hand forward, places the needle over a blue vein, prominent against my pale, thin skin.

"This is the real thing, Za."

"No." I look into his eyes. But I don't see anything there. Nothing but mania. Insanity. Cruelty. "Eli. Look at me!"

"Careful, these veins are so delicate, baby girl."

I try to yank my hand again, but I feel it.

A pinch.

His smile widens as he plunges the needle in.

My mouth falls open, fear seizing me.

Fear. And something else.

My feet feel heavy beneath me. I hear the needle drop.

My breathing slows.

There's a warm blanket covering my body and Eli doesn't seem so bad. The glass in my feet, my back, none of that is so bad.

This is euphoria. This is...

I fall forward and Eli catches me. "That's it, baby girl."

Warmth spreads through my chest. My limbs. My toes. My face.

"That's it." He rubs my back, holding me close. "Does it feel good, baby?"

Good? This is more than good. This is...this is ecstasy.

"Does it feel good now?"

46

Eli

SHE'S SO BEAUTIFUL. In the passenger seat of the 370Z, her mouth open as she leans against the door, snoring softly. She's so damn beautiful.

The sun is coming up now and after holding her on the couch in her living room all night, I can say *that* was the best part of this entire fucking year.

Cleaning up the glass on the floor of her apartment, picking it out of the bottom of her feet and that sliver in her back that went through her shirt…not so great. Despite what she probably thinks, I didn't really want to hurt her.

I've never wanted that.

When I first laid eyes on her when Alex brought her to our house, I knew I'd do anything to get her. To keep her. To have her. She was exactly what I wanted, and unlike every other girl who tried to own me, who tried to get me to own them, she was content to do whatever the fuck she wanted to do.

And what she wanted was what I wanted too.

But she just didn't know it. She didn't know Alex wasn't the one for her.

And then Rihanna failed in getting Zara to dump him, and then she was on me. Rihanna wanted me, but I didn't fucking want her.

She was a means to an end.

But I dealt with Rihanna.

And I'll deal with Alex too.

As I turn into my driveway, Zara still snoring softly in the passenger seat, I know I've already dealt with the most important thing. I've already made sure she knows she's mine. That the time for games is over because I'm tired of watching everyone else fuck around with her. I got what I wanted, making Alex watch me fuck her, and now I'm done with that shit.

She's mine now.

47

Alex

IT'S Saturday morning before I get to her apartment.

Saturday morning, and the sun is almost up, but I drove as fast as I could. I tossed and turned in my bed at my parents' house after dealing with Mom's lawyers and Dad blowing up and walking out.

I tried to let it go. I told myself she might've just fallen asleep. I told myself that she's okay. That she's been exhausted. That I trust her, and she's fine.

But I couldn't sleep, and I don't exactly trust her, so I drove.

I run up the stairs to her apartment, wishing she had a fucking car so I could know if she was here. She won't answer her phone, hasn't answered my texts since she told me she missed me too.

And that was it.

I knock on her door, softly at first.

No one answers.

Kylie isn't here. I know, because I called her, too.

Nothing. No one comes to the door. I don't hear movement inside.

I knock again, louder this time. I wonder if her neighbors will come outside, but I hear music thumping from one of these apartments, so I'm not too worried about it. Fuck, even if they were all dead asleep, I don't give a shit.

I slam my hand so hard against the door the third time, it just fucking pops open.

What the fuck?

She would have locked it. If she was okay, if she was here, that door would be locked and even I couldn't have broken the lock by knocking on the door.

I step inside.

It's dark as shit, and I'm worried she's asleep and I'm going to scare the hell out of her, but she would have locked that door.

And I smell it then, when I step further inside, closing the door softly at my back.

I smell the sharp tang of alcohol, and my stomach sinks.

I feel sick, and I put my hands on my knees, closing my eyes as my stomach heaves. I swallow it all back down.

Opening my eyes, I try to get myself the fuck together.

It's just alcohol, I tell myself. It's just alcohol and that's okay. It could be worse. I should've taken those bottles, I should've dumped that shit out, but it could be worse. It could be worse and maybe she's just asleep in bed. Maybe she just drank too much and we can deal with that. We can fix that.

I flip on the light in the kitchen and blink, my eyes adjusting.

And then my head starts spinning.

There are bottles of alcohol lined up on the counter—thankfully, some still full—and there're no cups or shot glasses or anything that would indicate she had a party but there's something red on the floor.

My mouth goes dry as I step closer, squatting down to look.

There's an empty feeling in the pit of my stomach, the hairs on the back of my neck standing on end.

That looks like blood.

Just a drop, but what's worse is the floor is faintly wet, like it was just cleaned or...

I stand to my feet, the room spinning around me. I head to the little pantry, open up the door and grab the white trash can, yanking it out so I can see inside of it better as I flip the lid off.

I heave again, stepping back from the can.

There're broken bottles inside, and paper towels with more blood. And something else.

There's something else, almost hidden beneath a bloody paper towel, but not quite.

Not fucking quite.

There's a fucking needle in this trash can.

I can't think. I can't even hear anything but a loud ringing in my ears. I storm down to her room, screaming her name, kicking her door open and flicking on her light.

She fucking wouldn't.

She wouldn't.

She would never.

"Zara!"

I yank back her covers but she's not there.

She's not fucking here.

I GET HOME IN NO TIME. THE SUN IS AN ORANGE BLIP ON THE horizon, the air is cool when I hop out of my Jeep and slam the door shut. I barely notice any of it. I unlock the front door of the house, flick on the lights as I slam it closed.

My gaze goes to the stairs. I'm going to drag Eli's ass out of bed and he's going to help me look for her. I don't care that he's a sick fuck, I don't care that we aren't talking anymore. He's going to fucking help me.

I already called her mother, found her number online, but she didn't answer. She probably sleeps with her phone on silent like every other dumb fuck on this planet.

I debated calling the police, but I'm not sure that would help yet. Not yet.

I go to storm up the stairs, calling Eli's name, but then I freeze, something catching my eye down the hall and through the sliding glass doors in the kitchen.

The tiki torches are on, the soft underwater lights making the blue surface dance with the light breeze. And the sun is rising ever-so-slowly. All of that gives me enough light to see by, but I still don't believe it.

I take a step past the stairs, down the hall.

I feel like I'm walking through concrete. I feel like I'm going to faint. I feel like I won't make it to the end of the fucking hall.

There's no way.

Maybe I'm delirious because I didn't get any sleep. I'm seeing things because I'm so tired and dealing with Mom's shit and Dad's bullshit and thinking about Zara and feeling guilty for leaving her.

No, this can't be what I think it is.

That can't be her, lying on her back on a beach towel, stripped down to nothing but her underwear, her hands resting on her stomach.

And that can't be Eli, sitting beside her, his feet in the water as he stares at her.

That can't fucking be what I'm seeing.

I try to swallow but it's like my throat is made of sandpaper. My heart is slamming around so hard in my chest, it's actually aching. This isn't right.

None of this is right.

Did *she* go to *him*? Is that what this is?

But it's fucking not even six in the morning. And that alcohol, and the *fucking needle*...

I clench my hands into fists and walk down the hall, forcing my steps to be steady and even. Forcing myself not to run. I can't run.

I can't run.

I get to the sliding glass door and neither of them look up. I think I see Eli's mouth moving, like he's talking, but I can't hear what they're saying.

I realize there's a small, circular speaker next to Zara.

Music is playing.

I recognize it, because it's something I introduced Eli to.

Memory, the acoustic version by Dear Agony.

What the hell. What the hell. What the fucking hell.

I reach for the handle of the door, take another deep breath, but it doesn't help. It feels like all the oxygen has left my brain.

I pull the door open.

Eli stops talking, and he turns to look at me.

Zara picks her head up, frowning my way.

Then Eli's lips curve into a slow smile. For a moment, I'm frozen by that smile. It makes my stomach churn. I don't know what the fuck it means.

And then he says, "I was wondering how long it'd take you to get here."

And I fucking lose it.

48

Zara

EVERYTHING STILL FEELS STRANGELY warm and oddly
fuzzy, but I sit all the way up as Alex charges at Eli, knocking
them both over into the shallow end of the pool.

The creepy music that Eli put on for me is still playing and
I can only watch, transfixed as Alex and Eli both go under,
and then both pop back up.

I draw my knees into my chest, wrapping my arms around
myself. I'm shivering, my nose is running, and I know it's cold
but it's not *that* cold. I know I should yell at them, tell them to
stop. I know I should fucking do something, but I don't know
what to do.

I don't know what to do and my brain is still trying to
process what Eli did. The words he told me before Alex came
storming out here.

That he loved me.

That he was sorry.

That we couldn't do that again.

That he was going to take care of me.

I lift up my hand.

My veins are stark against my pale skin and there's a slight bruise already, where he injected me with…my brain can't hold a thought.

"You motherfucker." That's Alex's voice, and he's trying to push Eli under. He's trying to push him under the water as they wrestle in the shallow end, a tangle of arms and anger and water spraying on the surface. "You stupid motherfucker."

He doesn't even know. He doesn't even know what he did. He doesn't know.

Eli laughs. He just laughs, and it sends a chill down my spine. I pull my knees in closer, resting my chin on one.

Maybe they'll just kill each other. Maybe they'll just fucking kill each other and I can sleep again and go home and pretend none of this happened. Maybe their bodies will be at the bottom of this pool.

Eli steps back, shoving Alex off him. He backs up on the stairs, gripping the railing. The same one I was lying beside when he shoved me under water, holding me down.

Alex pulls his shirt over his head, throws it off to the side of the pool, opposite me. My tired eyes take in his tan muscles, his tall, lean frame.

Eli is still laughing, gripping that railing. He has a white t-shirt on, and it's soaked, sticking to his every muscle.

"You think she actually wants you?" he taunts Alex, his voice cold. "You think that this week actually meant some-thing to her?"

Alex's gaze narrows, but he turns to look at me, because he's unsure. And I'm not sure what he sees in my expression, but I see his face fall. His lips part, and the tension seems to leave his body as he turns to face me more fully.

"Zara," he whispers. The music has stopped, and a strange silence settles over their backyard. The sun is rising, bathing us in orange and yellow.

I glance at Eli, but he is watching Alex with a self-satisfied smirk on his face.

He's a fucking psychopath.

Maybe I knew that from the very beginning. When he showed up at my apartment for no reason. Maybe that's part of why I liked him.

That's why girls like assholes, I think to myself. There's something appealing about being with a man who does not give a single fuck about anything. Anything but you.

But what about when he ruins you?

What then?

"Tell me it isn't true," Alex pleads with me, his voice cracking.

I run my hand over the back of my nose, force myself to meet Alex's gaze. He's so beautiful. He's so damn beautiful.

He doesn't know the truth.

He doesn't know what Eli told me. He told me he put Rihanna up to ruining me and Alex. He told me that he was the reason she kissed him after practice. He told me it wasn't enough, and then she wanted him, and he didn't want her.

He wanted me.

"Did you kill her?" I asked him. "Did you hold her under?"

He shook his head. "I didn't need to. When I pushed her, that's all I had to do. She killed herself, Zara. She drowned herself."

"It was always going to be him, wasn't it?" Alex suddenly demands, sending a spray of water toward me. I gasp, shivering.

I can't get the words out. I can't speak.

Alex wades through the water toward me. "It was always going to be fucking him. You two…" He turns to glare at Eli, who is glaring right back. "You two are fucking unbelievable. You two are fucking…psychos. You're fucking insane. Was this always a fucking game?" He turns back to me, his hands gripping the concrete ledge of the pool.

He left me once. He left me after that night with Eli.

But he came back for me.

And he stayed with me.

This week, he stayed.

That's when it was all real for me.

"Fucking answer me!" he screams at me, planting his hands flat on the concrete to haul himself up.

But Eli moves fast, and he jerks him back, his arm wrapped around Alex's neck. "She's not yours anymore, Alex. Let her go."

I get to my hands and knees, crawling forward. My body is so cold and I'm shaky and my nose is still running, and I can't fight either of them. I can't pull them apart. I can't stop them with my hands, but my words… Maybe I can stop this. Maybe I can fix this.

Alex doesn't even fight Eli, and Eli must sense it because he loosens the hold around his throat without letting him go as they float back in the water, Alex's gaze still on me.

"Fucking say something, Zara!" he screams at me, the tendons in his neck under Eli's arm stark against his skin. "Say something!" he pleads with me.

The concrete is rough against my hands, against my knees, but I crawl to the edge of the pool, darting my eyes back and forth between Eli and Alex and back again. Eli is staring at Alex and Alex is staring at me.

What's real?

Which one is real?

The psychopath? The asshole? Neither of them?

Am I fucking real?

Eli's words echo in my head: *Does it feel good now?*

No. No. No.

"Eli." My voice is hoarse, and I'm still staring at Alex. He's waiting for me to heal him. Waiting for me not to break his heart.

"What did he do to you?" he demands, and Eli pushes his forearm tighter against Alex's throat, cutting off the last word.

I shake my head, my hands trembling beneath me. "He... he..." I can't get the words out.

Alex grabs at Eli's arm, trying to yank him off. He succeeds, long enough to say, "I fucking know he did! What did he do to you? I saw it." His voice cracks and Eli is still glaring at him, holding Alex's back to his chest with the force of his forearm. "I fucking saw it in the trash, Zara, I know that he did something to you!"

Eli slams his forearm back against Alex's throat and I see Alex gag from the force.

I stand to my feet, my knees trembling.

Eli glances up at me, his eyes narrowed as he chokes Alex. Alex tries to force his arm off his windpipe, but Eli is the wrestler. Eli is the one with the power here.

And not just in his strength.

Alex is strong, too.

But Eli knows things, he told me. He has secrets.

"You think you hurt Cari that night?" Eli says, his voice low, a smirk pulling on the corners of his mouth.

Alex freezes, no longer fighting, his eyes wide. His face turns an alarming shade of red as Eli cuts off his air supply.

Cari. This must be the girl. Eli told me he knew the truth.

My fingers are trembling as I hold my hand to my mouth, unable to breathe. To think. To speak.

"You think it was you, huh? You fucking idiot." Eli laughs, his mouth against Alex's ear, but he speaks loud enough for me to hear him. "It was me."

My hand falls from my mouth.

"She wanted it, but she was too fucked up to remember she did. And then you, being the fucking hero, rip me out of her bed before I was able to get inside of her. You fucking prick." Eli's arm slams harder against Alex's throat, his other hand gripping his own wrist to keep the pressure tight.

Alex's mouth falls open, but I know he isn't getting air. He isn't getting air.

"Eli, no." My voice is little more than a whisper and I don't even know if he's heard me. He doesn't look up, he just keeps talking, making my heart cave in on itself with his every word.

"You fucking idiot, you slept against her door, keeping me out. But jokes on you because then you both woke up from your fucking drunk coma and she thought it was you all along."

No. No. No.

Eli seems to remember I'm here, listening. He glances up at me. "Don't worry, baby girl," he says softly, his voice strained with the effort of choking Alex. "That was before I met you."

He must misread the look on my face because he frowns and says, "Trust me. She wanted it. She was just too fucking drunk to remember it in the morning."

"Eli, you're going to kill him." The words come out in a rush and Alex is staring at me, his hand limp on Eli's forearm, barely hanging on at all.

His face is turning purple.

His beautiful, beautiful face.

"I know," Eli says with a smile. "And you're going to help me bury his body."

"Eli, no. No. No!" The last word comes out as a scream.

Eli looks furious. "This is our way out, Zara. This is it."

I glance around the backyard for something to use as a weapon because he's going to kill him.

He's going to kill him.

I see the net to clean the pool, hanging off the little shed where they keep their lawnmower. As fast as I can—which isn't fast at all, considering I'm still in the midst of the comedown from what Eli did to me—I run to it. My sore feet skim over the bare grass and I grab the net, running back.

Eli is laughing.

Alex is trying to shake his head.

I dart around the stairs for the pool.

"Don't do something stupid, baby girl, or I'll kill you too."

And then I jump, aiming the metal pole, horizontal, onto Eli's head.

The water is fucking freezing. It's all I can do to hold my breath as I sink under, but I feel it. I feel the pole connect with Eli's head, jarring my grip. I let go, because I don't have a choice. If I want to push back up to the surface under this freezing water, it's the only thing I can do.

Let go.

I let go and then I push on the balls of my aching feet, stinging now with the water, to the surface.

But someone stops me.

Someone holds me down.

And I don't need to look up to know who it is.

49

Alex

I'M GASPING FOR AIR, my lungs burning with it as I massage my throat, but there's no time for that. There's no time because my roommate is a fucking psychopath and he's currently holding the girl I love under water.

He's going to kill her.

He did it. I know he did. Without him telling me, without her confirming it, I fucking know that needle was his doing. And the blood? I bet it was hers.

And I bet he made her bleed.

He made her fucking bleed.

He almost sent me to fucking prison.

He let me think that night was my fault.

He said fucking nothing.

He put a needle in Zara's veins.

He goaded her into fucking around with him.

He almost killed me.

He's killing her.

I lunge for him in the water, doing exactly what he did to me, my forearm going around his fucking throat.

I haul him backward, and he stills in my arms, probably trying to conserve his strength. I know he knows how to fight better than I do, but between the two of us, I'm the fucking angriest, and that shit has to count for something.

Zara bursts up, to the surface, panting and rubbing water out of her eyes, shaking her head, trying to clear her vision.

God she's fucking beautiful.

She sees me, but she sees the net, too, and she grabs it.

Eli is still strangely calm in my arms.

I loosen my hold.

And that's exactly what he's fucking waiting for.

He lunges toward Zara, apparently wanting to get to her more than me right now. But Zara is ready, too.

She holds up the net like a shield, horizontally. He laughs because he's fucking insane, and grabs it, pulling it almost effortlessly from her arms.

She grits her teeth, not waiting for him to attack. She attacks him, her hands going for his face.

And I'm right behind him, to help her.

This time, I don't go for his throat.

This time, I cross my arms and bring them down over his fucking head, forcing him under.

Zara's mouth falls open and she steps back, out of his reach.

He struggles against my arms, but underwater, and with me having the advantage of being above the surface, he can't get up. He can't break loose.

When he tries to, I just wrap one arm around his body, keep the other on his head, forcing him to stay under.

He's still struggling, and Zara is staring at me with wide eyes. Those beautiful fucking ocean and emerald eyes.

She's in a bra and underwear, and she's shivering, her hands down by her sides, but she doesn't look away from me.

Time passes.

I don't know how much, but soon, Eli's struggles are more sluggish. Less violent. Soon, it's easier to hold him under.

Soon, he stops moving altogether.

"Alex." Zara says my name with a hint of desperation, but she doesn't move toward me. She doesn't look down at Eli.

I don't speak. I just swallow down the lump in my throat as Eli stops thrashing beneath my hands.

"Alex," she whispers again, "you don't want to—"

"Did he do it?" I ask her quietly as Eli goes still beneath me. "Did he stick that fucking needle in your vein?"

She doesn't answer me, but she doesn't need to. I can read the answer on her fucking face.

That motherfucker.

I don't let go of him.

I don't let go, and as the sun fully rises and casts the world in a promising shade of orange, I still don't let go.

I don't let go until I know Eli is gone.

Until I know I'm safe.

Until I know Zara is safe, and Eli Addison will never fuck with her ever again.

50

Zara

"I SPOKE TO HIS FATHER. He said he...he said Eli always had problems. Since his mom...you know, tried to hurt him." Alex swallows, laces his fingers through mine. "He was seeing a psychiatrist, but I guess he just stopped going."

I close my eyes, feeling the tears pricking behind them. I hear Eli's voice in my head: *Your scars are beautiful, baby girl.*

But other words spring to mind, too. Words that cut soul-deep. His confession. A girl's life stolen too soon.

"Zara."

I look up into Alex's dark eyes, those faint glimmers of amber that mesmerized me before I even liked him at all.

Funny I thought he was such an asshole.

The people with the biggest hearts always have the thickest armor.

His head is leaned against the black seat of his Jeep, and I see his throat move as he swallows. "Zara. I'm sorry I let him get to you. I'm sorry I left. But we're free now, you know? We're free and I want to put this behind us. I want to make you the happiest fucking girl in the world—"

"That's not your job."

"Let it be my job."

"Alex." I swallow down the lump in my throat. It's been three days. It's been three days, and I can't believe it. I can't fucking believe it. Three days, and none of us were charged. We told them what happened. About the needle and the heroin and the pool and the…

We told them about Rihanna too.

About Eli's confession, that he pushed her in. Eli's father didn't bother trying to push a case against us because Eli is a fucking psychopath and turns out, more people knew it than we thought. Turns out too, that Cari, the girl he assaulted, remembers much more than she originally let on, not wanting to turn everything into a scene. I kind of hated her, imagining her let Alex take the fall for something she knew wasn't his fault.

But she was terrified of Eli.

And I can understand that now.

"Yeah, baby?" Alex asks me.

"What're you doing today?"

He smiles, but it's sad.

He came over to the apartment, and I agreed to talk in his Jeep, not wanting to be in that place for another minute. Kylie came home Sunday, the day after Eli died. I've cried in her arms, but we haven't spoken about it. And Mom… Mom is overbearing. I needed space from her. I need space from everyone.

Except Alex. Because he was there. He knows. He did it. He saved us both.

"Whatever you want," Alex answers me.

I turn to stare out my window. "Let's go to the beach?"

He squeezes my hand. "One condition."

I let my eyes flutter closed, basking in the feel of his calloused fingers looped through mine. "Anything."

He laughs. God, I love that laugh. Full of so much fucking life.

"In that case, maybe more than one condition."

I turn my head and open my eyes, taking in his sharp jawline. Those beautiful lips. The line down the center of his bottom one.

So fucking attractive. Full of love. Like his soul.

I arch a brow. "Don't test your luck, handsome."

He smiles, his dimples flashing as he scrubs a hand over his tan face. "Shit," he says softly.

"Hmm?"

"I love it when you call me that." He laughs again. "Handsome."

"Don't dodge the question."

He runs his thumb over the back of my hand. "Spend the weekend with me there."

My eyes widen. "At your parent—"

"Hotel."

I hold his gaze. Tell him what I've been thinking for nearly two weeks now. "I'm not very fun without the drugs, Alex." It's hard to get those words out. To get my mouth to acknowledge my heart's fear. To confess to him what I've thought for some time. Why I almost chose Eli over him, even in the end.

Because Eli would've never expected me to get clean. Eli would've let me kill myself. It wasn't his job to fix me, of course. But he would've left me when he graduated. He would've left me when my addiction spiraled out of control. And with that heroin, it would've been quick.

I can still feel it.

Alex presses his lips together, a crease between his brow. For a moment, we just stare at one another but then he finally says, "I much prefer you without them, Zara."

I blow out a breath, trying to loosen that knot in my throat. "Makes one of us."

I can still feel it, if I close my eyes and think back to that night. I can feel the ecstasy. The dream. The way the world hugged me tight like a warm blanket. And Eli was there in my perfect bubble, watching over me.

It made me so happy, so warm, I didn't care. I didn't care about anything but that moment.

It lasted for hours.

It didn't last nearly long enough.

"Zara." Alex's tone is serious, his fingers flexing around mine. I turn to stare at him, still holding back the tears. I don't want to cry anymore.

"Let's go to the beach, yeah?" he asks me, running his thumb over the top of my hand. "We'll stay as long as you want. We can stay until Halloween, if you want to. We can dress up or not and go out and drink orange juice, or not. We can do whatever we want."

I rub my thumb against my sternum, the pain in my chest nearly unbearable. And I don't know what it's for. I don't know what it's for and I don't know if I want to know. I don't know if I'll ever know.

Eli is being buried this weekend.

I want to tell Alex that. I want to tell Alex we should go to the funeral, but then I think back to Rihanna Martinson's funeral. Eli comforting her mother.

Eli Addison, the fucking murderer.

I don't think he was born insane. Maybe his mother broke something in him. Maybe she didn't. Maybe it was the brother he's never met. The pictures she sent that felt to him like she was poking at him. Telling him how he would never be Adonis. His middle name. His father told us that.

He never told anyone. Not even Alex.

Was she crazy, too? Did she know how much she hurt him? Did she only want to reach out?

I don't know.

I'll never know.

"Do you regret it?" I ask Alex, unable to hold it in. We haven't discussed what he did. He held me that night in his arms, in my bed. And we didn't talk about it.

He looks out the driver's side window, and I see him swallow. "He was my friend, but I never really knew him." He laughs without humor. "He was my friend, and my roommate, going on four years. But I never fucking knew him."

I close my eyes, resting the side of my head against the seat, still facing Alex. "I don't think he knew himself."

Silence echoes in the confines of the Jeep.

It's so heavy.

It's so fucking heavy, but Alex doesn't let go of my hand.

"I don't know if things could've been different. If he had gotten help. And I'm not a murderer, Zara." He turns to look at me and I pry my eyes open even though they're so fucking heavy, too.

Everything is just too much.

"I'm not a murderer," he says again, his voice cracking. "I'm not," he pleads with me, even though I didn't say anything. His dark eyes are shining with unshed tears. His voice breaks: "I'm not, but I couldn't let him do that to you. I couldn't risk him doing that to you again because I love you, Zara. I love you, princess."

He chokes on those last words and I climb across the console, sitting in his lap, my legs stretched out over the passenger seat. I let him bury his head in my neck. I wrap my arms around his shoulders, feel him sob against me.

"I'm so sorry," he whispers, his fingers digging into every inch of my body he can find as he sobs harder. "I'm so sorry, but I couldn't let him… I couldn't let him hurt you."

And when the tears flood my own eyes, I just let them. I just let that knot loosen in my throat and I let my heart ache and we cry together.

We cry together over someone who might never have cried for us.

We hold each other, and we don't let go.

Not for a long, long time.

51

Alex

HALLOWEEN NIGHT, we go to the boardwalk. There's a carnival, clowns on stilts walking along the bridge over the canal, people dressed up in costume. The smell of funnel cake and popcorn in the air. There's not a lot of people here, considering it's the off-season, but I think Zara likes it best that way.

I know I do.

I throw my arm around her shoulder, tug her close to me and kiss her hair. She cut it, at a place on the coast, and it's to her shoulders now, all neat edges and healthy ends. I didn't really know anything about that, but she pointed it out to me. She told me the "straggly parts" were gone, and I never ever thought her hair looked "straggly", but whatever. It looks good as fuck, just like it did before. Though she looks older now, in a good way. Classier, maybe. Except for the fact she's in a nearly translucent black, long-sleeved top tucked into her skin-tight skinny jeans, and she's not wearing a bra so maybe classy isn't the word, but I don't care.

She knows I'm not going to share her like he did, and so

long as she understands that—which she said she did—then I don't care what she wears. She could walk around fucking naked for all I care.

Which makes me think of when I pulled down her bikini top at that fucking party and that fucking video I've painstakingly tried my best to erase from everywhere. She doesn't seem to care about that though.

Our past lives, as she likes to call them. Even though they weren't that long ago.

She does act like a different person. Quieter, not too... hyper. Because she's sober. But she's kinder, too. And I think she loves me more.

I kiss her again as we get to the middle of the bridge and she comes to stand at the edge, against the wood railing. It's close to ten o'clock, and the stars shimmer on the surface of the water which is, grudgingly, I have to admit, really damn romantic.

I wonder if she's thinking the same thing, but she just slurps on the orange juice in a plastic cup she has in her hand and I can't tell. I don't know where her mind is right now. I've asked her probably a hundred times what she was thinking the past week, so I let it go for now before she gets sick of me.

But I can't stop staring at her. At her sharp cheekbones, those long, dark lashes. And even in the night, even under the stars and the moon, I can see the blue green of her eyes. They're Caribbean eyes. That's the best way to describe them. Beautiful, like the sea, but better than the view of it we've got right now.

"Are you okay?" The words come out before I can stop myself. I've never had a lot of self-control, and I guess that hasn't changed.

She turns her gaze to me and it's a little hard to breathe. Especially when her pink lips turn up into a smile and the stud in her nose catches the starlight. She looks like fucking magic.

Okay. I'm obviously in love.

"Why do you ask?"

I notice that she didn't answer my question, but I let it go, pulling her even closer to me, so her head is against my arm. She smiles a little, clutching her orange juice, and I glance out at the canal. Out of the corner of my eye, I see a fucking clown on stilts, but I don't care. I ignore him, and the kids running and screaming from his path.

"I just want to know how you're really doing," I whisper into the dark.

She wraps her arm around my back, and I turn back to look at her, her eyes searching mine.

"Truly?" she whispers, and I feel myself tense, getting ready for her words. They may not be what I want to hear, and I have to be okay with that. I want her truth, even if it hurts. I've poked and pried so many times the past week. Probably too many times. I know it's not good for her recovery, but I can't walk around on eggshells when I'm with her all the time either and I always want to be with her.

"The truth would be best," I tell her quietly.

She squats down, my arm falling from around her shoulder, and she sets her orange juice cup on the wooden planks, then stands back up and circles her arms around my neck, standing on her tiptoes even though she's in gray, heeled booties. Another new word I learned from her.

"I love you, Alex Cardi."

I can't explain the feeling in my chest when she says those words. I can't explain how it swells and nearly bursts and I regret all the bad from before, all the shit I said about her. Did to her. All the fucking bullshit with my ex-roommate and how I left to go to the coast, and he was able to get his hands on her all over again.

I regret letting him ruin my life because I didn't want to relive a night that wasn't even mine to stress over. I regret what happened to Cari, but I can't say I'm not happy it wasn't fucking me.

It wasn't fucking me.

I did what I could.

I've always tried to do what I could.

Except where Zara is concerned. I did hurt her. And I almost drowned her, too. I almost fucked everything up for us.

"Do you?" I ask her, but I can't hide my smile.

Especially when she jumps up to plant a kiss on my head. I catch her, pick her up by her thighs, which she wraps tightly around me, making my dick fucking rock hard in no time flat. I'm aware there are children around us and those stupid clowns but it's fucking ten o'clock. If someone doesn't want their kids to see two idiots in love, they should take them elsewhere.

And when some woman mutters, "Get a room," I offer her my middle finger without pulling my tongue out of Zara's mouth.

She laughs against me, pulling back and flicking my nose. "You're awful," she tells me, and I know she doesn't mean a fucking word of it.

"You love me," I say against her neck, pulling her skin between my teeth.

She wraps her legs tighter around me, rocks her hips. I swear to God I would fuck her right here, except I don't swear to God anymore and I don't want anyone else to see my girl.

"Let's go back to the hotel?"

She licks her way down my throat, but finally pulls back, her face flushed and her eyes bright, and she nods.

Once we're there, her naked on the bed and waiting for me, I sink to my knees on the mattress and run my hands up her thighs, eyes taking in every inch of her smooth, pale skin.

In two days, I'm meeting her mother again. Tomorrow, she's having brunch with my mother, who is in an in-patient rehab. My father is a pussy and went away to some pastor retreat in Utah which I'm sure will do absolutely nothing for him, but I don't care.

I just want her to meet my mom, and I want to meet hers, and I want to go back to school and walk arm-in-arm with her to class, and take her to the gym and we can start working on that business plan of ours.

My inheritance is already in my account and has been for some time. I took money out of it for my legal fees from last fall, and I did it again for the shit with my ex-roommate, but there's plenty left, and Zara herself isn't poor. We could really start something.

Build an empire.

"What are you thinking about right now?" she asks me, propping herself up on her elbows, a slight frown on her face.

I glance at her naked before me, and my cock stirs.

She sees it and smiles. "What were you thinking of before you just looked at me like that?"

My hands slide up her thighs, over her hips, her torso, her breasts because I can't fucking resist them, and then to her face as I lean over her, settling myself between her thighs.

"Two things." I wiggle my hips against her. "I was thinking about your scars."

She goes rigid, so I keep talking: "If you don't want to tell me, it's fine. But it broke my heart a little, that you thought I didn't notice them. I always did. I always have."

She swallows, averts her gaze. "I used to hurt myself," she admits, and that fucking nearly tears me apart. "Because I didn't think I was, you know, worthy of anything. And it felt good. It felt good then."

I run my thumb over her lip. "I'm so sorry, princess." I take a deep breath. "When was the last time?" I ask her, since she seems willing to talk about it. "When was the last time you didn't feel worthy?"

She keeps looking down between us. "When you told me you wanted your father to like me. When you told me you wanted me to be more respectable."

Those words sear through me. Thinking of what she did

to herself because of what I said. Of her admission, right now. Her vulnerability.

My heart fucking breaks. "God, Zara." I blink back my own tears, gripping her face just a little tighter. "I'm so fucking sorry. I was…" I hang my head, and surprising me, she runs her fingers through my hair. Her touch sends a shiver through me, but I don't look up. "I was fucking stupid." I pick my head up, meet her gaze. "And you're so worthy. I'm so sorry, Zara."

She smiles at me, her fingers still in my hair. "I've wanted to tell you that for a long time. But now that I have, tell me your other thought. You said you were thinking two things."

I don't want to. I want to grovel at her feet. Tell her I was a stupid moron. I want to beg her to forgive me but I think she already has. I think she has because we both made mistakes, and neither of us knew what love was.

But we had to grow into it. It's part of growing up, and we did that. Together, we did that.

I blow out a breath. "I was thinking of what our life is going to look like a year from now."

She smiles faintly, but I see something else in her expression, the dim light from the bathroom giving me just enough light to gauge her emotions by. And now that she's not on drugs, she's full of them.

She said she wasn't fun without the drugs, but she's more fun. She might be quieter, but she laughs more. She teases. She's serious, too, and she's everything.

She's everything I've ever wanted. I'm always thinking about her, and us, and what we're going to do together now that this shitty chapter of our life has passed.

I tip her chin up, turn her head to face me. "What?" I ask her, worry in my tone, but I can't hide it. And I don't want to. I want her to know how I feel. "What do you see when you think of yourself in a year?"

She runs her hand through her hair, and I watch her throat bob as she swallows. "I think I'll be a broke philosophy major without a job and a shitload of debt from student loans."

Relief courses through me, because those problems are solvable. Those problems are too fucking easy.

She trails her fingers over my shoulder, eyeing my bare chest, a smirk on her lips. "And I think…no, I hope you're still here." She meets my gaze, her fingers still against my skin. "I hope you don't leave. I hope you still find me fun a year from now. I hope you don't mind that I'm really awkward and I'm kind of boring, and I don't really do shit when I'm not high and I actually kind of hate parties and also…" She bites her lip, laughing a little. "Also football."

I grab her hand, press it to my mouth. "I already knew that," I tell her. "About the football. The rest?" I suck on her index finger, and then the next one, and the next one. I love the way she wiggles underneath me, like she just can't wait for me to fuck her.

Yeah, neither can I, but I'm going to, just for a minute.

"I love you for who you are. I'm getting too old for parties," I tease her, "and it's a shame you got over them before you even turned twenty-one, but," I shrug, "less boys to flirt with you so fuck it. I don't care."

I drop her hand and she runs it through my hair.

"Who knew you could be so damn romantic?" she asks me, grinning.

I lean down and kiss her, her lips parting for me, her hands going around my neck. "I'm not. I just really, really like you."

She drops one hand, and reaches between us, grabbing my aching cock. "I like you, too. And this. A lot. It's the biggest one I've ever seen."

I'm not sure, exactly, what to make of that or how to feel about it, but I just laugh anyway and she guides me inside of her and it might make me sound like a fucking idiot, but when I'm inside of her it feels like home.

. . .

LATER THAT NIGHT, SHE'S CURLED UP BESIDE ME, HER MOUTH open as she drools on my chest. It's actually pretty sexy, especially the way her spine feels beneath my fingers as I draw circles down her back, staring up at the dark ceiling.

But Eli's words come back to me, and although I hate thinking his name, although I hate thinking of him, and although sometimes the way he felt bucking against my hands makes my skin crawl when it passes through my mind, I can't help but smile as these words: *And you can't breathe for her, too. She'll pull you down in that grave and bury you with her.*

He was a fucking psychopath, playing me as well as he played her.

But I buried him.

I fucking buried him, and it's Zara I want. Zara that wants me.

And when I imagine my future, she's in it.

Because this girl? The one whose head is against my chest? Yeah. I didn't save her. That girl saved me.

EPILOGUE

THREE YEARS *Later*

Zara

"I'm closing this fucking place."

"No, you can't, someone is coming right—"

He flips the switch for the closed sign on the gym, pulls down the blackout shade and steps back, retreating into the shadows.

I clamp my hand over my mouth, trying to stifle my laughter as there's a polite knock on the door.

We're supposed to be open 24/7.

Alex looks at me, his dark eyes gleaming, and then he scoops me up, twirling me around and when a little giggle slips past my lips because I've got my hands on his bare shoulders, he clamps his hand over my mouth, lowers me down to whisper in my ear, "Shh, princess. We don't want to get a bad review, yeah?"

I slap his chest, but we can see through the wall of tinted windows the person walking away, glancing over their shoulder and shaking their head, irritated.

"That was horrible business!" I chide him, smacking his chest again as he sets me down on my feet.

"I don't give a fuck," he tells me, keeping his arms locked behind me. "I want to spend the weekend with my wife."

I try to bite back my smile because it seriously is horrible business and weekends are a great time for us. "You could've called Dwight. He's been dying to take some of his clients here." I grip my husband's arms as I turn to take in our gym. We've got ninety feet of professional grade turf, for football, soccer, sled pulling. Olympic bar cages, a café, a yoga studio, a fucking sauna.

Whatever anyone fucking wants, we've got it.

Castle Cardi Fitness might have a dumb name, Alex's doing, but it's the most popular gym on North Carolina's coast.

We thought taking over Grove Community might not bode well for all the displaced congregants, but turns out, they love it.

And in the classroom at the very back, down a long hall past the bathrooms and change rooms and showers, I teach Stoicism to people every other night.

No, seriously. They come in droves, wanting to know how to get through fucking life. I thought it would be a joke. Alex kept pushing me to do it after I got my yoga certification and taught a few classes a week at night.

He kept telling me to use my philosophy degree, especially since I bought every book by Ryan Holiday and the fucking Stoics, too, and read through them every damn week, quoting shit at him to help him control his own temper.

"It isn't manly to be enraged," I'd tell him. "Marcus Aurelius said so."

To which he would roll his eyes and slap my ass to show me just how manly he was.

It was fascinating how much I learned, after school. I mean, I got through college, earned my degree, but turns out, you learn a lot more when you're not high as fuck, whether it's on Adderall or not.

Now, we have addicts in recovery or wanting to be in recovery come for my talks. We have teenagers looking for ways to handle adult problems. We have couples who own big businesses come for tips on handling stress, the Stoic way.

It's like a big NA meeting but we're Stoics Anonymous.

And Alex? Alex is like a god to the kids he runs football drills with. He's a godsend to the people he trains, and he runs a few of his own meetups to discuss personal and business growth.

He reads a lot of Robert Greene, which translates well in his talks on things like how to spot psychopaths and the best way to deal with them—drown them...okay, not really, but...kind of.

Right now, he looks like he wants to take me to the Olympic-sized pool we have in the very back of our facility where the baptismal pool used to be and fuck me on one of the towels.

But he'd never actually put me in the pool.

I don't swim anymore.

"Fuck Dwight. Fucker is off with the guys to Vegas this weekend."

I cock my head, surprised. "Really?" I ask him as he pulls me closer and I wrap my arms around his neck. "You didn't want to go?"

He wrinkles his nose, as if I've personally offended him. "Fuck no. I want to be with you."

I glance at the closed door. "Alex," I say, trying to keep my voice stern even as he kisses my forehead and smirks down at me. "We can't keep the place closed. It's bad for business. We're a 24/7 facility and we agreed we wanted someone on staff at all times." I glance at the clock on the wall beside the door. "The night girl isn't going to be here for another hour."

Alex laughs, boyish and loud and it makes my heart swell. "The 'night girl'?" he repeats.

I glare at him. "Well, I might actually remember her name if she didn't always look at you like she wanted to suck your dick."

He rolls his eyes. "She does not want to suck my dick, princess. And even if she did, I wouldn't let her. This dick is only for you." He pulls me so far against him, I can feel said dick, and three years after we officially started dating, two years after we got married, I'm still amazed by just how damn big that dick is.

I reach for it and his hands slide down my back, cupping my ass through my yoga pants.

"Keep doing that, Za, and I'm going to fuck you right here in the lobby." He shoves me up against the reception desk to prove his point, bending his head to kiss my neck.

I run my fingers through his thick, bronze hair and breathe in his dark, woodsy scent. "Aren't we supposed to meet your mom for dinner?" I ask him as he bites my neck and I lurch against him, the hairs on the back of my arms standing on end. I'm in a sweaty sports bra, my hair hasn't been washed in days and I really, really need a shower, but Alex does not give a fuck.

He trails his mouth lower, over my collarbone, tugging down my neon pink bra. His tongue licks my breast, his fingers on my back, and I know without seeing it that his thumb is brushing over the scar from the glass in my apartment that night.

The one Eli Addison gave me.

We don't talk about Eli much.

But sometimes, when I see that scar in the mirror, when I get too close to the edge of a pool, I think about him.

Sometimes I wonder what if?

What if things had worked out differently? What if I'd never grabbed that net? What if I'd never jumped in the water? What if I'd believed his bullshit, about needing me? About wanting me? About loving me?

Alex pulls back, cups my face in his big hands. I lock my own around his neck and smile up at him, forcing Eli from my mind.

What's done is done and I can't change it.

Maybe Eli Addison suited my temperament for a little while. My crazy. The old me. Maybe the sexual shit we did was good and maybe we had some strange sort of fun, fucking around with everyone around us. Including my now husband.

But I couldn't have lived my life with him.

He would've left me when he graduated, or he would've killed me himself. Or I would've gone on to worse drugs. Worse things.

A worse life.

He would've moved on to someone else. Someone else to break.

"What're you thinking about?" Alex asks me quietly.

I meet his gaze and wonder if he knows. When I think of Eli, I always have this strange sense that Alex can read my mind. Like the three of us are still somehow morbidly connected, even though Eli has been dead for three years.

The thought makes my heart flip in my chest. My stomach drop.

Still. After all this time.

He's dead.

I knew him for half a year, and most of that time I was fucked all the way up. But even if it was for the bad, he changed my life.

And without him, I wouldn't have the man in front of me.

I stand on my tiptoes and kiss Alex on the lips. He kisses me back, but then he picks me up, puts me on the counter at the desk behind me, and steps between my thighs.

"Princess," he whispers, pressing his brow to mine. "You know you can talk to me about anything, right?"

I force a smile, slide my hands down his back. "I know, handsome."

He softens, his shoulders relaxing as he sinks closer to me, gripping my hips. "I love you, Zara Rose."

"I love you, too, Alex Christian."

And I do.

I love him.

I just think a part of me died with Eli in that pool, too. A part of me that was wild and reckless and a little insane. A little off. That part of me died and I'm not so sure I don't sometimes want her back.

Sometimes, I just want to go off the fucking rails again.

As happy as I am with my life, with my husband, with the community we've put together in the same town he grew up in, with his mom nearby, and mine coming every other weekend, and Kylie and Ian working as pharmacists at the clinic just up the street, as much as I love this life, sometimes I just want to go a little fucking wild.

And I think only Eli would understand that.

My heart aches a little, imagining it. Imagining if I had gotten clean, if Eli had gotten counseling. If we had put our crazy together for good instead of evil. Instead of a way to pass the time. To entertain ourselves.

What would we have been, then?

One single decision changed my fate. Picking up that net and jumping into that water, not letting him drown Alex.

That changed my whole life.

For the better.

Definitely for the better, because this man in front of me is everything.

But there's always that voice in the back of my head.

"I cancelled on my mom," Alex says, jarring me back to the present. His eyes are searching mine. "I thought we'd go to the boardwalk, then see a movie?"

It's summer, and the boardwalk is always crowded on

Friday nights, but it's kind of nice. I've gotten used to being in crowds without being on something. It's like I can just disappear in them.

And with Alex's arm around me, I never feel awkward or strange like I used to as a teenager. I just feel loved.

I just wish that was enough.

I wish feeling loved was enough to tame my fucking restless soul.

But I just have to get through that one day at a time. One hour at a time. One minute.

Maybe one day I'll stop thinking about him.

Maybe one day I won't be in love with a ghost.

"That sounds perfect," I lie to Alex. "That sounds like an amazing night."

He kisses me again and I feel my phone buzz in my back pocket. After we're done losing ourselves in each other on the counter in our gym, I read my text as Alex heads to the bathroom.

Jax: **I'M OUT, ZA!**

I bite my tongue, holding back my smile as another text comes through from Jax.

Him: **I've got some good shit. You still down at the coast? I can come over.**

I glance over my shoulder, toward the hallway Alex disappeared down. Jax spent two years in prison for possession with intent to distribute, but it seems like he's ready to get back in the saddle.

I send him a heart, think of all the ways he touched mine. Then I block his number and delete his texts from my phone.

AFTERWORD

As someone who has many antisocial traits, this was not a manifesto against psychopaths. This ending was bittersweet for me in many ways.

A bonus scene is available on my website (authorkvrose.com) if you're interested in reading more about Eli. You can also find two books about his time in high school in *Ominous: Book i* and *Ominous: Book ii.*

ACKNOWLEDGMENTS

First thanks goes to those of you who made it through this book. I appreciate you. I swear to God I have the best readers on the planet, and that means **you.**

Thank you, too, to Christina, Kandace, and Taylor, for reading this sh*t in its rawest form. I am so grateful to you three.

On that note, thanks to my reader's group. God, I love you all.

I need to include my husband in this somewhere, so…this is that. Thank you for everything. I love you.

And as always, I couldn't write a word without music.

ABOUT THE AUTHOR

K.V. Rose is an author of dark romance. She lives with her family in Toronto. She's usually drunk on coffee or rum. Sometimes both at one time. You can find her on social media nearly everywhere at AuthorKVRose.

▼

pinterest.com/authorkvrose
instagram.com/authorkvrose
facebook.com/authorkvrose
goodreads.com/authorkvrose
authorkvrose.com

ALSO BY K V ROSE

Unsainted Series

These Monstrous Ties

Pray for Scars

The Cruelest Chaos

Boy of Ruin

Like Grim Death: Part 1

Like Grim Death: Part 2

Ecstasy Series

Ominous: Book i

Ominous: Book ii

Razer Rabbits Series

Verglas

Made in United States
Orlando, FL
22 December 2023

41579105R10243